The Green Eyed Butterfly

Kiffany Dugger

Cover Design by: Jamacia Johnson
Edited by: Courtney Owens, Nikkea Smithers and Angelique Parker
Printed in the United States

ISBN: 978-0-615-26547-6

Reviews

This is nothing short of a satisfying read just right for those who love to be entertained as well as made to think when they pick up a book. Dugger has managed to do what some seasoned authors fail to accomplished: she made her story resonate while at the same time flow. That's a feat she should be proud of. Hands down, one of my favorite reads of the year!
-C. A. Webb "Conversations Book Club-

"...The Green Eyed Butterfly is a work of imagination laced with suspense, lies, deceit, and romance. As readers journey with Seth, the true and shocking nature of her existence unfolds. The characters are linked as if they're in a small world of their own and the eye-popping suspense will leave readers amazed....
- The RAWSISTAZ(tm) Reviewers-

"...Dugger's penchant for macabre and suspense is duly noted in this chilling novel, and all the way to end she keeps us spellbound, restless, and in great anticipation with every turn of each page. Her ability to create complex characters and place them in dense psychological contexts shows style and skill (almost unseen in debut novels). That stated, Dugger is off to a good start, and The Green-Eyed Butterfly may very well be headed for classic status. Let's hope that this novel can rise above the mess of books that have recently flooded the shelves, and make its way to a position of respectable quality reading. Good work, Kiffany!"
-Push Nevahda Review-

"I absolutely fell in love with The Green Eyed Butterfly. It was full of suspense and kept you begging for more and more. Seth St. James, the main character, took you on a long journey of twists and turns as she sought after her true identity. Her emotional highs and lows made me feel completely sane, but kept me rooting for her at the same time. This is a very unconventional book. It definitely isn't your everyday mystery novel!!! You will never guess the ending!!! It was an awesome read!!!!"
-Cyteria Ray-

This book is dedicated to the loving memory of my grandfather
Carl "Daddy Carl" Dugger

Acknowledgments

Thank you Lord for blessing me each and every second. Thank you Lord for blessing me with the vision and resources to publish this book. You are awesome!

To my mother Delbra "Elaine" Dugger, my grandmother Ada Dugger and my aunt Etheldra "Thell" Haynie for loving me with all your heart and soul and teaching me that God is everything. Mommy, words can never express my gratitude for your role as mother and father. To Mose, Dolly, Saquetta and Rodney Henderson (Vikki and Donovan) for your unconditional love.

To: Johnny Jones for encouraging and believing in me. Monica, thank you for encouraging our friendship. To: Sholunda Rucker for your tough love and believing in me even when I didn't believe in myself. To: Kim Sturgis and A.S. Butler for sharing my vision and seeing the bigger picture. To: The Houston/Sip crew for constant support and encouragement. To: Consuela Fontenot for ministering to me and giving me that final push. Thanks Mic Fontaine for my daily pep talks. A special thanks to Dr. Rocelious Goodson keeping me healthy and sane in my midnight hour!

Thanks to my family and friends in my hometown of Batesville, MS and Detroit, MI for your love and support!

Thank you, my spiritual father Pastor Ralph Douglas West for your continued support and encouragement.

Chapter One

As I stood in the mirror staring into my inexplicable green eyes that were filled with so much sadness and pain, I caressed my locket and inhaled the memory of my past. I remembered the day that I discovered I was different. When I was five years old, I noticed I was the only one in my family with green eyes. My mother, father and sister all had brown eyes or a version there of. After looking in the mirror and becoming distraught over my discovery, I ran crying to my father. I cried because I was different and not at all like everyone else. My father tried his best to convince me that I was special, but at five years old all I knew was, I was the odd one out. Later that day, my father took me outside where he'd captured several butterflies in a net. He sat me down on the steps and explained to me that each one of the butterflies were different, but they were all still part of the same family. He showed me how beautiful each one was and told me that I was equally as beautiful. He called me his green-eyed butterfly. My father is dead now and each time I think of him, I think of that moment when he made me feel so special and so beautiful.

I tried to gather myself and recover from another restless night. As the cool sensation from my washcloth soothed my face, I realized that was the first day of spring. The flowers in my garden were in bloom. The sun was shining through the terrace doors in my bedroom and the birds were singing the melodic song of spring. Everything was so full of life but there was a familiar peculiarity lingering in the air. It was the twenty-year anniversary of my family's death, and that day was almost a carbon copy of that day.

The strangest feeling came over me. My stomach was uneasy and twisted in knots as nausea filled the pit of my stomach. I grabbed my stomach and combed through my medicine cabinet in search of relief, and after finding nothing there, I retreated from the bathroom and walked downstairs. I poured a glass of soda to settle my stomach and as my bare feet touched the cold marble, I tiptoed across the floor making my way outside. I walked out onto the veranda and stood at the edge of the pool to catch a few rays of sun. As I dipped my foot into the water, I felt a warm wind sweep through. This wind was unusually warm, but refreshing. Texas spring breezes are usually humid and stifling but this particular day's wind was like a breath of fresh air. As I looked toward the clear blue sky, I closed my eyes and let the wind move through my body. I breathed in the fresh air and visited my safe place in my mind.

My fraternal twin sister Nicolette and I were eight years old playing behind our house in the field of wildflowers. The summer time was the best time of year at our house. We would play outside until dark. I was always the tomboy who loved to catch bugs and chase rabbits through the field, but my favorite thing to do was catch fireflies or lightening bugs, as they're known to be in the country. I'd put them in a jar and poke holes in the top so they could breathe. It was so amazing to me to see the light flicker in the darkness from the bodies of those tiny insects. We would make wishes by the light of the flies. Our wish was always the same: we never wanted the day to end.

I felt the warm tears roll down my face and was jolted back to reality. My sister was not there, "I will never be eight years old again and my family is never coming back." Reciting these words seemed like a ritual to me. I would repeat them daily; hoping that one day I would actually believe what I was telling myself was actually true. Every night my prayer was that I woke up free. Free from the memory of having parents, free from the memory of having a sister and free from having a so-called normal life. I had come to realize that it was my destiny to live with that shit for the rest of my life. Why were Mattie and I the only ones to survive our family's terrible tragedy? And what is my purpose? I believe there is a being that "they" call God. I pray to Him because I see Him through others and I have seen what He has supposedly done for them. Mattie believes in Him like they're best friends or like He's a member of the family. Someone is watching over me and continues to save me in spite of myself, so I have to conclude that it must be God.

As I turned to reenter my home, I stopped to acknowledge my reflection in the glass door. Just as I did every morning, I stood there and tried to convince myself that I was in fact Seth St. James. I tried to convince myself that Noel Etienne Toussaint, the name my mother had given me at birth, no longer existed. I was twenty-eight years old and I still had a hard time understanding just who I was. Each day I learned to live with the past and my nightmares started to be fewer and farther between. They used to occur every time I closed my eyes, now they just occur every other time.

There is a burden that the living carries. It is the burden of life. It's the burden of remembering the dead. All that I have left are my nightmares and the locket that was given to me by my father on my eighth birthday. My sister Nicolette had received an identical locket that day. Every morning I light three candles, one for the memory of each of my family members, my mother, my father and my sister. I ask God's blessing upon them and their souls. I also asked Him to continue to bless me and protect me from this veil of evil that seems to cover me.

As I continue to stare at my reflection, I was ashamed at who stood before me. I had done some things in my life that I'm not proud of and could never utter to another living soul. Sometimes I didn't know where the urges of deviance and unconcern for human suffering came from. There is something that lives deep inside me that just won't rest. It feeds off my pain and misery. Sometimes it seemed as if there were two people inside of me, one good and one bad. I found myself struggling internally to just do the right thing. I asked myself, "What is the right thing?"

My mother used to sing a lullaby to my sister and me before we went to bed. I believe it went something like, "Rock a bye baby in the tree top; when the wind blows the cradle will rock; when the bough breaks, the cradle will fall and down will come baby, cradle and all." After the death of my family, I'd sit and sing that same lullaby to myself searching for comfort. As years passed and life became even more confusing, I realized that the song was far from comforting. At first it seems to be a soft and soothing tune that lulls children into a secure world filled with naivety and innocence. But once the song has been repeated over and over, it becomes a part of you, and soon you begin to realize that the song tells a tale of an innocent child plunging from atop a tree branch to an uncertain future. And that is no fairy tale; it's actually a prelude to a nightmare.

If you've ever wondered what happened to the baby after she fell from the treetop, after the wind blew and the cradle rocked...have I got a story for you. I'd like to tell you that she picked herself up, dusted off and kept on moving, but that would be a lie. I'd like to tell you that she lived happily ever after in the enchanted forest with prince charming, the seven dwarfs and whoever else lives in fairytale land; but that would be a lie as well. I'd like to tell you lots of colorful anecdotes that warm the heart and soothe the soul but they would all be lies, and if there's one thing I'm tired of, it's lies.

Chapter Two

Once my stomach began to feel better I went back inside. My mood was less than desirable and I needed to get to the store. I was expecting the arrival of the new Cavalli Spring Pumps and I wanted to be the first to unpack the boxes. Spending time at my boutique was the one thing about my life that I truly enjoyed. I named the store Anna Marie's after my mother.

Before going to my room to prepare for the day I stopped by Mattie's room to see what her plans were. When I opened the door she was coming out of her bathroom. She looked a little disoriented, so I asked, "Are you alright this morning?"

She clutched her stomach. "I don't know what's wrong. I woke up with an upset stomach."

I looked at her and said, "That's weird, I woke up with the same feeling." I told her that I'd drunk a glass of soda and felt better.

She walked over to the terrace and opened the door and to walk out. "Somethin' ain't right about this wind. It's unusually cool and sweepin' through mighty swift. I feel like it's gonna storm, but the sky is as blue and clear as ever."

There was s so much unspoken tension between Mattie and myself. I was ashamed to admit that my resentment toward her is of a selfish and somewhat sadistic nature. I have always wished that it was Mattie who was killed that night instead of my mother. Don't get me wrong, Mattie is great in her own way, but she's not my mother. She refuses to discuss the past and once she even said, "Just let the past be the past". She said that uncovering the past could hinder my future. Mattie never ever wanted to talk about the past. Even when I was a little girl and needed an explanation of what had happened to me and to my family, she would always shut me down. I never understood her silence, they were my parents and Nicolette was my sister. I was a child and I needed that connection. When I was ten, one of the kids at school asked about my parents. I told them they had been killed in a car accident and that's all I knew. I never shared with anyone the fact that I had a twin sister. It was like I appeared from nowhere and was born from no one.

I asked Mattie if she could tell me about my parents when they were young, or anything at all about them. I needed to know something. I needed to talk about them and I needed to keep their memory alive. Mattie told me the same thing she told me the night they were killed, "Never to mention them again". I guess that conversation is what set the tone for my relationship with her from then on. I have harbored resentment for her since that conversation. I don't hate her or even dislike her, but I must admit that I am uncomfortable around her and I don't ever know what to say. How could she rob me of the memories of my own flesh and blood? How could she not encourage me to hold on to the past, instead of forgetting it? As I got older and started to dissect the night my parents died, I figured maybe she felt I was too young and she wanted to protect me from whatever we seemed to be running from. I waited for her to come to me and say, "It's time you knew about your past." But she never did, and she hated the fact that I still wore the locket.

When I was a child I kept it in my jewelry box and never wore it. When I started attending high school and my true personality emerged I began to wear my locket. I it was all I had in the entire world. The first time she saw it around my neck she told me to take it off. She was afraid that someone would see the picture inside and ask questions. I couldn't believe she had the audacity to try and stop me from wearing what was mine. I couldn't take it anymore. I just snapped and it was then that we had our first argument. I'll never forget that argument. Her words, "grow up...you need a tougher skin" still ring in my ears.

It became clearer to me that Mattie was afraid or still mourning her own past and she could not help me because she couldn't help herself. With that being the case she should have been empathetic to my situation. There was no point in us discussing the locket because my mind was made up. It seems like when we left Georgia, Mattie's spirit changed. She tried her best to be there for me, but she just couldn't quite get it right. There was a veil of sadness that covers her. It's unexplainable to those who didn't live inside our world. She too, had pain and sadness in her eyes. There is also an air of guilt and shame. Mattie knew everything about my parents and I know in my heart that the answers I need lie somewhere deep inside of her.

I suppose a part of Mattie's seemingly uncaring attitude is the way that her own family treated her. Mattie grew up the daughter of a minister in a Parish outside of New Orleans. She was raised in a strict Baptist household. At the age of sixteen she was raped by a neighbor and became pregnant. Since the neighbor was her father's associate minister and a prominent citizen, they said she was lying and trying to ruin his reputation. Mattie stayed with her parents until she was ready to have the baby. They kept her hidden in the house away from the outside world. A midwife delivered her baby, and after she gave birth, she was allowed to hold her baby for only a few minutes before it started to cry and gasp for air. As the baby was being taken away she noticed what looked like a dark bruise in the shape of a perfect rectangle. It was the baby's birthmark. Tired from the labor, Mattie drifted off to sleep. While she slept, her mother woke her and told her that the baby had choked to death. At that point Mattie was confused and couldn't understand what had happened. She said she became paralyzed and numb all over. All she knew was that her baby was a boy. After she was told the news about her baby's death, her mother told her she could no longer stay in their home. She was told she'd disgraced the family with her lies and she could no longer live with them. She encouraged Mattie to leave and never return. When she left her parents' home, no one would take her in. She slept outside, finding shelter wherever she could. One day she met a minister and his wife outside of a gas station and without question, they took her in. She rode to Jackson, Mississippi with them and never looked back. She stayed with them for a while. After she began working at the local college and saved some money she was able to move out on her own.

As I walked down the hall to my room, I held on to the significance of the day. I wondered if Mattie remembered. How could she forget? As I continued my morning beauty regimen, my mind weighed heavily on my mother. She was one of the prettiest women that I'd ever seen. Her skin tone was rich, like honey and it was smooth and flawless. She had high cheekbones, full lips and thick eyebrows. Her hair was jet black and silky and lay down to the middle of her back. She always wore it straight, without curls.

My mother had a distinct smell. She always wore the perfume my father had ordered especially for her. They discovered it on a trip to Europe; it was called Serenity. My mother loved the name. She said when she heard the word Serenity, she thought of life with her children and husband. She said she found genuine happiness when my sister and I were born. The fragrance is over twenty years old and it's very hard to find, but I found a seller on the Internet and purchased two bottles. I only wear it on special occasions. Since I was feeling a little blue that day I decided to wear it. Maybe a soak in the tub before work and a few drops of Serenity would make me feel better.

After my bath, I dabbed Serenity on my pulse points and as I inhaled the delicate scent, I could smell my mother. Although the perfume is the same, the scent is different. It's like Serenity was made just for her. It worked with her body chemistry and created an intoxicating bouquet that transported me to a safe and happy place. I stood there with my feet glued to the bathroom floor. My throat felt as though I'd swallowed a golf ball and I tried to take a breath, but I couldn't swallow. I stood there, staring into a space free from pictures and whatnots, just a bare spot on the wall. I remembered the last time I hugged my mother; it was just seconds before she died. Sadly, my last memory of her is watching her take her last breath. I watched her chest move up and down as she inhaled and exhaled, with her mouth wide open as she fought for her life. I stared into her eyes hoping to see a light, instead I saw nothing but darkness. Her eyes went cold. My arms were limp and my voice was mute as I tried to reach out to her. Finally, she inhaled and never exhaled.

I spent my days wondering what was going through her mind as she stared into my eyes. As she looked at her child, her own flesh and knew that she was leaving me all alone in this world with no protection or a mother's love. The moment that life left my mother's body the bough broke; the cradle fell and I tumbled out battered, bruised, scared and worn.

As I stood there, still paralyzed, I was startled by the sound of the perfume bottle falling into the sink. I scrambled around trying to stop the bottle from rolling around in the sink. Luckily nothing spilled out. The sound of the glass hitting the marble brought me back from the past, and I gathered myself together and headed out to work.

When I arrived at the store, Isabelle was already there. I had three other people who worked with me, four if you included Mattie. Isabelle Batiste-Covington is the wife of Robert Covington. He played for our local professional football team. He's been in the league for about twelve years and it was about time for him to retire. I always teased her about her name. I told her it sounded like she should have been movie star or a singer with a name like that. Isabelle hated wasting her days doing nothing so she worked with me. She was very down to earth and is one of those real sista's who could adapt to any situation. She was every bit of five foot four, but believe me she was nothing to play with. Her family was originally from Louisiana, but she grew up in Florida. When she was excited, somehow the two accents mixed and you didn't know what the hell she was saying. When Isabelle was relaxed and in her comfort zone, which was most of the time, she was in rare form. Once a customer walks through the door or the phone rings you'd think she was June Cleaver. She kind of reminds me of what I like to call ghetto bourgeoisie. I like Isabelle for the simple fact that she's real, she's authentic. You could count on her telling you exactly how she felt straight to your face. I didn't feel like I had to wear a mask or pretend to be someone else around her. She's a five foot four ball of fire.

When I walked into the store Isabelle greeted me with a big perky hello as usual. She had to be the happiest person in the world. I guess I would be, too, if I'd lain with her husband every night. He was absolutely gorgeous. I didn't usually pay attention to the hazel-eyed, lighter complexioned, curly haired type. I usually went for the Terrell Owens, Mandingo brother.

I greeted Isabelle as I walked through the door, "Good morning, how's it going with you today?"

"Everything is fine as wine with me"

"Yes, and you sound like that's just what you've been drinking this morning." We both laughed. I always liked to start the day off on a good note. I asked Isabelle if the new Cavalli's had come in. Isabelle knew it was the reason I came in earlier than usual.

She said, "Yes they're here. There are two pairs on your desk. Of course one is for me and the other one is for you."

"You know me so well."

"That I do. You're a woman after my own heart...a heart made of the finest Italian leather."

If Isabelle and I didn't have anything else in common, we both loved shoes and handbags. I shuffled to my office. The pumps were sitting on my desk arranged like a work of art. Isabelle had taken them out of the box so that they'd be the first things I saw when I walked in. I tried them on and they were a perfect fit. After trying on the shoes, I stayed in the office to finish some paperwork. I must have lost track of time because I was in there for over an hour. I felt the need for a cappuccino, and walked out to the show room to tell Isabelle I was running across the street because I needed a fix. She asked me to pick up her a green tea.

When I returned, I noticed a gorgeous black Mercedes in front of the store. The car fascinated me because Isabelle and I had looked at a similar car a couple of days ago and I was considering buying a new car. The car I wanted was every bit of forty thousand dollars, and I was really trying to be practical. I was happy with my Range Rover and wouldn't consider parting with it just yet, but I wanted a sports car for those days that I wanted to be grown and sexy. When I walked into the store Isabelle was standing near the counter talking to a little girl. She was the prettiest little girl, about four or five years old. She had long braids and gorgeous dimples. She reminded me of myself at that age. There was something familiar about this child; I think it was her smile and her eyes. She was so wide-eyed and innocent. I walked up to her with a huge smile and said, "Hello there, aren't you pretty as a peach." My mother used to say that all the time. I always wondered how pretty a peach really was.

The little girl looked at me and started to laugh and said, "I hate peaches."

"Oh ok, how about pretty as a doll?"

"Pretty as Arielle?"

"Who's Arielle?"

Isabelle looked at me like, Duh and yelled out, "You know, the Little Mermaid." I had no idea who The Little Mermaid was. I just said ok so I wouldn't embarrass myself. The little girl smiled and buried her chin in her chest. I asked Isabelle if she was in the store with someone. Isabelle pointed to the dressing room.

"Her mom is in the dressing room, trying on that new salmon two-piece."

"Really, you've got to have the perfect skin tone to wear that shade of pink. Did you show her the new shipment of shoes?"

"Of course, and she went crazy for them...for some reason she re-minds me of you. Give her some green eyes and she could pass for your sister, fraternal of course."

"If she reminds you of me she must be gorgeous."

We laughed and continued to make small talk. In the middle of our fun the child's mother came out of the dressing room with the suit and shoes on. The lady twirled around in one spot and admired her reflec-tion in the mirror, "This suit is absolutely perfect, and I love these shoes. They were made for this suit." When I looked at the woman I was absolutely stunned, I couldn't move. I guess since Isabelle just mentioned the lady's eyes, they were the first thing I noticed. Her eyes were haunting. As our eyes connected I flashed back to the last time I looked into my sister Nicolette's eyes. The lady stood still, not moving a muscle. We just stared at each other, as if we were trying to figure things out. I heard the little girl say "Mommy, you look pretty...I like it, can we buy it?" I guess the little girl's voice snapped us out of the trance.

"Of course honey, mommy loves it. Let me get dressed, it's almost time to go to Pizza Palace."

The little girl jumped up and down at the thought of going to Pizza Palace. I was still standing in the same spot when Isabelle walked over and touched my shoulder. "Are you ok?" she asked.

I shook it off. "Yes of course, I guess the Cappuccino must have me a little off."

Isabelle walked back behind the counter. "I told you about that stuff. One day you're gonna run out of here so hyped up, we won't be able to catch you."

I stood there trying not to get caught up in my own world. I tried not to be overwhelmed by my fantasy that one day my long lost sister would just waltz back into my life. While I was listening to Isabelle, I noticed the little girl was wearing a gold locket. I've always been fascinated with lockets. Each time I see someone wearing a locket, I think of Nicolette and hope that I will find her locket someday. I have always pictured someone finding her locket in the rubble and remains of our house. I bent down on one knee in front of the little girl. "That is a beautiful locket. I have one almost like it." I grabbed my neck trying to find my locket, but I wasn't wearing it. I must have left it at home.

The little girl asked, "Where is it?"

"I guess I left it at home today. May I see yours?"

"Yes, but my mommy said I'm not allowed to take it off, only she can take it off."

"Oh no, I just want to look at it. You remind me of my sister."

"Really, what's her name?"

"What?"

"Your sister, what's her name?"

"Did I say that? I'm sorry, that's not what I meant."

I'd gotten so caught up in the moment. I never acknowledged Nicolette outside of my internal thoughts. I held the little girls locket in my hand. As I began to examine it I discovered it was missing a diamond chip. Beads of sweat began to surface on my forehead. I turned the locket over and noticed an N written in manuscript. There were no other letters just the N. Just as I was about to ask the little girl her name her mother called her.

"Noel, Mommy's ready."

I slowly pulled myself up from the floor as the woman was coming out of the dressing room. I felt my legs getting weaker as my breathing became heavier. I couldn't help but acknowledge the little girl's name. "Noel, that's a pretty name," I said to the woman as she walked over to us.

"Yeah, I've always loved that name."

"Yeah, uh what's your name?"

"My name is Lauren, I just moved here from Dallas. I'm a realtor. Things weren't turning over in Dallas too quickly, so I needed a change of pace."

She handed me one of her cards and said, "I'm sorry I didn't catch your name."

"I'm sorry, it's Seth and I own the boutique."

"I was passing through looking for some great shopping and your store caught my eye. I've been meaning to stop for some time now."

"Yeah, it's in a great location. We've got some great stuff, if we don't have it we can definitely find it for you."

"Well, I'm certainly pleased thus far. I love the atmosphere."

Through our entire conversation, I tried to look into her eyes to see if there was something more, but I just couldn't get it together. There was still something very familiar about her, like we had something in common. There seemed to be one too many coincidences. I wanted to just come out and ask her, "Are you Nicolette?" but I knew that I must have been imagining this whole bizarre incident. Finally, I snapped out of my fantasy and realized this was just an ordinary woman shopping with her daughter. I instructed Isabelle to give her a twenty percent discount and sign her up for our correspondence list. I told Noel that it was nice meeting her. Actually, the most bizarre thing was that Lauren and I really did bear a striking resemblance, but Noel was like a miniature version of my sister and me. I guess the saying is true, we all have a look alike.

I said goodbye to Lauren and retreated to the back. Once again, my imagination had gotten the best of me. There have been days when I think I see Nicolette on the street, in a restaurant or even in the crowd at a football game, but this was different somehow. My head told me that Nicolette was dead, but my heart always seemed to overrule. I realized I was still holding Lauren's card in my hand. As I went to place the card in my Rolodex, I noticed the name of her company, NMT Realty. In my mind I interpreted that as, Nicolette Marie Toussaint.

Chapter Three

After reading the card, I bolted out of my office and asked Isabelle where Lauren had gone. I was told she'd already left. I ran back into the office and grabbed my purse and keys. I told Isabelle I was leaving because I wasn't feeling well. I barely heard her response because I was already in my truck on my way to the house. As I peeled off doing eighty miles an hour down the street, things were beginning to come back to me. I was eight years old again. I started to remember things that I hadn't remembered before. It was like it was happening right then, and in living color.

We were laughing and playing in our family room. Nicolette and I loved to play hide and seek with my dad. We played every Saturday without father and they became our special days, so when Daddy wanted to play on a weeknight, we were excited. I remember we were all sitting in the family room watching television when we heard a car pull into the driveway. My father went to the window to see who it was. After he closed the curtains, we heard a car door slam as he told us we were going to play hide and seek. He told us not to come out until he found us. He instructed Mattie to play along with us; he wanted the whole family to play.

I heard my mother say, "I'm not playing any games. I'm staying right here with you." My mother kissed and hugged us and nodded for us to go and hide with Mattie. Mattie grabbed our hands and we went off through the house and out the back door. Nicolette and I broke away from Mattie to find our own place to hide. We ran back into the house to find better hiding places.

Mattie whispered, "Come back here," and motioned for us to follow her out of the door. I heard voices coming from the front of the house that were not familiar at first, but they were very distinct. I know that at least two of them were white. This was highly unusual because we'd never had white people in our home before.

We knew of white people, I went to school with white children and my father had white business associates, but I'd never seen or heard one in our home before. As the voices began to catch up with us and grew closer, Nicolette and I scrambled to find a hiding place. I was excited because I'd never played hide and seek with anyone other than Daddy and Nicolette. Mattie must have been excited to play as well when she heard the voices coming closer, because she bolted out the back door. I knew she'd found the best hiding place; she was hiding in the field behind the house. When I heard my father arguing with the men and my mother begging them to do something, I realized we weren't really playing a game at all. What was she begging for? I wasn't sure at the time, but in hindsight I can conclude that she was begging for her life. Suddenly I heard my mother shout "Oh my God." I heard loud noises that sounded like firecrackers. I saw my mother run into the kitchen holding her arm and begging the men to leave the house. She was crying and holding her left arm where blood was shooting out as if from a water fountain. I was so scared I couldn't move. In fact, I couldn't do anything but just look and listen. I looked straight across the room at Nicolette and saw the fear in her eyes. This wasn't a game at all. Something terrible was happening and I was afraid we were going to die. I just knew the men were going to find us. My mother pulled at my father with the strength she had left in her right arm, but my father just stood there looking at her saying, "I'm so sorry, Anna." My mother began hitting my father in his chest and that's when I heard another gunshot and watched as my mother fell to her knees. She fell down to the floor as if she were sitting up in a straight back chair. I heard another gunshot and she fell backwards with her knees still bent. When her body hit the ground, her right hand fell to the floor as if she were reaching out to me for help. A few seconds later I heard two more gunshots and my father collapsed on the left side of my mother, right next to Nicolette. After my father collapsed, I heard footsteps as the men left the kitchen.

A man with a raspy voice and a thick southern accent asked where Mattie was and another man answered, "Mattie doesn't live here. She has her own place, plus it's her bingo night." The man was right. It was Mattie's bingo night, but she told us earlier that a tree had fallen on the roof of the recreation center during the storm a couple of nights ago.

As my father lay on the floor bleeding to death, I heard one of the men tell the other, "I want this house and everything in it burned to ashes. Make it quick, we don't have much time."

I heard the voice of another man; (it was safe to assume he was a black man with a thick accent). "Look we didn't say anything about the kids."

The man that seemed to be in charge said, "When Nolan and Anna die who will get the kids and the money?"

The other man answered, "Mattie does, but I manage the estate."

I heard someone say, "That may be, but if the kids are dead, you control everything and there are no provisions for the kids deaths. Mattie gets a settlement, but she won't get everything, you or I control the estate, and I trust you'll settle your end of this."

The black man with a thick accent hesitated for a moment before he said, "And I trust this will all be in black and white."

The white man seemed to be in agreement. "I am officially Nolan's lawyer so, it's all legal."

I heard the other man say, "I still don't like this."

The white man said, "You better get used to it real quick."

Suddenly, I smelled smoke and the two men that were left in the kitchen left the room, I assumed to find what they were looking for. When the men left, we ran outside. Mattie was waiting for us and as we ran into the field she yelled for us to come to her. We ran to her and she held us and wiped our tears. She was so calm and we were hysterical. I watched as flames flew from our house like bolts of lightning. I couldn't stop crying. My Mommy and Daddy were still in the house. What the hell could have gone wrong? Mattie did her best to try and console us. She wiped our tears and said, "Ok girls, everything is gonna be alright. I'm going to take care of you."

All of a sudden, Nicolette ripped herself from Mattie's arms and ran toward the house screaming and crying. "Mommy, Daddy!"

I leapt up after her, but for the first time in her life she was faster than I was. She was way ahead of me and by the time she reached the back door, the entire house exploded like dynamite. I stopped dead in my tracks and fell to the ground. After a few minutes I lifted my head and watched as my whole life went up in flames. That was the last time I saw Nicolette. Could that really be her walking back into my life after twenty years, or did I just want it so badly that I was willing to believe anything? It had to be her, there were too many coincidences. Her daughter's name is Noel and she was wearing a locket similar to Nicolette's. There was a diamond missing in the same place that was missing in Nicolette's locket. The lockets were made just for us. There is no other piece of jewelry like it in the world. My father had their old wedding bands melted and molded into the lockets and the diamond chips were from my mother's original stones in her wedding ring. Our initials were also engraved on the back.

As I drove erratically, tears rolled down my face and clouded my vision. Someone more powerful than me had to be driving. I switched from lane to lane hoping I would make it home. Had I finally lost it? Did my cheese slip off my cracker? Was I finally cracking up? I turned my purse out on the passenger seat looking for my Paxil; I think I'm on the highest dosage prescribed. My doctor has been trying to get me to see a psychiatrist. She doesn't know what specifically has gone on in my life, but she does know that something just isn't right with me. I couldn't find my medication. My breathing became shorter and shorter. I hopped onto the toll way and got off at my exit. I set the world record; I turned a twenty-minute drive in Houston traffic into eight minutes. When I arrived at the house, I hopped out of the car. I was running so fast I almost lost one of my pumps. I left the front door wide open with the keys still in the lock. In my haste, I failed to notice Mattie standing on the other side of the door.

As I ran up the stairs to find my medication, Mattie yelled out to me, "Girl what's wrong with you? Slow down before you fall on those steps!" I ran straight for my medicine cabinet. While searching through the cabinet I looked down on the bathroom counter and saw my locket lying next to my bottle of Paxil. Of all the days in the world, I chose that day not to wear my locket. If I had worn it, maybe Nicolette would have recognized it. We could have embraced each other and cried like in the movies. All she needed was to be sure that I was her sister. She has to feel what I felt. My head felt like something inside was trying to pound its way out. My mind was racing a hundred miles an hour, the room was spinning, and I could hear my own heartbeat. I clutched my chest and felt the sweat soak through my blouse. Beads of sweat were gathering around my hairline and it felt like hot pins were sticking me all over my body. I tried to rip my blouse off, tearing the fabric causing buttons to fly everywhere. The next thing I knew, I'd fallen to my knees and I felt the cold tile on my flesh. Mattie was standing over me calling my name.

"Seth, Seth."

"What?"

"Seth, what in the world is going on? Are you alright?"

"It's Nicolette."

"What?" Mattie let my head go and I bumped it on the floor. I hadn't mentioned Nicolette's name in a very long time.

"What did you say?"

"Nicolette; I saw her today. She came into the store; I know it was her."

"Oh, my Lord! I knew this would happen one day...I think it's time for you to spend some time away for a while. It's been too long; time has passed. You've been holding on to stuff that you should have let go of a long time ago. You need help, baby. You're losin' it. You have made yourself physically sick. Look at you. You all passed out on the floor like you hyped up on some type of drugs. You don't sleep, you keep an ulcer and you have no life..."

"Just stop, I'm not crazy I know it was her. I'm not crazy...I can't be crazy!"

"How do you know it was her, did she tell you who she was?"

"No, of course she didn't just say she was my dead sister. She was with a little girl, her daughter. The child's name was Noel. She was wearing a locket like mine except there was a diamond chip missing and the initial 'N' was engraved on the back."

"Do you hear yourself? All of this is a coincidence. Lockets are given as gifts every day. Your lockets were engraved NMT not just N."

"I know but the locket was worn and old, there were two letters missing."

"Look, Seth I know that you are hurting, so am I. I have cried every night for twenty years. I cry for the child and the family that I lost all over again. I cry for you because I see the pain in your eyes and I know there is nothing in this world that I can do for you... Nicolette died twenty years ago when the house burned right before our eyes. You saw it yourself. You and I are the only ones who survived...please don't do this to yourself."

"But I know it was her. My heart tells me it was her. When I looked into her eyes I saw what I see every time I look in the mirror...I saw my very own eyes."

"Baby, I know what you think you saw. Do you know how many people out there resemble you and how many kids look just like

Nicolette as you remember her? I would love for this to be true, but it just can't be. I know what I saw that night and I know what I've felt for twenty years. Our family is dead and gone...all of them. It's time you realized it too. "

At some point, I realized she'd spoken of how she has suffered and how time has passed and how I need help to get through this. All I hear are the words of a hypocrite coming from her mouth like trash and poison. Has she really cried every night? If I need help so badly, then why hasn't she ever tried to help me? Why is it we don't talk about my family and why have I had to keep this bottled up inside for so long only to have everything fester like an incurable disease and eat away at my soul until there is nothing left for me to do but give up?

After Mattie left the room the Paxil must have taken effect because I woke up the next morning lying on the floor. My body was stiff and contorted from the position I'd lain in the entire night. I gathered myself from the floor and walked over to the sink. After washing my face, I stared in the mirror trying to figure out what the hell was going on in my life. I became overwhelmingly exhausted. Everything around me was cloudy and unclear and my mind was restless. Maybe Mattie was right. I had finally slipped over to the other side. I was tired of being tired. I needed to get away. I wanted a break from the store, a break from Houston and a break from Mattie. She was a constant reminder that I was an orphan. I had no mother, no father and no sister...no blood ties at all. Because my parents had been orphans as well, I didn't know who to reach out to. When I was younger and still filled with the idea that we were the victims of a simple robbery, I wondered why my mother refused to play hide and seek with us on that night. And why did Mattie follow orders so quickly? Mattie knew more than she'd ever admit to and she knew we were in danger as well. Why else would she insist we change our names and never speak of our old lives again?

This was no ordinary robbery. The men knew my father and they knew him well. They knew about Nicolette, and me, and they knew that Mattie was a part of our family. They knew our bedtime and where Mattie lived. They knew our habits and my father's personal business. I keep replaying the scene in my mind trying to match faces with the voices. I hear the voices and the footsteps in my sleep and I hear them when I'm awake. Every man that I pass on the street I wonder if he could be one of the men responsible for this hell that I live every single day. It seems that as days pass I become more preoccupied with unanswered questions. Details are much more important to me now. I have started leaving myself little notes with details about the conversation between the men on that night twenty years ago. Each time I think about that night, something new sticks out in my mind and I jot it down on a piece of paper. The pieces of paper are like pieces to a puzzle that I just can't seem to solve. Something is missing, there has to be a link that can help me solve this puzzle. I've started replaying conversations between Mattie and myself since that night, over and over in my head. Some things she says don't quite make sense.

Maybe Nicolette seems alive to me because she is my twin sister. She's my flesh and blood we shared life inside my mother's womb. We have been a part of each other since conception; as long as I'm alive she will always be alive. The problem is I don't think I could live without her. I stand here today in front of this mirror before God and whoever else is watching or listening and acknowledge for the first time that Nicolette is dead. She will forever be eight years old. She's dead...God damn it she's dead...there I said it, she's dead...They're all dead. I am an orphan...no mother...no father...not a damn thing. I have no children; I have no husband; I have nothing, I have no life...I am dead.

Before I knew it I'd punched a hole in my bathroom mirror and my fist began to bleed I put my hands over my face as I felt the blood drip down my arms and into the sink. As I removed my hands from my face and looked at the blood they were covered in, I couldn't help but remember my parent's blood. This was the same blood that covered my hands after I touched my father. The same blood that I didn't want to wash off for hours after my family was gone. This blood was the connection to my family. We were linked through it. I was the only one left and now my blood was shedding. My cuts were deep and my hands were burning. The blood wouldn't stop and I didn't try and stop it. I was wounded; I'd been wounded for twenty years. My hands were now bleeding along with my heart. My mind wasn't stable and it continued to roam. I could hear my mother's voice calling me...Noel...I could hear my father calling me...Noel...Nicolette called out...Sissy, Sissy.

I could hear the men say, "Torch the house, burn it to the ground." I could hear my father say, "I didn't mean for it to happen this way."

I could hear Mattie tell me, "We all we got now; we got each other." All of these people were talking at once; their words were running together and making one long drawn out conversation in my head. The room started to spin and my vision became cloudy. I started to scream and I begged for the voices to stop. I screamed and I screamed. I picked up the scissors that I'd used a few days ago to trim my hair. I grabbed a handful of my hair and started cutting. I held the hair in my hand and dropped it into the sink; the hair was all clumped together with the blood from my hands. I started randomly cutting hair and watching it fall. I stopped and looked in the mirror. I looked into my eyes, they were dark and distant; the light was fading from them just as it had faded from my mother's as I watched her die. I no longer knew this woman staring at me. She was a stranger; she'd invaded my life and was here to destroy what was left. She helped me realize my sister was dead. I looked around my bathroom, which was completely white. White towels, white rug and tile; white everything! What kind of person has an all white bathroom? My bathroom was always spotless and now it was stained with red blood it was no longer pure. It was soiled just as my childhood had been soiled. I looked at my chopped up hair, my bleeding hands and wild eyes; I grabbed the scissors and stabbed myself in the chest. I felt my body move in slow motion. As I spun around the room, I heard the voices of my mother, my father and sister again. They were getting louder and louder. I could feel people around me but no one was there, except Mattie. I opened my mouth to call her name, "Please help me Mattie...Please help me." I could see her lips moving and tears flowing from her eyes, but I couldn't hear her voice. As my body hit the floor, I felt cold. I lay there on the cold tile as my body became cooler and cooler. Finally, I felt a calming wind sweep through my body. I am free...I am rested...I am ready to move on.

Chapter Four

I was lying in the psyche ward strapped to a hospital bed. Judging from the fact that my mouth tasted like hot garbage and the room smelled like day old piss, I assumed that I'd been in that place for a few days. Everything seemed hazy to me. I was seeing things as if I were in a tunnel. As I began to focus, everything moved in slow motion. I realized that I couldn't move. I looked around the room then lay there staring up at the ceiling and wondering; is this my lot in life? I guess I'm immortal, I can't die. I guess, like others who were so blessed to be alive, I should find God and walk around saying "Halle-lujah," "Praise God," and "He sho' is good...He saved my life!" Is that what the hell I should do? Well Hallelujah, thank you Jesus, hot damn I'm alive...what a fuckin' joke! I started laughing out loud while I struggled with the restraints on my arms. I screamed for someone to come and take them off. I felt trapped like an animal in a cage not even half my size. I couldn't put my hands near my face or any other part of my body. My mind was restless. My body felt warm and filled with adrenalin.

I yelled and screamed, "Get this shit off of me! Let me out of here! Please let me go." I started trying to lift myself, thinking that I could possibly somehow chew through the fibers of the restraints and get the hell out of there. I guess I thought I was Willa the Rat Queen and could gnaw my way out of there. I could hardly even lift my head.

The more I screamed, the more my screams went unanswered. I lay there shaking my head from side to side screaming, "Let me out of this mutha fucka! Let me out of here! I want to go home." To this day I can't begin to explain to you what I was truly feeling. Unless you've ever experienced this loss of control, you can never imagine the power that insanity holds. One day I'm walking around maintaining some sort of life and draped in designer gear, living in a beautiful home and driving a luxury automobile that some people would go into debt just to say they own, but there I was strapped to a bed at the nut factory. Where are Jack Nicholson and the Indian Chief when you need them?

I was lying there staring at the ceiling still trying to figure out how to get out of there, when two huge men followed by a nurse burst into my room. I swear to you, I have never seen a strait jacket before in my life. I honestly thought they only existed in the movies, but they are very real. The men walked over and released my restraints. They grabbed my arms. I started kicking and screaming and trying to fight them. At one point, I thought I was free. I felt my foot touch the ground and I slid off the side of the bed. I tried to slip between the two orderlies, but the nurse grabbed my legs and yelled for another nurse to come in. The other nurse came toward me with a syringe filled with what must have been a sedative. I felt a sharp prick on my skin and I saw the nurse come toward me with the jacket.

I heard someone say, "When she comes to she's going to be a hand full, she needs to be moved to solitary." After that, the events of the next few hours are completely unknown to me. I woke up in a room without windows; just a door and a bed. I struggled to sit up straight. Once I was sitting upright, I made my way off of the bed and tried to walk to the doorway. When I looked out I saw another room directly across from mine and couldn't see much farther than that. I walked around the room that was about the size of a jail cell. I walked from one end of the room to the next trying to figure out what the hell went wrong. I walked and walked. I must have walked at least a mile. Finally, I became tired and slid down the side of the well-cushioned wall. I sat there propped against the wall with my eyes wide open. I don't even remember blinking. I whispered to anyone who could hear me, "Please help me, help me."

I sat there with the cold floor pressed against my skin. It was just me and the thoughts inside my head. I had no sense of time. I didn't know what day it was. I didn't know what time it was. I sat there and begged for help until I couldn't speak anymore. Seconds passed, minutes passed, hours passed and finally the day passed. The next thing I heard were keys rattling in the door. I assumed it was morning. The door flew open and a nurse with a tray of food walked into the room. She placed the tray down on the bed and leaned in front of me.

Before she could even ask me if I was ok, I looked up at her and said in a low voice, "Get the fuck out of here and leave me alone." I placed my foot on the ground and tried to gather my balance and she headed for the door. I didn't want to be bothered by anyone. I stayed on the floor against the wall and continued to sit there.

Finally, I closed my eyes and transported myself back in time. I was a little girl again. Nicolette, Claude Jr., Victoria and I were outside chasing lightening bugs. We were running and playing and enjoying the night air. Our parents and Uncle Clark were sitting out back telling stories and watching us enjoy childhood. We sang songs and told corny knock-knock jokes. Just as everything began to feel so real, everyone started to get farther and farther away from me. I stretched my hand out, but I was unable to reach them.

I opened my eyes, and begged for someone to help me. My room seemed to be filled with lightening bugs and butterflies. The butterflies were swarming around my head and I could see the light flickering from the bodies of the lightening bugs. My arms were bound and I couldn't shoo them away.

I began to cry. I asked "Why?" and rocked back and forth and cried some more. While I was sitting there, I looked toward the ceiling and began speaking to God. "Dear God, please...I need you right now Lord...down here on earth. Please, on top of everything else please don't let me lose my mind totally. I don't know what I've done to deserve this, but I'm sorry and I beg your forgiveness. Please Lord, have mercy on me...Please have mercy on my soul..."I must have cried until my tear ducts were bone dry.

After I couldn't cry anymore, I whispered, "Please help me." After I could no longer whisper, I rocked and rocked, until I'd rocked myself to sleep. Seconds passed, minutes passed, and hours passed once again. Another day came, this time I met the nurse at the door and told her not to enter my room. She stood in the doorway with another tray of food and I told her I didn't want any food.

"I don't want anything. Now get the hell out of here, and leave me alone."

She looked at me with a puzzled look and said, "Look, at least let me take you to the bathroom."

Without saying a word I walked over to where she was standing between my room and the hallway. I spread my legs apart and squatted. I pissed right there on the floor in front of her. When I was done, I turned around and walked back into my room.

"I'm finished, thank you." Without saying a word she slammed the door.

I continued to walk the length of my cell. I begged for my sanity and begged for mercy. I walked and I prayed, I prayed and I walked. My prayers switched to curses and my curses switched to praise. I was having a very personal moment with my God. It was just the two of us, but then I invited my mother to come into the room. I took my place on the floor because that's where I was most comfortable.

My mother sat on the bed and I asked her, "What took you so long?"

Her reply was, "I didn't think you were ready to see me just yet, so I came when I thought you needed me." I sat there trying to figure out if this counted as being insane, I was sitting there talking to my dead mother.

I looked up at her and she said, "Baby, you can't do this to yourself. You do know that you are not crazy."

"Well then what do you call this, the latest fashion craze?" I started moving in my strait jacket.

"No, you've lost control. This is totally understandable in your situation. You can't lose control. You have a purpose. You're alive for a reason. There's a thin line between sanity and insanity. Now you just need to cross back over into the land of sanity. I need you. I need you to help me...I can't rest if I know you're in pain. I've been restless for twenty years. I've tried to watch over you, but I'm fading and I'm tired. There is so much that you don't know..."

"I know Mama, please tell me. Tell me what happened."

"Baby, I wish it were that easy. You have to find out on your own." Just when it seemed that I was getting somewhere, I heard the door open.

I sprang up from the floor almost losing my balance and yelled, "Get the hell out of here; get out." The nurse was telling me that I needed to eat. I told her I didn't want any food and to get the hell out. I stood there jumping up and down in one spot. I lost my balance and fell to the ground. I lay there wallowing like a fish out of water. She closed the door and yelled through hole in the doorway that she'd be back with another sedative. I didn't have much time. I needed to get my mother back. I called for her to come, but she never came. This made me furious and I began walking, yelling, cursing and screaming. When I couldn't go another step I collapsed against the wall again. The nurse came back with another nurse. I heard her say it was a mild sedative. She told the other nurse to see if she could make me eat a little of the soup she'd brought with her. I didn't fight. I couldn't fight. I couldn't remember the last time I'd eaten.

I looked up at the nurse and told her, "I need help...I need to find my mother. Please can you help me?" She was actually very nice, she told me she would try and help me, but I knew she couldn't help. Before the nurses left, they helped me onto my bed. I lay there on the bed drifting off to sleep. I remembered my mother's lullaby.

I lay in a fetal position and started singing to myself; "Rock a bye baby, in the tree top, when the wind blows, the cradle will rock, when the bough breaks, the cradle will fall and down will come baby, cradle and all." This song rang in my head as I lay there trying to gather my thoughts and cross back over to sanity. While I was singing to myself, I could hear my mother's voice. She joined in with me and I could actually feel her with me. A sense of comfort and calmness swept over me. I stretched my body out and decided to rest.

Chapter Five

The next morning I woke up in a regular hospital room. It wasn't the same as before. The room was larger than my original room. There were no arm straps or strait jackets to restrain me. I was fresh and clean and my hair was braided. I really wasn't down with the corn-rows, but at least I didn't look like a wet chicken anymore. While I was lying there, a nurse walked into the room. She was vibrant and friendly.

"How are you feeling this morning?"

I looked up at her and said, "How the hell do I look?"

She smirked and said, "You look a whole lot better than you did when you first got here. And thank God you smell better."

I laughed to myself and said, "I can imagine."

I asked her how long I would be staying there. She stated she didn't know and I would have to speak with my doctor about that. The nurse also informed me they'd been consulting with my primary care physician to try and get some background information on me. My family doctor assured them I wasn't dangerous, there was just something emotionally wrong with me and she couldn't figure out what it was. If trying to commit suicide didn't make me crazy, then what was I? The nurse told me they'd done a series of neurological tests. She said everything seemed to be fine, but the doctor assigned to me would update me on what was going on. Before she left the room, she told me I'd received several visitors and calls while I was in solitary. I asked her if they knew I was in solitary. She stated she'd only told them I was unable to see visitors right now. Patients in the psych ward weren't allowed visitors until their probationary period was up. I told the nurse I didn't want to see anyone anyway. A look of concern came over her face. While she was talking I remembered her telling me she would help me find my mother the night before. She was also the person that fed me when I was in solitary. She walked over to my bed.

"Well your family has been here every day to see you." She stated.

"I don't have any family."

"They seemed like family to me."

"Everything ain't what it seems."

"Alright then...just trying to help," she said softly.

"I'm beyond help. I don't want to see anyone."

She stood there for a moment with a look of pity in her eyes and said, "You don't even want to see your mother."

"My mother is dead." She looked confused and yet embarrassed at the same time.

"I'm sorry, I just thought..."

I looked up at her and said, "Don't worry, it's ok, she's been dead for twenty years. I know what I said to you last night, but I guess it was the sedative talking for me."

The nurse placed her hand on my shoulder and told me everything would be ok and she left the room. As I looked up toward her, there was something familiar and comforting about her. I searched my mind and tried to think of how our paths could have crossed. I looked into her eyes, they seemed to be all knowing. She was a strikingly attractive woman with distinct features. Her skin was fresh and clear. Her jet-black hair complimented her olive skin tone, which glowed like rays of sunshine. As she parted her full cherry lips, her bright comforting smile was revealed. She appeared to be my parent's age, if they'd been alive. As she walked across the room to refill my water pitcher, I noticed her regal frame. She glided across the floor with confidence. She was tall, about five foot nine. She wore a long braid that cascaded down her back.

After filling my water pitcher, she walked over to my bed and said, "You know when our loved ones die they continue to live on in our hearts." She touched her chest as she spoke. "As long as you keep her in here, your mother will live forever. That's where I keep my mother."

I asked, "Is your mother dead too?"

"To be honest I don't really know. It's a long story, but we lost touch so long ago. Things were so different way back then. People where different. Some things you just have no control over and you just have to flow with the tide, I guess."

At that moment her eyes grew sad and distant. I didn't want to be intrusive, so I reluctantly held my questions. As I watched her visit some far away place, I assumed the place where she kept her painful secrets, I noticed that she too had green eyes. Her eyes were not like mine they were a dull shade of green almost hazel. They almost looked transparent. At that moment, I felt like I could see right through her eyes and into her soul.

She batted her eyes vigorously and said, "Oh, would you look at me. I'm bringing you down with my sentimental woes!"

I sat up in my bed and placed my feet on the ground. "Oh no believe me, you can't bring me down. I've got no place to go but up!" We both laughed. I realized I didn't even know this woman's name, so I asked her.

"I'm sorry, I didn't get your name."

She extended her hand and said, "My name is Iris, Iris Clayton."

"Well Iris, Iris Clayton, I'm sure you know my name by now." She laughed.

We sat and talked for a long time, making small talk. We didn't get too personal, just friendly banter. Finally out of curiosity I asked her where she was from.

She looked over at me, tilted her head and said, "I'm like a leaf in the wind, and my home is wherever I land." At that moment, it was as if a fresh breeze swept through my body. I felt warm and safe. Iris removed herself from my bedside.

She said, "Well, Seth, I think I've bent your ear long enough. I'll be sure and check on you later.

As she began to exit my room I noticed her arm. It appeared to be inflexible. I remembered that she did basically everything with her right arm. Whatever her affliction, she hid it quite well. In passing, her imperfection might have gone unnoticed. Just as she turned to leave she looked back at me and smiled as if she were telling me that everything was going to be alright.

I sat on the side of my bed trying to sort through my bizarre, yet comforting, visit from Iris. Suddenly, I heard the doorknob turn. I thought it was Iris returning, but instead it was an impeccably dressed black man standing in the doorway.

As he entered my room he said, "Hello I'm Dr. Batiste, how are you feeling today?"

"Fine I guess."

"Well you look better."

"Thanks, that seems to be the consensus around here."

"I just call it like I see it." Dr. Batiste informed me that he was not my medical doctor. He was assigned to be my psychiatrist while I was there. I had been checked out and everything seemed to be fine physically. He said I'd undergone a neurological exam and everything seemed to be ok. He confirmed what the nurse had just told me. He'd spoken with my primary physician and there wasn't a reported history of any mental illness. I acknowledged that I was being treated for anxiety along with depression. Dr. Batiste informed me that he wanted to release me to a Mental Health facility for observation, something not too restrictive, sort of like a retreat. I asked him how long would this observation take. He recommended thirty days in order to develop an effective treatment plan. It all depended on my progress and my evaluation. His job was to evaluate me while I was a patient at the hospital and to refer me to another facility. I asked him if he could suggest a facility, I was ready to leave that place already.

"Judging by the information I was provided with, I assume you don't want a state supported facility you would prefer something a little more private."

"You mean because I can afford it."

"You said it I didn't." What was this? Showtime at the Apollo? Everyone here was so full of wisecracks. When he noticed I wasn't amused, he remarked, "Tough room."

It's kind of hard to laugh at anything while you're lying in a psyche ward. Dr. Batiste told me he wanted to keep me in the hospital for a couple more days just to be safe. With a straight face I said, "To make sure I don't nut up again."

He laughed and quickly hid his smile, "Yeah something like that." He said he had a few suggestions for treatment facilities. He recommended one in particular called Serenity Springs. He was on staff at the facility and he wanted to continue to see me and set up my treatment plan. I asked him why he needed to be the one to see me, he never heard me say one word until twenty minutes ago. He told me his sister Isabelle worked with me and he wanted to do anything he could to help me. He'd heard wonderful things about me. First of all, I was shocked to find out that he was Isabelle's brother. Then, I immediately informed him that it was a conflict of interest and I definitely did not want Isabelle in my business. I guess I just wasn't paying attention. When I heard his last name I never thought to ask if he knew Isabelle. It really is a small world after all. He assured me that whatever we discussed was strictly confidential and he would never risk losing his license or getting sued. He just wanted to help. I agreed to go to Serenity Springs upon my discharge from the hospital. I stayed at the hospital for a few more days and then I moved thirty miles from the city to Serenity Springs.

Once I reached the new facility, I mainly stayed in my room. I sat by the window and stared out at the other patients. I tried to imagine why each of them had come here. I wondered if any of their issues came close to mine or was my situation unique. I really didn't think I had anything in common with any of those people. I couldn't believe that at this time last week I was lying in a cold dark room bound by a strait jacket. I thought to myself, if that could happen to me, and I know I'm not totally insane, then what had these other people been through. I was extremely uncomfortable. I wasn't interested in making friends with anyone. I was only planning to be there for the minimum of thirty days and so far I'd counted every tree I could see on the grounds. I discovered the different types of flowers that grew in the flowerbeds. I knew the exact number of tiles on the floor in my room and how many footsteps it took to reach the door from the window. My room was on the back end of the property and the view of the flower garden reminded me that as a child I would wake up every morning and thank God for the trees and my mother's beautiful flowers. Nicolette and I couldn't wait to play in the field behind the house. Or, if it were autumn, we would run and jump in the grass and leaves, playing hand games like Miss Suzie and Tweel Leel Leet. My mother would often play Little Sally Walker with us. Sometimes our friends from the nearby homes would come over and play.

There were children who lived approximately half a mile down the road on each side of us. The houses were spaced pretty far apart, I guess because everyone liked their privacy. We lived on an old country road where there were a few other houses. Private homeowners had purchased the land. Some of them owned horses and others, enjoyed the open space and the land. My closest neighbors were Victoria and Claude Shaw, Jr. We called her "Vicki" for short and we called him "Claude Junior". Sometimes we would just call him "Junior." My parents and the Shaw's were good friends. My father and Dr. Shaw were as close as brothers. My father always said Dr. Shaw was a good man as well as being very resourceful. I remember the last time I saw Vicki and Claude, J. It was the day before the fire. We were playing at our house. Claude, Jr. was nine and a half, he was the oldest. Vicki was our age. Claude and I would always get into a fight. He was so bossy because he was the oldest. I used to take up for Vicki and Nicolette. This time Claude Junior had made me so mad, I clocked him in the head with a rock. His head was bleeding and he wanted to go home. I remember telling him, "Claude Junior, don't you come back here until you learn how to treat girls." Of course I got in trouble for that and couldn't play outside for the rest of the day. After Claude's mother cleaned him up, he and Vicki came back to play. Nicolette was allowed out but I had to stay in. I sat by my window and watched as they played. Claude looked up at me and stuck his tongue out. I guess it was a reflex; I stuck my tongue out at him and put my middle finger up. As I remembered that day I pressed my forehead against the window and began to laugh.

Dr. Batiste said, "So she does know how to laugh," I had no idea he was standing there.

"How long have you been there?"

"Long enough to catch you laughing."

One of the things we had to do before being released from the hospital is attend group and individual therapy. Dr. Batiste let me know my group would meet at 1:15 in the yellow room. I asked him if that was the pre-menopausal, midlife crisis, homicidal, sisterhood of crazy heifers group. He looked at me and smiled.

"No, it's the 'do whatever I can to get the hell out of here' group."

"Why doctor, you have a sense of humor."

"Yes, and if you tell anyone, I'll deny it."

He touched my shoulder slightly as he spoke to me and I felt a slight shiver. It wasn't the kind of reaction you get from a cold wind or a frightening thought. It was pleasant, warm and friendly.

When I walked into the room, I realized that I was one of the only two black women in the group. I greeted everyone and took the seat closest to the window. I figured when I got bored I could look out the window and imagine I was somewhere else. The therapist walked in and the group began. She introduced herself as Leah Anderson, she said we could call her Leah. She sat right next to me. She asked each of us to introduce ourselves and tell why we were here. Most of the women said they really didn't know what happened, they had just snapped and lost it. Some explained they were feeling unstable and needed to get away. When it was my turn, I introduced myself and told them I was there because I was tired and I needed some rest so I stabbed myself. Everyone seemed to be shocked at my cavalier approach to my situation. I knew they'd all tried to commit suicide because that's how they grouped us until we made progress. I didn't respond to the blank stares and open mouths. I sat there waiting for the next question. Time passed and we listened to one another's stories. I gazed out the window and turned to look at them every now and then just to acknowledge that I was still there. I guess it was my turn to share.

"We haven't heard from you Miss St. James, wouldn't you like to share with us today?" Leah prompted me.

"Will that help to get me out of here any quicker?"

"Actually, not really, but it can aid in your progress."

"I'd rather just listen. I really don't have anything to share."

"There's no need for you to be afraid to share with us. Everyone here is in the same boat."

From across the room one of the ladies decided to speak up.

"Yeah, we all have the same issue here, you're not alone. When my husband left me after fifteen years of marriage I knew I was hangin' on by a thread so I took some time for myself and checked in here."

Another woman said "I know what you mean, when my husband told me he was leaving me for his secretary, I cut the crotch out of all his pants and set his car on fire in front of his whore's house. You should have seen that bitch crying."

I sat there and listened to those women cackle over stupid shit. I thought to myself, get a perm and a younger man and get over it. Leah was sitting there letting everyone vent.

Finally she turned to me and said, "See you're not alone, everyone here has issues that need to be worked out as well." Was she out of her mind? I didn't have anything in common with these nutty heifers. I couldn't hold my peace any longer.

"What? You people have no idea what pain is. Your husband's left you and you're feeling a little down so you checked into the Beverly Hills nut house for wayward wives to ease the pain. So they left big deal! They probably left a long time ago and you were all trying too hard to be the perfect little housewife to notice. He's been fuckin' the secretary and the babysitter since way back when. You want to know why I'm here? I'm here because I saw my mother and father killed right before my eyes. I saw my sister get blown away in an explosion after our house was set on fire. A few weeks ago I almost attacked a woman in my boutique because I thought she was my dead sister...so hell naw you don't share my issues, you're not even in my league...this is not a vacation for me, this is my life... so excuse me if I don't want to share with the group. You want to know why I'm here? I'm here cause I'm alive, got dammit!" The room was quiet as I bolted from my seat and my chair flew into the wall. As I exited the room you could hear a fly fart on the windowsill. No one said a word.

I went back to my room and sat by the window. I closed my eyes and tried to find Vicki, Nicolette and Claude Junior again. I tried to find the trees in the woods. I tried to find the dandelion field. I tried to find a way out of this place through my mind. Something had to give. It was time for me to find myself. The group session confirmed that I did not belong here. It was time for me to go. I needed help that much is true, but I couldn't get it here. I don't need some lady looking at me asking me how I feel about things. I don't need a therapist, I need a private detective. I'd been there for three weeks and I needed to get back to my life. I needed to learn how to live with what I now knew to be true. Nicolette is dead, but most importantly I needed to know why. While I was trying to relax Dr. Batiste entered my room.

"Hey...everything alright?"

I removed myself from the windowsill and walked past him and sat in the chair. "Why...what have you heard?"

"Well, I heard you didn't exactly enjoy your group session at all."

"That's an understatement," I said. Dr. Batiste sat down in the chair next to me and pulled off his glasses revealing gorgeous brown eyes.

"To be honest, you did just fine. You may not realize it but you have made progress. It wasn't what I had in mind, but it was progress nevertheless."

I was totally puzzled "What...do you need a bed here as well?" He dropped his head and laughed.

"No, what I mean is you finally verbalized what has been consuming you all these years and what was making you feel as though you were losing control. I bet you've never told a living soul what you told the group."

"No, I've never told anyone about my past."

"You were holding so much inside and it was growing like a cancer eating away at the lining of your soul until you snapped...you're right you don't belong here. You need something more intense." He must be the crazy one. I was not going to another hospital.

"Look, I am not going to another institution, I've had enough of this One Flew Over the Cuckoo's Nest shit...I'm going home...I'm not crazy!"

"I know you're not crazy, you're in pain. I was referring to individual sessions with a psychiatrist. I'm talking about psychotherapy. I want to discharge you and schedule private sessions for you."

I don't know what it was about Dr. Batiste, maybe it was his professional yet compassionate demeanor, but I was ready... ready to free my soul.

"Well doctor since I'm paying for this we might as well start now. My real name is Noel Marie Toussaint. That was the name my mother gave me when I was born. When I was eight years old a group of men came into my home and killed my parents in cold blood. It wasn't a robbery, it was a planned execution. My twin sister Nicolette was killed as she tried to go back into our burning house. The house exploded and I never saw her again. The only survivors were me and my surrogate grandmother Mattie. I don't know what happened, but the older I get, I feel that this is deeper than just a random robbery. I believe my father was into something that he couldn't get out of. I believe my Uncle Clark had something to do with my family's death and I also believe that Mattie knew what was going on, but she has never spoken a word about it since we left Georgia and changed our names. So, no, I'm not crazy. I'm sad, mad as hell, and I need some answers. I need to know what happened to my life."

I could feel the tears roll down my face. I felt relief even though my journey was just beginning. Dr. Batiste looked into my eyes. It was the look of pity, but also of understanding. When I looked at him I thought about Isabelle, she had the same look the day I met Lauren. She knew there was something wrong, she's always known. I made up my mind to open the door to my past, to exorcise those demons. It was time for Mattie to tell me everything she knew about my father. There are some things that happen in life that you just can't shake. They leave you numb and helpless and sometimes you can't even speak a word. You just pray and hum Amazing Grace, how sweet the sound that saved a wretch like me.

Chapter Six

I was ready to be discharged from the hospital so I called Isabelle. She was the only one I felt comfortable with. On the way home, Isabelle and I made small talk. We talked about the weather and the boutique. We talked about the latest entertainment news and world affairs. I could tell she wanted to ask what made me flip out, but she was afraid. This was the longest car ride that I'd ever taken. I noticed things that I'd never seen before; buildings, landmarks, trees and neighborhoods. My eyes were open and I was more in touch with my surroundings. Everything was so much clearer.

I think we were both relieved when we finally reached my house. I thanked her for the ride and told her I'd call her later. I opened the door to my house; it seemed like for the first time. As I walked up the stairs, I inhaled the fragrance of my surroundings. I walked upstairs and into my room, it was as neat as a pin. Everything was in its place, just the way I liked it. I put my bag down next to the bed and walked into the bathroom. The broken mirror had been replaced. The towels and rugs were clean and my locket was lying next to the sink. I picked it up and put it around my neck. This was now truly all I had left of my family. There were no other pictures, locks of hair or other tangible mementos to hold on to. I cleaned the bathtub and prepared my bath with my favorite milk and honey bubble bath and a capful of baby oil. I poured myself a generous portion of Cognac.

I undressed in front of the mirror and for the first time I noticed myself. I noticed my beautiful skin tone. I noticed my curves. I noticed everything. I looked into my own eyes and saw myself. I didn't see my mother and I didn't see my sister, I saw me. My eyes were beautiful and bright. The hair that I attempted to destroy was absolutely gorgeous; it was now in its natural state. For years I'd worn my hair straight down my back because that's how I remembered my mother wearing her hair. I was probably the only woman in the world who still gets her hair pressed.

Suddenly, as I looked at my image in the mirror, I realized my own existence and the miracle of my life. All Mattie's talk about God the creator, the way maker, it must have been true. My life was spared for a reason. I have attempted suicide twice in my life, each time I was saved. While I was at Serenity Springs, I started reading the Bible and praying to God again. I remembered Him from the days of Sunday School and Vacation Bible School. I've tried to do this on my own and I hit rock bottom. For so long, I've lived my life as if I were alone. Isabelle was the only person that I've felt close to in a long time. If I were to ever learn how to love someone as a sister or like family, I would begin with her. I was tired of being alone. I needed people. I needed friends. I needed family. And, I needed Jesus. Hell, while I was at it...I needed a man.

Once I was finished with my bath, I walked into Mattie's room. I'd never entered her room other than to talk to her or to leave her laundry or something trivial. She wasn't there and this time my visit was different. It was as if I were on a mission. Unconsciously I started going through her drawers and looking under her bed. I was looking for something, but I had no idea what it was. I searched through her closet. I searched the shelves and I got down on my knees and searched the floor. Behind her winter coats I found a small chest, sort of like a footlocker or cedar chest. It was just small enough to fit inconspicuously behind her winter clothes. I was so overwhelmed with curiosity. What could be in there? Most people keep things like, baby clothes, photo albums and other mementos. I sat there contemplating on opening the chest. I knew it was wrong, but my gut kept telling me to open it. It was like the chest was saying, "Open me." The strange thing was it seemed to call my name, but it wasn't saying "Seth," it was saying "Noel." I looked around to find something to pick the lock. There was nothing in there that would open it. I ran to my bathroom and got my fingernail file and a few bobby pins. I ran back to the closet and sat cross-legged in front of the chest. I opened one of the bobby pins and tried to open the chest. I was beginning to get frustrated when the phone rang. It scared the shit out of me. My heart was beating so fast and I lay on the floor for a few seconds. The phone wouldn't stop ringing so I decided to answer it. It was Mattie.

"Hello, sweetheart...happy to be home?"

How ironic that she would call while I was snooping through her things. I tried to sound happy to hear her voice.

"Of course, I couldn't wait to get back...I feel much better...when are you coming home?" I really didn't care when she was coming back;

I just wanted to know how much time I had to snoop through her things.

"Actually, I just told Isabelle that I am on a church retreat, I didn't want anyone to know where I was...Barbara got a deal on a cruise and we'll be gone for ten days." A cruise! What the hell! And since when did she go anywhere with Barbara?

"It sounds like fun, where are you going?"

"We're going to a few islands in the Bahamas and we're going to stay a couple of days in Montego Bay." She seemed to be scrambling for words.

I thought to myself, Montego Bay is on a totally different Island. What was she up to? Before I could say anything about her geography mix-up, she said her time was running out on the payphone and she didn't have any more quarters. I was wondering what happened to her cell phone, but I just let it go. Obviously, she didn't want me to know where she was or what she was doing.

Before I went into the hospital, she was receiving calls from a man. That was cool with me. It was obvious she was being illusive about her whereabouts. It made better sense to me if she was going on the cruise, or wherever she really was, with him. Maybe she'd get a life and move in with him. Before getting off the phone she did make it known that she'd left her cell phone at home on the charger by mistake so I wouldn't be able to reach her. I looked over at the charger and it was empty. I guess she trusted me enough to know that I didn't frequent her room, so her lie would have gone undetected. I concluded that she was off with a man. She still had some fire I supposed. We said our goodbyes and hung up the phone. As I prepared to walk back into the closet, the phone rang again. This time it was Isabelle.

"Hey girl, how's it going? You settled in yet?"

"I sure am, I took a long hot bath and now I'm hungry."

"Really...well, order a pizza, and I'll come over with a chick flick." Without hesitation I agreed. I walked into the closet and retrieved my hoodlum tools. I felt bad about snooping. Just as I was getting ready to turn out the light in the closet; I looked down to make sure that everything was back in its proper place. As I stared at the trunk, I couldn't resist opening it. I reached up and pulled the bobby pins from my hair and popped the lock. The first thing I noticed was an old photo album. The album was old and worn. The cover was torn and some of the pages were cracked and dry-rotted. I could hear the cellophane cracking as I opened the album. The first picture was one of Mattie when she was much younger. She was absolutely breathtaking. Her skin was smooth and dark like pure cocoa. Her hair was jet black, her eyebrows and lashes were thick. Her eyes were round and bright like full moons. She had deep dimples and a round face. Her hair was parted down the middle and draped over her shoulders. This was clearly not the woman that I saw each day. The woman that I shared my home with was perhaps a shell of the woman staring back at me in that photograph. She now wore the look of worry and sadness. Lines, wrinkles and bags replaced her smooth skin. Her jet-black hair was accented with strands of gray. Although her hair was still long, it had remained in the same long braid for the last twenty years. It seemed like her hair turned gray overnight.

I examined the picture and tried to visualize what Mattie was like as a teenager, but the person in the picture was so unfamiliar to me that I couldn't make the connection. I continued to flip through the album. I was so excited to see pictures even if I had no idea who the people were. I continued to browse through the album, assuming they were pictures of her parents, sisters, aunts, cousins and friends. As I turned the pages, one after another, my eyes grew wide with amazement as one particular photo caught my attention.

It was a picture of my mother, father, and my Uncle Clark. I couldn't believe my eyes; it was like a hallucination. I was so nervous and my hands were shaking as I peeled back the cellophane that covered the picture. I peeled the picture off the page and held it in my hand. I outlined their faces with the tips of my fingers. I was crying so hard, I could hear my tears falling on the pages of the album, and I just let them fall. I didn't want to let go of the picture long enough to wipe the moisture from my face. This was the first time that I'd seen a picture of my parents in anything other than my tiny locket. This time I could see facial features and imagine their individual personalities. My mother was gorgeous. Uncle Clark and my father were so handsome.

Uncle Clark and my father grew up in a group home together. They were like blood brothers. I could only imagine that they would have become more striking with time. I could imagine them sitting around smoking cigars and drinking well-aged cognac as distinguished gentleman do. I thumbed through the album to find more pictures, but that was the only one I could find with my parents in it. I wanted to take it and tuck it away for safe keeping among my treasures, but I knew it wasn't mine to take. How could I ever explain finding the picture in the first place? I wanted to have a copy made, but I was afraid that it might get damaged in the process. I sat there for what seemed like an eternity staring at the picture. It was like I was trying to make them jump off the canvas and come to life. I sat there so long my backside was numb. I couldn't help but grow angrier at the thought of Mattie not sharing these memories with me. Why did she hate me so, and why did she want me to suffer?

I rummaged around in the trunk to see what else I could find. As I held my hand to my mouth to mask the gasp that escaped my lips, I couldn't believe my eyes. I reached into the trunk and pulled out the clothes I had been wearing the night my family was killed. They were neatly folded and stuffed into a plastic bag. I opened the bag and pulled them out. I could still smell the smoke from my burning house. The clothes were still dirty with soot. They even had small traces of blood from where the debris from the house hit my face. In an instant I began to remember that night all over again. The memories were flowing like water from a faucet.

After my family was killed, we stayed in Georgia for a few weeks until Mattie could figure something out. We went back to Mattie's house after the fire and she immediately started preparing for us to leave, but where, I didn't know. Shortly after we arrived at her house there was a knock at the door. She'd sent me into the other room to hide in the closet. She told me not to come out for any reason at all until she came in and got me. She took a piece of folded paper out of her bosom and told me that if anything happened to her, call the number on the piece of paper and ask to speak to Detective Charles Jonathan. I was so confused I didn't know what to do. I ran and hid in the closet just as I was told to do. I was tired and cold. The reality of losing my parents and my sister had not set in at that moment as I hid in the closet. I hadn't opened my mouth to say a word since Mattie dried my tears in the woods and calmed me. When I heard the knock at the door I thought the men found Mattie's house and had come to kill us as well. I ran and hid in the closet, I piled clothes on top of me just in case they looked inside the closet. I couldn't hear what was going on outside. I must have dozed off because when Mattie opened the door, she woke me up. As I sat on the edge of her bed and looked down at the floor, she prepared my bath water. We both smelled like smoke and we were dirty from lying in the grass. We walked a good ways that night to Mattie's house until someone stopped and picked us up. As the water ran in the tub, she sat down next to me and put her arms around me. She stroked my hair and wiped my dirty tear stained face and tried to console me. "I know you don't quite understand what has happened to you. I really can't explain it myself. Everything is going to be ok. Your mother, father and sister have gone to heaven and they're not coming back, it's just you and me now. You have to be a big girl and you must understand that things are going to be very different from now on. We are going to have to leave Georgia soon and we can never, ever come back here."

I began to cry uncontrollably. The reality of losing my family had finally hit me, and I wanted to go home. I told Mattie I wanted my mommy and my daddy and I wanted to go home now.

"You can't go home ever. The house is gone and so is everyone else, honey. It's important that you remember this." Mattie told me that I would have to change my name. I could no longer answer to Noel. I wiped my tears and looked over at Mattie. I wanted to know why I had to change my name.

"But...why? I love my name."

Mattie said, "There are some bad people out there who can never know that we're still alive. The only way we'll be safe is to change our names."

I was more confused than ever. More than anything I was scared as hell of the bad people. I would do anything to be safe, so I agreed to change my name. Mattie told me my name would be Seth, like in the Bible. Adam and Eve were blessed with Seth after Cain slew Abel. He gave Adam and Eve a second chance at having a child. I'd received a second chance at life. My life was spared and my new name was just a substitute for my birth name. It took me years to get used to having a name that should belong to a boy, but eventually I accepted it.

Our next step was to find out where to go. Mattie took out a map of the United States that I had left there a few weeks ago and told me to pick a place on the map. I picked Texas because I liked the shape of the state. At the time I really didn't care about Texas, I really didn't even think we were going anywhere. I waited every single day for my parents to walk through the door. I figured they were off on a vacation and took Nicolette with them. My feelings were hurt, but I would forgive them for leaving me if they'd just come back home. The day after the fire, I woke up and waited for my parents to come; I waited the next day and the day after that. Mattie insisted that I stay in the house; I couldn't even look out the window. When she had to leave the house, she locked me inside all by myself. Every time someone came to the door she would make me hide in the closet. It seemed that Uncle Clark visited quite a bit those few weeks before we left. The police came to the house one day. They weren't normal police; they were dressed in suits. I was tired of hiding in the closet, so I hid under the bed and I was able to hear the conversation. They asked about my father and they asked about Uncle Clark. They wanted to know where she was the night my parents were killed. She told them that she was there at her house. She stated she went to play bingo, but when she arrived she found out the roof at the bingo hall had been damaged in the storm a few nights before. Since she didn't drive, she stated this particular night Uncle Clark had driven her. She also stated that after she left the bingo hall, she cooked dinner and Clark fell asleep on her couch. I knew she was lying, but it really wasn't significant at the time. The fact that was puzzling me was that she informed the police that Uncle Clark had been there. I don't remember the police or Uncle Clark coming to the house.

After the night of the fire Mattie never called me Noel again. She drilled my new name into my head. Not only had my first name changed, but my last name as well. It became, St. James. Mattie's last name was James so she simply put the "St." on the front of it and from then on we were Mattie and Seth St. James, beloved grandmother and granddaughter. She changed her first name from Madelyn to just Mattie. That really wasn't a drastic change for her because we called her Mattie anyway. I guess Mattie was tired of hearing me ask to go home. She couldn't make me understand why we couldn't return. On the day we left Dillon, she had the cab driver ride by our old house on the way to the airport. When I realized we were finally going home my heart started beating fast and I couldn't keep still. I looked up at Mattie and smiled, I was so excited. She didn't smile back, she just sat there. We slowly drove by the house. There was nothing there but a bunch of trash and the remains of what used to be a house. The land was dark and ugly with patches of burned grass and left over flowers. The area was partitioned off with yellow tape. The dandelions were no longer in bloom and the trees behind the house looked like a scary wilderness. My heart sank to my feet and tears rolled down my face. I didn't look at Mattie; instead I rested my chin on the door and began to slowly die deep inside of my soul.

Chapter Seven

I was startled by the sound of the doorbell. I'd forgotten all about Isabelle and the pizza that I'd ordered. I placed the picture back into the album and put the album behind the chest where I'd found it. Now that I knew where it was, I could go back and look at it whenever I had the chance. As I walked down the steps, I fanned the tears and wiped my face. I took a deep breath and answered the door. I was happy to see that it was the pizza guy and that Isabelle hadn't arrived yet. I had time to dry my tears.

Isabelle arrived only a few minutes after the pizza arrived. She asked how it felt to be home. I told her it felt great. I could look at her and tell she really wanted to know what was going on with me. Something inside of me said, "Tell her". Only her brother and a room full of minivan driving, pill popping, soccer moms knew my story, and it sounded so farfetched, they probably thought I was having a psychotic episode. Isabelle was sitting at the kitchen table across from me.

The whole house was silent. Finally, I said, "Do you ever wonder about me?" She looked at me as if to say, can you be more specific?

"I mean, about me as a person, where I'm from, about my family?" She dropped her head and looked back up at me.

"Yeah, I do...you never talk about your parents or any of your family for that matter. I know you're not from here, but you never say where you were born...and I guess what puzzles me is that you said Mattie was your grandmother, but you don't resemble her at all...There are a lot of things I wonder about you, but I just figured since Mattie seemed to be your only family...your parents were dead or just not around."

"Well you're on the right track...my parents are dead and they never knew their parents." She immediately had a look of sadness as I began to tell her about my mother's family. "My mother never knew her parents or so I believe. She was given up for adoption at birth. She was very fair skinned and said growing up she didn't feel like she was a hundred percent black, whatever that means. As a child she was referred to as 'high yella' and 'half breed.' When she turned eighteen and became emancipated from the state of Georgia she was told by her caseworker that her mother was indeed white and her father was black. My mother's final caseworker had been around for a longtime and the story of my mother's existence had been passed down through the agency. As the story goes, her mother was from a well-known white family in Georgia and her father was the hired help. After her mother became pregnant, she refused to tell who the father was. When my mother was born it was clear that she belonged to a 'nigger'. Later on that night, after my grandmother gave birth, two black men that worked for the family were found hanging from an old oak tree in the woods behind the house. Two others got away and never came back. My mother was given to a midwife that lived in one of the family's row houses. The midwife died when my mother was five and she became a ward of the state. At that time there were no families for black children. My mother was bounced from place to place until she was eighteen. A few months before my parents were killed, she told Nicolette and me about her past. She told us our father was helping to find answers as to who she really was. Sometimes we would hear my mother crying in her room. My father caught us listening one day and told us my mother's heart was broken and she was trying to find her way. Of course, at the time, we had no idea what he meant, but I would find out years later. After my mother's death, and even now, I dream of her walking in the woods behind our house searching for Nicolette and me in the dark. She would call out to us, but she couldn't see us and we couldn't see her. She would always tell us that she was lost and couldn't find her way. It seemed the closer I got to her, the farther away she became. I'd always wake up before I found her. One night, while Mattie, Nicolette, Mama and I were watching television, as we waited for my father to come home, Mama began to tell us about a white woman who used to visit her as a child. It was like she didn't even realize we were in the room with her. They called the woman Missy, and she seemed to find Mama wherever she would end up. Missy would bring toys and clothes to the children in the foster home. She would bring special gifts for Mama. My mother didn't believe Missy was the lady's real name.

On her last visit a Black man dressed in a black suit and hat came to the door and said "Miss Ginny we better go now, you're gonna be late for your appointment." 'Missy' or 'Ginny' left and never returned. That was the last time my mother saw her face to face. She was sixteen years old at that time. When my mother graduated from high school she received an envelope with a card and ten thousand dollars in cash tucked inside. The card was signed Missy. My mother was never given the names of her parents, or exactly where in Georgia she was from. Mama said there was always a warm and familiar feeling about Missy. When she learned of her past she assumed that Missy was her mother or at the very least, someone who knew her. After my mother finished reminiscing, she looked at my sister and me and made us promise to never forget her after she was gone and to always let her memory live in our hearts. I was very uncomfortable that night and I began to worry about my parents dying and leaving us orphaned. There was so much pain in my mother's eyes that night, it was like she knew she didn't have long to live. When I look in the mirror, I see the same look in my eyes and I feel her pain. I now know exactly what her pain felt like. My only comforting thought is knowing she can never feel that pain again.

As for my father, his parents along with his younger brother were killed in a car accident. My father was the only survivor. There were no family members on either side willing to take on an extra burden, so he grew up in a group home for boys until he turned eighteen. He knew exactly where his family lived in Louisiana, but he had no interest in contacting them or keeping in touch. My parents met in college. They both went to Tougaloo College in Jackson, Mississippi. That's also where they met Mattie. She worked in the cafeteria and basically took care of my father while he was in school. She says he was like her own son. After my father met my mother, Mattie cared for her as well. The three of them had an uncanny connection with each other. None of them had any biological family. They were all orphans with no one to love them, but each other."

Isabelle spoke softly, "My goodness, I can't imagine how it feels not to have family around."

I said to her, "You are blessed to have the love of your family. Don't ever take it for granted."

Isabelle hesitated before she asked, "Do you mind if I ask what happened to your parents?" I froze for a moment and tried to figure out whether or not to reveal my secret. I took a deep breath, but before

I could respond, Isabelle stopped me. "I know it has to be painful but it seems like you're ready to talk about it."

I took a deep breath "I'm ready to talk about everything...I just don't know if you're ready to hear it."

"I think I'm a pretty good listener."

"No Isabelle, it's much more complicated than that. If I sit here and tell you everything I've been keeping inside of me for the past twenty years...you'll become part of me...you'll become my family. You will bear the burden of keeping my secret." She looked straight into my eyes.

"You are family to me. I feel like you know every inch of my life, and I want to know about your life. Since I felt us getting closer in spirit, I hoped that you would let me into your world and tell me why your eyes are so full of sadness."

I walked over to the refrigerator and poured us some wine. I took a sip from one of the glasses and handed the other to Isabelle. She looked at me as if to say, "Damn, is it that serious?"

I sank down slowly into my seat and repeated the same speech that I had given her brother. As I told her the story and relived it in my mind, I gave her more details than I'd given Dr. Batiste. I expressed my reluctance to continue to trust Mattie and my desire to find out the truth. I sat there and spewed information like it was rehearsed. I knew the whole story backward and forward. When I finished speaking, I sat back in my chair and waited for her response. Her eyes were filled with tears as she sat speechless, trying to comprehend all that I had told her. At first she had no idea how to respond to such a powerful and bizarre story, and when she finally was able to respond, she said my story sounded like some kind of underworld fiction novel, but she could look into my eyes and see that it was real.

She touched my hand as it rested on the kitchen table. "You think Lauren is your sister don't you? Her daughter's name is Noel and the locket...." It was like she was trying to piece things together.

"When I first saw Lauren and Noel, I thought she might be my sister, probably because I wanted it to be true. But I guess rationale set in and I realized she can't be alive because I saw her die in the explosion. The day I saw Lauren, I lost it...I couldn't take it anymore. To be honest, I didn't wake up that morning and plan to attempt suicide, it just happened...it was like I was standing there outside of my body watching myself and ultimately lost control."

Isabelle got up from her seat and paced around the kitchen in disbelief.

"How in the hell have you held this in for so long?"

"I held on to the belief that Nicolette might be alive...I don't know why, but there was always something inside of me that said she was alive. After that day at the store, and I guess a month in the psych hospital, the feeling went away and reality set in. Coming to the realization that Nicolette was dead seemed to wake me up."

"So where do we go from here?"

"We?" My heart jumped as I took in her words.

"Of course, you can't go through this alone and from what you just told me I don't think Mattie can help you...nor does she want to. You shared this with me for a reason...I know I can never take the place of Nicolette, but I'm here and I'll be the best sister I can be." We embraced each other and I felt no regrets concerning my confession.

Isabelle asked me why I thought my parents were murdered. I told her months before my parents were killed my mother seemed to pay extra attention to us. It was as if she knew something was going to happen. She kept us in her eyesight at all times. She even began volunteering at our school. My father's business partner, Uncle Clark was spending more and more time at our house. He wasn't married, but I remember my mother referring to him as a 'ladies' man'. He used to bring different women around all the time. We had more aunts than anyone. I loved Uncle Clark, he was always so much fun. His real name was Ellis Clark Winfield, but he hated that name, so everyone called him Clark.

My father went to Tougaloo University, and Uncle Clark went to college in Georgia. After they graduated and settled into life they hooked back up and went into business together. My father was an attorney and Uncle Clark was into real estate, among other things. My father always said Uncle Clark was a "different breed of man." He was more of a hustler than anything and if he could make a dollar, he would. Uncle Clark pretty much grew up on the streets of Louisiana until he was arrested at thirteen. That's all we knew about him. My father says they were all they had back then. They both had those Louisiana accents that drove the women wild. Clark's accent was thicker than my father's. Uncle Clark worked hard to maintain his, while my father worked hard to lose his. Sometimes if you closed your eyes, you couldn't tell them apart by their voices. My father used to tell stories about the things he and Uncle Clark would get into when-ever we all got together. My parents would argue about Uncle Clark and his crooked ways. I don't think Mattie was too fond of him either. There was something odd between Mattie and Clark. It seemed like he had this secret contempt for her. She tried her best to make him welcome, but for some reason he just wasn't receptive to her. One night, I heard my mother tell my father that Uncle Clark was going to get him into something he couldn't get out of one of these days. My father told her Clark was his brother and he owed him his life. My mother told him he didn't owe Clark a damn thing. She said he owed his wife and kids the truth and an honest life. When you're a kid these things don't mean much, but when you're an adult and your parents died the way mine did, it means a whole hell of a lot. My father's relationship with Clark and his so called "business associates" seemed to be the only thing my parents ever argued about. My mother always referred to Clark as being slick, but for some reason she felt pity for him. She said he was too scared to be his own man. She was always nice to him and welcomed him into our home but you could believe she was watching him. Once, I heard my mother say that Clark was going to lose himself trying to keep up with my father.

Isabelle and I spent the rest of the night going through some notes that I'd taken and we discussed the possibility of hiring a private detective. We were sure the information we needed wasn't going to jump out at us, we needed professional help. I told Isabelle I would spend every penny I had to find the truth. Since I just appeared from nowhere and my past was sketchy, I was sure Isabelle was wondering how I made my living before opening the store. It was clear I was pretty well off. I informed Isabelle that my parents left life insurance policies with Mattie named as the beneficiary in case anything hap-pened to them. Each of my parent's insurance policies totaled two million dollars. And of course there was money in the bank and all kinds of other assets that were left to Mattie. That was the one positive thing I could say about Mattie, she has always done right by me financially. We didn't waste any of the money, but we lived comfortably in a suburban neighborhood. Mattie spent the rest of her working life as a kindergarten teacher. We lived a middle class life. I tucked away half of the money that I have so that when I found Nicolette she would have her share. I didn't know what kind of life she'd led. I didn't know if she ever went hungry, if she was scared or if she even remembered what had happened to her. And now, since I have acknowledged that she is in fact dead I will spare no expense in finding out why she and the rest of our family were murdered.

As I sat there feeling confident about what I'd shared with Isabelle, I remembered one significant detail that I'd forgotten to mention about myself. There is another secret that has haunted me. Although not as ancient as the subject at hand, it still remains tucked away in the confines of my mind. This is a secret that I am not willing to share with anyone outside of my internal thoughts. Isabelle looked at me with such empathy. She began to shed tears for the little girl that had been lost all those years. As I looked into her eyes and dried the tears that she'd shed for that little girl that fell from that bough that was broken, I wondered if she would shed those same tears for the cold blooded murderer that lived inside me. I guess the saying is true, "One sin just leads to another and so and so on."

Chapter Eight

When we first moved to Texas, Mattie and I lived across the street from Dr. and Mrs. Benjamin Stein. Dr. Stein was a dentist and his wife Grace, drank all day and night until she passed out. They seemed like a loving family, but soon it was like watching a bad picture develop. You wait for this great picture, but it turns out to be a blurry distorted mess.

I found out the Stein's had a secret. Mrs. Stein was a raging alcoholic. She'd probably been abusing alcohol her entire life. They had a son named Benjamin, but because Mrs. Stein drank during the pregnancy, he'd been born with abnormalities and was moved to a residential treatment center for physically and mentally disabled children at the age of six. I am not certain of his official diagnosis, but I know whatever it was kept him from living a normal life with his parents.

Mrs. Stein and Mattie used to talk all the time. After Benjamin was born you would think Mrs. Stein would stop drinking, but she continued. Eventually between the guilt, the depression and the drinking, she slowly killed herself. Grace Stein was from old money and she'd paid her husband's way through dental school. She'd majored in fashion design in college. She knew he would never leave her as long as she was his meal ticket.

He absolutely despised her because of what her drinking had done to their son. In his eyes, they were married in name only. They even slept in separate rooms. I don't recall ever seeing them leave the house together unless they were going to visit Benjamin. Dr. Stein visited Benjamin every chance he could. But not Mrs. Stein, she couldn't stand to look at her mistake. She knew she was the reason Benjamin was damaged.

They both seemed to be decent people in spite of their circumstances. Dr. Stein was always friendly. He always had some corny comments that made me laugh, as if he were Red Foxx. He was fairly attractive, but other than that there was nothing spectacular about him. He was tall and lean with dark hair. Mrs. Stein was quite the opposite. In fact, she was gorgeous. When we first met, she reminded me of a model in a magazine. She was about five feet, nine inches tall with long jet-black hair that bounced when she walked. Her lips were a natural shade of rose and she took great pride in her tan. She had high cheekbones and a great figure as well. When I was younger I wanted to be just like her. I was so fascinated with Mrs. Stein because she reminded me of myself. On the surface she appeared to have it all, but deep down her soul was lost and tortured.

Because I wasn't very sociable, I would occasionally spend time at the Steins. At that time I didn't know Mrs. Stein was an alcoholic. Either she hid it very well, or I just didn't notice, because I was a kid and didn't know what was going on. Mrs. Stein became pregnant with Benjamin. After he was institutionalized, Mrs. Stein began drinking more than ever. She would wander across the street day and night when Dr. Stein was away from home. She'd have a glass of cognac or gin in one hand and a cigarette in the other. We always knew when she'd mixed her lights and darks, she'd be in rare form. Some days we would actually have to run out to the middle of the street to get her before she got run over. She would strip down and dance to whatever music was playing in her head. Other times she would sit and talk to Mattie until she passed out. Mattie would put a throw across her limp body and let her sleep it off. When she was really lit up, she would ramble on about Benjamin and how she loved him and how sorry she was that he'd turned out the way he had because of her drinking. I felt so sorry for her because I knew how it felt to live with guilt and pain. My guilt was different though. I couldn't figure out why I lived and the rest of my family was gone. Mrs. Stein told Mattie that Dr. Stein would sometimes spend days without speaking to her.

They had a housekeeper named Emma, who managed all of the household needs. She would sometimes come over and talk to Mattie, telling her stories of the foolishness over there. She told Mattie about their unnatural relationship and how she couldn't understand how they could live like that.

To her credit, Mrs. Stein did attempt to stop drinking and that was a shitty mess. I'd never seen anything like it before. She was dead set on quitting on her own. She didn't want any professional help. She knew the consequences of quitting on her own, but she felt she deserved to suffer, and suffer she did. Both Mattie and Emma kept a pretty close watch on Mrs. Stein during her ordeal. Emma's own father had been an alcoholic and died from liver failure when she was seventeen years old, so she knew what to expect. Mrs. Stein went through horrible spells of vomiting and her eyes were beet red because she wasn't sleeping very much. Sometimes she would sit and talk to Benjamin, and her mother, who had been dead for ten years as if they were sitting right next to her. She had a terrible seizure and was hospitalized. She'd transformed into someone totally different. She was not the Grace Stein that I was once in absolute awe of as a child. She weighed less than a hundred pounds because she had stopped eating. She rarely spoke to anyone and on those rare occasions when she did speak, I found her breath so offensive, I had to sit across the room and talk to her. Her skin turned pale and her lips were chapped and ash white. She was frightening to look at. Finally, she balled up in her hospital bed and died. When they found her, she was in the fetal position cradling a picture of Benjamin. I think she was a victim of life more than the alcoholism.

Dr. Stein remained oddly reserved during the entire ordeal. It was as if he was waiting for her to die. Not even two days had passed after her death when he brought Benjamin home and hired a nurse to care for him twenty-four hours a day. He asked Mattie and Emma to pack Mrs. Stein's things and once they did, he gave it all to charity. It was clear he was changing or simply becoming who he'd always been.

Occasionally I would go over to sit with Benjamin when he gave the nurse a few hours off. I'd never noticed the way he looked at me before or maybe this was something entirely new. I remember on one particular night we were in the room with Benjamin when Dr. Stein looked at me as if he were undressing me in his mind. He seemed so different to me at the time. He was much more handsome and vibrant. He'd started wearing brighter colors, instead of the drab brown and black he'd worn before his wife died. He'd bought a new sports car and had become the life of the party, when before he'd been so reserved and quiet. He'd actually yell clean across the street just to say hello to us. I began to see features that I'd never noticed before. He was attractive but that was the extent of it at that point. We laughed and talked for a good while. Benjamin laughed or gave his version of excitement.

Dr. Stein thanked me for the time I'd taken with Benjamin and complimented me on my maturity. We talked about my plans for after graduation and what had motivated him to become a doctor. For the first time he even spoke of his relationship with Mrs. Stein, saying he harbored resentment and contempt for her even though she was dead. He told me things about her that I never would have imagined. It turned out that they married because she had told him she was pregnant while they were in college. They got married right away and then mysteriously; she suffered a miscarriage while he was away visiting a friend. He also told me she'd threatened to commit suicide if he ever tried to leave her. He told me about the insane rages she'd have; cutting up clothes and breaking furniture. According to him, she'd drained him of any type of normal life. I felt uncomfortable hearing these things about Mrs. Stein. These were things that she never discussed during her life and I was sure she didn't want them discussed now that she was dead. I understood his pain and frustration, but I also felt her shame. Dr. Stein should have let her rest in peace. She had suffered ten times over for her reckless lifestyle. We all have crosses to bear, but the fact remains, he chose to stay with her all those years so it couldn't have been all bad.

After Benjamin fell asleep, things got a little too comfortable, and yet creepy at the same time. Dr. Stein seemed to be flirting in his own way. I cut the conversation short and helped him straighten up the house in preparation to leave. It was at that time that he told me he had a few things of Mrs. Stein's that he saved especially for me. Even though she had some nice couture I was still uncomfortable wearing a dead woman's clothing. I thanked him and explained I was uncomfortable with the idea of wearing Mrs. Stein's clothes. He said he wasn't thinking, he just knew that the items would look nice on me. While we were standing in the closet he reached up and turned out the lights.

Somewhere between the light switch and the closet door his hand ended up my shirt and he began kissing my neck. He said he'd been watching me develop into a woman and he was very much attracted to me. He said he knew he was wrong, but couldn't control himself. The whole time he was in my ear and up my shirt he kept saying how wrong he was and I knew it was wrong, too. I knew I had no business in this man's bedroom. I wasn't even legal yet, plus I was pure, never been touched a virgin. I resisted, but deep down I really don't think I wanted to stop him. It wasn't like I would sit up and dream about him or anything, I never really noticed or acknowledged him as being a real man before that night. To me, before that night, he was always just my neighbor. I guess I wanted to feel something I thought I needed to feel.

I wasn't interested in kissing him at all. There was something about kissing him that seemed so personal. I knew I was wrong on so many levels, but something inside became almost like an animal. I was curious and I wanted to get it over with. I grabbed him by his waist and started unbuckling his belt. I reached up and pulled his shirt over his head. His body was so white and when my brown hands touched his bare white skin, the contrast was unattractive to me. In my mind, I removed myself totally from the room. Instead I pictured myself on one of those soap operas that Mattie liked to watch, with the steamy yet fake love scenes. I stuck my hand down inside his boxers so I could prepare myself for what I had to work with. It wasn't bad considering I'd never touched a penis before. I guess it was considered average. I didn't tell him I was a virgin, I figured he'd find out soon enough. He would either feel guilty or whole again because I had never been touched. Most virgins in my situation would have been nervous and apprehensive especially since I was being seduced by Dr. Stein. It was clear to me that he wasn't going to stop until he got what he wanted. When I touched him he was hard as a rock. At that point, the male anatomy became intriguing to me and I wanted to look at it up close and see what it looked like in real life. I never thought that my first dick would be pink. Unfortunately the lights were off in the room and I couldn't see a thing or the thing.

Dr. Stein picked me up by my inner thighs and we moved to the bed. He was kissing me all over my body and pulled my clothes off piece by piece. He was like an animal let out of its cage. I'd lost all inhibitions. I didn't care that he was fifteen years older than I was, or that he was white or even that he was the husband of my newly deceased neighbor. I just wanted to do it. I wanted to be touched. At that time my virginity, like everything else in my life wasn't important to me.

Dr. Stein touched me inside, with his middle finger, as he kissed my breasts. He was sucking my nipples as though he was trying to get a taste of chocolate milk. While he was moving his finger inside of me I felt this overwhelming heat. The next thing I knew his tongue was inside of me and he kissed me inside with this tongue. It felt like I was melting all over the place. My knees became weak and I tried to push his head away but he resisted and grabbed my hands while he was still inside of me. He kissed the inside of my thighs and then my stomach and moved up toward my breasts. I was thoroughly enjoying all of it. Then he whispered in my ear. "Are you ready?"

I nodded and prepared myself for the unknown. He tried to slip inside of me very slowly and when he discovered my secret, he didn't say a word about it.

While he was working his way inside of me he began to moan and groan and even said, "Damn!" Once he moved in and got real comfortable it changed to, "Damn! Oh Shit! Got Damn!"

His response was turning me on and made my body feel like fire. The more he moaned and groaned the more excited I became. The crazy thing was his response to me was more exciting than the actual sex.

"Your pussy is so good; I never knew it could be this good." His words made me feel powerful, and somehow I flipped him over and climbed on top of him. This was even better and he wouldn't shut up. The louder he became the more involved I became. He sat up suddenly and turned me around; I landed on my stomach. Then he grabbed my legs and pulled me close to the edge of the bed. He stuck his dick in and I could feel him going much deeper inside me. He told me to bend over and raise my butt up higher. I was face down in the sheets. He was growling and yelling.

"Oh...Oh...yes...yes ... Damn!" He was so loud, I was afraid he would wake Benjamin. I could feel his sweat dripping on my cheeks as he started moving really fast. I could hear our bodies as they made contact with one another, making a clapping sound. He yelled out to let me know he was cumming and it was at that point that I began to feel let down. He was moving and poking and I wanted him to finish. I kept thinking that I wanted him to hurry up and be done. Finally he stopped moving and let out one big moan. He collapsed on the floor and lay there until he fell asleep, curled up naked on the floor. I looked down at his naked body and realized I had the power to make a grown man revert back to a childlike position. I didn't even try and wake, him nor did I think to check on Benjamin. I dressed quickly and left.

As I walked back to my house I thought, "Is this how it's supposed to be?" It seemed as though I had been watching a bad picture develop;

sort of a blurry distorted mess. When I got home, I took a shower and really didn't give it a second thought. I didn't know if my emotional capacity to care about relevant things had something to do with seeing my parents and sister killed or if there was a side to me that just didn't give a damn. I'd just lost my virginity to my neighbor who was fifteen years older than me. It wasn't love. I just simply liked him as a neighbor and I held a special place for his helpless son. I didn't care or express any remorse for what I'd done. I finished my shower, put on my pajamas and went to sleep.

Of course things were different between Dr. Stein and me after that. The day after I lost my virginity, or should I say gave it away, I went over to see Benjamin as if what had happened never did. The nurse, who was off the day before, was back. Dr. Stein asked to see me in his study. He invited me to sit down. He sat in the chair in front of me and reached out to touch my hand, but withdrew. He apologized for taking advantage of me, saying he didn't realize or even think about it being my first time. He said he couldn't control himself and he was wrong. He also apologized for being insensitive about his wife's things. He handed me a small box and told me he was sure that it couldn't make up for what had happened but it was a reflection of his embarrassment. I took the box in my hand and opened it. It was a pear shaped diamond necklace. He said he knew I wore nothing but the best. This wasn't embarrassment; he was paying for some pussy. What he was really saying was, "I know I was wrong, but I still want to fuck you and there are benefits if you keep this up." That was my interpretation of it all. As I stood up, I placed the box on the desk and reached over and grabbed his crotch. I unzipped his pants and pushed him down in the chair. I straddled him and rode him as I watched his eyes roll back in his head. That was it, I was officially down. A diamond necklace became earrings, and then high-end clothes, and finally cash.

Mattie was always busy with church, Mrs. Stein was dead, and Emma was now working for Dr. Stein at the office. Mattie had no business at the house other than visiting Benjamin every now and then. I had her convinced that I was visiting Benjamin. I had my own car so I could come and go as I pleased. I told her I was working at a boutique in the Village to account for all of the high-end clothes; that and the fact that we were well off and I got a monthly allowance kept her questions to a minimum. When I turned twenty-one, she gave me full control of my own money and that was cool. I didn't need to touch it because Dr. Stein was paying me. He was absolutely sprung. He didn't even bother to date women his own age or any other women for that matter. We hung out at the house a lot when the nurse was off and sometimes we would meet at different places. He basically paid me to stay in town and attend college. But then he began to talk about "our" future. He wanted me to get my degree and assumed that when I graduated from college, we would actually be together. He'd definitely moved into a comfort zone. I decided I wanted to try living on campus to get away from what had become my own comfort zone. I was never really all that sociable in high school. Mattie agreed that I should move on campus in order to meet new people.

I let my roommate Karen in on my relationship with Dr. Stein. It turned out that she was a ho' from way back looking for an opportunity. I encouraged her to seek out an older lonely man. I told her the things to look for and to choose older white men. They love beautiful black women. I told her to look for someone who was married and clearly unhappy, but wouldn't leave his wife.

She hooked up with a man who was a doctor as well, a cardiologist named Winston Ruben. His wife was a pill popper and a poster child for plastic surgery 'gone bad'. His children were older and attending college out of state. It wasn't long before Karen was living the life; driving a new car, wearing designer clothes and she was preparing to move out of the dorm. She told Dr. Rueben she needed money for her tuition and he gave her three thousand dollars. On that same day, I lost my wallet and had to cancel my credit cards and bank card. She gave me a few hundred dollars without blinking. She told me she owed me that for turning her on to 'the game'. She jokingly said I should be a pimp but quickly corrected herself and instead said, "I mean a Madame."

That idea stuck in my head for weeks. I did a little research and came up with an idea. More and more girls began asking Karen about her 'friend'. No one knew about Dr. Stein and me. She told them how I had given her some helpful information. The girls began coming to me with questions, so I charged them for my information. I began giving small classes in my room about how to catch and keep a sponsor. I didn't limit it to older white men. Depending on the potential of the girl and her ability to handle certain situations, I put them onto some hardcore players. Shortly after I started my business venture and learned more about what I was doing I began to screen the girls more carefully. It was a learning process and I made a few mistakes, but once I worked out all the kinks, everything ran smoothly.

Chapter Nine

There are some beautiful girls out there who just never realize the power that they hold. They had more to offer than just their looks or their bodies. These were the ones who were looking for someone to give them the attention they craved. They needed someone to dote on them and make them the center of the earth if only for one moment in time. Those were the girls that I targeted. They had low self-esteem and needed confidence. Self-confidence is often the key to life.

A woman who holds herself in high esteem will never consider being pimped; she will be the one in control. She thinks too highly of herself to be controlled. Her game is to maintain control or at least keep it even. Men really don't matter to her because she knows that for her they come a dime a dozen. But she's no fool, and is still able to recognize a good catch when she finds one. If she's down for you, then she has your back no matter what, like a real woman should. She won't deal with a weak man. She won't respect him because she needs the challenge.

The girls that I chose were quite the opposite from me. The way I figured it, any woman could prostitute herself, but it took a true deviant to convince someone else to sell her body. I had mind control over the girls. I had the power to convince them that they were either queens of the world or they were the most worthless pieces of trash. I wanted the best; nothing ghetto or unrefined.

All my life, even in high school, I was somewhat of a tomboy and most of the very few friends I had were guys. One friend in particular was someone I went to high school and junior high with. His name was Alex Young. Alex had lived next door to me for years and we were tight. I had his back and he had mine. He kept me out of a lot of trouble. I went through a rough patch during high school, and had become the poster child for the bad attitude disease that plagues us once we become teenagers. I was one of the girls who carried a box cutter.

I remember when we were in the eleventh grade and Alex had gotten into a fight with a guy named Prentice Mayweather, III. Prentice was always bothering someone and shooting off his mouth and on this particular day he chose Alex to pick a fight with. Everyone was standing around waiting for them to fight. That was during the days when people actually fought fists to cuffs. Finally, when the name calling was over a few punches were thrown. Prentice's brother Malcolm jumped in because Alex was tagging the hell out of Prentice and when he did, I dropped my backpack and jumped on Malcolm's back. There we were, fighting like a bunch of wild dogs. Somehow it turned into an all out mess. Since Alex was on the basketball team they all jumped in as well. Prentice had a million cousins and they all jumped in, too. Needless to say, it was complete mayhem around school after that. When you saw Alex, you saw me and vice versa. Everyone thought we were messing around, but we were just friends. Don't get me wrong, Alex was a great catch. He'd always been fine, but I was never really attracted to him like that back in the day.

There was something about that day and about that fight that frightened me. I never knew I had that much hell cat in me. With each blow I landed I felt victorious and full of life and I wanted more. I just felt like I wanted to fight all the time. It was as if there was something brewing inside me and I couldn't control it. When I was sent home and Mattie found out I was fighting a bunch of boys and didn't get more than two scratches on me, she told me she couldn't blame me. She said it was in my nature. At the time I found her comment odd and disturbing, but I didn't bother to question her.

After high school, Alex received a basketball scholarship to the same University that I attended. We hung out in college as well and our relationship remained strictly platonic. After the local NBA team drafted him, we began to hang out even more. I would take care of different odds and ends for him that he didn't have time to take care of. Since he was single and was an only child, I was like his family. He knew about my little escort business and he'd used my services a few times. Some of the girls would do me a favor just to say they were with Alex Young. Pretty soon I started getting calls from his teammates and other quality clients. The clients understood that I was the proprietor and everything went through me. I never ever had clients of my own, I didn't care who they were. Dr. Stein was my only conquest of that nature. Against Dr. Stein's strong protest, things between us began to taper off and soon became nonexistent. It wasn't easy, he had become very confrontational and possessive. Some extra muscle that I had on speed dial in case one of my girls needed help with a situation paid Dr. Stein a few visits for me. I really felt sorry for him, but I had him to thank for inspiring my business venture.

Sex for me was never something that was romantic or even really necessary. I didn't run around like a nymphet. Don't get me wrong I enjoyed it, but only with certain people. I guess I was a pimp with principles. I had one guy in particular named Ron. I was with him for a while and I made it clear that it was just physical; don't even ask me to be your girlfriend or some crazy shit like that. Love was not a luxury that I could afford.

Business was so good and I did so well that I expanded my employees beyond my regular college girls. I had three girls who hadn't attended school with me. I had fifteen girls working for me. We cut college guys out totally and only dealt with a certain type of clientele. In a year, I had men calling from out of state requesting certain girls when they came to town. Pretty soon I had foreign dignitaries using my service. Sometimes the girls would figure out they didn't need me and became independent. I didn't mind because every time one left there was another girl waiting to take her place and it was tax free money. A few clients were police officers and some were political officials. I made sure I stayed connected. I couldn't afford to get caught, so I was extremely careful.

I never talked to the clients. I'd have them leave a message on a designated voice service. The girls each had a cell phone that was strictly for business. Alex's agent had a friend that owned a hotel and all he wanted was pussy whenever he needed it, so he let us use his rooms. Now to be clear this was strictly an escort service that provided a companion for those special occasions. I never pressured or encouraged the girls to engage in any type of sexual activity. They were free to make their own choices and act accordingly. If they had questions regarding sex, just like any friend, I would give them helpful advice. I never told the girls to go out and sell pussy as long as they gave me my initial commission. It really wasn't as easy as it sounded. There was a lot of trial and error. A lot of girls weren't cut out to be escorts and I understood that. For some reason, I possessed a cold, hard, don't-really-care side. Some of the girls needed mentoring more than others, but some just wanted the money and whatever came along with it.

Everything was fine for quite a while. I didn't have to show my darker side until one of the girls decided to challenge me. Angel was one of the more rebellious girls, actually she was the worst. She was one of those ghetto chicks who dressed a little better than her regular clique and was going to school, so she thought she was the shit. Angel's real name was Ramona Chambers, but I guess she thought she should be called Angel. Angel was so out of touch with reality that she actually thought she had some class.

Once during a meeting, she told me she felt like since she was doing all the work, she shouldn't have to give me as much money as she'd been giving me. It was ironic because I was actually trying to give her some slack because she decided to do a party for a few of Alex's teammates that were welcoming the rookies and new players to the team. She'd broken several rules. I didn't allow the girls to participate in parties. It was my number one rule because things could get out of hand and I didn't want anyone getting hurt. If a client was doing drugs or heavy drinking, my girls were instructed to leave immediately. We simply did not deal with that shit. This crazy heifer went all alone, to a party filled with testosterone driven athletes. She not only put on a solo strip show but she had sex with several of the guys for free. What the hell was that all about? The free part didn't concern me as long as she gave me my normal cut. I guess she didn't think I would find out, but one of Alex's teammates thought things may have gotten out of hand because she ran from the back crying while trying to put her clothes on. She also left her purse behind. He was concerned about whatever happened getting around. I asked him not to contact her again and I told him I would take care of it. I considered myself a fair person.

My plan was to talk to her privately. I figured she'd just gotten in over her head while trying to be a big girl. She was not one of the girls who could actually handle herself in that type of situation. She called me out in front of everyone and told me I needed to reconsider my percentage. She tried to convince the other girls that I was taking advantage of them. I really didn't know where this all came from because up until that point I was always understanding and cooperative.

I asked one of the girls to check to see if anyone was in the hallway. We always had our meetings at the hotel in a corner room on the top floor or a room without residents on either side of the room just to make sure we were secluded. After the girl came back into the room and reported that the hallway was clear, I balled up my fist and punched Angel straight in her mouth. When she fell to the ground, I took my foot and held it firmly against her throat and leaned over her. I told her I would beat her until she couldn't see if she ever tried that shit again. As I was talking to her with my foot on her neck, I felt adrenalin rush all through my body. I let her stand up and grabbed her by her hair. I pulled her head back and explained to her that I really wasn't the one to play with. I let her hair go and asked one of the girls to get the bitch a wet towel.

Everyone was in complete awe. They'd never seen that side of me. It was at that moment I realized I had the heart to pimp, so I must have the heart to do other shit. I calmly apologized to everyone in the room and reminded them about the rules. I assured Angel in front of everyone that if she even considered pressing charges against me she would never utter another word in this lifetime. I took the towel from her and wiped the blood from her face. I walked over to the ice chest and prepared an ice pack. As I was wiping the blood, I told her she'd made a terrible mistake. I also explained to her that I can be her best friend or her worst enemy, but there was a thin line between them both. I then stated that I no longer needed her services after that night and she could easily be replaced. I explained to the girls what she'd done so they would understand that I meant business and I had a zero tolerance policy. Angel apologized and asked for a second chance. I told her, "NO" and asked her to leave.

That incident bothered me the whole night. I didn't exactly know what to do, but I did know that something was wrong. My mood switched back and forth and my instincts were telling me that I couldn't let Angel get away with disrespecting me. I also had this feeling in my gut that she would turn me in. I sat contemplating about what to do. Finally, my phone rang. It was my girl, Monica. She told me Angel was trying to get some of the other girls to set me up so that she could, as she put it, "Teach that bitch a lesson!" I knew it was true because I could always count on Monica. She'd been with me all four years through college and she was ruthless. It was like Monica showed up from nowhere. She came to me about the business and she was always there when I needed her. There was something honest about her and I never had to worry about her betraying me. We had gotten each other out of a few unfortunate situations and she joked about being my guardian angel.

Monica was straight from the projects in Chicago and looked like she'd just stepped off of a runway in Milan. She was five foot ten and had the perfect body. She had a smooth cocoa complexion, big brown eyes and wore her thick curly hair in a natural short cut. She was gorgeous, but if she caught you looking at her the wrong way...she'd cut you. She appreciated her natural beauty and made a lot of money. There were times when she would offer me more money than my percentage, but I never took it. She didn't suffer from low self-esteem and didn't have any of the other characteristics that some of the other girls possessed. She was hard and wanted to make money. She was the one who encouraged me to kick a little ass every now and then just to keep everyone in line.

Without hesitation, like someone else was controlling my mind, I changed my clothes and drove to Angel's house. As I pulled around the corner, I saw her standing in the doorway, waving goodbye to a man that was obviously on his way out. She was wearing a silk robe which she held together with one hand. I pulled around to the back of her house, parked my car and walked calmly around to the front door and knocked. She opened the door and I didn't even give her a chance to say a word. I hit her in the face with the palm of my hand curved upward and as she lay on the floor begging for mercy, I saw that her nose was broken. My intention was to scare her, but now I had a bigger problem. I was sure she would be so set on taking me down that she'd go to the police. My whole operation would be ruined and I couldn't have that, there were too many prominent people involved. I stood still for a moment trying to figure things out. It seemed like in an instant, my problem was solved. I felt an overwhelming burst of confidence. I felt hard and cold. I didn't say a word. I grabbed a pillow from the couch, placed the barrel of my gun in front of it and pumped two holes into her chest.

Before I left, I ransacked her place to make it look like a robbery. Angel had a troubled past and had been known to strip and prostitute. Luckily there were empty condom wrappers on her nightstand, that would play in my favor. She'd just had sex with someone, so he would be the prime suspect. I tried to make it look like the perfect crime scene. I found myself getting too involved with what I was doing. I had to stop myself because I was getting carried away, but there was something about that very moment that gave me a rush. It was like a high or a buzz. I quickly gathered myself and got the hell out of there.

After leaving her house, I went home and burned every stitch of clothing I was wearing, including my underwear. I'd worn my gloves while I was in her apartment and hard sole shoes that wouldn't leave a distinct pattern in her carpet. I wore a stocking cap with a skullcap over it to make sure every single hair on my head stayed covered. I showered roughly, scrubbing my skin clean.

My heart was beating fast and I was scared as hell. I couldn't believe what I'd done. I didn't tell a soul. I was afraid that when her body was found one of the girls would tell the police about our fight. I was hoping they'd think she was just another whore who was killed by a pimp or john. For days, I walked around like nothing had happened, but I was dying inside. I'd prayed a vain prayer that God would make everything go away and continued to walk around reciting prayers in my head. I promised the Lord that if he got me out of that mess, I would give up my business.

Monica insisted I was on edge, she kept telling me to calm down, even though at that point, she didn't really know what I'd done. I could tell she knew something was up. No one said a word about Angel. Luckily she wasn't well liked by any of the other girls.

Finally the day came when Monica called me and said, "Did you hear about Angel?"

"No. What's up?"

"She was found dead, her body washed up on the shore in Galveston. They say her apartment had been ransacked."

I tried to hold my composure. I couldn't believe what I was hearing.. I was stunned and my whole body was numb. I'd left her lying on the floor in her apartment. The whole event was so bizarre. I couldn't make any sense of any of it. I replayed that night over and over trying to figure out if I'd missed a step somehow. Had I blacked out and thrown her into the river? I was starting to feel as if I was going insane. I asked Monica if they had any leads. Before I could retract my statement, I realized my mistake. Criminals always want to know if there are any leads.

Just when I was about to ask another question, Monica said, "They think it was a serial rapist. Another woman was raped and murdered the week before in her same complex and the killer disposed of the body in the same area."

My heart sank to my feet and I felt some sort of relief. Then Monica said the weirdest thing.

"I guess that bitch learned her lesson." She paused for a moment before she continued, "Seth, I want you to remember that I always have your back no matter what."

That was her way of telling me that she knew what I'd done. My question was how did she know what I'd done and what had she done? Time went on and no one ever questioned me. I'd gotten away with my crime and I had a little help along the way.

After Angel's murder, things had to change. Several other episodes with new girls trying my patience or trying to see just how far they could go seemed to pop up. Once the girls got a taste of money and power, they'd grow balls that needed to be clipped real quickly. I found myself becoming even more heartless and cold. I became more and more restless. It takes low self-esteem and an ounce of greed to pimp yourself, but it takes a cold heart and a heavy hand to pimp someone else. I was growing weary of the life that I'd created. I started having nightmares and dreams about my mother telling me about my lifestyle. There was a very delicate emotion when it came to my mother. The dreams about her seemed so real. We would sit up and talk about certain things. Sometimes when I was awake I could swear that I heard her voice chastising me for what I was doing. I was becoming more and more violent and unconcerned about others. All through life, I had relied on my dead mother's parenting versus Mattie's. My mother started whipping my ass from the grave. I dreamed more and more about her and in every dream she was disappointed about my lifestyle. The escort business was wearing me thin. I began to think more and more about where my personality was coming from. I was letting the power affect me. I felt as though I was beginning to lose the civilized part of me. I clearly had a dark side.

I gave up my business and passed the torch on to Monica. We'd been together throughout all four of our college years and she was ruthless enough to handle the business. She'd always been there when I needed her and I never had to worry about her betraying me. Monica graduated Summa Cum Laude and went on to law school. We try to keep in touch even though we've become so far removed from what we used to be. We never discuss the past. We have an unspoken rule to just let it be.

Chapter Ten

A few months passed. I relaxed for a while and hung out with Alex. He'd opened a men's clothing store and made me one of the managers (on paper). I went in a few times a week and went over the sales figures and did paper work just to make sure he wasn't being taken advantage of. I was given full reign as to what was to be sold in the store. Just so I could explain my income and wouldn't get caught by the IRS, Alex introduced me to his financial planner and I began investing my money. I let my money make money.

Alex had been traded to another team, so I helped him settle in before the season. Even though his store was very profitable, he turned his lease over to me and sold me the store and its contents. After acquiring the store, I had a huge going out of business sale and sold all the men's clothes and turned it into a women's boutique named after my mother. Alex and I continued to keep in touch. I became his personal stylist because he had no fashion sense. I still continued to help him with his personal business.

Everything was going well until a weekend trip to Miami and a mixture of some dark and light liquor turned into an unexpected night of awesome sex between Alex and me. I really can't tell you what happened. All I know is I had a few drinks and he had a few drinks and together we were as drunk as Cooter Brown. He whispered in my ear that he wanted me so bad.

I asked, "What is it that you want me to do?" I looked into his eyes and I knew that that was a dumb question. Before I knew it, he bent down and kissed me. The next thing I knew we were in the back of a limousine tongue wrestling. I'd never been that turned on before. I climbed on top of him and started kissing his neck and his chest. The limo stopped and we jumped out and ran up to the room. We couldn't get out of our clothes fast enough. No one said a word. The room was pitch black, which I was grateful for because if I knew exactly what I was doing, if I had even glanced at his face, I would have stopped. Before I knew it, he had me against the wall holding me up by my thighs with his hands. My feet were off the ground and his tongue was inside of me. My whole body was quivering and I couldn't get my thoughts together. It was as if my mind was gone. I don't know where, but it was gone. I begged him to put me down but he wouldn't stop. I came so hard I was dizzy and just dumbfounded. After I was literally taken off the wall we lay down and made love.

It was like nothing I could have ever imagined. He kissed me and I almost melted. He kissed my neck like he kissed my lips soft and tender caressing the nape with his tongue. He caressed my breasts. They fit so perfectly in his mouth as he manipulated my nipples with his tongue. I looked at his beautiful smooth ebony skin. Looking at my caramel colored hand placed on his sun kissed skin, the contrast was stunning. We were two distinctly different shades, but we were the same. I was engulfed by his hue and intoxicated by his scent. He licked me from my breasts to my navel and back up to my lips. As we kissed he slipped inside me and I was lost, I became part of him and he became part of me.

For the first time in my life, I'd made love, It wasn't just sex, it was spiritually stimulating. I just wanted him to take control of every part of me. He was so ample I could feel him way beyond the normal limits, yet he was gentle and so sensual. With every single stroke I could feel his passion and my body trembled. He looked into my eyes and told me he loved me and he was truly in love with me. At that moment, I knew I was in love with him. I caressed his face and told him I loved him. His strokes became more commanding and passionate. He lay on my chest and I wrapped my legs around his perfectly chiseled body and enjoyed holding him as I basked in the thought of him exploding inside me. I felt a thrust of passion move through my soul as I felt him getting firmer while inside of me. Just as I was about to explode, I heard him moan softly in my ear. I didn't say a word, I just clenched his back with my legs and let him feel me melt all over him. We exploded at the same time and just lay there holding each other. All of a sudden my legs started to shake and I exploded again in a final climax. We were both speechless. There was nothing to say and we lay there breathing like two animals in heat until we just drifted off to sleep.

The next morning I stood by the window and admired the beauty of the city. I stared out at the ocean and got lost in the emotion of thoughts of the night before. I glanced over and thought to myself that I couldn't ruin his life. There he was, lying there so content and fulfilled. As the sunlight shined through the window, I couldn't help but smile. Alex was one of those rare men who accepted you for who you were. He didn't try and change you and mold you into what he wanted you to be. Physically, he was the perfect specimen. He had this huge Jalen Rose smile and deep dimples that light up the room. Even though he wore his hair bald most of the time or a close fade, his hair had the perfect wave pattern. It was soft and curly. I loved to feel his hair in my hands. I stood there and tried to rationalize why I slept with Alex but I could only admit to myself that it was because I really wanted to. I tried to convince myself that I could actually make this work, but the more I tried to convince myself, the more I knew it wasn't going to happen. There was something inside of me that a man like Alex should never encounter. I knew that I was capable of anything... including hurting him.

When he woke the next morning the topic of conversation was the question 'where do we go from here'. I suggested we keep what happened in Miami, in Miami. I really wasn't in the mood to talk about it and the sun was killing me. I was so hung over, I prayed for death. The remaining days of the trip were truly awkward. We tried to continue like nothing had happened, but it was very difficult. I thought about him all night. For a few weeks after we left and returned to our homes I couldn't get that night out of my head. I would dream about it whether I was asleep or awake. Sometimes I would get shivers up my spine. I felt more for him than just something physical. We shared one another's soul. I was so in love I became physically ill. I couldn't eat and I barely slept. In the same instance, I was having nightmares. I was dreaming of waking up next to pools of his blood. I would look over and see a knife in my hand. I was so afraid of hurting him.

One night, Alex popped up at my house and told me how he felt and that he wanted to get married. I told him I couldn't marry him for reasons he could never understand. He told me he knew I loved him because he could see it in my eyes. I didn't deny my feelings, but I could never give him what he needed. Alex walked out of my life that night and now I started to only see him on television. I have tried so many times to pick up the phone and call. I wanted so bad to just tell him that I loved him, but I was scared to lose someone else that I loved. The last time I saw him was at Benjamin's funeral. As always he was looking as suave as usual. He'd hired a professional stylist to assist with his fashion deficiency. Coincidentally, Isabelle's husband Robert, and Alex share the same agent. Robert kept me pretty well informed. Whenever he changed his address or his phone number, he would always send a note to the store to inform me of the change. The note always consisted of the new address or phone number and ended with, 'Still waiting'.

Chapter Eleven

I woke up the next morning to the annoying sound of someone ringing my doorbell. As I turned my head to check the time, I realized it wasn't morning at all. It was actually 12:03 in the afternoon. Somehow I'd managed to sleep half the day away. Ignoring the doorbell, I pulled the cover over my head. A few seconds later I heard someone beating on my front door. I kicked off the cover and jumped out of bed. I grabbed my robe, headed out the bedroom door, and ran down the stairs. I didn't even bother to ask questions, I abruptly opened the door.

"Yes?" To my surprise, Dr. Batiste was standing on the other side of the door. I grabbed the sash to my robe and tied it around my waist. I ran my fingers through my hair.

"Dr. Batiste, what are you doing here?" I said.

He stood there holding a rather large envelope in his hand. As Dr. Batiste stood in front of me, immaculately groomed and well dressed in his leisure attire, a refreshing breeze emitted his enticing fragrance that immediately heightened my curiosity. As he began to speak, he became less of a doctor and more of a man. I calmed my libido and awaited his response.

"Please forgive me for just dropping by like this, but I just can't seem to get you off my mind."

I raised my eyebrow and said, "Excuse me?"

"Oh no, I mean your situation, your past. I couldn't stop thinking about your story so I decided to do some research."

I stepped aside and invited him in. "Please come in."

I escorted Dr. Batiste into the den and excused myself to freshen up. I brushed my teeth and washed my face and threw on some sweats. I put my hair back into a ponytail and joined him in the den.

"I'm sorry, I seriously overslept. I guess I was happy to be back in my own bed."

Dr. Batiste smiled and said, "That's certainly understandable."

Everything was severely awkward. I could tell he was uncomfortable, but I didn't know why. I said, "So what kind of research did you do? I guess my story was pretty hard to believe, since you felt the need to check it out for yourself."

He quickly became defensive, "Oh no, that's not it at all. I know that at this point you probably have a lot of questions about what happened and you need closure. The only way to find closure is to confront the issue. I just thought I'd get you started." I really didn't know how to respond. Ideally I wanted to start healing, but I was afraid of what I might find. My eyes were glued to the large envelope resting on Dr. Batiste's lap and I grew more anxious. I wrung my hands together and waited for him to say something.

There was an awkward silence and then I said, "Is that for me?"

Maxwell took a breath, "Oh, yeah. But you have to be absolutely sure you're ready to do this."

The hair on my neck stood at attention. The envelope seemed even larger. What could possibly be inside? I reached out and said, "Please just let me see what you have in there." The envelope's journey from his hand to mine seemed to take forever. The moment seemed to move in slow motion. As the envelope finally reached my hand, I grabbed it and held on for dear life. With my hands shaking and sweat outlining my brow, I unlatched the clasp, reached inside, and slowly pulled out a piece of paper.

Dr. Batiste said, "It's a copy of your death certificate." There it was in black and white: "Noel Marie Toussaint D.O.B. April 27, 1976; D.O.D. August 8, 1984. Cause of Death: asphyxiation." He pulled out a second piece of paper. This one read, Nicolette Madelyn Toussaint. D.O.B. April 27, 1976 D.O.D. August 8, 1984. Cause of Death: asphyxiation.

At this point I became physically ill. My stomach was skydiving. The envelope fell from my lap and that's when a third piece of paper slipped out. This was a copy of a newspaper clipping. I reached down and picked up the envelope from the floor to retrieve the paper. The headline read: Local Real Estate Tycoon arrested for Murder of Business Partner and Family. The next two headlines read: Ellis Clark Winfield Acquitted of Business Partner's Murder. Toussaint Family Deaths Ruled an Accident.

With a faint voice and tears in my eyes I said, "Where did you get these?

"I pulled them from the microfiche archives at the library...I figured this would be a start and if you wanted to look further we could...I don't know how far you're willing to go, but I'll help you in any way I can." As the tears began to flow my eyes burned and my vision became blurred. Dr. Batiste knelt down in front of me and wiped my tears.

"Are you alright?" he asked softly.

I let out an awkward laugh. "No, I'm not...It says here, that my Uncle Clark was arrested for my parents' murder. The night they were killed I never saw any faces, but I remember hearing voices...my God this is really too much!" I placed my hand on the side of my head. I was trying to soak up the news articles. I closed my eyes and remembered Clark's raspy voice. I remember when I thought Uncle Clark's voice was so fascinating. It was like he was hoarse all the time. Then a light bulb came on in my head. "I remember hearing Clark's voice."

I was so overwhelmed, I started to hyperventilate. I jumped up and ran toward the kitchen. Dr. Batiste scrambled around trying to find a paper bag. I grabbed a glass and ran to the faucet for a drink of water. After drinking the water I sat down on the kitchen floor. I could feel a panic attack coming on. I tried to fight it, but I felt a burst of hot air come over my body. I felt like hot pins were sticking into my flesh. My stomach became weak and it hurt. I began sweating and my hair became soaked. As I pulled off my clothing, I searched for a cool place on the floor. Finally, I just lay there balled up in the fetal position, begging for this unbearable feeling to go away. As I drifted off to another place, I could see Dr. Batiste standing over me. I heard him say he'd be right back, but I couldn't respond. All I could hear was the front door slam and then a few minutes later it opened again. As I lay on the floor I could hear the rapid movement of his feet as he ran back into the kitchen. I felt him grab my arm and then I felt a sharp prick. My body went numb and I could no longer feel anything.

I woke up in my bed, dazed and confused. I looked over at the clock, it read 6:18 pm. I remembered Dr. Batiste being there earlier. I removed the covers to find myself fully dressed again. On my way down the steps I was greeted by the tantalizing smell of marinara sauce.

I thought to myself, "What the hell is going on?" I walked into the kitchen and found Dr. Batiste standing over a pot on the stove, stirring.

"Dr. Batiste, what in the hell are you doing?"

He laughed, "Well you were in no condition to do much of any-thing earlier. So I decided to stick around to make sure you were okay. I watched a few movies and came in here and found something to cook. I gave you a mild sedative so I knew you wouldn't be out all night." All I could do was stand there; I was truly embarrassed. I tried to find the right words, but I couldn't think of anything to say.

Finally, he said, "Why don't you go upstairs and take a shower? By the time you get yourself together, dinner will be ready." I looked at him like he was crazy.

"Dr. Batiste I don't think that's a good..." He quickly interrupted me.

"Look, if I wanted to take advantage of you, I could have hours ago. You were so out of it, you wouldn't have known anything. I'm just trying to be nice. Trust me, my intentions are honorable. And please call me Maxwell!"

I stood there thinking, I really hope he doesn't think that he's going to be my therapist now. There was no way in the hell that would happen. I think he saw seen me naked. I stood there contemplating about what to do. Finally, I said what the hell. I turned and went upstairs to freshen up.

Maxwell and I sat around eating, sipping wine and just talking about the things that grown folks talk about. We talked about poli-tics, religion, entertainment news, music, movies...you name it, we discussed it. We talked about how he and Isabelle struggled growing up and the sacrifices she'd made to put him through school. He was human and genuine.

At some point I noticed how fine he was. He was no longer hiding behind his lab coat and starched shirts. He was casually dressed in a pair of carpenter jeans, the type that's a little baggy, but fit the ass just right. I could see the imprint of his manhood in the front of his jeans. He looked like he was growing another leg. He'd taken his shirt off and his t-shirt hugged his chest and outlined his biceps. His skin was smooth and clear like pure chocolate. As we sat for a little while longer, I felt myself getting lost in his mesmerizing brown eyes. As I hung on his every word, I couldn't help but be taken by him.

Before we realized it, the time had slipped away. It was 12:15am. Maxwell suggested it was time he left. I agreed and he prepared to leave. He told me he'd had a great time and enjoyed our conversation. The truth was I enjoyed him as well and I didn't want him to leave. I really just wanted to lie in his arms and fall asleep. I wanted to let go and feel uninhibited. I wanted him to wrap his big biceps around me and hold me close and never let go. I wanted to get lost in his chest. I wanted to feel his kisses on my bare skin and feel his sweet breath in my ear. I wanted him and everything he had to offer. Instead, I walked him to the door. Of course, there was the awkward moment of kiss or no kiss, hug or handshake. He reached around my body with both arms and pulled me close and kissed me on my forehead. My head fell on his chest and I stood there frozen for a few seconds. We both pulled away at the same time. "I'd better go."

I stepped back and said, "I think you better."

We were like magnets unable to separate. We looked into each other's eyes and he grabbed me with his left hand. I could feel the palm of his hand at the small of my back as he caressed my face with his right hand. He pulled my face closer to his and kissed my lips, parting them with his tongue. As he entered my mouth our tongues became one, searching for each other. My entire body became warm and my legs weak as I wrapped my arms around him and he held me tighter. He slowly kissed me as we tried to break away. Without saying a word I looked into his eyes and gave him the approval. He picked me up in his arms and carried me up the stairs to my bedroom. All I could think about was how I knew I needed to plant my feet on the ground and let this man go home, but I didn't say a word.

Once we reached my bedroom, he closed the door with his foot and placed me on the bed. He asked me if I was sure this was okay. I assured him that I would be all right. With his tongue he slowly outlined my lips and moved down to my neck. He gently suckled my neck and caressed my stomach with his warm hands. As he was kissing my neck I caressed his head. His hair was freshly cut and felt like soft cotton in my hands. He pulled my blouse over my head before he resumed his position. I removed his shirt and the rest of his clothes followed. His body was absolutely flawless. He had the sexiest coffee colored skin tone. His body was perfectly chiseled like a stone statue, and his skin was as smooth as satin. I felt his warm body on top of mine skin to skin. He kissed my neck and then gently suckled my breasts manipulating my nipples, making them erect. I could feel the inside of my body becoming warm. He slowly moved from my breasts; his tongue tenderly touched my navel. He slowly moved back up to my breasts and with his left hand he caressed my thigh and slowly placed his middle finger inside of me. His touch made me quiver with anticipation as it sent a sudden chill through my body. He searched until I found pleasure. Once I'd found pleasure, he grabbed both thighs and spread my legs apart. As I felt his affectionately wet tongue, he entered me creating a warm creamy explosion of ecstasy. As he searched for more treasure, I could feel my temperature rise. Finally, my legs started to tremble and my body exploded from the inside. My body was relaxed and as I rolled the condom on his manhood, I prepared for my next exhibition. As he entered me, I grabbed his arm to accept his ample gift. I could feel my fingers as they gripped his forearm. I opened up and he gently made his way inside and we began to explore each other. With each stroke I could feel my soul shake so much I could hardly contain myself. He whispered in my ear that he would never let me go. He begged me to hold him tighter. I wrapped my arms around him so I could feel every inch of him. Just when it seemed he had given me all of him, I felt more. I couldn't help but call out his name as he went deeper and deeper. He couldn't believe how inviting I was. Somewhere along the way we got lost in time and space and explored every possibility of the night. I felt my body began to lose control of its orgasmic functions and my mind went on a journey beyond earth. Once I was relaxed and basking in my achievement, I felt Maxwell's body grow anxious as he expressed a passionate whimper and a pleasure filled moan. We fell asleep in each other's arms, with him still inside of me. He'd achieved his orgasm and he was still able to successfully lie there, still inside of me as we slept locked in a warm embrace. I thought I hit the jackpot with that one.

Chapter Twelve

I woke in the morning feeling absolutely wonderful. I looked over at Maxwell and watched for a moment as he slept. I really didn't know what the hell I was doing, but it felt good. As Maxwell slept, I prepared for my morning shower. We had slept with the French doors open and the humidity was less than bearable. I closed the doors and turned the air conditioning on before stepping into the shower. The water felt good against my skin as I turned the shower to full blast. I let the water roll down my back as I stood under the spray. The water was warm and soothing. I reminisced about the night before, and how for the first time since Alex, I'd given myself body and soul to a man and it felt great. I knew that we were probably moving too fast, but somehow I felt safe because there was something very familiar about him. Even though we'd made love, I still wanted to take things slow, if that was possible at that point. For some odd reason, I began to think about Alex. Why was I thinking of Alex Young when I had a perfect specimen of a man in the other room? I splashed some water on my face and shook my head as if to bring myself back to reality. After I stepped out of the shower I could hear Maxwell tossing and turning in the bed. I heard him call my name. I told him I was getting out of the shower.

"Why didn't you wake me? We could have showered together." I heard his feet hit the floor.

I laughed, "Don't you think I need some time to myself?" I walked over to the linen closet and retrieved an extra toothbrush and placed it on the counter for him. He looked up at me and smiled.

"I see you're prepared for overnight guests," he said.

"A wise woman is always prepared."

"Hey, I ain't mad at cha...when I finish with this I'm gonna put it right next to yours where it should stay from now on."

I couldn't help but laugh. Was he was serious?

"I'm serious." He said as if reading my thoughts. "Last night wasn't just last night...I told you yesterday I was here for you and that's what I mean." The moment was too serious, I needed to break it up.

"Please just brush your teeth and don't worry about the resting place of the toothbrush." He laughed.

"I love a funny woman, ha ha ha." He grabbed me, and we started to wrestle. Suddenly, as we rolled around on the bathroom floor, I heard the doorbell ring.

"Damn, its 9:30 in the morning... who the hell is at the door?" I looked up at Maxwell.

"Are you expecting someone?" He asked.

"No. Maybe it's Isabelle. She said she wanted to go out for breakfast this morning. I guess I'll go see." I was half dressed, clothed from the waist down, so I grabbed a t-shirt from my drawer on the way down the stairs. On the way out the door I reminded Maxwell that if we were going to breakfast he needed to go home and change so he should get moving.

I yelled, "Just a minute!" While running down the steps and pulling my shirt over my head, I almost tripped. As I approached the door, I was so frustrated that I didn't even bother to ask who it was or look through the peephole. I just assumed it was Isabelle and opened the door with this big smile on my face. It wasn't Isabelle though. It was Lauren, the girl from the boutique. What the hell was she doing at my house and how did she know where I lived? I was stunned so much so that I couldn't even speak. I stood there with the door and my mouth open. She broke the silence.

"Hi, Seth you probably don't remember me, I'm Lau..."

"Lauren from the store. You're Noel's mom." She let out a sigh of relief.

"Yes, yes...I apologize for showing up unannounced but I stopped by the store one day and Isabelle told me you were in the market for a new house. She knew I was a real-estate agent looking for new clients. I stopped by several times and you weren't there and no one knew when you'd return. They said you'd taken some time off...I didn't know if you were ok...I, I did some research and found your address...and I know..." Her voice trailed off as she stood there fighting with her words, moving from side to side.

"Look, Lauren I don't want to be rude, but I really can't talk to you now. I can't explain it, but...I just can't talk to you, it's really not a good time for me...I'm sorry." I looked at my watch and said, "Do you know, it's still considered early for a Saturday morning?" I wondered why she'd be soliciting clients on a Saturday morning.

"Please I just need to talk to you." She pleaded. "If I can't help you, I promise I won't bother you again." Her eyes were becoming watery and she was making me nervous. She couldn't keep still, and ran her fingers through her hair as her eyes danced around from one place to the next. This was truly a weird little situation we had going on. I told her I still had her card and I would call if I needed her.

I tried to close the door, but she pushed her hand against it, stopping me from closing it completely.

"Noel!" She cried out.

I stopped right where I was standing and didn't move an inch. I was frozen. I was paralyzed and numb.

I looked up toward the sky and said, "Please don't do this to me." I said to myself. "She is outside my house trippin' and I'm in here about to freak out again. Come on, get it together." I was trying to talk myself out of an anxiety attack.

I guess the air from the outside pushed the door open. As I stood inside the house on one side of the door, Lauren stood on the other side. The door opened and we both stood there silent and immobile. The only thing I could feel was my heart beating and tears rolling down my face. I didn't even realize that I was crying. I was so stunned that I didn't see Isabelle pull into the driveway, nor did I hear Maxwell come down the steps or feel him standing next to me.

"Seth! Seth are you okay? Seth!" Isabelle and Maxwell were calling my name. I could hear them, but I couldn't respond. I wanted to move. I wanted to reach out and grab Lauren and hold her. I wanted to ask so many questions. I wanted to know where she'd been...what she'd done and what she'd seen? Was this really Nicolette? Could this possibly be the moment I've waited for all my life? There she was, standing right there at my house, on my property and in my eyesight. She was less than three feet away from me. The only thing separating us was air. I was straddling the fence between certainty and doubt. I contemplated letting her in my house, but wrestled with the thought of slamming the door in her face. Within sixty seconds, I'd played a hundred different scenarios in my head. For a moment I thought I was losing my mind again. I blinked my eyes and shook my head trying to lose the moment. Finally, I just gave up. Maxwell clutched my arm.

"Seth, who is this? What's going on?"

With every fiber of my soul I took a deep breath and said, "It's Nicolette; my sister."

Maxwell was dumbfounded. He just stood there and said "Damn!"

Nicolette stepped up and reached out to me. At first, I just stood there for a long time while she held me and then I embraced her with everything that I had. If that truly was Nicolette, God had blessed me beyond what I ever deserved. If that isn't Nicolette, I could tuck that overwhelming feeling of immense joy away in my emotional psyche and cherish it forever. As we pulled away from each other we held each other's faces in our hands. I touched her cheeks and caressed her hair. This was my sister; my flesh and blood. She grabbed me and hugged me so tightly we fell into the door. No words were spoken just the sound of happiness. I was so enmeshed in the idea of Nicolette being there I forgot there were others around us. Finally, the silence was broken.

"I can't believe you are really here, I feel like I'm dreaming. Is this really you?" Lauren was still crying. Maxwell ran into the kitchen to get us some water, he returned in record speed. I guess he didn't want to miss a moment. He handed one of the water glasses to Lauren.

"Here you go Lauren, Nicolette...here." Isabelle took both of us by the hand and led us into the sitting room. I'd forgotten that Maxwell was a psychiatrist until he intervened.

"This seems really overwhelming for everyone, I think. If the two of you don't mind we need to first find out where Nicolette or Lauren came from and what's going on here. There needs to be some sort of rationale."

I was caught up with all of the excitement, I forgot to be rational. What if she was a fake? One of the newspaper clippings said she was dead, and then there was the death certificate. But the certificate didn't mean anything because there was one for me as well.

"Maxwell is right we need to be rational." I finally said. I gathered myself and wiped my face. I began to speak to Lauren.

"Lauren, I don't know you from the man on the moon. You just show up at my house and tell me you're my dead sister. As much as I want you to be Nicolette, I can't just start inviting you to Sunday dinner. You have to understand this."

Isabelle agreed with me. "That is so true. Seth has been through a lot...this is just too heavy right now. This all seems to be too coincidental." Lauren dropped her head, she couldn't stop crying.

"I knew I was taking a chance by coming here, but when I saw you at the store and looked into your eyes, I saw your reaction to my presence and knew that you had to be Noel...you just had to be. I needed you to be her. I'd been driving by the boutique for weeks before I had the nerve to stop in that day..." I stopped her in the middle of her sentence.

"How did you know where I worked anyway? How did you even wrap your mind around the idea that I could be your sister? How did you know anything about me?" I could tell that she was getting agitated, she took a breath before she spoke.

"When I saw the name of the store one day, I was immediately intrigued. But I thought it was just a coincidence. Another time I was passing through and I saw you standing outside. At first I thought it can't be you, but I kept passing the store. I've sat in my car day after day just trying to build up the courage to come inside and finally, one day I did."

I reached for the locket around my neck and realized it wasn't there. I guess she knew what I was looking for, she reached in her pocket and pulled out her locket and handed it to me.

"I believe you have one just like it." As I held it in my hand, I turned it over to the back.

Lauren said, "Both M's have worn off, and the T is fading as well. It's been through more than you can ever imagine. Just open it."

Before I opened the locket I asked Isabelle if she'd go upstairs and see if my locket was on the bathroom counter. She agreed and ran up the stairs. I took a deep breath and opened the locket. There, inside the locket, was a picture of our family; my mother, my father, Nicolette and myself. It was the same picture that was in my locket. All I could say was, "Where have you been?" I took her hand and held it in mine...I held my sister's hand. I touched her flesh, and we were breathing the same air. I was speechless. I didn't know what to say. I just couldn't think of any words. Isabelle returned. I took the locket from her and opened it. I showed everyone that the lockets contained identical pictures. Isabelle and Maxwell looked at each other in amazement.

Isabelle said, "Well, I'll be damned."

Maxwell fell back onto the couch. We all sat there like forever it seemed. No one knew what to say. The moment was extremely awkward and I was truly overwhelmed. I walked around the room in circles examining Lauren. I stared at her so long. I thought she was going to disappear or combust. I was so confused. My thoughts ranged from immense joy to overwhelming doubt. I wanted this woman to be my sister, but I had to maintain some sort of level head. Lauren was sitting on the couch with her feet planted on the ground and her legs clamped together as if she were afraid to move or say anything. As I paced the room, everyone watched her every move. No one knew what to say. I stopped and turned to everyone and then looked directly at Lauren.

"Why should I believe that you are my sister? Why, after all these years, are you just now trying to find me? What made you even think I was alive?"

She kept her position on the couch and said, "I know it's hard for you to take this all in at once, but to be honest I really wasn't sure if you were alive or not. I'd always hoped that you were. You have to understand, that night was extremely traumatic for me and it's taken me all this time to even admit that any of it had actually happened. When I saw you for the first time, I was just motivated by a possibility."

I had to understand that this was traumatic. Was she serious? "Lauren, it's been equally difficult for me as well, so I think I can honestly say that I know what you've been through. I'm sure you can understand my reluctance to simply accept the possibility that you are who you say you are. This last month, since the first time I laid eyes on you, has been pure hell in every sense of the word. I'm just beginning to live a normal life." She got up from her seat and joined me in front of the mantle.

She said, "Look Noel..."

"It's Seth."

"I'm sorry, Seth. We can't stand here and measure how difficult it was for one or the other. All I know is that I was born Nicolette Toussaint and I've lived the last twenty years hoping that this was all a dream. I don't want anything from you but the chance to talk to you and possibly get to know you."

I wanted this woman to be my sister. She looked like me, she had an identical locket and her daughter's name was Noel. To me that was more than coincidental. I just wanted to grab her and say, "I know you're Nicolette," but I was afraid. I was afraid that I was dreaming and I'd wake up in the nut house again. Everyone was mentally worn out from the events of the morning. Lauren seemed to be very disappointed that I couldn't just simply accept her right then, at that moment.

She walked over to the couch and grabbed her purse and said, "Listen, I shouldn't have come... I'm sorry. I have to get going. Noel's with the babysitter and I need to pick her up. Please just forget any of this happened."

"Lauren, you just can't walk in here, drop a bomb like this and just waltz out and never return. That's not how this is going to work. I suggest we discuss this like rational people. All I know is you can't just up and leave my house and never come back, that's just insane."

Isabelle and Maxwell both agreed that my idea was best. Isabelle said, "Seth is right, you can't just drop this here and leave. It's not healthy for either of you. If you are actually Nicolette, it would be a shame for the two of you to miss out on getting your lives back together because of fear."

Isabelle and I went to the kitchen to prepare a pot of coffee. As we stood side by side at the kitchen counter, she asked me about my feelings toward Lauren. I told her that for so long I'd felt in my heart that Nicolette was alive. I knew my parents were dead, even though for some reason I could never really truly grieve for my father. There was something about his spirit that I just couldn't connect with. I dreamed of my mother quite frequently and for a while I would sit up and talk to her as if she was there with me. I hoped that my father would come to me or I could settle my apprehensions about his involvement in their murder.

When I was a child, I remembered the father that I'd known since birth and as I got older and became obsessed with the past, I couldn't help but remember my father's last words, "I didn't mean for it to happen this way." Something about that just didn't seem right. I loved my father dearly and I missed him like crazy, but I just was not at peace with him. I couldn't feel him like I felt my mother or like I felt Nicolette. Isabelle asked me if I thought my father had anything to do with what happened. I told her I'd seen enough movies, read enough books and watched enough television to know that it's possible. If he had anything to do with it, I needed to know why. I knew my father was a good man and he loved us, but I think he became involved in something that he couldn't get out of. My mother was always on him about doing business with Uncle Clark. After I read the newspaper clipping I figured Uncle Clark must have been tied up in there somewhere. That, along with hearing his voice in my head, I knew he was there that night. I told Isabelle about the man with an accent and the raspy voice. Clark had a very distinctive Louisiana accent and his voice was husky. He spoke slowly and pronounced every syllable. I guess you could consider him cool. I stopped walking and looked at Isabelle.

"Isabelle, I have replayed that night in my head over and over for twenty years. I've gone over every possible scenario. When I was at Serenity Springs, I decided to put more of my thoughts on paper, I wrote down everything that stood out in my mind." Isabelle suggested we listen to what Lauren had to say about that night.

"We all need to sit down and go over what you remember and what she remembers along with the newspaper clippings that Maxwell found so we'll have somewhere to start. Plus, you need to find out what Mattie knows, because she knows something."

I contemplated telling her what I'd found in Mattie's closet, but I kept that to myself.

"You are definitely right; Mattie knows more than she has ever admitted. She'll be gone until Sunday that'll give us enough time to find out if Lauren is really Nicolette." Isabelle looked puzzled.

"How are you going to find that out for sure?"

"You forget? I am dating a doctor."

"What?"

"Girl I'm talking about a blood test...you know DNA."

"Damn girl, that never even crossed my mind."

"Once I came to my senses earlier today, that was the first thing that crossed my mind."

"But Seth, she looks just like you, and her daughter could be your child."

"I know and she has Nicolette's eyes..."

"She has your eyes. The girl looks more like you than her own mother."

"I know. I still have to be sure. This is all so bizarre. People are crazy, and I do have some pocket change. She could be trying to get over on me. Think about it, I was in the psychiatric hospital and I blurted everything out. One of those people in there could be conspiring to get their hands on my money."

"Damn girl, you're right. But you have to admit everything she has said so far has been true and only you would know."

"Yeah, I know." Isabelle was being so supportive. She really made me feel at ease.

"I want to thank you. Anyone else would have thought I was crazy and abandoned me by now, but you have been my rock." She touched my hand.

"I have always been here for you. I was just waiting for you to open the door to your heart...besides if you're going to be my sister-in-law, we can't have you losing your mind. I need somebody to shop with." We both laughed and continued to prepare the snacks.

As I suggested, Lauren came back over with Noel in tow. After lunch we cleared the dishes and set Noel up in the room with a movie and a monitor. We could hear her, but she couldn't hear us. We all gathered in the living room. Isabelle, Nicolette and I all sat on my sectional, each person maintaining an adequate amount of space. Maxwell sat close to me. He was there just in case things got too emotional.

I guess I was so anxious, I just simply blurted out, "Where the hell have you been for the past twenty years?" It was like she had been waiting to answer that question forever.

"For the past twenty years, I have been living as Lauren Davis and to be honest, I don't remember how I got out of the fire. I remember running toward the house and that's about it. I don't remember the actual explosion. When I woke up I was in a children's home. There were kids in there with all kinds of emotional problems. A few days after I woke up, a policeman came to visit me. He came in my room alone...no nurses or therapist, and told me that my parents, sister and grandmother were all dead. The bad people had come and taken them away and if I ever talked about any of them to anyone, the bad men would come and take me away as well. He told me I could no longer call myself Nicolette. He said my new name was Lauren. He told me I could never tell anyone about our conversation and that if I ever opened my mouth and told anyone about our conversation or about my family, I would be hurt. For a long time, I had nightmares every night…I don't know if there was something medically wrong with me or if he had just scared the hell out of me. For two years I didn't say a word. No one ever told me how I got there and I really didn't care. I was told my name was Lauren Davis, and my parents had been killed in a car accident. I knew that was lie, but I was scared. I was told I was found by a police officer at the scene of the accident. Of course we had no family so I became a ward of the State of Georgia just like mamma was." Tears rolled down her face as she took a breath. Isabelle handed her the box of tissue that was resting on the table. My fears had been confirmed Nicolette had not lost her memory. She had remembered every detail and she shared the same pain that I'd felt.

"When I was ten and started to speak, they felt I was ready to be adopted. A couple outside of Los Angeles adopted me and that's where I grew up. I was an only child and I didn't interact much with any other children. I stayed to myself and thought a lot. I never ever told my adoptive parents anything. I've never told one single person. I've gone through college, had a child and gone through life with no one. Since the day I left for college, I have stayed away from my adoptive parents. They have no idea where I am. After two years in college, I quit school and got my real estate license. I'd already done well for myself when I had Noel. I feel guilty for the way that I've treated my adoptive parents, but I just can't bring myself to truly love them like they want me to."

The room was filled with silence for a few seconds. I told Lauren I knew how it felt to shut the world out. I told her that even though Mattie was a link to my past, I could never bring myself to love her like I guess I should have. Lauren told me that even though the policeman told her that I was dead she knew that I had to be alive because she knew I had been hiding in the woods, but hope was just too much for her to live with. She figured the men must have found us and killed us too. She reached into her bag and pulled out several pieces of paper with sentences and words all over the place. She told us she spends a lot of time trying to piece things together.

"Whenever I remember something about that night, I write it down…when I turned eighteen I requested my files from the state…this is all that I could get."

Maxwell reached over and pulled out the big envelope full of papers and postit notes that I'd been writing on as well. The envelope also included our death certificates and newspaper clippings. There were death certificates for the entire family including Mattie. I couldn't understand why Mattie would have a death certificate, but I guess she needed one in order to conceal her identity. We both fell to the floor and started sorting through the papers on the coffee table. Lauren was overwhelmed when she saw her own death certificate. She held it close to her chest and cried her eyes out as if in mourning. She placed the certificate back on the table and we both began going through the papers again. Isabelle stopped us and suggested we first sort out what I'd written from what Lauren had written. We still needed to discuss what she remembered about that night as well.

Lauren told us there were some things about that night that she couldn't recall. She said she'd blocked a great deal from her memory, it was just too much for her to handle as a child. We sat there for hours trading information. The longer we sat there, the more we realized that Lauren didn't know much more than I did. We talked about basic childhood stuff. One thing that we did agree on was that Clark was there that night and so was an unidentified white man. Lauren became very uneasy when we talked about Clark. There was something in her eyes that told me she'd thought long and hard about Clark's involvement. She said that she knew in her heart he definitely had something to do with all of this. She spoke with so much passion and contempt for Clark. We also came to the conclusion that judging from the last words our father uttered, he was twisted up in this mess somehow as well. At the end of the night everyone was tired, confused and frustrated. We weren't any closer to finding answers to our questions than we had earlier. Maxwell and Isabelle were fading and drifting off to sleep. Finally, it was time for everyone to leave. They gathered their things and prepared to leave. Before everyone left, I remembered that I wanted to discuss a blood test for Lauren and myself. I'd been putting it off all day. I didn't know how to work it into a conversation. It was almost like asking your husband asking for a paternity test for your newborn that favors your green-eyed minister. It was very awkward.

Finally, I said, "Before you guys leave there is something I need to address."

Maxwell said, "Sure baby, what is it?"

"Actually, it concerns Lauren." Lauren looked a little puzzled and concerned.

"What is it Seth?" I lowered my head and prepared for her reaction to my request.

"Lauren, I'd like to have a blood test to determine whether or not you really are Nicolette." Lauren smiled and said, "You don't have to explain, I keep telling you how much I understand how you feel. I honestly do."

I walked over to the mantle and said, "The only problem is, we can't just waltz into a hospital and request a blood test. Can we?" I looked over at the doctor for an answer.

Maxwell responded, "I can arrange to have it done, no questions asked. I have some favors to collect on. We can do it on Friday, the lab tech owes me a huge favor."

I was so happy, I wanted to jump up and kiss him.

Isabelle said, "Well I guess it's settled then. We get this done on Friday and everyone will be relieved. You two just have to make sure you're ready for the truth."

Lauren finished gathering her things and said, "All I know is that in my heart, I know you're my sister and this test will just confirm what we both know is true."

I detected a little animosity from Lauren toward Isabelle's statement. I could understand both Isabelle's and Lauren's concern. Isabelle was concerned with my feelings and Lauren was frustrated with us doubting her.

Lauren told me that back in Los Angeles, she'd worked at an escort service and got involved with the owner. She became pregnant with Noel and he refused to believe that Noel was his. He beat her up, put her on a bus and threatened to kill her if she ever showed up again. After hearing that story, I felt so ashamed of what I'd done as a madame. I didn't share that part of my life with her; it was too close to home. It saddened me to know that she'd led such a challenging life. I know it sounds crazy that our lives could be somewhat parallel. I sold sex and so did she. I couldn't help but wonder if that could somehow be genetic, but from whose side of the family. The girls that worked for me could have easily been my sister. I thought about Noel's father and added him to the list of people who had hurt the ones I loved and would someday have to pay for what they'd done. I wanted to right all the wrongs in her life. I wanted to punish those who had ever hurt her and made her feel as though she was worthless. I wanted to be her protector, just as I had been when we were kids.

Chapter Thirteen

When Friday morning came I jumped out of bed. I was anxious to meet up with everyone at the hospital. Lauren would meet us there as soon as she dropped Noel off at school. Isabelle was coming to pick me up from home and Maxwell would already be there. I got dressed and Isabelle scooped me up. I was so excited, I could barely sit still. We pulled into the parking garage; Isabelle parked the car and turned to me.

"Are you sure you're ready for this?"

"I have to be. Either way it goes, I have to know."

"What if it turns out to be negative?"

"Of course I'll be disappointed, but I have already accepted the fact that Lauren might not be Nicolette. And if she's not Nicolette, there has to be an explanation as to how she knows so much and why she's pretending to be someone she's not. So, I guess I'll either have to hug her because she's Nicolette or I'll have to whoop her ass for lying."

"Well you know either way, I've got your back."

"Now that, I am sure of."

We hopped out of the car and made our way into the hospital. Maxwell met us in the lobby. We all waited for Lauren to arrive. She was late and I was getting anxious. I hoped she wasn't backing out. For her sake, I hoped she was who the hell she said she was. We decided to go ahead and draw my blood first while we waited for Lauren. As the elevator doors parted, I saw Lauren as she exited. She looked up with a smile on her face.

"I'm so glad to see you guys. I thought I was too late and went on up to the fourth floor. I thought I'd missed you." I was so relieved, but frustrated at the same time.

I said, "No we've been waiting down here like we planned. I was afraid you'd changed your mind."

She leaned over and hugged me and said, "Oh no, I'm ready." We rode the elevator to the fourth floor without saying a word. When we reached our destination, Maxwell led the way down the hall.

He took us into his office and said, "Ok ladies, Charlotte is going to come in and take your blood. I'm going to take it to the lab here in the hospital. I have a buddy down there who will get it back to us pretty quickly. I'm gonna go out and get Charlotte and we'll be back in here in a few minutes. Is everyone ok?"

I was so nervous. "Yes everyone is just fine. Now, can we please get this over with?"

Maxwell smiled and walked out the door. We didn't say a word. What could I say? "If you aren't Nicolette, I'm gonna kill you?" I think that would have been a little inappropriate. Charlotte came in and took our blood and while Maxwell took the samples down to the lab, we sat in his office and waited. When he returned he suggested that we go and get something to eat while we waited. I told him I was too nervous to eat, but everyone suggested I go anyway and watch them eat.

They ate breakfast and we made small talk. We were trying desperately, not to discuss the 'what ifs'. While we were sitting there, I couldn't help but bring up the Mattie factor. I stopped swirling my spoon around in my teacup and looked up at Lauren.

"Lauren, there is something you should consider."

She put her fork down wiped the corners of her mouth and said, "What is it?"

"Well, I just want you to be prepared for the possibility of Mattie not accepting you right away. She doesn't want to have anything to do with the events of the past."

"With all due respect Seth, I could care less how Mattie feels. I know you're my sister. You and my daughter are the only people that matter in this situation. If Mattie doesn't want to accept me, I can respect that. I'll deal with her when that time comes."

I was so relieved because I didn't need those two bumping heads right now. I felt more confident that everything was going to be ok. We sat in the restaurant for two hours making small talk. At some point it became tedious and I just couldn't take it anymore. Just when I was about to excuse myself from the table, Maxwell's phone rang.

He looked at it, held his finger in the air and said, "It's the lab, hold on."

I sat there on the edge of my seat waiting for him to hang up. When he was done he motioned for our server and told us the results were ready and we needed to get to the hospital. He paid the bill and we all piled into Isabelle's car. That was the longest drive I think I've ever taken. I stared out the window the whole time. I lost myself in something playing on the radio and for a few moments I didn't have to think of the results. We pulled up to the hospital yet again. This time I felt my stomach get weak and beads of sweat well up on my forehead, threatening to roll down my face. While we were walking toward the hospital, Maxwell came up beside me and put his arms around me and kissed me on my cheek. He didn't say a word, but I knew what he meant. We took the same journey to the fourth floor as we had earlier. Maxwell instructed us to go to his office and wait while he went to the lab to get the results. Only a few minutes passed before he re-entered the room.

He stood there with a manila folder in his hand. He told us that he hadn't looked at the results yet. He wanted to find out when everyone else did. We all sat there in silence as he opened the ominous folder. His eyes grew larger, as he dropped his head and put his hand over his mouth. He had a look on his face that could only be described as perplexing. He looked at me, then he looked at Lauren and then Isabelle. Finally he said, "Well, Seth...Lauren, you two are definitely sisters."

My heart must have stopped for a few seconds. I couldn't catch my breath. I just sat there like a statue. I didn't reach out to my sister. Instead I sat there holding my hand across my heart, with tears streaming down my face. I could hear Lauren sobbing next to me. Isabelle and Maxwell didn't say a word. They were speechless. I laid my hand down on the couch between Lauren and myself and took a deep breath. A few seconds later, I felt Lauren's hand in mine. All we could do was sit there, holding each other's hand. I felt like if I looked at her or even if I blinked, I would wake up from that dream and lose her. I don't know how long we'd sat there or even how we left the office and ended up outside the hospital. While we were standing there, I reached over and grabbed Lauren and hugged her. I hugged her so tightly we could barely breathe. Once we let each other go, we said our goodbyes for the moment and went our separate ways. She went off to pick up Noel. Isabelle and I went back to my house.

On the way home Isabelle said, "I am so happy for you. I can't believe all this is happening. I know this is a stupid question, but how do you feel?"

"To be honest, this feeling can never be described. It's on a totally different level that I don't believe has been created yet."

"So where do we go from here?"

"I want to get through the ordeal of telling Mattie. After that who knows? I do know that I want to find out what happened that night more than ever."

"Well, Mattie will be back the day after tomorrow. I think hiring that private detective is a good idea. The only thing is this is such a delicate situation I wouldn't even know where to begin."

"Don't worry about that, I know a few people who can find out any and everything, and never ask questions."

"Tell me...why am I not surprised?"

"Believe me you don't want to know. I haven't always owned the boutique." I left it at that.

We arrived at my house and I was exhausted. All I wanted to do was rest. I went directly upstairs to change into my comfortable clothes. Isabelle went into the guest room to change. She decided to stay over since Robert was still out of town. We were waiting for Max and Lauren to come over. We decided everything had been too tense the last few days, so we needed to sit around the house smoke a few cigars and get drunk. Isabelle and I got a couple of old Black movies from the seventies. I cooked a pan of lasagna and found some old music. You know from when music meant something, made you sing and feel good all night long. When Maxwell and Lauren got there, we danced, told stories, cursed, played spades and the dozens. I promise I don't remember when I'd had that much fun. We didn't think about what had transpired just days before. It didn't even seem like Lauren and I had been apart for twenty years or that Maxwell had only been in my life for a few days. I stopped for a few moments and watched everyone around me as we enjoyed ourselves. Everyone seemed to click and get along just fine. I was happy that Isabelle welcomed my sister into our lives with open arms...I was happy, but I still felt incomplete. The only thing that could seal this for me would be to find out what had really happened to us.

While Isabelle and Max were passed out on the floor beneath my feet, Lauren and I managed to stay awake for a few more minutes. One of those seventies classic hits that make you say 'that's my jam' was blasting on the stereo. Even though we were born in the middle of the seventies, we still remembered hearing our parents play those old tunes. The eighties still had quality music as well.

The CD changer shuffled to a song called 'All Cried Out', which was a big hit back in the day. I remember rewinding the tape trying to write down the words, so I could put them in a letter to Heath Tolbert that said, "I like you, do you like me? Circle yes or no." Heath was the cutest boy in the sixth grade. Back then I was into light skin and curly hair. I remember standing in front of the mirror with my hair brush pretending to sing to Heath. Boy, if I could sing, I would have been lethal.

"What were you doing when this song came out?" I turned to Lauren with my question.

"Girl, I was in the sixth grade crying my eyes out over Randall Johnson."

"Randall Johnson!"

"Yes Randall Johnson. He had it goin' on! He was so cute with his Jheri Curl...."

"Oh girl, no you didn't. A Jheri Curl...Lauren?"

"That's what I said, a Jheri Curl. You know you wanted one."

"OK, I admit I wanted a Jheri Curl. I even started wearing my hair wet so the kids would think I had a Jheri Curl."

"Well Randall was cute. He wore one of those red jackets...you know the kind that went down into a V in the back?"

"Yeah, the kind that Michael Jackson wore."

"Yeah, you remember...anyway he used to waltz into class with his books in one hand and his Afro-pick in the other hand. They used to make these Afro-picks with a little spray pump on the end so you could put your activator in it."

"Girl yes, I remember. That activator would have the whole class room smelling like collard greens."

We laughed so hard that we almost choked. A few more songs popped up and we had a story for each one. For some reason I wanted to know if she'd gone to her prom.

"Lauren, did you go to your prom?"

"No, I stayed at home that night. I really didn't want to go. It was kind of weird. I felt like, maybe if my real mother and father couldn't be there I didn't want to go. I didn't even want to go to my graduation. My adoptive parents made me go to that. Did you go?"

"To graduation?"

"No, the prom."

"No, my best friend and I stayed at home and watched movies all night. We sat back in his backyard and got drunk drinking wine coolers."

A disappointed look appeared on Lauren's face. "You had a best friend? What was he like?"

I sighed, feeling a little sad myself. "He was this boy who lived next door to me. We were really close all through grade school and even after we graduated from college. We drifted apart, though. I haven't talked to him in years."

For some reason she seemed to be relieved, but she faked it and said, "I'm sorry to hear that."

While we were sitting there, she asked me about Isabelle. I guess she felt like Isabelle was snoring so loud she wouldn't hear our conversation. "What's the deal with you and Isabelle?"

I felt her discomfort concerning Isabelle. I didn't know if it was jealousy or just the fact that she just didn't trust anyone. "Isabelle is a wonderful person. I've known her for a few years now. I guess she's the closest thing I've had to a real friend in quite some time. Now she feels like a part of my family. I really don't know what I would have done this past month without her. She's great, you'll see."

Lauren didn't give me the response I was hoping for. She took a sip of her drink and looked down at Isabelle lying on the floor and said, "I guess we shall see."

Lauren's comment sounded harmless on the surface, but it was the look she had in her eyes. Right then I knew she and Isabelle may not have been the best match. We sat there until we drifted off to sleep. When I woke up the next morning, Isabelle and Maxwell were in the kitchen. Isabelle was making pancakes and Maxwell was sitting at the table waiting for the food. I walked into the kitchen and rubbed Maxwell's head. He leaned over to kiss me, but I turned away; my breath was foul. I desperately needed to brush my teeth. From a distance, I said good morning to everyone and grabbed some juice from the refrigerator.

Isabelle said, "Good morning, you look as bad as I feel."

I felt like I had been licking shag carpet all night. I said, "You just don't understand, I feel like day old shit. Lauren and I stayed up a little longer than you guys."

She looked over at me and said, "I know...I caught the tail end of your conversation." I immediately knew what she was referring to.

"Please don't be thrown off about it. I just think Lauren has a hard time adjusting to meeting people." Isabelle flipped over a pancake and turned the bacon making it sizzle as the aroma filled the air.

"I can understand that. I thank you for defending me. I guess you sensed the same apprehension I did." I took another sip of juice as I listened to her response.

"Yeah, but I'm sure it'll pass and if it doesn't, I don't need you two women acting up. I will definitely handle it."

Isabelle took a sip of her coffee taking in what I just said. "Oh it's not you that I'm worried about."

I put my juice down on the table and walked over to her. "Come on Isabelle, are you still worried? The test proved she's my sister."

Isabelle turned to me, "I know, but you have to remember that you don't know anything about her except the fact she's your blood sister. You don't know anything about her mental state."

Maxwell decided to put his two cents in. "Baby, Isabelle's right. She was raised in a group home for two years before being adopted. That, in addition to the trauma she experienced on the night all this craziness happened, can drive anyone crazy."

I knew he didn't mean any harm, but I said, "Yeah like me."

He tried to comfort me. "You know that's not what I meant." I smiled.

"I know, I was just teasing you. Actually, I was going to suggest that you recommend a therapist for her. She does seem like she might need some professional guidance."

Maxwell walked over and kissed me on my forehead. "Anything for you baby."

The smell of food cooking must have awakened Lauren. She walked into the kitchen with her nose in the air. "Something smells great."

"It's Isabelle's famous pancakes." I replied as she took a seat and joined us.

"Well Isabelle, I guess you're just a regular chef around here," she remarked.

Isabelle smiled and simply said, "Yes, I love to cook."

Of course I cosigned, "Isabelle can make anything. She needs to open her own restaurant."

Maxwell agreed, "Robert and I have been trying to get her to do that for years."

Isabelle said, "I guess one day, I'll seriously consider it. Right now we're trying to start our family so, it's not a priority."

I took a sip of my juice and said, "Yeah that's right, it's time for you two to make me a little niece or nephew."

Lauren quickly responded, "You already have a niece who is blood related to you."

I looked at Lauren and saw claws and horns. I couldn't figure out how we'd gotten to this point. A few days ago everyone seemed to be getting along well. I scrambled for a response, but Maxwell saved me.

"Isabelle, is the food almost ready? I'm so hungry my stomach is about to pass my chest."

Without hesitation or a thought toward Lauren's comment, Isabelle said, "When you all get back from washing your hands, breakfast will be ready."

She never batted an eye as she continued to prepare the food. I don't think she was too worried about Lauren. If anything, she was more worried about me. Isabelle could definitely take care of herself.

We were all seated at the table, eating the breakfast that was really more like brunch, and making small talk. I was mid-sentence, telling everyone about how I needed to clean up and prepare for Mattie's return on Sunday, when I heard the door open. The next thing I heard was Mattie's voice bellowing through the house as she passed the living room and entered the kitchen.

"My goodness what happened in here?" I was shocked, she was a day early and I wasn't at all prepared. I stood up as she covered her mouth and acknowledged her embarrassment. She didn't know I had company. I didn't know why she was shocked, there were unfamiliar cars in the driveway. I struggled to find the words to greet her.

Isabelle recognized my dilemma and ran over and hugged Mattie.

"Welcome home, how was your trip?" The look on Mattie's face said she was still wondering who the two strangers were.

"My trip was wonderful...I'm sorry I don't believe I've met either of you."

I made the introductions. "Well, this is Maxwell, Isabelle's brother and my new friend. And this is Lauren."

A huge smile came over Mattie's face. "Well Maxwell, welcome to our humble abode. I hope to see more of you around here. Lauren it's nice to meet you."

Lauren was uncomfortable with my introduction of her. I guess she wanted me to introduce her as my sister. Clearly, this was not something that I could just spring on Mattie. I suggested that Mattie take her things upstairs, get settled and come back down so that we could talk. She looked puzzled, but she didn't question me. Maxwell helped her take her things upstairs. When he returned, he suggested maybe he and Isabelle should leave. I begged them to stay. I most definitely needed them to stay.

Once Mattie was settled, she walked into the kitchen and poured herself a cup of coffee. "Whose little girl is sleeping in the guest room?"

Lauren immediately answered, "She's my daughter, Noel."

Mattie didn't bat an eye, she said, "Well she is absolutely adorable." Lauren thanked her. I sat there not saying a word, trying to figure out where to start. I decided that if I was going to do this, I needed to have some proof. I excused myself and went to the safe in my office where I had put the blood tests. When I returned to the kitchen, I sat down and invited Mattie to sit down next to me. I placed the envelope on the table. Mattie placed her coffee mug down and looked with her brow furrowed in deep concern. She knew something was wrong.

"Is everything ok? Are you feeling all right? Something is wrong, I can tell...what is it?" I could see her frustration.

I said, "No Mattie, nothing is really wrong. I guess it's how you look at the situation."

Mattie said, "What situation?" She looked from one face to the other as I took a loud and very deep breath. I swallowed a big gulp of courage and motioned for Lauren to come over to where we were sitting. I couldn't hold it in any longer.

I turned to Mattie and said, "There is no easy way for me to say this to you, and so I'm just going to say it." I gestured toward Lauren with an outstretched hand and said, "This is my sister Nicolette. She really is alive."

Mattie's body became extremely relaxed. She looked up at Lauren, placed her hand on the table and looked down at the floor as if she were trying to find her words there. She looked over at Maxwell and Isabelle and then back at me and said, "I can't believe this. You just won't quit, now you've dragged this woman in here off the street and tried to convince me that she's your sister who's been dead for twenty years. This takes the cake! It's too much! I can only assume they know everything!" Mattie gestured toward Maxwell and Isabelle as she moved into rage. I jumped up and tried to calm her, but the only way I could get her to listen was to show her the blood test.

"Mattie I have proof. We took a blood test. Here read it." I handed her the envelope. She stood there a moment before taking the envelope from my hand. She slowly reached in and took the piece of paper out and read it. She clutched her chest and put her hand over her mouth as the paper slipped out of her hands and onto the floor.

"I can't believe it! I just can't believe it!" She sat there shaking her head from side to side. She didn't embrace Lauren like I was hoping she would. She just sat there staring at her as if she was waiting for her to disintegrate or something. It was Lauren who moved first.

She reached up and hugged Mattie saying, "It's true Mattie. It's me Nicolette. I'm alive."

Mattie didn't return her affection. She pulled away and said, "What happened to you? Where have you been?"

"After I left the group home in Georgia, I was adopted by a family and had been living in L.A. for the past twenty years. I relocated here to get a fresh start, when I saw Seth one day and knew right then, she was my sister. It took me a while, but I worked up enough nerve to go into the store."

"You're the woman she saw the day she came home and lost it."

"Yeah, I guess that would be me."

"Why did it take you this long to try to find us?"

"Why weren't you trying to find me?"

"Because, we thought you were dead. We saw the house explode. I saw the burning debris knock you down. I saw it with my own eyes...how did you escape the fire?"

"To be honest, I don't remember who saved me and I don't know why, I'm just glad that I'm here with you and Seth. I missed you so much. I need you...my daughter needs a family." Mattie's face told me that she still wasn't comfortable with our new family dynamic. I didn't say a word. I sat there quietly and let them express themselves.

Mattie looked at me and said, "Listen, I know you're ecstatic about this whole thing and I know what this piece of paper says, but this is truly too much for me to handle right now. Lauren, I'm sorry if I don't seem very hospitable, but I'm stunned to the point of being absolutely numb. As a matter of fact, I need to lie down. I feel ...". Unable to finish her sentence, she made her way to the doorway and headed for the stairs. I ran after her to make sure she was ok. Everyone ran behind us. I assured them she'd be fine and walked her up the steps. I escorted her into her bedroom, pulled back the covers and helped her into bed. She reached up and grabbed my arm.

"Seth, something just doesn't sit well with me. I know this is what you've wanted all along, but I have this feeling in my bones. It's the same feeling I had leading up to your parents' death. You may think I'm old fashioned, but I know more than you give me credit for. That paper might say that girl is your sister, but we still don't know a thing about her. We need to take this very slow. You can't afford a relapse."

I appreciated Mattie's honesty. She and Isabelle were saying basically the same thing. I knew they wanted the best for me. They wanted to protect me. Deep down I knew they were right, but now that I knew Lauren was my sister, I wanted to make sure she was taken care of in every way possible. I wanted the chance to be the sister she's never had. Isabelle and Mattie were just going to have to accept her, because she wasn't going anywhere. I made sure Mattie was resting before I turned out the light and closed the door. I walked back downstairs and entered the kitchen. I explained to Lauren that Mattie needed some time to get used to this. Lauren was upset.

"I should really leave now. I need to get Noel and leave. We'll come back later. I really need to leave." She couldn't finish her sentence without crying. "I really thought she would be happy to see me. I thought the blood test would convince her. I don't know what to do."

I wiped her tears and embraced her, "Don't worry, that's just how Mattie is. She doesn't deal well with emotions and she's emotionally dead right now and extremely careful. She doesn't mean any harm. She's just been through a lot. You should understand that." Lauren's mood changed as she had become angry.

"I'm tired of understanding! I have to understand everyone's feelings and no one is trying to understand mine." I tried to calm Lauren down, but she was still very irrational. She went upstairs, woke Noel and darted out the front door without saying a word. I stood there in the front door and watched as she got into her car and sped off.

Isabelle came to the door and said, "Come on honey, just let her go. You know she'll be back."

I was glad Isabelle was still there. I went into the living room, plopped down on the couch and started to cry. I cried and I cried. The weird part is I had no idea what I was crying for. I should have expected Mattie's reaction. Although I didn't know the news would make Mattie physically ill, I knew it would be difficult for her to handle. I should have known because when I first laid eyes on Lauren, it drove me crazy. In my mind I had envisioned a happy reunion. I pictured everyone laughing and crying and just so happy to be with each other.

I sat there alone thinking to myself. Where do I go from here? At my request, Isabelle and Maxwell left me alone. I could hear them in the kitchen cleaning the breakfast dishes. I wanted Isabelle to come in and console me, but at the same time I wanted to be alone. I wondered how Mattie was handling things upstairs. I couldn't begin to imagine what was going through her head. I sat there and looked down at my hands resting in my lap. I stared at the shredded tissue in my hand. The pieces were all over my lap. I brushed the particles from my clothes, but they remained in the same spot perhaps making things worse. I became frustrated from the lingering white specks so I jumped off the couch and went into the kitchen.

I immediately asked the question, "Do you think I'm crazy for wanting this thing to work out? Are my expectations so unrealistic?"

I didn't address my question to anyone in particular. I didn't care who answered. Isabelle and Maxwell looked at each other as if they were mentally trying to decide who would answer my question.

Finally, Maxwell said, "Yes, I think your expectations of a happy family this soon are unrealistic. You know how Mattie reacts to you and the two of you have been together for a very long time. So logically, you couldn't expect Lauren, with a painful and haunting reminder of the past, to come in here and be humbly accepted by Mattie. You also have to take into account that this could be a major setback for everyone involved. Lauren carries painful memories as well. Like you said before, we have no idea about her mental state, sister or no sister." Maxwell made good and logical sense.

Isabelle agreed with him, adding, "Seth you just have to give it time. I know you want your family back together, but honey this is going to take some time. Whether you like it or not, this is not going to get any easier. I can tell already that Lauren is going to want all of your attention for herself and anyone she sees as a threat is going to be a challenge for her."

I listened to what they both had to say. I guess I wasn't seeing things as clearly and rationally as I should have. I walked over and grabbed the broom and started sweeping the floor. While I was sweeping I saw Isabelle look in the direction of the door. I looked over and Mattie was standing there.

Isabelle said, "How are you feeling Mattie? Why don't you come over and sit down. Let me fix you some iced tea." Mattie came over and sat down at the table.

"Thank you, baby. That would be nice." I asked Isabelle if she would fix me a glass as well. She pulled out four glasses from the cabinet and we all sat at the table. "So, how are you feeling?" she asked looking at me.

I quickly answered. "Actually, I feel pretty good. I think some time away did me a world of good."

Mattie turned to Maxwell and asked, "So where did you two meet?"

Maxwell gave her an embarrassing smile and said, "Well, it's quite interesting. I met her at the hospital. I'm a doctor."

Mattie looked at him with a puzzling look on her face. "So I guess you're attracted to the eccentric type." We all laughed because it was really very funny. What she was really asking was whether Maxwell dated all the nut jobs at the funny farm.

Maxwell laughed and said, "I noticed Seth a long time ago when I used to visit Isabelle at the boutique, but she never noticed me. I knew she wasn't crazy. Well, after I did extensive testing and confirmed she was harmless, I took a chance."

Mattie took a sip of her tea. "I guess you didn't know what you were getting yourself into. I assume that since you two have met the new addition to our family, you know our secret."

Isabelle answered immediately, "Yes we know all about your past, but we don't care about any of that. We just want to be here for support."

Mattie reached over and touched Isabelle's hand. "For some reason I sincerely believe you mean well. It's this Lauren girl that I'm worried about. I'm just not comfortable with her. I don't know; I can't explain it. Isabelle replied, "I feel the same way Mattie. Even though the blood tests proved they really are sisters, I'm just not comfortable with the situation either."

It was time for me to jump in. "I appreciate everyone's concern, but with all due respect, it's really not anyone's decision to accept her but mine."

Mattie became agitated again. "Now that's where you're wrong, it affects my life, too."

"Yes, but she's my sister, which means it has an even bigger effect on me. For God's sake, she's my twin. What's the damn problem?"

"Hold on Seth, don't get testy with me. My only concern is trying to find out what she wants from you, because she wants something. I can see it in her eyes. Not to mention she can open up a doorway to the past that really should stay closed."

At that point I remember thinking about Mattie's fear of confronting the past and said, "What is it about the past that you're not telling me? What has you so worried, Mattie?"

She took a deep breath before saying, "Look Seth, I am happy that you're home and you're ok. I admit, not talking about the past all these years contributed to your breakdown, but I cannot and will not talk about it. Not now, just like you, I need time." How much time did she need? Hell, it had been twenty years.

"I can't tiptoe around your feelings anymore. It's really not about you, Mattie. I do understand that your life has been affected too. I'm really sorry about you being tied up with my family and this whole mess, but the fact still remains, you are involved. If you don't want to face your past that's fine, but don't block me from my healing process. Now either you are with me or you're against me. There are no gray areas."

Mattie didn't say a word, she just quietly sipped on her tea. The room remained silent and no one moved. They simply stared at us to see who would make the next move, so I decided to move. I walked up the stairs, closed my bedroom door and waited for the day to pass.

Chapter Fourteen

When I was a kid I used to watch this show that was centered on finding long lost loves. The show was a drama and it had adult content, but it was always fascinating how, after so many years had passed, people still longed for their first love. I automatically thought of Alex. I guess Alex would always be my first and only true love. The truth, is the night that Alexander Young walked out of my life, I lost another part of me. Another piece was taken from my soul, making me feel even more incomplete. It was that night that I realized the variations of love. The emptiness I had felt in my heart from Alex's departure was different from the emptiness or the loss that I felt for my family. I also found the true meaning of a broken heart. I felt so hollow inside. I think I was more pissed off at myself than anything. My pride wouldn't let me beg him to come back to me. I couldn't position my mouth to make the words 'I'm sorry' come out. Not a day went by that I didn't take the piece of paper with his number written on it and contemplate calling him. Each time I saw Robert, I hoped in my heart that he had some word from Alex. I hoped for anything: a hey, hello, how are you, how are things going.

Sometimes Robert would say, "Your boy asked about you," or something like that. Instead of asking for further details I usually just said, "Oh yeah" or sometimes I'd say "really?" I always acted unconcerned, like I could care less. The truth is it's hard for any woman not to think of Alex. Alex is one of those men, whose smile makes you feel good when he walks into a room.

It was my favorite day of the week, Wednesday. We usually got new shipments at the boutique on Wednesday and I was expecting a few new pairs of shoes. I think I had more shoes and handbags than anything. As always, Isabelle had arrived first. As I drove up, she was turning on the lights in the store. As I came through the door she greeted me with her usual hyper "hello."

"Hey girl, it's Wednesday, you know what that means."

With a huge smile on my face, I said, "Of course, new shoes are coming."

"Girl, how many pairs of shoes do you have?"

"I know you are not talking...a woman who had her husband build her a closet just for her shoes. Don't get me started on our handbag collection."

"Ok, you got me. Let's just say we're even, " she stated.

"Alright then, but you know you need some help."

"What Jimmy Choo can't cure, I don't need."

"Amen, thank God for Jimmy, Roberto and whoever else can turn a cow into my best friend."

I walked around checking the store to make sure everything was ready for business. Since it was Wednesday, my entire staff would be in. Kelly would be in after her eight o'clock class and Quincy had a half day on Wednesdays so he'd be in after lunch.

It was almost the end of the month, so I had a lot of paperwork to do. I told Isabelle I was going to run across the street to get some tea, and of course she ordered her usual. I ran across the street and picked up our beverages. On the way to and from, I made small talk with the rest of the shop owners. I caught up on some quick gossip. Everyone commented on how well I looked. They said I must have had a hell of a vacation. I just smiled in agreement. I thought to myself, a trip to the funny farm might do a whole lot of folks some good. I darted back across the street so our drinks wouldn't get cold. When I stepped through the door, Isabelle said Robert had just called. He wanted to make sure I was at the store because he was stopping by on his way to work out. He told Isabelle he had something for me. I wondered what it could be. But I knew it had to be something about Alex. Maybe he did more than ask about me this time.

There I was hoping to hear a word from Alex when not long ago I decided to focus my attention on my relationship with Maxwell. The old saying was true...there are just some people that will always hold a special place in your heart. Isabelle reminded me that Lauren, Maxwell and I were joining them for dinner at their house tonight. I told Isabelle I hadn't forgotten, and then let her know I would be in the back doing paperwork. I spent a good part of the morning doing paperwork, placing orders and managing our accounts. It was mostly a lot of busy work. I was so caught up that time flew by fast.

My desk was covered with papers, PostIt notes and all sorts of chaos. I was one of those people who didn't function well in clutter. I stopped for a minute and looked around at all the mess and instantly became agitated. I sat back in my chair and massaged my temples and tried to map out some sort of plan to tackle the tornado in my office. I sat there at my desk just staring at the wall. You know how sometimes you just get off track and forget what you're supposed to be doing, so you just stare into space to try and figure out your next move? While I was sitting there, I heard a knock at my office door.

I figured it was Robert so I just said, "Come in." I waited a few seconds and the door remained closed, then I heard the knock again. Once again, I said, "Come in," but no one responded. Robert was always playing jokes and acting crazy, so I figured he was just exhibiting his usual adolescent behavior. I decided to pretend as if I were angry.

I sprang up from my chair and flung the door open, and as I did I said, "What the hell do you want?" To my surprise and downright amazement there in front of me stood Alexander Morgan Young. It was as if I had been hit by a truck; right in the center of my chest. My body was heavy. I was numb and speechless. I found it difficult to breathe. I stood there trying not to be obvious about how I was feeling and trying not to pass out, all at the same time. There he was, standing on the other side of the door, breathing the same air that I breathed. He flashed his beautiful white smile and it was like a lifeline allowing me to breathe normally again. My legs came back to life and I could feel the nerves in my fingertips once more. My spine tingled with anticipation as I stood there waiting for him to speak. It was as if I needed to hear his voice, just one word, and the temporary paralysis would free my feet and I could move from that spot. I looked up into his beautiful brown eyes and became lost. I found myself back to the moment our lips first touched. I felt a wave of warm air sweep through my body. Time was a wonderful thing and it certainly had been good to this man. I couldn't understand why his presence was affecting me to that magnitude. It was the shock of my life, seeing him with no warning, or maybe it was just seeing him, period. I could feel the heat rising from my chest.

I felt him touch my arm as he called my name "Seth...Seth." I snapped back from whatever trip I'd been on. It was amazing, the power that the flesh had to control the mind. I'd just experienced the early signs of menopause in thirty seconds. I stepped back and grabbed the door handle. I could almost feel my hand reaching up and snatching him into my office and throwing him down on the couch, but instead I welcomed him in and offered him a seat. As he walked by, I could smell his cologne and it brought back fond memories. He was wearing my favorite fragrance. There was something about that particular scent that took me to another world. Ok, it must have been a physical attraction because that's all I could think of at that moment...how fine he was. Ok, get it together, I felt better. I was really flipping out for a minute. It was just a temporary loss of control brought on by sexual repression. I realized nothing could ever top that one night in Miami.

Once I had gathered myself together, I sat down behind my desk. I was contemplating crossing my legs. I could feel his eyes all over me. I never wore skirts before and wouldn't you know I picked today to be half dressed. I was wearing a pink silk two-piece skirt and top ensemble. It was very form fitting. Of course I was wearing my friend Jimmy on my feet. I'd had my hair straitened and my makeup was tight, if I must say so myself. After I sat down, I tried to redeem those cool points that I lost a few moments ago. I did cross my legs. I decided he deserved a peek as I sat back in my chair.

I said, "Well, Alex Young...what a surprise."

He smiled, revealing his gorgeous dimples, licked his lips and replied, "So, I see." I guess we were going to play who could make who suffer more. I struggled to find the proper dialogue that would not make me appear too nervous.

"So I assume I can thank Robert for this visit?"

"Yeah, actually, I spent a little time on the West Coast rehabbing my knee. I have a four hour layover here, so I called him up to see if he wanted to hang out for a minute."

"Really? Doesn't your mother still live here?"

"Yes, she does, but she and her sister are on vacation."

"How is your mother?"

"She's fine, she asks about you all the time."

"Yeah, I haven't seen her since she moved to The Woodlands"

"Oh, yeah she loves it out there."

"I know. It's so nice out there and they have that great mall."

"It appears to be the prime spot for real estate."

"I know what you mean, I'm thinking of putting my house on the market. I was considering moving out there, it's just so far from the store though."

"Uh, um so are you and the doctor moving out there together?"

Well get to the point why don't you. Wasn't that cute...Robert had filled him in on my dating status. I was definitely not going to get into that with him. I looked up at him from an angle and simply tilted my head and said, "No." There was no need to ask where he had gotten his information. I quickly looked for something else to talk about. I spotted the mini fridge. "Can I offer you something to drink?"

He flashed another smile and said, "Will I get to see those pretty legs walk over here and get it?" No he didn't, how inappropriate. What was I talking about, who was I kidding? My intention was to sashay on over and let him catch another glimpse of what I knew he missed.

Since he wanted to be slick, I just simply said, "No actually you can just reach over there and get whatever you need out of the fridge yourself." He sat back on the couch and declined to take advantage of my beverage offer. There was a brief moment of silence, so I quickly picked up a new subject.

"Wow, this is the first time you've been in here since I changed everything."

"Yeah, I must admit this place is really, how do I say...bourgeois." I guess he thought he was funny because he almost choked on his huge smile.

"Oh really? And just what does that mean?"

"You know what I mean, it's really very nice. Stuff in here ain't cheap."

"No, it's not. We do cater to a more affluent clientele."

"Yeah, rich women like you and Isabelle who have nothing to do but shop all day."

"Whatever, Alex...can I interest you in a tour?"

"Yeah, why not."

I led Alex from my office and into the store. The first face I saw was Robert, standing there with this "big cat that swallowed the canary" grin.

Isabelle was standing there with this apologetic look on her face.

I winked at her, smirked at Robert and said, "Hi, Robert."

He smiled back. "Hello Seth, how are you today?" He was such a smart ass. Robert looked like he wanted to burst with laughter. I gave Alex a tour of the store and we reminisced about the days when his business was there. I'd totally redone everything, and the store had a totally different atmosphere. He seemed to be fascinated by my taste in fashion.

When we reached the shoe area he said, "I bet you have every shoe in here." That reminded me of the new shipment that should have arrived by then.

I grabbed his arm and said, "Thank you for reminding me, we should have gotten our new shipment in today." I walked over to the counter where Isabelle was.

"Did the new shipment come in yet?"

Isabelle walked around the counter and stuck her foot out. She was wearing a pair of gorgeous stiletto sandals. They were made of peacock feathers with calfskin leather straps. They were strictly for going out on the town and there were four other boxes that she hadn't even opened yet.

Isabelle said, "I opened the first two boxes and figured you would want to open the other ones. I wanted to share the excitement."

Robert and Alex looked at each other and said in unison, "Women!"

I stopped Robert right there. "Robert, please don't act brand new in front of Alex. I can remember when we spent the entire day looking for a specific pair of shoes for you not too long ago." Robert tried to defend himself.

"That's different. It was for a special occasion."

"Oh, do I need to remind you of the day you had us on the computer ordering custom made Ralph Lauren shirts where the logo and the shirt had to coordinate? Shall I go on?"

Alex started to laugh and said, "There's nothing wrong with a man taking pride in his appearance. Leave that man alone."

I smiled, "Well he started it."

For a minute it was like old times. Alex and I were laughing and talking like we saw each other every day. In the midst of our laughter I remembered how awkward I felt around Alex.

I looked at my watch and said, "So Alex, I imagine you and Robert are going to miss lunch and you don't want to miss your plane." I could tell that my lack of tact made Alex uneasy.

He said, "Yeah, heaven forbid I get stuck in Houston with you." Then he said, "Hey Robert, man I forgot my cell phone. Let me get it, then we can go." He looked back at me with an unsettling look, without saying a word. I looked over at Robert and Isabelle. They both gave me a disappointing look. Robert waved me over. Isabelle just stood there and nodded her head. I was totally confused, Isabelle was giving me the go ahead nod, but I was dating her brother. I followed Alex back to the office.

I knew I was wrong, I had to try and redeem myself. As he reached to get his phone I walked around him and stood behind my desk. I didn't know what to say. I couldn't say I'd made a mistake, I'm confused, I think I love you. That all sounded so juvenile and confusing. The only thing I could do was say his name. "Alex."

He looked up at me with the same disappointment as the last time I saw him. "Seth, did you really think I had a layover by chance? I travel too much to know how to avoid a layover, in Houston of all places. You know why I came, you know I came here just to see you. I could give a damn about spending time with Robert. That's my boy, but I see him all the time."

"Alex I really didn't know why you were here."

"Come on Seth, stop playin' me, and you. I saw the look in your eyes when you saw me. I felt the heat from your body. And I know you felt mine."

"Alex, please don't be silly."

"No, don't you be silly...silly enough to let me walk out that door again."

"Alex you can't just come in here and expect me to drop everything and do what you want me to do. Things are much more complicated now. You don't understand." He tossed his phone on my desk and I watched as his whole body, along with the tone of his voice changed. He was much more tense. He stared at an insignificant object as if he needed to gather his thoughts. Then he turned, looked over at me and captured my attention with his eyes.

"I don't think you understand. When I think of my life and my future, I think of you. I think of how we were the best of friends and how that can only intensify these feelings that I know we have for each other. What I don't understand is why you keep putting me off and denying what you know we can have together."

"Alex, I think that when friends cross that line, they can never go back. There are so many things about me that you don't know and that you could never begin to understand. I'm happy right now. I have someone in my life and things are going well. I think you should find someone and be happy." I couldn't believe those words were coming out of my mouth, let alone believe them myself. My heart and my brain obviously had not been introduced. I stood there struggling to understand what the hell I was saying. Maybe someone knew something that I didn't. Maybe there was a reason for what I was saying. Alex became agitated at that point.

"What makes you think I don't have someone? I'm just like you, lying to myself and settling for less than I deserve."

"Hold on, you don't know anything about Maxwell and I think you should respect him for who he is."

"Well Seth, just who is he?"

"He's someone very special."

"Someone special? Please, I know you. I know what someone very special means. It means he's your flavor of the month. He's your bandage to heal whatever troubles you have at the moment. You're gonna get tired and toss him aside, broken and fucked up in the head."

"That's your problem Alex, you think you know me. You think you know what I need."

"I do know you. I know that your favorite color is harvest gold, not yellow, not plain old gold, but harvest gold. I know your favorite movie is The Color Purple and when you're feeling low, you watch it because it lets you know that someone else's life is worse than your own. I know you wear a size two, but your favorite designer is Gucci because it runs a size larger and it makes you look like you have more curves than you do. I know that to this day, you have a phobia of white vans because we saw a movie about a kidnapper who used his white van to kidnap women. I know that when you go to McDonald's you order a number three, without onions or cheese and a Coke with extra ice because you like the sound that ice makes when you chew it. I also recall a warm spring day when I carried you on my back four blocks down a flooded street because I didn't want you to wade in the nasty water that came to my knees." He looked down for a moment and paused to let that sink in. Then he moved in closer to me.

"I know that every moment we spend apart is a moment that I am dying inside. I'm a full grown heterosexual male who is not afraid to stand here and admit to you and whoever else, that I love you with everything that I have." Alex tried to swallow the lump in his throat. He grabbed my hand and stared deep into my eyes. "Seth," he said gently. "I have the Father, the Son and the Holy Spirit. Now, I need you."

My heart sank to the tips of my toes. I could feel my face flush as I fought back the tears. There was nothing left for me to say. I looked up at Alex. That's when I noticed Maxwell standing in the doorway. I wondered how long he'd been there. For a brief moment, Alex and I were the only two people in the world.

Alex hadn't noticed Maxwell standing there. Before he turned to leave, he said, "This is the last time I'm going to walk in or out of that door, are you going with me?"

When Alex turned toward the door he noticed Maxwell. From the look in his eyes, he knew who Maxwell was. Ignoring Maxwell, Alex turned to me and said, "Well?"

I took a breath and looked over at Maxwell and said, "Alex Young, this is my boyfriend Maxwell Batiste."

Alex turned to Maxwell and sarcastically said, "Brother, you have my sympathy." He walked past Maxwell and out the door.

I was empty and confused as I watched Alex's shadow disappear down the hall. I'd just let him walk out of my life again and gave Maxwell false hope. He was not my boyfriend and I did not deserve him or Alex. As I stood glued to the spot I was standing in, I didn't bother to wipe the stain of tears from my face. I could not understand why I rejected Alex when I knew how I felt. I had come to the conclusion that I was one of those people who thrived on drama and misery. The sad part was the fact that Maxwell was still standing there with this dumb look on his face and it made me feel even worse. He stood with his hand stretched out saying, "What the hell was that about?"

The sound of his voice irritated me beyond belief and I responded by saying, "Please, not now Maxwell." At that point my feet became unglued from that spot and I rushed past Maxwell heading toward the front of the store. I walked through the door and looked around for Alex. He was not there and Robert was gone as well. I looked at Isabelle and she said, "He's gone."

As I ran my hand along the counter, I slowly walked back to my office. I passed Maxwell as if he were not even there. He followed me matching my footsteps, all the while asking what was going on. I declined to answer any of his questions. I couldn't think clearly and I could feel my eyes welling up with tears. I tried my best to hold on and to maintain what bit of dignity I had left. I reached behind my desk and grabbed my purse. I grabbed my keys from my desk and walked out of the store without saying a word to anyone. As I passed Isabelle, I noticed that Kelly and Quincy had made it in. I could see their mouths moving but I could not hear what they were saying. I suppose they were saying hello or attempting to exchange pleasantries, I really didn't know. I'd tuned everyone out and was in my own world. As I started my car, I saw Maxwell standing in the doorway looking as if he was in a fog of confusion. I didn't even realize that I was backing out in front of an oncoming car. I looked in my rearview mirror to find a man behind me flipping me the bird.

I pulled up to the house and noticed Isabelle's car in the driveway. I knew she stopped by to warn everyone about Alex's visit and my mood. As I approached the driveway, I noticed she was still sitting in the car. I parked behind her, grabbed my purse and got out of the car. I walked over to her car and knocked on the window. She was talking on her cell. She raised her index finger gesturing for me to wait a minute. I stood there for a minute waiting for her to finish. I wanted to make sure she didn't mention to Mattie that I had seen Alex. Lauren didn't know anything about Alex, and Mattie knew too much. I wasn't in the mood to explain. She finally finished her call and opened the door to get out of the car. As she opened the door she wore a half smile, half empathetic look. She crawled out of the car with her purse in one hand and her cell in the other. She got out, closed the door and rested on the car door. She reached up and touched my right cheek with her right hand. "Are you ok?"

I touched her hand with mine and tilted my head slightly, "I'm ok.... I just don't know what's wrong with me."

She removed her hand, looked at me and smiled, "Girl there ain't nothin wrong with you. You're in love, that's all. You love Alex and just won't admit it."

I stepped back a little, "You know it's crazy, I was just thinking the other day that if I had another chance with Alex, I would definitely take advantage of it, but when I saw him I acted like a total jackass. When I saw Maxwell standing there I felt even worse."

Isabelle showed me her cell phone and said, "When you pulled up I was talking to Robert on the phone. He said Alex was pretty pissed off, but I think he was more hurt than anything. Robert said Alex talked about you all during lunch. I got the impression that you won't be hearing from Alex again unless you make the first move. Even then if you're not standing there naked with 'I'm sorry. Please forgive me.' written on your body you can forget it."

I started to laugh. I could always count on Isabelle to lighten up the mood. I almost forgot to ask about Maxwell. I didn't want her to think that I didn't care about him so I made sure I put extra emphasis on my concern.

"So, uh what did Maxwell say?" She looked up at me and said, "Maxwell is going to be fine. I explained to him that you and Alex have a lot of history that has never really been resolved. I explained that you really can't deal with any binding emotional situations right now from him or Alex."

I turned my head and looked across the street. I needed to remove myself from the conversation for a minute. Isabelle commanded my attention by grabbing my hand. "Seth, are you listening?"

I turned to her and said, "Yes, I'm sorry my mind wandered for a moment."

"Yeah, that's been happening a lot lately."

"You know, sometimes I just don't get it. I mean, I look at my life. The way it is now. I have this beautiful house with a three-car garage in one of the most prestigious neighborhoods in Houston. My boutique is listed as one of the top ten places to shop. You're getting ready to open up another store in the Galleria. I couldn't ask for a better friend and family than you and Robert. I have my sister back and a beautiful niece, but I still feel empty."

"Honey, not even people can make you complete if your heart and soul is empty."

"I know. I've always known that my parents were dead. I was never sure about Nicolette, but I knew my Mama and Daddy were gone. It seems like having Nicolette back would make it all better, but I still feel uneasy, like something just ain't right, now more than ever I just want to know what happened."

"And I think you should find out."

"Me too. That's why I decided to go back to Dillon"

"Really? I think that's a good idea. You know that I'm right there with you, but how do you think Mattie and Lauren will feel about this?"

"I think Lauren will be ok with it, but I'm not so sure about Mattie."

"Well, do you know when you'll be able to make the trip?"

"Yeah, I'll leave on Friday. I have to make arrangements and tie up a few things here. I think I just want to go back to where I used to live and make sure that this isn't a dream or maybe discover that it is...I just need to do this".

"Well then, I guess we need to hop on that plane." I grabbed Isabelle's hand and held it real tight.

Lauren or Nicolette and I had missed birthdays, girl talk, good times and bad. She was my sister, but she was still a stranger, I couldn't feel the way that I should, at least not right then. She didn't know me and I really didn't know her. Could our blood ties alone help us to survive this together? I looked at Isabelle and felt grateful for her, but I wished I could share that same closeness with my sister. Before we went into the house, I asked Isabelle not to say anything about Alex. She agreed and we headed for the front door.

I heard voices coming from the kitchen as I entered the house. I decided to just walk in and announce my plans to go back to Dillon. Anyone who wanted to go with me was welcome. I walked into the kitchen, put my purse down on the table and kissed Noel who was sitting down at the table eating a brownie and drinking a glass of milk. I walked over and kissed Mattie on the cheek and affectionately touched Lauren on her shoulder. I glided through the kitchen like I was walking on air. At that moment, I didn't seem to have a care in the world. I knew I had something to say and there was no easy way to say it. I walked over to the fridge and grabbed a bottle of water. I poked my head out and asked if anyone wanted any. Isabelle and Lauren both said yes while Mattie declined. I handed the bottles over to the girls and took a big gulp of my water. I swallowed the water and placed the bottle on the counter. I stood there with both hands on the bottle and looked at everyone in the room, including little Noel.

"I have decided to go back to Dillon. I'm leaving Friday morning. Anyone who wants to go with me is welcome." I grabbed the bottle of water from the counter and stood there and looked at the faces of Mattie and Lauren as they stared at me with blank looks. Mattie pulled out a chair and sat down at the kitchen table. She rested her forehead in the palm of her hand. She looked to her left and to her right like she was trying to figure out just what to say. I looked over at Isabelle and Lauren, they were just standing there.

With her mouth full of brownies, Noel looked up and asked, "What's Dillon?"

Lauren walked over to Noel and brushed her hair with her fingers. "Dillon is where Aunt Seth and I lived when we were about your age."

As the mood changed, Mattie looked up at me and said, "Why in the hell would you want to go back to Dillon? Can't you just leave it alone?"

I was shocked and pissed all at the same. I was shocked because she never cursed, she didn't even really say hell or damn. I was pissed because I was tired of not knowing. I was tired of her not understanding my need to find some answers and possibly close the pages to this horror novel. I guess my frustration got the best of me. Before I knew it, I pulled a vacant chair back from the table and sat down.

We were eye level when I looked at her and said, "I am so got damn tired of this. You act like nothing ever happened. Like Dillon, Georgia is some fictitious place I made up in my head. Like we never had parents. You want us to act as if Lauren and I just dropped out the fuckin' sky like aliens or some other supernatural shit. I have tip-toed around you long enough. I have been so empty and have been feeling incomplete all these years. I was eight years old, a child, a baby, not much older than Noel. Neither one of us knows what happened to mama and daddy, but worst of all, we don't know why."

Mattie sat back in her chair and said, "I told you a long time ago to just let the past be the past. You think you want to know what happened, but you don't." She looked over at Lauren. "I knew when you came here it wouldn't be long before trouble followed."

With a very uncomfortable look, Lauren put her bottle of water down on the counter. When she did, she slammed it down so hard that some spilled out on the counter. "Trouble...what do you mean trouble? So my coming here is trouble? That's what you think?"

Mattie moved near Lauren. "I didn't mean that you were trouble. I just..." Her voice trailed off.

Lauren was very hurt and upset, "What did you mean? Because trouble is what you said and since I arrived here, you've been a little less than welcoming."

Mattie became very defensive. "I have tried my best to welcome you..."

"That's just it, you shouldn't have to try. When you came back from your trip and found me here, I saw the look in your face. It wasn't a look of joy; it was a look of worry. When I hugged you, you just stood there. You didn't even touch me. At first I was jealous because Seth was raised by someone she knew loved her, someone who was a link to the past, but the more I watched the way you two act around each other, the more I realized she was all alone just like me."

Mattie rose from her chair and looked at both of us. "You know what? You're right. I haven't been what I should have to Seth or to you since you've been here. I can't change any of it, nor can I sit here and promise that I will do better. Motherhood has been one heartbreak after another. When Seth came along and needed me, I simply didn't have anything left to give. I guess I figured as long as I was here to try and teach her right from wrong, somewhere along the way she'd learn to love herself. Well I guess I fucked that up too."

We all stood there for a while, staring at Mattie. I think everyone was more concerned that she'd just said, "Fuck." There was definitely more to Mattie's story. She was truly bitter over the death of her child decades ago. There seemed to be something more that she just wouldn't tell us. Whatever it was, she seemed terrified about it. More than ever I believed whatever Mattie didn't want to talk about was buried somewhere in Dillon.

Surprisingly she took her seat near the wall and sat back in her chair. As she caressed her temples, she looked over at us and said, "Look, you two are grown now and you've been through a lot. I admit that I have been selfish. I too, have secrets that I would like to keep as my own. You deserve to find out what happened. I just want you to prepare yourselves for whatever you'll find."

This cloak and dagger routine was getting old. My parents were shot and then set on fire. My sister who I thought was dead showed up on my doorstep a few weeks ago. It was time out for the society of secrets. Why can't she just tell me what the hell I needed to know? Just when I was about to ask her what the hell she was talking about, Mattie walked over to me.

"I am older than I should be and I am tired...just tired. This has taken me and consumed me." She pointed to her head. "I have decades of secrets up here. My secrets, your secrets, your parents' secrets, everyone's damn secrets. I can't bear this burden alone, so you two get packed up and run on to Dillon so we can all share these secrets. I can't protect you anymore. You deserve to know where you came from and what happened years ago. Dillon is a good start and that road you used to live on will take you where you need to go. There is someone there who will help you. Just don't ask me to tell you anything because I just can't."

This was the first time that she ever mentioned someone else knowing what happened. I needed to know who could help us. Who was she talking about? "Mattie who are you talking about?" I asked her. "Who can give us the answers we need?"

She seemed to be tired all of sudden, more tired and worn than I'd ever noticed. She was having difficulty trying to make her way to the kitchen exit. Just before she headed out the door she turned to us and said, "You will find everything you need on that old road."

In desperation Lauren walked over and grabbed her hand and said, "But there's nothing left! There is no house."

Mattie retrieved her hand quickly and said, "There's plenty there."

I could see there was no use trying to get anything from Mattie. She was beyond uncooperative and I was beginning to lose my patience. I could see the disappointment in Lauren's eyes. I could also see there was something else between Mattie and Lauren. It was almost as if Mattie couldn't stand her. Maybe she was mad because she thought Lauren had started everything.

Isabelle crept over to where we were standing and watched Noel drinking her milk. She wasn't paying any attention to us. Isabelle said quietly, "This is some creepy shit. Are you two sure you're ready for this?"

I sat down next to Noel. "I've got to be ready, if I don't at least try, I'm gonna wind up right back in the nut house."

Lauren shared my pain. "I know, I'm gonna be in the bed next to you."

Isabelle said, "I'm in it until the end. I just want to make sure that we know what the hell we're getting into."

I didn't think it could be that serious because whatever had happened, it was twenty years ago. Who could possibly hold a grudge that long? I felt I needed to down play the situation. "Look it can't be as bad as Mattie's making it out to be, I mean it happened over twenty years ago. If it was over something like gambling or money, my parents are dead so what ever happened is settled."

Lauren was still skeptical. "Obviously, you don't watch television or read books, people don't forget nothin'. And what if these people think we saw it happen?"

I was becoming slightly agitated. "Lauren, we don't even know who these people are. Daddy was a well-known lawyer. He had to have a lot of enemies. And let us not forget that Clark was a suspect."

"And do you think, if he is still hangin' around, that he'll be willing to tell us the truth? Clark ain't nothin' to play with."

"It sounds to me like you're having second thoughts. A few minutes ago you were down for whatever," I said.

"Look, I'm just thinkin' about what Mattie said."

"And I've been thinking about my Mama's chest being blown out in front of me, and my Daddy laying on the ground bleedin' and talkin' about he didn't mean for it to happen. Something is definitely wrong with that picture, Nicolette...Lauren...whatever."

"It's the same picture I see every night.. Do you think I want to believe that Daddy had anything to do with what happened? What if we find out he was involved...then what? Where will his memory go then?"

"You know as well as I do that there could be a possibility that Daddy had something to do with all this, but we just don't know that for sure. Since that night, I have felt you alive in my heart. I can still feel mama, but I can't even remember what color daddy's eyes were. I need to know why I can't feel my daddy's spirit." Things were getting a little out of hand and Isabelle interjected.

"Ok guys, look, we all know this is a very sensitive subject for both of you. It's clear that Seth is ready to find out what happened in your past and that means going a step further, to Dillon. Now Lauren isn't quite ready for that yet. Seth, you need to respect Lauren's feeling and give her some time. Lauren, you need to respect Seth's need to move on and let her go back to Georgia. Seth and I will go to Dillon this weekend and Lauren you can stay here. If you feel comfortable when we return, we'll tell you what we found out." Isabelle walked over to Lauren to console her. I was happy Isabelle reached out to Lauren in her time of need, maybe things between them wouldn't be difficult after all.

Lauren agreed with Isabelle's suggestion, "I think that's best for now. I thought I was ready but I'm not...I just can't right now. I have my daughter to think about and...I just can't." I understood where she was coming from, and I agreed that it would be best that she stay behind. I promised to share with her what we uncovered if she wanted to know.

Time slipped away from us and everyone needed to settle down for the night. Lauren and Noel left. Isabelle stayed for a few moments. Once the others were gone, Isabelle informed me that she was planning a trip to Georgia that coming weekend anyway. "I guess you should know that Robert and I were going to Atlanta this weekend. Alex is having a party and we were invited. Robert wants me to go and I really want to go."

I actually didn't know how to feel. The mention of Alex just reminded me of what a jerk I'd been. I cleared my throat "That's fine with me, Robert is your husband. He and Alex are friends and you want to go. Don't worry about me. We can't tip-toe around the subject of Alex forever." She smiled as if she were shocked by my response.

"There is something I forgot to tell you."

I wondered what it could be. I knew it had something to do with Alex, but what was it? I said, "What do you have to tell me?"

Isabelle hesitated a second, "Robert told me that one of the reasons Alex stopped by was to ask you to be his date for the party."

Just when I thought I couldn't feel any worse about the 'Alex' situation. If he'd asked me to the damn party instead of trying to confess his love, we could have worked up to the 'I'm still in love with you part'" I couldn't think of anything else to say, so I just stood there quietly. Isabelle knew I was at a loss for words. She said, "I thought you would want to know." She gathered her purse and her bottle of water. "Well I'm out of here, I know Robert is starving. I have three missed calls from him. I'll see you tomorrow."

I walked Isabelle to the door and turned off the lights in the kitch-en. I walked up the stairs thinking about the hot bath I was about to take. As I passed Mattie's room, I heard a faint sound. It sounded like she was crying. I stuck my ear to her door, she was crying. I knocked on the door and when she didn't respond, I slowly opened the door and peeked in. She was on her knees next to her bed. I didn't know if she was praying or crying, then I realized she was doing both. I sat down on the bed beside her and stretched out my hand to console her and then I realized I couldn't bring myself to actually physically console her. I drew my hand back and wondered about what to do. It seemed like such a difficult task. I knew the same resistance that wouldn't allow me to comfort Mattie was the same thing that created a wall between Alex and me. It seems that every time I'm put in a situation where I needed to be sensitive, something inside me said, 'no'. I looked down at Mattie and I wanted to reach out to her, I wanted to comfort her and tell her that everything would be ok. Instead, I sat there with my hands on top of each other resting in my lap. It was like I had paralysis or something. I looked toward the ceiling as if trying to find strength from somewhere. I looked along the walls and to the floor, but there was nothing. I couldn't possibly be that rigid. I couldn't understand why my affection was selective. I had little difficulty expressing affection with Isabelle or Maxwell, but Mattie was different. I could say I felt that way toward her because there was never really any tender moments between us, but I should have been able to reach out to anyone in need.

With everything that I had left in me from the hectic day I'd had, I unfolded my hands and placed one on Mattie's head. To my surprise I started to stroke her hair and in the next moment I found myself asking her if there was anything I could do for her. The last time we shared anything remotely tender was the day Lauren walked into the store and back into my life. Life with Mattie hadn't been all bad. I guess those last few months, we had been preparing for something emotionally and we had no idea what it was. I continued to stroke Mattie's hair and wondered where we'd gone wrong. At what point did I start resenting her? And at what point had she started regretting me? I figured that loving me too much would just remind her of the love she had for the child she'd lost. Sometimes it was more painful to love than to hate.

While sitting there on Mattie's bed, my mind began to wander and I forgot I was trying to console someone. I thought of my own mother and the night Lauren and I had heard her crying. I wondered what she was crying about. I wondered if my dad was telling the truth. I wondered if my mother missed her mother as much as I missed mine. No one could ever convince me that there was nothing special about a mother's love. Some people say love is love when it comes to family, but that's a pure lie. I would give my life to have my mother hold me, to feel her soft skin and to smell her sweet perfume. Each morning, I wake up feeling afraid that this would be the day I forgot what she looked like. Over the years she became more and more abstract to me. When I was younger I could hear her voice so clearly, as if she were standing in the same room with me. As I grew up it became a faint whisper. I thought of Mattie and never really realized her last memories of her mother were violent and cruel. Her last memories of her own child were equally as cruel. I began to feel the tears well up in my eyes and it seemed as though I could feel Mattie's pain. I made my way to the floor and knelt down beside her. I put one arm around her shoulder and I took her left hand in mine. I felt her body as she became more relaxed and comfortable. Her face was no longer buried in her palms. She looked up and began to recite the 23rd Psalm: "The Lord is my Shepherd, I shall not want..."

Without hesitation, we recited the entire Psalm. I did not ask why, I knew why. I needed the Lord to guide me on the journey that I was about to take. Mattie had given me her approval in her own way. After we finished, we both sat down beside the bed on the floor. She took my hand in hers. "There are some things that just can't be explained. I never meant for you to think that I didn't love you or even like you for that matter. Love is a luxury that some people simply can't afford. It seems like it takes so much energy to love. When I was child, I prayed my mother and father would love me like that Bible they were always reading told them to do, but they never did. When I got a little older I started lookin' for love in all the wrong places. One day, I thought I found someone who was willing to give me some attention. The associate minister at my Daddy's church was real nice to me. He told me I was pretty, and that I could do or be anything I wanted. I thought he was the best thing ever. He was much older than I was, so I saw him as kind of a father figure, nothing more. I was tall, skinny and dark as tree bark; I was so selfconscious. He had such a wonderful personality, or so I thought. He was half white. His father was white and his mother was black. He had these piercing blue eyes and black wavy hair. It was like he was the eighth wonder of the world. Oh, I trusted that man and I guess you could say I loved him like family. Well, one day he asked me to go riding with him to pick up something for the church. I didn't think anything of it, so I went with him. He decided that since it was such a nice afternoon, we should go riding in the country. I remember that day clearly. We rode out a little ways from town and he stopped the car on a private road. While we were sitting there he told me how he felt about me, he told me he loved me, although not like I loved him. I told him I thought he was nice and he reminded me of how I thought my father should be. He told me I had been teasing him all this time and he was going to teach me not to play with grown men. Well, he raped me right there in that car on that lonely road. I cried and I screamed and he wouldn't stop. When he finished he fixed himself like nothing had happened and handed me something to clean up with. Then he drove off. He was so unconcerned. He asked me if I wanted a soda or something as if we'd been on a real date. Then he drove me right back home and let me out right where he'd picked me up. I moved to get out of the car and that's when he told me to keep my mouth shut. He said no one would believe me anyway. I got out of the car, went into the house and cleaned up before my mama got home. I kept quiet and stayed away from him until I realized I was pregnant. When I told my parents what happened on that night, they told me I was a liar and that I threw myself at Rev. Nichols. I stayed in that house and endured so much abuse. You wouldn't believe these were people of God. I wanted to have my baby so I could love him, and he could love me. Unfortunately, after he was born I was told he'd been born dead. When I met your parents, I loved them like my flesh and blood and then they died, too. I met Clark and loved him like he was my own and he turned out to be the devil reincarnated. Do you understand what I'm trying to say? When you came along and needed me, I was so empty. I had nothing left to give."

Mattie dropped her head as if she were ashamed of what she'd just told me. I was shocked to hear that she cared for Clark as much as she did. I remember they barely spoke to each other unless they had to. I continued to hold her hand and cherished that moment. I wanted to ask her about the pictures in her closet, but I didn't want to ruin the moment. For the first time, I understood her a little better and didn't resent her as much. She put her hand on top of mine and said, "When your sister showed up, I didn't feel that special something that I feel for you. All I felt was, here are two more people I couldn't give my love to. I also knew there was nothing stopping you two from finding out what happened twenty years ago. That's what scared me more than anything."

"You keep saying that you're afraid of what we'll find."

"Baby it's not what, it's who you'll find."

I jumped up from the floor. "Who is this mystery person and why are you so afraid of him? Why won't you just tell me who he is? I mean, if it's Clark, I already had a good idea that he might be tangled up in this mess somehow."

Mattie looked shocked that I had mentioned Clark's name in that manner. "What...why would you think of Clark?"

"I remember hearing Clark's voice on the night of the fire. I also pulled up some old newspaper articles about him. They were saying he'd been accused of Mama and Daddy's murders."

"So you've been doing your homework."

"I had to...you won't tell me anything. I just don't think you understand how important it is that I find out what happened to my mother and father. But most of all Mattie, I need to know why."

"I understand...I understand that it's time we all found out so we can let it go, and start living the way we should. When I was downstairs earlier in the middle of my rage, I just stopped and realized that I am tired. And I know if I'm tired, then you must be exhausted."

"Why won't you tell us what we need to know?"

"To be honest, I don't even know the truth anymore. All I do know is that it wasn't an accident." Mattie struggled to get up from the floor. Once she found her balance, she grabbed hold of me and stood there for a moment. "I want you girls to remember that the devil is real, he's alive and breathin'. Seth, you are strong, you always have been. You have more of your Daddy in you than you know. I don't doubt for one minute that you can't take care of yourself, but your sister, Lauren...that's another story. She's always been timid and a little scared, and time hasn't seemed to change that. Something in her eyes just ain't right. She is much more emotional about things than you are. There's gonna come a time when emotions can't help you. That's when you'll need to forget about Lauren and handle things on your own."

I heard every word she said to me. It was like she was predicting the future or something. I couldn't help but wonder what she meant by the devil. I thought she was going a little too far with it, but I asked her what she meant.

"What did you mean when you said the devil is alive and breathing? Who is this person?"

Mattie looked at me with one of the most serious looks I have ever seen. Without cracking a smile she said, "You'll know exactly who he is when you meet him, forget what you heard. Kill him with kindness, this one you will have to fight with pure evil."

Chapter Fifteen

The next few days were hectic. I tried to make sure the shop was okay for the weekend. Isabelle and I both would be out of town at the same time. Kelly and Quincy would be there, but they couldn't do it alone. Mattie would be there to help and Robert's sister, Tracy, would be available as well. Tracy usually came in on the weekend just to keep her discount in good standing. The store seemed to be covered. That was one less thing I had to worry about. I still hadn't seen Maxwell in two days. For some reason his schedule was unusually busy. At first I thought he was bitter about Alex, but he still managed to call me almost every hour. To be honest my mind wasn't on Alex or Maxwell at that point. I hadn't talked to Lauren much since she left my house the other day and that bothered me more than anything. We'd spoken a few times on the phone, but that was all. She hadn't been to the house or the store and I hadn't made an attempt to see her. It was definitely something that would take time. We had two very different views on how to handle the delicate past we shared. I wanted to confront it head on and she wanted some time to let things soak in and become comfortable with being able to move forward. Within the last few days, my relationship with Mattie was starting to change. I found that we had more in common than I thought.

Time was winding down and the sun had gone down. My day was done. When the sun rose again, I would be on my way to Dillon. It was really beginning to sink in. I was going back to a place that I hadn't set foot in for twenty years. My stomach was all tied in knots. I called Isabelle to remind her what time to meet me at the airport. She told me if I called her one more time, she wouldn't go with me. I checked my suitcase for the fifth time, making sure I had everything I would need for the weekend. I walked over to my closet and stood there trying to figure out what was missing. I glanced over at the dress that I'd just brought home from the boutique earlier that day. I pulled it out and held it up to my body in the mirror. I hadn't tried it on before bringing it home, I just grabbed one in my size. It was a basic dark almost navy colored dress. It was a silk halter with a very low cut back. The waist was fitted and the dress stopped just above my knees.

I pulled out the shoes that came in earlier, the same pair that Isabelle had. The straps of the shoes were decorated in what appeared to be peacock feather. They were dark with hints of turquoise and yellow in them. My toes were out and the feather covered the top of my foot. As I twirled around in the mirror, I realized I had the perfect place to wear that dress. I thought of Alex's party. I figured either two things would happen if I showed up. One, he would be excited to see me or, two, he would tell me to go to hell. Either way it was worth a try. I took off the dress and grabbed my weekend garment bag from the closet and placed the dress and the shoes in it. I felt like I was preparing for the prom.

After retiring to bed, I became restless. I rolled over and grabbed the phone from the night stand and dialed Lauren's number. She picked up on the second ring as if she was waiting for the phone to ring.

"Hello?"

"Hey, were you sleeping?"

"Uh no, actually I just finished reading Noel her bedtime story."

"Let me guess, Ira Sleeps Over."

"You know it."

"Look Lauren, I need to apologize for the other day. It was wrong of me to be angry just because you need more time to think about things."

"It's ok, I was wrong too. I should understand your need to move on and finally put this behind you."

"The one thing that kept me going was the fact that for twenty years, I knew deep inside you were alive. AOnd just when I thought I was losing my mind, you came back to me like I knew you would. I know that Mama and Daddy are dead, but I guess I just need to know why, so I can move on."

"You've always been the strong one, even when we were kids. I remember Daddy used to say you had heart and weren't afraid of anything. Mama used to say you became more and more like Daddy every day. I was more like Mama, kind of reserved and level headed."

Excitedly, I said, "Lauren, I need to find out about myself. I need to find out why I think the way I do, why I make some of the decisions I make. There are things I've done that you wouldn't believe. I've always known I had this dark side. There is a side of me that even scares me at times. Sometimes I sit and wonder where I came from and where did Mama and Daddy come from. Who were they really? Neither of them knew where they had come from. They just knew they had each other."

"I know what you mean. I don't necessarily have a darker side, but sometimes I do sit and think about our grandparents and what were they like. I wonder where mama got her hazel eyes from that she passed on to us. I wonder where daddy got his loud laugh that sounded like he was the Count from Sesame Street." We both laughed. "You know what I mean."

"Yeah, I know what you mean."

Lauren was quiet for a moment, then she said "Just promise me you won't ever leave me like mama and daddy did."

"I promise. Don't worry. I probably won't find anything, after all it's been twenty years, but I have to try."

"You're probably right and I do understand."

"Well, let me try to get some rest. I've got a long day ahead of me."

"Ok, call me before you leave."

"I surely will. Goodnight."

Lauren and I hung up. I drifted off to sleep. The next morning I sprang up with no problem. I got myself together and headed for the airport. I didn't bother to wake Mattie. I felt it was best if I just called her later on. I didn't call Isabelle. I trusted she would be there. Sure enough, she was standing there waiting for me when I arrived at our departure gate. Soon after my arrival, Maxwell and Lauren showed up. I was shocked to see Lauren, but I was absolutely speechless when I saw Maxwell. I figured Lauren had changed her mind and decided to go. But what was going on with Maxwell? I wondered if they'd come together. When I saw Maxwell, I walked over to him. "Max, what are you doing here?"

He kissed me on my forehead. "I've missed you these last few days and I figured since you're my girlfriend I should be here for you."

As you can probably figure, I felt really small at that point. I thought I should take that opportunity to straighten things out. "Look, Maxwell, I..." He stopped me in the midst of my sentence and told me everything was going to be ok. I hugged him and let it go. My mood was different now. For some reason I was more comfortable when Isabelle and I were the only ones going. There were so many things that I wanted to talk to Isabelle about and Lauren was one of them. Now that she was going with us, I'd have to wait until another time. I was feeling guilty because I didn't feel more than I did for Lauren. I wanted desperately to see Alex, but I knew that was out of the question now that Maxwell was tagging along. It seemed like I had more pressure on me now than I ever did. I didn't say much after they arrived. When we got on the plane, I told Maxwell I was up all night and I wanted to sleep until we reached the Atlanta airport. He said he understood. Isabelle and Lauren sat away from each other. I looked over at Isabelle and I knew she could read my mind. As the plane took off, I settled comfortably in my seat and took a nap. Once we arrived in Atlanta and were outside getting the rental car, I took a deep breath and prepared myself for what was next. I dozed a little more during the road trip to our old house.

Chapter Sixteen

Everything was still the same on the road leading to our old house. Victoria and Claude, Jr.'s house was still there just as I'd left it twenty years ago. There were some changes to the landscape, but everything else was basically the same. The Richardson's house was still there as well. You could see the stables behind the house, just off the road. There were a few new houses. They were still spaced far enough apart so that everyone would have their privacy. As we were approaching our old property, I didn't know what to expect. I wasn't sure if someone had bought the land and built a new house on it or what. That's something no one thought of before we took the trip.

As we turned into the driveway, the sound of the tires treading on the gravel was so very familiar. I was amazed at how the pine trees that were planted a year before the fire had grown on the side of the driveway. It had the effect my mother wanted. At the end of the driveway there was an amazing sight. There sat our beautiful miniature mansion surrounded by sweet smelling Georgia pine trees, with a great big oak tree in the front yard that shielded the house from the sun. It was constructed from deep red brick made from that good old Georgia soil. The house was lined with beautiful rose bushes; red, white, pink and yellow. The shrubbery was neatly manicured and the lawn freshly cut. In the midst of the greenery were white rocks that decorated the walkway and the flower garden. There was a fountain in the front yard filled with chirping birds. As we stepped out of the car my heart almost leaped out of my chest. The front door opened and a tall fair skinned woman with long jet-black hair walked through the doorway. I couldn't believe my eyes. Lauren and I embraced each other. I focused my eyes to make sure I wasn't hallucinating. I was standing there looking at my mother in the flesh. When she realized who we were, she ran and embraced us. She was yelling for my father to come out of the house, but I guess she wasn't loud enough. We all hugged each other so hard until we fell to our knees. She knew exactly who we were. She'd remembered us. My mother grabbed our faces and outlined our features with her fingers. We sobbed uncontrollably and there were no words that could express what I felt. I cried and I cried.

I let go of years of hurt, years of pain and loneliness. The scent of my mother mesmerized me. She was wearing her favorite perfume, Serenity. My tears blurred my vision. My mother broke the silence.

"I knew you'd come back to me." She kissed our faces and embraced us once again.

"We thought you were dead."

"I know, my babies, my beautiful girls. They took you away from me and told me you were dead, but I could feel you; I knew you'd come back."

"But we saw you die...the house exploded..."

"They wanted you to think I was dead. Everything is going to be ok"

I was so happy to see her, I didn't need an explanation. I just wanted to hold her in my arms. I looked over to at Lauren. She was no longer there, but I could hear her calling my name, "Seth, Seth...wake up... Seth wake up."

I woke up with tears rolling down my face. It was all a dream

"Hey, you were dreaming. Are you ok?"

I wiped my face and gathered myself.

"Yeah, I was dreaming. I dreamed everything was still the same and Mommy was waiting on us to return. I could even smell her. It was too real. My stomach is uneasy. I need an antacid or something."

Lauren held my hand. "Well we made it...see, there's nothing here."

We pulled into the driveway a few feet away from where our house sat. When we reached the end of the driveway, just as Lauren had said, there was nothing there that symbolized life. Everything was dead. There was no dandelion field. The trees in the woods looked unkempt. The land looked barren. If not for the pine trees, there would be no symbol of life. My heart was beating fast and I couldn't even begin to imagine what was going through Lauren's mind. I looked over at her and saw the look of despair in her eyes. She'd been hoping for the same thing I had hoped for.

Somehow, I thought I would drive up and the old house would be standing just as I remembered it. I expected the dandelions to be in bloom. I expected our swing set to still be there and our toys to be sprawled out over the backyard. I expected my parents to be sitting around back drinking ice tea with lemon slices floating in it. When we pulled, up our parents were supposed to run to the car and greet us with open arms. They would want to know where we'd been for twenty years. I wanted them to tell us there was some sort of mix up and we'd been stolen away from them and they'd spent every waking moment looking for us. I wanted my mother to take me in her arms and kiss and hug me and outline my face with her fingers. I would do the same to her. I wanted to fall to the ground in a deep embrace and never ever let go. I wanted to hug my father and walk standing on his feet like I used to do every night before bed. He would walk Nicolette and me to bed. She'd be on one leg and I would be on the other. I wanted so much out of that little moment.

All that was left was the foundation to our house. Weeds and grass had grown alongside it. No one took the time to come out and clear the area. It was a horrible sight. My dreams were crushed. It was final. Everything that I'd seen in my nightmares was in fact a reality. The cold barren land was a reminder of what was going on inside of me at that moment. I felt Lauren touch my hand. I must have zoned out for a minute because I forgot I was still in the car. "Are you alright?" I looked over at Lauren and tears were rolling down her face. I really didn't know what to say to her. I had not properly prepared myself for that moment. When we pulled up, I was prepared for my fantasy to come true. I reached over and wiped her tears away. Maxwell and Isabelle were in the front seat looking at us with blank stares. No one knew what to say. What exactly can you say at a time like this, "Welcome home?" I seriously think not. I suggested we get out and take a look around. At that point, I really didn't know what we could possibly find out there that would help us.

When we got out of the car and our heels sank into the gravel. Nicolette and I looked at each other across the car and said, "Damn" at the same time. As we laughed with each other, we remembered how our mother used to get her heels caught between the gravel. She always carried a separate pair of shoes in the car just in case she couldn't wait to get out of the car in the garage. Maxwell and Isabelle looked puzzled. I told them to be careful with their shoes in the dirt. The grass was brown and hard as we stepped off the rocks. The four of us walking on the grass had a unique sound, like a small army going to battle. The grass crackled with each step. As my foot touched the foundation of what used to be my house, I felt overwhelmed. I could picture every detail of my old house as if it were right there, in front of me. I stepped onto the cracked pieces of foundation that were still embedded in the ground. I couldn't understand how no one had bought the land or taken care of it all those years. It was such an exquisite piece of landscape. Lauren and I reminisced about the good old days. As we stepped onto what used to be the entrance to the house she remembered the day she tripped on the rug and chipped her locket.

"Do you remember how clumsy I was?"

"Do I? I remember Mommy had to put those lace guards on your shoe laces because you couldn't keep them tied."

"I remember being so excited to get upstairs after school to change clothes, so we could play with Victoria and Claude Jr."

"Claude Jr. and I couldn't stand each other."

"Girl you know you loooved him."

"With his big peanut head and buck teeth. Every time he talked I thought he was gonna spit out a tooth."

"Oh, he wasn't that bad. Braces do wonders these days, and I'm sure he grew into that head of his. At least, I hope he did."

We both laughed, "You remember the day you convinced him to see if there really was honey in the tree, like in Winnie the Pooh?"

"Oh my God yes, he got stung by a bee and the other bees started chasing him...he jumped in our kiddy pool and almost drowned because he was screaming and fighting in the water."

"You tortured that boy."

"We tortured each other." Isabelle and Maxwell were laughing along with us. "Sounds like you guys had a lot of fun out her in the middle of nowhere." I laughed.

"You wouldn't believe how much fun the four of us had. Our parents had to make us come in when it was time. We did everything together."

"We sure did." Lauren's mood seemed to have changed within seconds. She put her head down and started walking toward what was once our back yard.

"I remember that night and running into the woods. I was so scared. Deep down I knew Mama and Daddy were dead but somehow I didn't want them to be alone. I broke away from you and Mattie and ran back so they wouldn't be. I don't remember the explosion. I just remember running so fast that I could hear my own heartbeat. My legs didn't seem long enough to get me to the house in time. The closer I got, the farther away it seemed. I kept thinking I couldn't leave them alone. The next thing I knew, I was sitting up in a home for crazy kids and some man was telling me who I was and who I wasn't."

As she described her fears, I ran the same event in my mind. I couldn't stop thinking about how amazing it was that she had survived. When the house exploded we could feel the heat and the impact out there among the grass and trees. It was amazing that she was able to walk away without any physical reminders, like burns or scars.

We showed Isabelle and Maxwell where our swing set used to be, along with our favorite tree and other features of the old house. All of a sudden Lauren remembered something. "Seth, do you remember when Claude Jr. took your doll and broke off her arms and legs and you took his G.I. Joe and set it on fire?"

"I almost forgot about that. Daddy whipped my ass for playing with fire."

"Yes and you felt guilty and convinced me to sneak out of the house in the dark to give G.I. Joe and Barbie a proper burial."

"Yeah, we buried them in a shoe box under that tree over there," I said.

"We got another whipping for sneaking out of the house and for being outside alone at night."

"I wonder if it's still there." We all looked at each other with raised eyebrows.

Maxwell tried to figure out a way to dig up the dirt. "We can use a stick to dig up the dirt. Come on, you were eight years old. How deep could you have buried it? You were a little deviant when you were young."

"Man, you don't know the half of it."

"And somehow I don't think I want to," he responded.

"Just remember that for future reference," was my final reply.

We walked over to the tree. Maxwell found a large tree limb that was lying on the ground and started digging. Sure enough the branch went straight through something and made a crushing sound. When he pulled the stick up a piece of a cardboard box came up with it. I reached down and started digging like I was looking for gold. I was excited. There, in the midst of the dirt were the remnants of the shoebox and the two plastic dolls. One was just the torso of Barbie with the arms, legs and head beside it. The other was a G.I. Joe action figure with singed feet and legs. We all laughed.

Maxwell laughed, "You two actually burned and buried a toy. You would make a great case study...you might be a little touched after all." Maxwell seemed to be quite comical today. I knew he was trying hard to lighten the mood.

Isabelle was marveling at the possibilities of the land. "I can't believe you guys grew up here. I mean, I know there is nothing here now, but I look at this land and the houses we passed along the way. All this clean fresh air."

She was right, the place was awesome. At that moment something hit me. I wanted to buy the land. I wondered who bought it or what happened after the fire. Everything was paid for: the land and the house. It was private property. Lauren was into real estate. She must have known how I could buy this land.

"Hey Lauren, how would I go about buying this property?" Her response was not really what I expected.

"What, are you crazy? Why would you want to buy this? Why would you want to live on these memories? What you're thinking is absurd." She was clearly offended by the mere suggestion.

"This is where we grew up. This is the place I dream about."

"Well this is the place I have nightmares about."

"Look, I know there are some painful memories here, but there are also some great ones. I look around and I see what used to be. Just standing here, in this air, gives me some sort of peace. I am standing on the same soil that our parents stood on. Don't you understand? I have longed for the day that I would breathe this air again. I don't know why, but I just want our old house, our old land, our old lives..."

"You want our old life? Buying this land is not going to bring our parents back. If that was the case I would have bought it a long time ago."

"What do you mean?"

"I check on this land every so often to see if it's on the market, and to see if there is anything listed that could help me figure things out"

"Why didn't you say anything?"

"There was nothing to tell, the only thing I found out was that this land is owned by a private company named Benson and Hawthorne."

"Benson and Hawthorne; are they from Georgia?"

"No, the company is based out of Los Angeles. I think the original intent was to try to buy this land along with other lots around here and build houses to sell. For some reason they never sold this land and it's just been sitting here."

Isabelle seemed to be intrigued by this information. "Well how long after your parents death was the land sold? If your parents were dead, then who sold it?"

"Well, I found out that Clark sold land to this company. We all know he would sell his own mother for money."

Maxwell thought it would be a good idea to try and find Clark. You two keep talking about this Clark guy. Why don't we try to find him?"

Lauren seemed to get even more agitated, so I jumped in. "The only problem with that is, a couple of days ago I was doing some research and I found out that he died in a car accident not long after our parents' death. I'm pretty sure it wasn't an accident." I pulled out a copy of the article that I'd gotten off of the Internet.

Lauren said, "He was a slippery little bastard. I guess he can't help us now if he died in a car accident. Like I said before, I can't find anything on Benson and Hawthorne. They don't have a website. I did find a number once, but it had been disconnected."

Isabelle was still confused. "I just can't understand why someone would hold onto a piece of land like this and not do something with it. It's like they just forgot about it."

Maxwell was intrigued as well. "What I want to know is why everyone is coming up dead? Now we know why Lauren thought you and Mattie were dead, but when I pulled up both death certificates it indicated that you died in the fire with everyone else..." Maxwell pointed to me. "And Mattie's death certificate stated she died of a heart attack. The article that I pulled up from the Internet stated that Mattie was Clark's alibi for the night of the murders. The death certificate was dated for approximately one month after the murders. She was found by a Dr. Shaw, who just happened to stop by to check on her."

Lauren jumped in. "You know that part has always puzzled me. When I first saw our death certificates, I noticed Dr. Shaw had signed them all. Until I read Mattie's death certificate, I always assumed everyone was dead because that's what the police officer led me to believe. But then I began to wonder why Seth's death certificate stated she died in the fire and Mattie died of a heart attack some weeks later. I couldn't understand why Mattie would leave you out there while she got away. When I ran away from you guys, both of you were fine."

Isabelle put her hand on her hip and pointed her finger into the air. "There's something about these death certificates, and this Dr. Shaw. Do you guys know anyone named Dr. Shaw?"

Suddenly, it hit me. I was so angry with myself. "You idiot!" I was talking to myself. I began pointing in the direction of Claude Jr. and Victoria's house "Dr. Shaw, Dr. Claude Shaw, Sr."

Lauren grabbed me by my arm. "Dr. Shaw...Dr. Shaw was our neighbor. We keep talking about Claude Jr. and Victoria. He's their father."

It still didn't make too much sense to me, I said "What would Dr. Shaw have to do with this?"

Maxwell looked over the fence and through the grass at Dr. Shaw's house. "At this point anything is possible, and no one is above suspicion. I think that if this Dr. Shaw still lives down the hill, we need to pay him a visit."

I was reluctant about that visit. "I don't know if he was involved, something tells me it's not quite that simple. I don't think it's a good idea to show up from the dead after twenty years."

Isabelle interjected, "But Seth, if he is the Dr. Shaw we think he is, then he already knows you two are alive."

I shrugged my shoulders and asked, "But what if he's not involved?"

Lauren put her hand on my shoulder. "I think I want to take that chance."

I had to admit, it did all seem to go together. But what would we do? Just burst in there and say, "Hey remember us? The two dead kids from next door that are supposed to be dead?"

It seemed to be getting warmer and warmer outside. I started to perspire. We uncovered a lot in forty-five minutes. There was something about this place that was making all of us think. Even Isabelle and Maxwell were feeding off the information that Lauren and I had gathered on our own. I was disturbed about the fact that Lauren didn't share with me the information about the property until now. I guess she'd hit a dead end and felt it wasn't important. I love her and I definitely want her to be a part of my life, but I was going to buy that land and she was going to help me find out whom I could get it from, she just didn't know it yet. I walked the land a little more, remembering the old days while Lauren stepped aside to make a call and check on Noel. Maxwell and Isabelle were standing off to the side talking to one another. I think they were giving me some time to myself to gather my thoughts. As I stood staring across the field at the Shaw house, I wondered if they still lived there and if they'd be willing to give me the answers I needed. I pondered in my head whether there was a possibility of Dr. Shaw being involved. Somehow it didn't seem like he would fit into this little puzzle. Everyone was right though, we'd come this far and I needed to see this thing through. Suddenly, I remembered Mattie saying something about someone being able to help us. She'd also said we'd find what we needed out here near the old land. Could she have been talking about Dr. Shaw or was there someone else around there that knew what happened? We'd just have to drive down to the Shaw's and hope they still lived there. Just as I was gathering my thoughts, a car drove past.

It was coming from the opposite direction and moving pretty fast. It passed by us and suddenly I heard the tires screech. I watched as the car backed up. It was a big black SUV. I could tell there was a man driving. We all walked toward the front of the property, where he'd parked his truck behind our rental. He sat there for a minute before he climbed out.

Maxwell looked at me and asked, "Do you know him?"

Looking back at Maxwell, I said, "What do you think?" I didn't mean to snap at him, but who would I have possibly known out there? The man got out of the SUV. I narrowed my eyes to make sure I was seeing what I thought I was seeing.

"Yeah, Lauren and I both know him, that's Dr. Shaw."

Maxwell's mouth flew open. "Well, I'll just be damned, speak and he shall appear."

Dr. Shaw got out of the car and I saw that it was him alright. He looked pretty much the same, just a little older. His accent was a mixture of a southern twang and proper pronunciation.

"Hey, there. How's everyone doing this afternoon?" He took off his hat, as only a southern gentleman would do, out of respect. I remember him always being so proper. Even though Dr. Shaw, Clark, and my father were good friends, his demeanor was different. He was reserved. For some reason his presence was like a breath of fresh air.

We all responded in unison, "Fine...and you?" He didn't seem to recognize Lauren or myself at that moment.

"I haven't seen you folks before. Are you lost or just sightseeing?" I tried not to look directly into his eyes. Lauren had wrapped up her phone call with Noel. Maxwell and Isabelle just stood there. I lifted my head and broke my silence. It was do or die. Either he could help us or he couldn't. Lauren turned and stood next to me.

"Actually, we used to be from around here, we're just visiting right now." The smile on Dr. Shaw's face disappeared as he clutched his hat, almost crushing it out of shape. He narrowed his eyes and moved in closer and grabbed his chest.

"Oh my Jesus!" At that moment he knew exactly who we were. For some reason my sarcastic side emerged.

"No, not Jesus! It's Nicolette and Noel Toussaint." Just as those words escaped my lips, a massive amount of heat came over me. I started to sweat and my stomach became queasy. Did the sight of him make me ill? I could feel the inside of my stomach moving around like it was trying to exit my body. I looked up at the sky and everything was spinning so fast. I said to myself, "Please don't let me hit this gravel." My legs became rubber and I couldn't stand. I grabbed my stomach and felt my body hit the ground.

Chapter Seventeen

When I came to, I was inside the Shaw house. It was just as I had remembered. Time had changed and so had the furniture, but it was generally the same. Dr. Shaw was applying a cold compress to my forehead and checking my pulse. He was calling my name. He told me that I'd had an anxiety attack, but would be ok. I sat up on the couch and gathered myself.

"How long have I been out?" Lauren sat next to me and brushed my hair back.

"Not too long. Dr. Shaw picked you up and rushed you here to his house." It was all coming back to me. I remembered feeling sick and seeing the sky spin around.

Dr. Shaw came in carrying ginger ale and saltine crackers. "Here this will help settle your stomach."

The truth was I just wanted him to tell me how he knew exactly who we were, since we're supposed to be dead. I figured I should already know the answer to that question. Isabelle was outside the room on the phone, checking in with Robert, as Maxwell quietly stood beside her. I rubbed my head and took a sip of the ginger ale. Lauren was shoving crackers down my throat. I fanned everyone off, sat up straight and looked around the room. There were pictures of Dr. Shaw, and I guess Victoria and Claude, Jr. I walked every inch of that room remembering how we would play in this room when we knew we weren't supposed to. I studied each picture as if I were trying to freeze their faces in my memory bank. Lauren sat there, looking like a lost child. I was much more fascinated than she was. I was overwhelmed with nostalgia.

"You know...I remember a time when we weren't even allowed to be in this room. Everything was always so neat in here, just like it is now. This was like a forbidden fortress." I laughed to myself as I ran my hands along his desk, the same desk from twenty years ago. I could still see the same crayon marks. "I remember when we got a whipping for writing on your desk with crayons. We came in here and made an art table out of it."

Dr. Shaw laughed. "Boy do I remember that; I was so mad at you kids. You all were bad kids."

Lauren looked at Dr. Shaw. "Were we bad enough to deserve what happened to us?"

I was shocked to hear Lauren shoot straight from the hip. She asked exactly what I was thinking.

Dr. Shaw rubbed his head. "You know, that's why I kept the desk just the way you kids left it, it was like you were still here." His eyes welled. He caught himself and quickly rubbed them.

"Look, Dr. Shaw, we don't mean any harm, but judging by your reaction today, I'm sure you can answer some long awaited questions."

He walked over to the window and looked back at me. "And you deserve to have those questions answered. It's time I let this go. It's time I got rid of this burden." Dr. Shaw rubbed his fingers through his hair. "Can I get you guys something to eat or drink?"

I didn't want anything he had to offer, except the truth. His name was all over our death certificates and his reaction to us had been really weird.

Lauren looked at him and said, "No thank you, we didn't come here for a tea party. If you have something to tell us, I wish you would get it over with, better yet. Did you have something to do with the deaths of our parents?"

Dr. Shaw seemed to be offended by that statement. Of all the nerve, he was offended!

He said, "I had nothing to do with your parents' death. To be honest with you, I really don't know what happened myself. What I do know, I am more than happy to share with you. You'll just have to be ready to accept what you're about to hear."

I asked, "What are you gonna tell me? That my father or Clark had something to do with the murders? Well we kinda figured that out already. So why don't you just fill in the blanks." He sat in his chair and offered us a seat.

Get real comfortable, it's gonna be a long night. First of all you need to understand that what I'm about to tell you is more complicated than my giving you information and having you listen. You need to pay attention to every single detail. It's also important that you know I always loved you kids. Your father, mother, Clark and Mattie were my blood family. Your father was a complicated man, though. He always had high hopes and dreams."

I looked at Dr. Shaw and said, "There's nothing wrong with being ambitious."

"No, Seth there's nothing wrong with ambition, but greed is altogether different."

I was startled by the fact that he had called me Seth. I didn't remember introducing myself as Seth. I watched as he settled into his chair and began telling a tale that was definitely made for the big screen.

"Well, see...back then things were different. It was a different time and place. Things were much harder for a black man, especially one with a mind of his own. Your father was one of the smartest people I ever knew. Even when we were kids hustling for money, doing odd jobs and running errands for local gangsters and number runners, your father would only spend what he needed and he'd save the rest. He taught me about saving for a rainy day."

Lauren stopped Dr. Shaw midsentence. "Hold on Dr. Shaw, you knew my father when you were kids?"

"Yes, I sure did. Nolan, Clark and I grew up in the same group home in Louisiana. We were like blood brothers..."

I shared Lauren's confusion. "This is the first we've heard of this. My father never mentioned that. Why is this the first time this has ever been mentioned?"

"Well, Noel..."

"It's Seth."

"Sorry, Seth. Actually I am the reason your father came to Dillon. Clark wanted to stay in Atlanta. This was too slow for him. Dillon was much too settled for Clark. He needed something a little more fast-paced."

Lauren was still puzzled by the new revelation. "Why didn't you all ever say anything? Of course we knew that daddy and Clark grew up together, but they never said anything about you. I just don't understand."

Isabelle had some questions of her own. "I mean...I agree, how can you never even acknowledge growing up together?"

"Well, it's simple, I didn't want to relive those days, and truth be told neither did Nolan. We were all reluctant to relive the past. It had been a hard life. We lived in that home and nobody cared if we lived or died. We were there only to make the check from the state fatter. When you grew up like we did, not knowing where you came from or knowing that your own family didn't want you, it was rough. We were all we had and we took care of each other. We were all different. Your father was extremely resourceful and very level headed. I was the shy one; I cared about people. Clark didn't give a shit about nothing but your father and me. Between the two of us, Clark depended on your father for everything, but even that relationship had its limits. Clark was reckless. He acted on impulse and had no regrets."

Dr. Shaw was very passionate about his feelings toward Uncle Clark. It was almost as if he hated the man. Dr. Shaw intrigued Maxwell, I could see it on his face and by the way he hung on to his every word. Considering he was a psychiatrist, Maxwell probably wanted to know more about Dr. Shaw's feelings toward Clark.

"If he was the person you say he was, why did you continue to associate with him? I mean he sounds like a terrible person." Maxwell moved in closer. Dr. Shaw took a seat in the chair next to Maxwell.

"Well doctor, like I said before, we were all we had and Clark was sort of like my protection. It's hard to explain. To be honest I never really knew what either of them was truly capable of until we got older."

Maxwell leaned forward, and asked, "What do you mean?" Dr. Shaw offered Maxwell a cigar and lit himself one.

"In due time son. I hope the smoke doesn't bother you ladies" We all told him we were fine and he continued his story.

"Before we graduated from high school and went our separate ways, we agreed that once we were able to, we would go into business together. You know, keep the money in the family. Your father went to law school. I went to medical school in Nashville and Clark went to business school. I moved here with my wife and then your parents came. Your father's law office, of course, was in the city. He'd hooked up with Clark and started doing land development and other things. My practice was also in the city. To tell you the truth, I wasn't too keen on being with Clark again after what happened some years before that."

Dr. Shaw had mentioned other things that my Daddy was involved in; I wanted to know what those other things were and what had

Clark done to betray Dr. Shaw's trust? So I asked, "Dr. Shaw you said my father was involved in other things; what were they?"

He was vague, and wanted to talk at his own pace. "I'll get to that later."

"Ok that's fine, but you seem to be leaving out important details."

He moved to the edge of his chair and placed his cigar in the ash-tray. The smell of the cigar was familiar. It started to make my nose tingle and I began to cough.

"Oh, I forgot the smell of my brand of cigar makes you sick."

The odd thing was I didn't remember him ever smoking a cigar in front of me, but I didn't ask about it. He seemed to be uncomfortable with questions at that point, so I blew it off. Once more, he continued his story.

"I just want to make sure you girls can handle what I'm about to tell you and that you understand we made some mistakes that I know I will pay for, for the rest of my life."

I was becoming very agitated with his pace and I needed him to say what he had to say. I was beginning to think Dr. Shaw was in this much deeper than we could ever have imagined. I guess Lauren felt the same way, because before I knew it she had jumped up from her seat. "Can you please get to the point Dr. Shaw? Just give it to us straight."

He took a long, slow drag from his cigar, set it back into the ashtray and began wringing his hands together. He ran his fingers through his hair and took a deep breath. "When we were about twenty years old, we all met up in Mississippi to visit your father one weekend. It was the first time we'd seen each other in a long while. Everything was going great that weekend and there were no signs that anything was about to go wrong. Your father took us to what we used to call a jook joint back then. It was like a little hole in the wall place where we listened to the blues, danced and drank."

I was growing more agitated. "Dr. Shaw, we know what a jook joint is."

"Your father introduced us to a young lady. Clark and the girl hit it off that night and they wanted to be alone. Your father and I wanted to go back on campus. We were tired, and half drunk. Clark told us he'd catch up with us later. Clark had borrowed a car from someone at school and drove to Mississippi so he had been our transportation. He took us back to the school and then he and the girl went off somewhere. The girl lived alone, so we thought they were going back to her house. A few hours later, Clark came back to the room and woke us up. He told us to come outside, he had something for us. We got into the car and drove off to a dark road. The girl was still in the car. She looked worn out. Her face was all bruised and her lip was busted. We asked Clark what happened and he said they were just having a little fun and it was our turn. Of course, I was scared as shit. I knew that Clark had beaten and raped this girl. She was really out of it. I begged him to take her home. I told him he should leave that night. I needed to get back to Nashville as well. The only problem was your father lived there and he would have the risk of her calling the police and involving him. She begged and pleaded with us to take her home. She promised she wouldn't say a word, but Nolan said we couldn't trust her. Clark said you could never trust a whore and he had this look of evil in his eyes that made me shake. The girl kept begging to go home and Clark just snapped, and started choking her. But what shocked me was when your father held her legs to stop her from kicking. I tried to stop him, but Clark reached in his pocket and pulled out a gun. With one hand, Clark chocked that girl to death."

I could not believe my ears! I dropped my head and let it hang there, seemingly lifeless. Isabelle grabbed my hand and clutched her chest as she commented. "Oh my God, you can't be serious!"

Dr. Shaw took another drag of his cigar. "I am as serious as I've ever been."

I needed to know more, so I asked, "Well what happened? Daddy never mentioned spending any time in jail."

Dr. Shaw smirked. "Oh, no we didn't go to jail. No one ever found out."

Lauren asked, "What happened to the girl?"

Dr. Shaw leaned back into his chair. "I was scared stiff...hell, I cried. At that point, we didn't know what the hell to do. We knew we definitely didn't want to go to jail, especially in Mississippi. The only place to send a nigga was the penal farm over in Parchman and that was no place I wanted to be. Clark said the only thing to do was to get rid of the body, clean the car and never talk about this again. We drove around for hours trying to find someplace to dump that body until we realized we were in the middle of nowhere. We were so out of it. We'd been driving and driving and were miles away from campus, almost in Louisiana. The sun was getting ready to come up and the sight of that body, plus knowing what had happened, was making me sick to my stomach. Finally, Clark pulled down a dirt road and we dumped the body into a field of tall grass. We needed to clean up before we left town and before Nolan went back on campus. Nolan said we could trust Mattie because she was like us. She didn't have any family and she loved him like her own son. So we went to Mattie's and told her what had happened. We cleaned up and Nolan went back to campus to get our things. Mattie burned our old clothes and we cleaned out the car that Clark had borrowed. I got on the bus and Clark got back on the highway. Mattie swore she would never tell a soul about what happened. Come to find out, Clark borrowed the car from some big time dealer that he was working for. He did odd jobs for him and that wasn't the first time he had blood on his hands. The man got rid of the car and kept our secret as well. But no one does anything for free. Clark never allowed us to forget that we were not so different from him, and the man he worked for never let us forget he knew all about what had happened."

This shit was crazy. This man was going to sit there and tell me that he and my father helped Clark hide a dead woman in the woods of Louisiana. Somehow this was as unbelievable as what happened to me. I looked around the room to see everyone else's reaction. Maxwell and Isabelle were scared to even look in my direction. Maxwell asked for a drink and Isabelle just sat there staring into space. At that point, I regretted deeply that I had gotten them involved. Lauren and I should have come alone. I knew the risk and I knew anything was possible. Uncle Clark was a real Mutha fucka. I knew then that it was he who was involved in my parents' death. It was his voice I had heard at Mattie's house. He had my daddy tied up in this some kind of way.

The story about the dead girl was unreal. I didn't know much about Dr. Shaw, but I couldn't see how my father could just let that go. And Mattie, no wonder why she was always at church, praying and calling on the Lord. She needed Him, she definitely needed Him. I knew I had no room to talk, I used to be a pimp.

I looked around the room and wondered what secrets everyone else had. I mean was Isabelle ever a stripper? Was Maxwell a transvestite? Just then I remembered Lauren had once turned tricks. What the hell else could possibly shock me? Not a damn thing! I needed to get some clarification. I wanted to know if Clark killed my parents and what was Dr. Shaw role in all of this.

I stood up and said, "So, Dr. Shaw, after hearing this colorful tale of murder and mayhem, did Clark kill my parents and what did you have to do with what happened down the street?"

He looked at me as if he was offended and shocked, but I really didn't give a damn. He need to quit bullshittin' and tell me what happened. Maxwell was on his second drink. Even Isabelle had a glass in her hand.

"Are you two alright?"

Isabelle took a gulp of her drink. "Yes we're fine, I do feel like I am at a dinner theatre or something, this shit is crazy."

Lauren pulled a cigarette out of her purse. "Hell, I know I can't take this."

I didn't even know she smoked. "Lauren, you smoke?"

She held the cigarette to her mouth struggling to light it. "I was trying to quit, but I need this. As a matter of fact, pour me a drink. A big one."

Now everyone had either a cigarette or a drink in his or her hand. One would sip and the other would drag. Pretty soon the room was filled with the smell of liquor, cigars and cigarettes, a real den of hell.

Maxwell said, "Ok, we still don't know why Mr. and Mrs. Toussaint were killed and you must know why Clark really died."

Dr. Shaw looked at me and said, "I see you don't believe a word I just said."

I looked back at him and said, "Well it is a little hard to digest."

He rose up from his chair and walked over to the wall and moved a painting to the side. He started fumbling with the combination on his safe. The door popped open and he pulled out an envelope. Inside the envelope was an old piece of brown paper. It looked like it would crumble at any moment. He walked over and handed me the paper. It was an old newspaper article. I read the headline, "Body of Negro Woman Found in Louisiana Field." The article stated there were no suspects. The woman was completely naked and her body was badly decomposed. Back then a dead black woman was really of no concern to anyone. She was just another lost nigger. The article made everything real. Who was my father? Even though he didn't kill her, he didn't make things right either. Dr. Shaw pulled out another clipping that read, "Atlanta Gangster, Johnny Case found dead in his car." The last clipping confused me. I had no idea who Johnny Case was.

"I don't understand. Who is Johnny Case and what does he have to do with us?"

Dr. Shaw took his place in his chair and said, "The man that Clark borrowed the car from was Johnny Case. He was one of the baddest dudes in Atlanta back in the day. Whatever he wanted, he got. He felt that since he kept our secret so well, we owed him, and we could never, ever stop repaying him. Even though Clark was now a college graduate and a businessman, he was still dirty. He did stuff for Johnny on the side and whenever he needed legal matters handled, he called on Nolan. And I was his regular physician, more so when he needed a cause of death or something like that. You understand."

Lauren was still puffing on her cigarette. "Yes we understand. You all were his do boys."

Dr. Shaw smiled, "I guess you could say that." He took a sip of his drink. "The truth was Johnny owned all of us. And for some reason he was the only person I have ever known Clark or your father to be afraid of. Clark had gotten into something he couldn't handle. Soon he started gambling and losing big money. He lost portions of the money from the business your father and he owned. Money started coming up missing from the account. Things were delinquent and Nolan got himself burned by trying to help Clark. Your mother couldn't stand this. Your parents started fighting and your mother threatened to leave Nolan. When things seemed like they were getting better, your father cut his losses and split, leaving Clark for a minute. Then Clark showed up one day and told us that some money had come up missing from Johnny and they were blaming him. It seemed almost a million dollars had come up missing from Johnny over the years and Johnny had finally found out. Between your father and Clark, someone was taking side deals and cutting into Johnny's business. Come to find out Clark had been selling drugs for Johnny and helping him beat people out of property. Your father was Johnny's attorney and had the authority to make decisions about money. When Johnny found out, of course he didn't want to hear whose fault it was. All he wanted was his money, anyway he could get it."

Johnny Case, drugs, gambling! What next? Were my father and Clark lovers? Were they on the down low as well? Who were these people? Were they really my parents? I finally knew where the dark side of my own came from. I grew up around thugs, thieves, drug dealers, pimps and murderers. I looked over at Maxwell. His eyes were wide open with anticipation of what was coming next. I almost thought he was enjoying it.

He said, "So Johnny had Mr. and Mrs. Toussaint killed because they owed him money. And Clark's car accident wasn't really an accident."

Dr. Shaw appeared stunned when Maxwell mentioned Clark's accident. "How did you know about Clark's accident?"

Lauren said, "Well we have done some research of our own. I am in real estate and I wanted to know who owned this property. I found Clark had sold it to a company called Benson and Hawthorne. Seth thought Clark was still alive, so she did some research and found out he was killed in a car accident."

Dr. Shaw seemed to be impressed. "Well, you're on the right track."

Isabelle was getting restless and she really wanted to get to the point. "Dr. Shaw, 'the right track'...what does that mean? Please go on with your story Dr. Shaw."

"I sure will. At this point, your father was in way over his head. He needed money to pay Johnny. He sure as hell didn't want to go back to a life of poverty. Around that time your mother's biological mother died and left her a substantial amount of money. It was enough to pay Johnny with enough left over to live off of. Your mother agreed to give Nolan enough money to pay his portion to Johnny, but of course Clark was broke, so that meant he would be killed. Anna told your father that after the debt was settled she wanted a divorce. She asked him to leave the house. Clark had convinced your father to believe your mother hated him because he knew she was having an affair with Russell."

I had almost forgotten about Russell. He was a good friend of the family. My parents knew him from college. Even though he and my father were cool, he was more of my mother's friend. This was still too farfetched. I knew my mother would never cheat on my father.

"Russell? My mother and Russell...please."

Lauren added, "Now all this other stuff might be true but, Mama and Russell? Hell no!"

Dr. Shaw agreed. "You are absolutely right. Your mother adored your father, but Clark was pouring it on thick. And if you didn't know better you would think there was a possibility of an affair. Your father became more and more jealous. He felt even more loyal to Clark, so he ended up paying off Clark's debt with Johnny as well. Of course a debt to someone like Johnny Case can never be repaid. Your mother gave Nolan one week to leave the house. Your father became uneasy about her. He was always paranoid, and worried that she didn't need him anymore. He and Clark began talking about having your mother killed and collecting her inheritance."

I felt a sharp pain in my chest. I leaped up from my seat. "I knew it! I knew my father was involved! The night he died he told us he didn't mean for it to happen that way. Do you remember that Lauren?"

"Of course, I remember. I have been trying to figure that out forever."

I glided across the room driven by something that I could not explain. The pieces of the puzzle were finally coming together. I always knew that he was somehow involved in all of this, but I just didn't want to admit it, or believe it.

"The night that my parents died, my father told Lauren and me he was sorry about all of this. I have spent hour after hour, minute after minute, trying to figure out exactly what my father had to do with all of this. That son-of-a-bitch."

I could hear Lauren begin to cry, she asked, "Did he mean to kill us as well?" Dr. Shaw walked over to Lauren to comfort her. He put his hand on her shoulder and held her hand.

"No, Lauren." He got up from the seat and paced back and forth within a few feet of us. "Are you sure you want to hear the rest?"

Lauren wiped her eyes. "Yes of course we need to hear the rest."

Isabelle interjected, "Are you guys sure? This is a lot for one day."

I sat between Isabelle and Maxwell. "I know you mean well, but we have to hear the rest, tonight." Then I turned to Dr. Shaw. "Please continue."

He returned to his chair and looked at all of us before he continued. "The plan was to have your mother killed and collect the insurance money and inheritance and keep you girls with him."

I had one question that desperately needed an answer.

"Dr. Shaw, how did you know all of this and not talk him out of it or even get killed for merely knowing this? How could you let my father do this?"

"Well Seth, I didn't know about all of it until a few days before your parents were killed. Of course Clark was weak and he got scared. He was more afraid of going to jail than anything. Even though Clark and your mother never really saw eye to eye, he didn't really want to kill her. But at the same time he was jealous of the attention your father gave her. So he initially figured he would suggest the murder and your father wouldn't go along with it. Clark thought your father would believe the 'Russell' story and simply leave. During this time your father started to lose his mind. He was unbearable. It was like he was possessed with power. Everything was about him and what he wanted. Clark got scared and thought he would be the next one to die so he ended up plotting with your father's personal lawyer. He was the one who had handled your mother's inherited estate. Your father used him to handle his personal legal matters as well. His name was Dawson Meeks. He was a white man who had a lot of authority. He could get anything done. He was supposed to help your father get back on his feet after he'd lost everything. Dawson needed a good Negro to help him in the community. He planned to run for mayor in the coming election."

Maxwell said, "Yes I remember him. Dawson Meeks was the mayor of Atlanta, but I think he was indicted over tax fraud, or something dealing with embezzlement."

Dr. Shaw revealed a big smile. "Yes, he most certainly was, but that didn't pan out. He's now a congressman. The thing was that no matter what your father had done, or was about to do, he was still controlled by someone else and he couldn't stand it. Just like Johnny, Dawson had your father under his thumb. Clark became even more reckless because he needed money. Dawson understood Clark would do anything for a dollar, and figured he would be more useful in the long run. After I found out about all of this, I immediately went to talk to Nolan. He decided to pack up the entire family, Mattie included, and move far away from everything. I too, had decided that I needed to get away from everything and everyone. Nolan and I agreed to just go our separate ways and start all over again. Well, Nolan and I talked to

Dawson about leaving and changing our identities. Dawson knew how to do everything. He was dealing in some shit I can't even put out in the air. We didn't know Clark and Dawson had teamed up. Nolan told Clark that he changed his mind. Nolan figured since they were brothers, and Clark listened to everything he said anyway, Clark would agree to cut his losses and leave town as well. Your father came to me one night; he was frantic. He told me he'd overheard Clark and Dawson talking. Clark had decided to have Anna and Nolan killed. He did have a heart though, you girls were not supposed to be harmed. Clark figured Mattie would take the two of you. Clark's plan was to kill your parents only. He had Dawson change your father's will. What they didn't know is that your mother was suspicious all along. She had become suspicious of them all, including your father. She gave Mattie two million dollars and a few other assets to care for the two of you. There were no provisions if you girls died. She never anticipated that, but I guess God was working on her side, so she left Mattie the money under no certain conditions. There were other things she had too. They were in safe deposit boxes and a few other places. Mattie knew your father was changing and they were in danger so she and your mother understood each other perfectly. Mattie didn't know everything, but she knew enough to be afraid. Anyway, one night Clark, Dawson, and two other guys came to the house. They shot your mother and to his surprise, they shot your father as well. Dawson had gone back on his word, and ordered the men to kill you guys as well. Dawson and Clark still denied any involvement in your parents' murders. I'm surprised they didn't try to shut me up, but I didn't know much. To be honest, I really and truly don't know whom to believe. Your father and Clark were displaying signs of insanity throughout this entire thing. Everyone was out for number one. Not a day goes by that I don't sit and think that there is something I'm missing, something I could have done to stop your parents' murders. I've blocked out quite a bit and refused to remember the rest. I just know that I look down across that field every day and grow weary trying to piece it all together."

I was still confused about certain aspects of the story. My father technically didn't have my mother killed. Clark had been the actual culprit or maybe Dawson. I do remember hearing Clark say we were innocent and he didn't want us hurt. But if Clark thought we were upstairs and we died, then how did Dr. Shaw know we were alive...who could have told him?

"Ok, Dr. Shaw, if Clark thought we'd died in the fire, then how did you know we were alive and why was your name on our death certificates and Mattie's? It doesn't make sense."

"There are two parts to that question. First of all, after I saw the fire, I called 911 and ran down the road. I knew exactly what had happened. I stood there and watched as my brother's house went up in flames. There was no one around that night. I stood alone and when I decided I couldn't stand there any longer, I walked down the road and went home. I left the scene and went home to tell my wife and kids what happened. They have never really recovered from that. Your mother was the best friend Brenda ever had."

Isabelle interjected, "Who is Brenda?"

"Brenda was my wife, she died a few years ago of breast cancer."

Isabelle said with compassion in her voice, "Oh, I am so sorry to hear that." Dr. Shaw dropped his head.

"It's okay. My life is made solely from pain." At that moment I felt sorry for Dr. Shaw. He'd seen so much death and deception. His life was never really happy. He lived with so many lies and secrets. I wonder how he survived. Dr. Shaw lit his cigar again and continued with the story.

"After I went home, I thought of Mattie and I wondered if she knew what had happened. So I told my wife I was going to check on her. When I got there, she was so dirty and she smelled like smoke. I knew then that she had been there that night. She reminded me of a time when she had helped me one night, and that now she needed my help. She told me after she'd seen the men come to the house, she was afraid Clark had something to do with it. Of course she couldn't tell the police because Clark wasn't the only person involved. Plus, if Clark went down, the two of us would go down with him. Her, for what we had done in college and me, because of everything else I'd done since then. It was like a domino effect, so I agreed with her. We needed to figure out a way to get rid of this life once and for all. She took me to the closet where you were fast asleep and told me we needed to get you out of there as soon as possible. Since I was the doctor and technically the physician on the scene I could sign the death certificates. For all the authorities knew, everyone including Mattie was in the house that night."

Maxwell interjected again. "But Mattie's death certificate stated that she had died of a heart attack weeks after the fire. After she had told the police she had been with Clark on the night of the fire."

"Exactly Maxwell, that became a problem when the police stopped by the house that night to inform Mattie of what happened. They started asking her questions about Clark immediately. We later found out that one of Johnny's boys had been arrested. Instead of turning on Johnny, they tried to make it look like Clark was running everything. They found out your father was working for Johnny and somehow tried to tie that all together. After the police left, Mattie told me she was afraid of Clark and she told me something that shocked the hell out of me." Dr. Shaw took a deep breath and looked over at us as we sat there barely breathing. "Mattie told me Clark was her biological son."

Isabelle began to choke on her drink. We rushed over to help her. Her eyes were watering and in the midst of choking she begged Dr. Shaw to go on. "Please, please go on." I was too afraid to say a word. Lauren's mouth flew wide open.

Dr. Shaw started to laugh, "I see our reactions are the same. Let me tell you, I know this is some bizarre shit, but Mattie told me the night she helped us get rid of the evidence, she noticed Clark's birth mark on his back. She remembered her child had a birthmark on his back just like that one. It was some weird patch of hair almost like a square shape. She said of course at first it seemed to be too much of a coincidence so she just let it go. She thought her child was dead anyway. She said it just ate at her and ate at her. One day she looked at Clark, listening to him laugh, and noticed he had the same strange haunting laugh that his father had. Other things about him stood out. She said she studied him more and decided to do some research of her own. She found out her parents turned him over to the state as an infant because they were ashamed of how he was conceived. They thought he had been adopted by a couple in Louisiana just a few miles from where he was born, but actually he'd been sent to the group home. She said she confronted him with this information and once she convinced him it might be true, he made her have a blood test. The test proved he was her son and from that moment on, Clark hated her and made her promise never to tell anyone, or he would kill her. She said Clark was definitely something evil, just like his father, and she was afraid of him. She figured if she agreed to be his alibi, she could somewhat redeem herself with him."

I couldn't believe I had lived with that woman all of my life and she'd been holding that inside all of these years. Clark's upbringing was not her fault. She had no way of knowing. I could only imagine what she must have felt while missing her child all those years. To think he was dead, and then to find out he's alive, only to have him hate her and wish death on her. I felt tears welling up in my eyes and I felt an enormous amount of guilt for resenting her all these years. At that point I didn't know who to feel sorrier for. There are so many victims. My thoughts of Mattie made me miss a portion of what Dr. Shaw was talking about, but when I came back to my senses he was still talking.

"...After I found out about Clark, I realized it was getting late and I needed to get home. Well, to my surprise he'd come back to Mattie's house while I was still there. He needed to make sure she told the police just what they needed to know. I was praying inside that you, (he nodded toward me) would not come out of the closet. It was a blessing you were sound asleep. Clark sat there and explained how he didn't mean for you girls to die. He said it was a good thing Mattie wasn't there because now she could be his alibi. She told Clark after the suspicion had settled down and the police were off his back, she wanted him to see to it that I was the person to sign the death certificates. That could not have come at a better time, since I was at the scene and had witnessed the fire; I was able to sign the death certificates. After Clark left, we decided that, in a few weeks Mattie would have a heart attack. I would be the one to find her after I stopped by to check on her one day. The one good thing I had acquired while dealing with Johnny Case, was a lot of friends. I managed to get you and Mattie new identities. I had a friend who owned a funeral home. He came and carted you and Mattie out in his van. Because I had been the one who declared Mattie dead, an autopsy was not necessary. He signed off on the papers stating he had cremated Mattie at my request since I had been her only living relative. I told them I was her nephew." Dr. Shaw laughed to himself. "You two stayed with my friend overnight, and the next day Seth and her grandmother, Mattie St.

James were on their way out of town. I was so worried because Texas didn't seem to be far enough away, but Mattie was very careful."

Lauren began to cry. "What happened to me...how did I end up in that place?"

Dr. Shaw looked at her with a puzzled look. "To be honest with you, that is the one question I cannot answer. I never saw you again after that night, Lauren. I was shocked to see you today, I really thought you were dead. I'm sorry I can't help you, but I do think I know who can." Here we go again with another piece of the puzzle. Everyone else was dead. Who else could possibly help us? Mattie obviously hadn't known my sister was alive.

"Actually there are two people who might be able to help you." He was pissing me off now.

"Would you mind telling us who? I'm getting a migraine," I said to Dr. Shaw as I held my temples.

"I know this is frustrating, but I want to make sure you understand everything. There was a police officer Clark and Dawson used to keep around. He was first on the scene that night...after me of course. This is a long shot, but if someone found you it had to be him or someone who was in on the whole thing and didn't have the heart to kill you. His name is Officer Charles Brandenburg." We all looked at one another.

"Isn't he the man who told you your family was killed in a car accident and your name was Lauren?" Maxwell had obviously been paying close attention to all of the details in my past history. Lauren grabbed her chest.

"Yes, that's him. I will never forget that man. There was something about his eyes. He could look right through you and make you believe anything. Do you know where this officer Brandenburg is?"

Dr. Shaw nodded his head. "I sure do. He lives in a convalescent home in the city. He's been there for a few years. He had a stroke some years back. I'm one of the doctors on staff there and I see him twice a week. I didn't even know he was still alive until I ran up on him doing my rounds after he was admitted.

"Well, does he know who you are?"

"I think he does, but he's never said anything. I really don't want him to say a word about any of this to me. We just make small talk and polite chatter."

"Do you think we can see him? Do you think he will remember our father?"

"Of course. I don't think you ever forget things like that. We can go tomorrow, if you like."

I was still wondering about this other person who would know what had happened. Before I could say anything, Maxwell spoke. "So who is the other person who might be able to help?"

Dr. Shaw bit his bottom lip. "The thing is I don't know if you're ready to see him, if he'll be willing to help you."

I yelled, "Please just tell us who it is!"

"It's Clark."

"Clark? What are you talking about? Clark is dead!"

"Clark is as alive as you two are."

"Ok, we saw his death certificate and read the newspaper article."

"You also saw your own death certificates and read articles about yourself...do you still not understand what he is capable of?"

Clark was still alive. I must say, I wasn't surprised at that point. I didn't think anyone was. We'd heard so much crazy shit that night m I was still confused, not to mention my frustration. I wanted to pull my hair out right then and there. All I heard was maybes, and possibilities of who actually killed my parents. I started to wonder if Dr. Shaw had killed them. That was a possibility too, but I had to conclude Clark had been the one who'd done it. He was the only one alive.

I was tired and my mind was weary. This was all too much to handle in one sitting. I looked at my watch and it was already 9:30pm. We had been there since one o'clock. Technically I had worked an entire day. I needed something strong to ease my mind. I knew that as soon as I put my head on the pillow, I was going to dream about all that garbage. The night needed to end soon. I asked Dr. Shaw to continue with his information.

"Clark was getting in deeper with the whole Johnny Case thing. Since he was suspected of your parent's murder, they were trying to use him a scapegoat. So Clark arranged for a meeting with Johnny and the guy who'd fingered him for the murder in the beginning. While Clark sat in the back seat of a car, he shot Johnny and then shot the other guy through the front seat. Of course they both died and there was no way he could stay here after that. He came to me that night and told me what he'd done. We waited, he needed to hide out for a while. One night, when we thought everything had settled, we went up to Willow Road and pushed Clark's car off the road and down the hill. It rolled down and hit a tree and exploded. I gave him his new driver's license, social security card, credit card and everything he needed to start a new life. His new name is Stewart Benson."

We all said, "Benson and Hawthorne."

"Who is this Hawthorne person?" I asked.

"Your guess is as good as mine. When you guys mentioned it, that was the first I'd heard of anyone named Hawthorne. I guess maybe someone was stupid enough to marry his crazy ass. Or maybe it's his new business partner. With Clark you just never know."

I asked Dr. Shaw, "Do you know how to contact Clark or Stewart or whoever he was going by these days?"

Dr. Shaw snapped "Hell no, the night he left, he was dead to me. I never ever want to see that bastard in my life. All I know is I heard he was out west someplace. Even that was too much information for me." He continued. "When he left I tried to pick up the pieces of my life. I needed God to forgive me and I needed to live my life right from then on. The death of you and your parents...well your parents...did something to my soul. It fucked up my whole family. My kids were sad, my wife was heartbroken and it took us a very long time to get through it. If they only knew half of what I'd done, it would have destroyed my family. You don't know how many times I wanted to slit my own wrist or shoot myself in the head, but I had a family to think about." As he fought back tears, he said, "If you really want to find Stewart I'm sure it won't be hard since you know his new name." He dropped his head in shame. "Look, I owe you guys so much and I'll do anything I can to help you, even if that means laying eyes on Ellis Clark Winfield again."

Emotions overwhelmed me, I walked over and hugged Dr. Shaw. I was confused about why I'd reached out to him at that moment, but it just felt like the right thing to do. "It would so easy for me to hate you, but in a way you saved me. You didn't know that Lauren was alive and you were a victim of this dark twisted world. I have lived my whole life with misery, hate and pain. I am tired and I'm drained. I know what it feels like to want a family."

Lauren came over and hugged him as well. "Yeah, I agree. I just want to hear what Clark has to say. I don't blame you Dr. Shaw. I mean I am a little uncomfortable with some of the choices you made, but it seems like you were caught up in something you just couldn't get out of. There is something about a snake that can take your entire soul and make you do whatever he wants. Clark had everyone under his spell, including my father. I believe he's nothing but pure evil. And of course we can't deny our father's involvement in this. I guess it didn't work out like he'd planned."

I'd really had enough for one night. I was hungry and I needed a bath. Dr. Shaw offered to take us out to eat. I desperately wanted pizza, so we ordered a pizza and ate that while he filled us in on Victoria and Claude Jr. He showed us pictures of them. Victoria was absolutely beautiful and Claude, Jr. was very handsome. Victoria was married without children and Claude, Jr. was still single.

Lauren said, "See, I told you braces are a great investment. Claude, Jr. got those bucked teeth fixed." We immediately asked if we could see them. He said they lived in the city, but he wanted the chance to explain everything to them first. We all agreed that would be best. I would have loved to see them again. I couldn't wait to hear about every inch of their lives. I wanted to know everything. I looked over at Lauren. She seemed distant. I reached over and hugged her and told her I loved her. I told her we would definitely find out what happened to her when we talked to this Brandenburg character. She hugged me back and I could feel the moisture from her tears on my shoulders. As I caressed her hair, I knew she felt lost and needed to find her way.

Chapter Eighteen

After hearing Dr. Shaw's confessions, my vision became clear. I looked over at Maxwell and realized for the first time that he looked almost like Alex. They had similar features; the only major difference was their height. Alex was about six-foot-six, Maxwell was six-foot-two. They both had that smooth chocolate skin and dark curly hair. Alex had the brightest round brown eyes with long beautiful lashes and thick eyebrows. Alex was more physically defined. His body is absolutely perfect, like chiseled stone. Ironically, Maxwell wore his clothes better, but as far as I was concerned, it was Alex who never had to wear another thing in his life. The night we made love it was like he was peeking into my soul. Maxwell and I had not connected that deeply. Even though our physical relationship was great, I still couldn't compare it to that one night I'd had with Alex. The night was the direct result of a lot of time and caring that we'd put into our friendship over the years. Even before Alex walked through the boutique doors earlier that week, I had been thinking more and more about him. I thought about the way I treated him and the way I had treated myself by denying his love. Sometimes I thought of how different my life might have been if we were together.

I was so private and selfconscious about people. I didn't know if I could deal with the attention that came with being the wife of a famous man. Whenever the team came to town, I made sure I attended the games. I wanted to be close to him even if it was in the midst of thousands of people. For some reason I thought he knew or could feel that I was there. When he came out of the locker room, I always see him looking around through the crowd for something or someone. I just wanted to jump up and yell, "Here I am, over here!" But I never did. I just sat there and admired the view. I was so proud of the way he turned out.

Even though he was well known by everyone all over the world, he was still very well grounded. He enjoyed the simple things, the things that really mattered. I remembered one time when we were in Miami and he needed a shirt to wear that night. We searched all over the mall for a black shirt. We went to a high-end store and they were selling a simple black t-shirt without a design just a plain shirt, for a hundred dollars. I told him to get it because I was tired of looking. He commented that no matter how much money you have there are some things you just shouldn't do and paying a hundred dollars for what looks like a t-shirt is one of them. We left the mall and went to the discount store down the street. He purchased a shirt for fifteen bucks and looked great in it. I loved just hanging out with him, the long talks about life or just plain bullshit. I hoped he'd found someone to love and someone who would love him back unconditionally. It was hard meeting people when you were in his position. You don't know if they want you for you or for what you have

Robert felt it was his duty to report any changes in Alex's life. He informed me about the fact that Alex didn't have a steady girlfriend, nor did he have any children thus far, that we knew of. Deep inside, I wondered if there was ever a chance for us to put the past behind us and move on in whatever direction it was meant for us to go. And then I woke up and face reality, loving me is not easy and Alex does not deserve my wrath.

Robert still had hope that we would get together that weekend. He was very disappointed when he found out Maxwell had decided to join us in Georgia. Robert wanted to give us the chance to take care of as much as we could before meeting him in Atlanta. Robert knew about my relationship with Maxwell, even though Maxwell is his brother-in-law and he loves him, he knew where my heart lied, even better than I did. Robert felt that I deserved all the happiness I could get. He said if I loved Alex half as much as he appeared to love me, then I need to stop acting like a fool and get with the program. Robert said he wouldn't dare tell Alex what was going on, but that I definitely should fill him in on my past. Somehow being in the same state with Alex brought a feeling of peace. I wanted so badly to drive straight to Atlanta and tell Alex everything.

My mind was so far gone. I'd actually planted my feet on the same soil that used to be my home. Dr. Shaw had answered more questions in one hour than I could have ever imagined. As I looked at his face I could see the relief in his eyes. He'd wondered for years what had happened to Mattie and me. Who would have thought all of this was happening on that lonely little back road in Dillon, Georgia where the black elite escaped the corruption of the big city? There was one thing

I was sure of, I knew where my dark side had come from and I knew why I never connected with the memory of my father. I knew Uncle Clark had something to do with my parents' murders. I just didn't know to what extent and to be honest I still wasn't sure what really went down.

As I stood on the back porch of Dr. Shaw's home, I didn't reminisce about the old days. I knew once and for all, those days were behind me and there was no use in holding on to the memories anymore. They all seemed like such a big lie. The memory of my mother would still remain alive in my heart, especially now that I knew the real reason she died. I owed it to her to keep her with me always. I was ready to find the last piece of the puzzle, and was ready to move on. There was something inside of me that told me there was much more I had to learn. I had Lauren and Noel and a newfound respect for Mattie. I should have known better than anyone that people had their own demons to fight and that determined the way they live their lives. Mattie had carried so many of my secrets as well as her own. She couldn't afford to let anything compromise our new life. After I talked with Dr. Shaw, I called Mattie to let her know we were all right. When I told her we were at Dr. Shaw's house, there was an unspoken silence between us. For the first time, we both understood each other and were actually one in the same. She was excited to find out we were with Dr. Shaw.

She said, "Oh, praise God." There was a brief silence and then I heard the sounds of her sobbing on the other end. I didn't interrupt her. I knew she was purging herself from decades of silence and secrets. In the midst of her crying, she said to me, "Claude is a good man. You listen to what he has to say. If there is anyone you can trust, it's him."

I understood what she was saying, but the human part of me was still uncomfortable with the information I had learned about his past. Mattie knew me too well.

"Seth, I know you, if it weren't for Claude, you and I might be dead. He had nothing to do with your parent's deaths. He tried to talk your father out of it. You have to understand that Claude's life was not his own. I promise you the devil was alive and here on earth for a while."

I was tired and didn't feel like asking her any questions right then. I knew she was talking about Clark. I figured she would take some time during my absence to deal with the fact that we knew her secret. I didn't even tell her Clark was still alive. I really didn't think she could handle it. On the other hand, I figured she'd always known he was out there somewhere. The devil never dies. I told Mattie we would be there just a little while longer and we would also be going to Atlanta to meet Robert the next day. She immediately asked me about Alex.

"Will you be seeing Alex while you're there?"

"Excuse me, how did you know..."

"Don't worry about how I know anything. You just make sure you know how to get to Lakeland Hills."

Lakeland Hills? This heifer knew where Alex lived? "Now just how do you know where Alex lives?" I asked her.

"You're not the only one who loves Alex. He's a good boy, always has been."

"Mattie, you know I'm seeing Maxwell now."

"I know that. Maxwell seems to be a good person, but he's not and never will be Alex Young." That was so true. He wasn't Alex and he never would be. She could tell I didn't want to discuss Alex, so she switched the subject to Lauren.

"How's Lauren dealing with this?"

I took a deep breath. "She's handling it well. She's not a push over."

Mattie laughed, "If she's anything like you, then she's tough alright." I reassured Mattie we were going to be fine.

Mattie continued, "You take care of yourself and remember what I said about your emotions getting the best of you. I know how you are. You can be a real hell cat when you have to be." Mattie was right I had always been the one to fight and raise hell and she knew I would kill for my sister.

As I thought about my conversation with Mattie, I began laughing to myself. Maxwell came out and brought me a glass of water. The air was warm and there was no cool breeze coming through. Maxwell stood beside me.

"A penny for your thoughts..."

"Just thinking of the old days, of old friends."

"Really? Anyone you want to tell me about? I hope it's not an old boyfriend."

"No, just someone I miss. There are a lot of people I miss."

I moved away from Maxwell and sat in one of the patio chairs. I held the glass of cold water in my hand and took a sip. As I felt the cool water make its way down my throat, I looked out into the yard and started talking.

"You know, before I started finding pieces to this puzzle, I never thought of how other people were dealing with life. For years, I've been the only person living this hell. I never thought about how Mattie was feeling. Ad I never could have imagined in a million years how Dr. Shaw and his family were feeling. I've lived in this glass bubble that was mine and mine alone as if there was no one else in the world living the way I was. I never stopped to see anyone but myself."

Maxwell took my hand. "It's perfectly normal for someone who's been through what you've been through, to go through life removed from everything." I pulled away from him and settled back into my chair.

"I feel even more guilty about my relationship with Mattie. Did I ever truly give her the chance to be what I needed her to be?"

"The truth is, those few years after your parents' murders were the most difficult years of your life and you needed more from her than she gave you...she even admitted it herself. You can't change your past relationship with Mattie, but you can change how you two interact in the future." Maxwell took a seat beside me and scooted to the edge, then he leaned in closer.

"I know you don't want to hear this but, your mother is gone and she will never come back. Mattie lost her son and even if we do find him, he is still lost to her. You and Lauren need a mother and Mattie needs children." At that moment I felt more for Maxwell than I'd ever truly felt, but it wasn't anything near love or even passion for that matter. I don't know what was going on but it seemed like what I felt in Texas was not what I felt there, and before I knew it I was caressing Maxwell's hand. I told him he was a good friend.

"I just want to say thank you Maxwell, You have been a great friend and I really appreciate you."

Maxwell drew his hand away. "Friend?"

"Yes, I mean we are friends...please don't start the name game. We said there weren't going to be any labels right now."

"It's not the word friend, it's the way you said it. You said it as if you were letting me know there isn't more to our relationship."

"Maxwell this is not the time. I can't even go through this with you right now. To be honest all I need you to be is my friend and if you have a problem with that, then I understand if you need to go back to Houston." I held my temples and dropped my head. I started to feel my boiling point., I needed to step back and calm down.

I continued. "Look, you said you were here because you wanted to be here as my friend, that is all I need. I can't handle anything more from you. Forgive me for being selfish, but for the first time everything is becoming so much clearer to me. I can finally put my finger on something concrete."

"I understand that, but what happens when all that comes together and you need more than just a friend?"

"I'll deal with that when the time comes."

I was so pissed and for some reason I just felt like he was truly being insensitive. Had I led him on? I mean I told him from the beginning what I wanted and didn't want. All I know is I couldn't handle someone needing me right now. I felt like I needed to walk away. I got up from my seat, placed the water on the table and left Maxwell sitting there. I walked into the living room, everyone was sitting around talking like old friends. I stood there for a minute trading niceties and nods of agreement, but once I looked at the car keys sitting on the table I knew that I needed to get away, if only for a few minutes. I politely excused myself and asked Isabelle to accompany me outside. Out of concern, Lauren excused herself as well. I told them I needed to go for a drive by myself, just to think. Isabelle understood that I needed time and space. Lauren said she would stay because she wanted to talk more with Dr. Shaw. She was having the time of her life listening to old stories about our childhood. Isabelle said she would see if Dr. Shaw would drive them back to the hotel. Before I walked out the door, Isabelle reminded me that Atlanta was just a forty-five minute drive. Lauren seemed puzzled by this statement.

"Atlanta? I thought we were picking Robert up tomorrow."

Isabelle patted Lauren on the shoulder and told her there would be girl talk later. On my way out the door, I looked up and saw Maxwell standing there. Isabelle pushed me through the door so we could talk.

"He is my brother, but he's not Alex. You deserve all the happiness you can get...just go," she whispered as she made a whisking gesture with her hand.

I hopped in the car and drove straight to the highway. I looked up and read the sign: Atlanta, fifty-nine miles. I paused before I entered the actual ramp leading to the highway, but only for a second. I took a deep breath and drove straight on. I keyed in 1226 Lakeland Trace into the navigation system. Everything was so different about the city. There was nothing there that I could identify with. When I was a child everything was so much bigger than it was now. I guess I'd grown into everything. Time on the highway passed without a single thought of my parents. I was rehearsing what I was going to say to Alex. Before I knew it, I was pulling into Alex's community; of course it was gated. There was a security guard housed in a glass and brick bungalow. He came out and bid me, "good evening" and asked whom I was there to see. I told him I was there to see Alex Young. He told me he needed my name so that he could check the list. He checked the list and said there weren't many names on the list, but mine wasn't one of them. I told him I wouldn't expect it to be. We were old friends who grew up together and I hadn't seen him in a while. He looked at me as if to say, yeah right.

"Listen officer...sir or whatever, I can assure you that I am not or never have been anyone's groupie or stalker. Alex and I grew up together. I was in Dillon, I thought since I'm this close I might as well check on him and see how he's doing. If you want, you can escort me to his house yourself." He looked around.

"I can't leave my post, but there is another officer patrolling the neighborhood. You look harmless but they come in all different forms nowadays. I'll call Mr. Young and see if he would like some company." I leaned over and reached in my purse. I figured it couldn't hurt to try. I pulled out a hundred dollar bill and handed it to him. It wasn't folded. It was new and crisp. He smiled, folded it and put it in his pocket.

"I'm going to let you in. But if you go up there and act a fool, I will tell the police that you forced your way in here, do you understand old friend?" I put my car in drive.

"You can do whatever you have to do, but right now will you open the gate, please?" I drove through the gate and realized I didn't even know if Alex was home. I didn't know if he had company or if he even wanted to see me. I reached his house. It was the last one at the end of the cul-de-sac. I pulled into the circular drive, took a deep breath and got out of the car. My heart was beating so fast, I could hardly catch my breath. What a little deceitful heifer I was. I'd just told Maxwell I was just looking for a friend and there I was looking for Alex. I didn't want to just be his friend, or did I? Hell, I didn't know what I wanted. I checked my breath, popped in a Tic Tac, unraveled my ponytail and rang the doorbell. While I was waiting for Alex I realized I had on a pair of jeans, a t-shirt and a pair of sandals that were killing my feet. I hadn't refreshed up my makeup. I backed away a couple of steps, thinking about returning to the car when I heard someone fumbling with the door. I turned in haste, there was no way out. I thought, please let him have a maid or a professional homeboy or somebody else who answers the door. Whoever it was didn't ask, "Who is it?" or anything. Was he just going to open the door? I tried to calculate the amount of time it would take me to dive off of the porch and get behind the bushes before that handle turned and the door opened. I was on the last step, preparing to lunge forward when I heard the door open. I fell off the step and almost hit my ass on the concrete. I regained my balance and turned slowly so that I wouldn't break my ankle in the shoes from hell. I threw my hair out of my face and stood up straight on the steps. My breasts were lopsided from my acrobatic performance. I grabbed my under wire and popped them back into place and took a deep breath and smiled, showing all thirty-two of my pearly whites.

"Alex. Hi. I was in the neighborhood and I..." He interrupted me.

"Well, I'll be damned!" He was shocked. At first he stood there for a minute and just looked at me without saying a word.

"I know I look bad, but it is summertime in Georgia and this air isn't exactly cool."

"You look just fine to me."

"I hope I'm not interrupting anything."

"No, I was just relaxing."

He flashed those pretty white teeth, those deep dimples followed and I felt a heat wave...and it wasn't from the weather. I swear he'd gotten taller or maybe he was just that smooth, I really didn't know. "Wake up and compose yourself, you did not come here to lose control," I said to myself. I didn't really know what I was there for, but I hoped to hell that I found. I realized I was still standing on the porch, and he had the door wide open.

"Are you going to cool off the entire neighborhood or can I come in?" He shook his head as if he were daydreaming.

"I'm sorry. Come on in." I could feel his eyes glued to me as I passed through the doorway. I ran my fingers through my hair to make sure everything was intact. I jumped as he slammed the door and turned to look at him. He was standing there with his hands stuffed in his pockets, looking at me.

"You look well."

I look well, that was so very polite. "Thanks, you look fine...I mean...well yourself." I looked around and noticed everything was so clean and neat. I knew he had to have hired a decorator because Alex would be content with a sectional and a big screen television, with a refrigerator full of strawberry pop. I felt the warmth from his body as he passed me. I could smell his cologne, which was absolutely mesmerizing. I got lost for a brief moment in the fragrance. I watched him walk that slow sexy walk as he led me through the house. He was bow legged with calves like tree trunks. Alex was simply fine; I mean there was no other way to describe him. He was six-foot-six and two hundred and sixty pounds, all muscle. He had on a pair of jogging pants, a t-shirt and those god-awful flip-flops. Alex caught me admiring his assets as he turned to lead me into the den.

"Can I get you something to drink? I have some strawberry soda." We both laughed at the same time. "But of course you knew that...you know me so well." I dropped my head and blushed. He went into the kitchen; I sat there and looked around the room. There were a few photographs, mostly of him and other athletes or other famous people. I glanced down at the table between the chair that I was sitting in and Alex's recliner. There was a picture of us in Miami. I picked it up and smiled. He caught me holding it when he returned to the room. I tried to put it down, but I dropped it on the table. The look on his face was serious.

"Its ok, go ahead and look at it, I look at it all the time." He handed me a glass.

"So what's up? To what do I owe this unexpected visit? I thought I'd never see your face again in this lifetime."

"Like I said, I was just in the neighborhood."

"Robert told me you and Isabelle were in Dillon on business and he would be meeting you tomorrow. He also told me that his brother-in-law decided to follow. I guess you have a little tag-along crush who's trying to date you."

"What do you mean trying to date?"

"Seth, you don't date, you take people's souls and keep 'em in a little jar beside your bed."

"I think my feelings are hurt."

"Come on Seth, you know better than that. I don't even think you have feelings."

"Well, maybe you're right. I don't have the best track record."

Alex reached down and put his hand on my knee. "So what's up? What's really going on? I mean after all these years... Me leaving my phone number for you anywhere I could...sending messages by Robert...you coming to my games and trying not to be seen..." He let his voice trail off.

"What are you talking about, me coming to your games? I never..."

"Please stop, I'm a single man and in every house that I own there is a picture of you. My boys know that you're not my sister or my cousin. And I talk about you as if you're a legend. So people know what you look like. I just want to know what's up. I am man enough to admit that I can't handle a casual little visit. So before you get comfy and I have to ask you to leave, what's up?"

Damn I felt like Thumbelina! I understood where he was coming from. I did just drop out of nowhere after I went through the trouble of avoiding him all of those years. Not to mention acting a fool the other day.

"I just needed to see you. I've been going through quite a bit lately and I just needed...well, I need you."

He smirked. "Seth, you've never needed me or anyone else. Do you need me for the night or a few hours...What could you possibly need me for other than that?"

Although I deserved Alex's reluctant attitude, I wasn't going to take too many more snide remarks. "You can never begin to understand what I've been going through."

"The good doctor's not what you expected?"

"No, it's deeper than that, Alex."

"Please, you don't worry about shit...I really don't even know if you know how to be deep."

180

That stung right in the center of my chest. Was he still bitter, or was that what he really thought of me? I could see that I had hurt him more than I realized and he was not giving me any slack. At that point, I just wanted to get the hell out of there. I leaped up from my seat and headed for the door. I guess I didn't realize I was starting to cry until I felt tears rolling down my face as I gathered myself to leave.

"You know what? I guess it was a mistake coming here, and I'm sorry for what I did or didn't do to you. I won't bother you again."

Alex grabbed me by the arm. "Look, Seth I'm sorry, I just didn't..."

I snatched my arm back. "Didn't what...know I had feelings?"

"Well."

"Well, I do and I am hurting deeper than you can ever imagine."

"Please, I'm sorry. I guess I'm still a little bitter."

"You guess...a little?"

Alex shot me a serious look. "Ok, sometimes I really can't stand you."

We both laughed but I knew he was serious. Alex took me by the hand and led me back into the room. "Come on, sit down and let me get you some tissue and some water, just don't move."

By this time, I couldn't control my sobbing. Alex came back into the room and said, "Oh, my God what's wrong?" He knelt down in front of me and wiped my tears with his hands. He held my face in both of his hands. They were so massive, I was buried in the midst of his fingers. He kissed my forehead and held me close.

"Seth, you're scaring me. I've never seen you like this before. What's wrong?" I took his hand in mine and looked up to the sky. I needed all the strength I could get, to tell my story one more time. By this time I knew it inside out, and now I had even more details to add.

"Alex, I'm not who you think I am."

He smiled. "Well whoever the hell you are, I hope she's a lot nicer than that bitch I saw earlier this week!"

I got up from my seat, looked around the room and tried to find an object that would help me focus. I located a picture across the room. It was the picture we had taken the day he was drafted. I realized at that moment that he was who I was destined to be with. We'd been there for each other, through thick and thin. I had been running all of my life and I was finally all run out! I'm empty.

"No just listen...before I moved to Texas, I lived in Dillon with my mother, father and my twin sister Nicolette." I didn't look at Alex but I could feel his body relax as I heard him sit back in the chair.

"My parents were killed in what I thought was a robbery. Some men came into the house, killed my mother and father and set fire to our house. Mattie, my sister and I ran to the field in the back of the house to hide, but my sister ran back into the house. Once she reached the house, it exploded." I looked down at Alex and saw that he was stunned. His eyes were wide and his hand was resting on his head.

"Are you serious? Please tell me this is a practical joke."

I knelt down. "Look at me...do I look like I'm kidding?"

He took a deep breath. "No, no not at all."

I continued. "Mattie and I were all that was left of my family. After a few weeks we changed our names, our identities and moved to Texas. My real name is Noel Toussaint. For the past twenty years I thought my sister was dead, but a few weeks ago she showed up at my store. I freaked out, tried to commit suicide, and ended up in a mental hospital for a month. I mean I had a full episode, straitjacket and all. I convinced myself she wasn't my sister. About a week after I came home from the hospital, she showed up on my doorstep and told me that she was my sister. We had a blood test done and everything."

Alex was having a hard time wrapping his mind around the information I was pouring out to him. "What the hell...you tried to do what...commit suicide? Robert didn't even tell me!"

"I know, I asked him not to."

"Damn, I had no idea."

"Well, that's not all."

"You mean...there's more?"

"Oh, yeah..."

I lifted myself up off the floor and sat down beside him. "I found out earlier today that the man I knew as my uncle plotted with my father to kill my mother. It turns out my mother, who had been given up for adoption when she was a child, inherited almost five million dollars from her biological mother after she died. My father got himself into a few bad business deals and he was growing deeper in debt. My mother figured out what was going on and was planning to leave him. My Uncle talked him into killing her for the inheritance. Somehow, things got crossed and my father was killed as well. My uncle, who was raised in a group home along with my father, was Mattie's biological son; the same son her parents told her had died at birth. They turned him over to the state because he was the illegitimate son of a minister. He never forgave Mattie for accepting the story about his death and not trying to find him. He made her swear to never tell anyone who she really was. Upon my parents' death, they left Mattie two-million dollars and various other assets. Clark and my father's personal attorney were in on the whole thing. They altered the will, and Clark ended up with everything else. Mattie never told Clark that I'd survived. She kept me hidden until we left Georgia. Clark is still out there alive somewhere, and I'm trying to find him, so I can figure out exactly what happened to my family."

"I am sorry if I seem insensitive, or confused, or whatever it is I feel right now. I just really don't know what to say. This is so much to accept in one sitting. I mean how do you feel about all of this?" Alex could not bring himself to get past the story I'd just told him. He paced back and forth holding his head. "I'm sorry that's a stupid question. You tried to commit suicide. Oh my God, Seth...I didn't know." Alex's reaction was genuine and I almost felt sorry for him.

"You have a sister...well does she look like you? I mean...what the hell?"

I actually found myself trying to console him. While I was holding his hands, he realized how much I needed him. "I am so sorry...I want you to stay here with me tonight. I don't want anything from you. I just don't want you driving back to Dillon alone tonight. If you really have to leave, I'll drive you." He rubbed his temples.

"This whole thing is so bizarre, but I do believe every word of it. The one thing I don't agree with is you trying to find this Clark person. If he's the way you described him, then I don't want you anywhere near him. We can hire someone to find him."

I was uncomfortable with his use of the word we. What did he mean, we?

"You have way too much to lose to get into this crazy mess," I said.

Alex took me by the hand. "When you walked through my front door and stood over there and told me this, it became "we." Do you think I'm gonna let you walk out of my life again? Hell naw! You go tell Dr. whoever, thanks for everything, but he has got to go, and I mean that."

What was there left for me to say? "Ok, I understand how you feel, but we just can't jump right into anything."

"Girl, please. I've known you since I was nine years old. I remember when you were a pimp and a hustler. I know everything about you. We're not jumping into anything and we're beyond foreplay. We need to get right to it." I couldn't help but laugh. He was right about one thing, I did need to talk to Maxwell.

"I know you're worried about me, but I need to find Clark on my own. Dr. Shaw is going to help me and so is my sister Lauren."

He looked at me with confusion. "Who the hell is Dr. Shaw?"

I guess I'd forgotten to mention Dr. Shaw. "He's an old friend of the family who grew up with my father and Clark. He knows everything."

"Are you sure you can trust this dude?"

"Yes, I'm sure. Plus, I think Dr. Shaw has some old favors that people owe him. I'm not going in completely blind."

Alex held me close to his chest. "I just don't like it, I really don't." He pulled away for a few minutes. "You do know that you're staying here tonight, right?"

"I'll stay, but I didn't bring a change of clothes. All I have is on my back."

"That's okay. We can toss them into the washing machine. You can sleep in my bed, I'll sleep in one of the other rooms."

"Actually, I would prefer to sleep with you, if you don't mind. I mean I just want to..."

"It's ok, I know what you mean. I'll run you some bath water with your favorite ghetto bubble bath."

We both said at the same time "dish detergent!" We laughed as we walked upstairs. I was completely comfortable with Alex. He prepared my bath and put my clothes in the machine. While I bathed he cleaned up and got the DVD player ready for a movie because he knew that I had to fall asleep with the television on. We needed to laugh so he popped in a standup comedy DVD. He set out one of his t-shirts and a pair of his boxers for me and we settled under the covers and acted like an old married couple. We talked a little more about my feelings about everything and my plan for finding Clark. Finally, he kissed me on my neck and told me how much he'd missed me. I told him I'd missed him as well. At that point I hadn't given a thought about Maxwell. He probably knew where I was and what I was doing.

I drifted off to sleep and slept through the night without my night-mares or thoughts of the past to haunt me.

As I woke up the next morning to the frigid temperature from the air conditioning, I felt Alex's warm embrace as he kissed me good morning and we began to appreciate the creation that is "us." I felt the nectar from his warm kiss as he caressed my neck with his juicy lips. He moved slowly to my breasts as my nipples waited erect in anticipa-tion of his gentle suckle. I could feel my clit pulsating with excitement as he sucked my breasts. I felt the strength of his hands as they ca-ressed my body and I quivered with expectation. My stomach trem-bled as he outlined my navel with his tongue. I was helpless as the warmth of his breath tickled the doorway, entering my southern comfort. My spine relaxed, and my body melted as the moisture from his tongue lubricated my inner walls and allowed my sweet juices to flow. My knees shook as I melted from the inside out, while Alex manipulated my warm creamy center. I could feel my mind go weak and body lose all control. Just as I felt I couldn't endure another magnificent second of his oral tantalizing, he retreated from my southern comfort, spread my legs and entered me with his ample manhood. My inner walls wrapped around him making my sweet soul wetter and warmer. I felt him in the depths of my walls as he gave me every single inch of him. I wrapped my legs tightly around his body and we embraced exploding into unbridled ecstasy. As I felt my eyes widen and my nails grip his flesh, the warm moisture escaped my body and he simply whispered in my ear, "Good morning," and we both fell back into a deep sleep.

Chapter Nineteen

When I woke up for the second time, I turned to glance over at Alex and he wasn't there. I figured he was either downstairs or maybe he'd run out for a minute. I sat on the edge of the bed and realized that the room needed a woman's touch. More specifically, it needed me. As I was gazing around the room, I noticed my jeans, t-shirt, and unmentionables were neatly folded at the foot of the bed. It made me smile. Inside the bathroom, I found towels and a toothbrush waiting for me as well. After I'd brushed my teeth and washed my face, I turned the shower on. I couldn't wait to get into the shower. I quickly removed the t-shirt and boxers. The warm spray massaged my body and I savored every drop on my skin. The water soothed me as it ran through my hair making it feel heavy as it covered my head and my neck.

I closed my eyes and I saw my mother. The water seemed warmer and more inviting. She told me everything was going to be just fine and that I would find my way. She said I could trust Dr. Shaw and that I needed to find Clark. She also told me not to worry, I would be protected. When I found Clark, all of my questions would be answered. I would be free to live my life. She told me that Clark was my light, but he was not my salvation and he would lead me to the person who would clear my path. She reminded me that Satan was once an angel and that he is a master of disguise. Sometimes we fear those who breathe the most fire, but we welcome those who seem as gentle as a lamb. She warned me to beware of the wolf in sheep's clothing and to take care of Nicolette. She did not call her Lauren. My mind began to race and I became more confused.

Just as I was about to ask what she was talking about, I felt water hit me from the back and from each side. I felt like I was in a car wash. Alex was behind me and had turned the side showers spigots on. I could feel water coming all around me. I stood there laughing because it scared the hell out of me. My mother was gone and I had no idea what her message meant. I made a mental note to discuss it with Isabelle later. At that moment, it was Alex who had my full attention.

He stepped into the shower with me. He'd been out running and needed a shower pretty badly. I stood in front of him and watched the beads of water drip from his magnificent body and outlined his tight abs and firm backside. I reached down for his manhood. As he pinned me up against the shower wall. Then he grabbed both of my legs and held them up while he entered me, holding me close as his passionate thrusts made me tremble with excitement. The water created an even more intense eroticism that could only be described as mindblowing. As our tongues touched Alex pushed deeper and deeper inside of me. He was moaning and muttering.

"Damn, Damn...Got Damn." His verbal burst of excitement made me tremble even more. I felt a warm sensation sweep through my body as I exploded. Alex's thrusts became more vigorous as he shouted, "Damn Girl..." Then he rested his breathless body against mine. As he released my legs and I planted my feet firmly on the ground, he stumbled out of the shower and onto the chair in the opposite corner of the bathroom.

As I watched him sitting there, panting with satisfaction, all I could say was, "Damn!" I stepped out of the shower and walked toward him.

"So when are you gonna let the good doctor go?" He looked me straight in the eye as he waited for my answer. I explained to Alex that I had to let Maxwell down easily. I couldn't just spring a breakup on him.

He raised his eyebrows and stood up, walking toward me. He held my shoulders, keeping eye contact with me as he spoke. "Look, I know you're trying to be nice, but I'm not. Now when you get back to Dillon, you pull him to the side, and tell him. And that's about as understanding as I'm gonna be." He wasn't compromising about this at all.

"Ok, but he has been there for me and I do respect him. I do consider him a friend."

Alex dropped his head and then picked it up to look at me. "You picked a fine time to grow feelings, but I do understand. I just don't want anything to mess this up. I respect your decision. I need to get ready for my party anyway. You are coming, right?"

I pulled my lips together and raised my shoulders. "Well, no...let me explain. Robert and Isabelle are going, but I need to spend some time with my sister. We planned to go to dinner and then hang out."

Alex smiled and kissed my forehead. "Why don't you bring her with you? I can introduce her to some of my boys." My heart wouldn't let me say, "no" to him.

"Ok, Alex. I'll bring her along," I said without skipping a beat.

I looked at the clock. It was getting late and I needed to get back to Dillon to change so we could stop by the nursing home and then head back to Atlanta. I got dressed and kissed Alex goodbye. I told him I would call him later. I didn't want to tell him that I was going to see Brandenburg. He gave me a key so I could get back into the house if he wasn't home.

I dreaded seeing Maxwell...I mean, what could I possibly say to him? I didn't feel guilty about Alex, but I felt an obligation to Maxwell because he'd been there when I needed him. It was my fault anyway. I shouldn't have mixed business with pleasure. He would also have to bear some of the blame. What kind of psychiatrist would get involved with a patient? He should have known that I needed temporary emotional support. At any rate, no matter whose fault it was, it was coming to an end.

When I arrived at the hotel, I prepared myself to face Maxwell. I unlocked the door and stepped into the room. I could hear the sound of the shower and thought, "Good, I can buy a few extra minutes before our conversation." I went through my suitcase to find something fresh to wear. As I was searching for shoes and my shirt, I heard the water stop. Shortly thereafter, I heard the door open. Maxwell walked out half-wrapped in a towel. It was official, I had no feelings for him beyond friendship. It was like a light switch, I turned him on and then off again. I admit that he was gorgeous standing there in that towel. After all, I am a woman, and I do recognize an attractive man. We were both waiting for the other to speak.

"Hi." I spoke first.

"Hello." One-word responses were always unpleasant. He sat on the bed and proceeded to put lotion on his body. "How was your evening?"

I pulled myself up, sat on the dresser, and let my knees dangle. "It was pleasant."

"Really? Did you see Alex?" Bam! There it was. I could finally exhale.

"Yes I did."

"So how was your visit?" This was taking too long.

"My visit was okay. It was something that I should have done a long time ago."

Maxwell laughed to himself. "So where does this leave us, or should I even ask?"

I looked down at my feet and watched them dangle for a moment before I looked back up at him. "Do you just want to hear me say it?"

"Yes I do."

"To be honest, I have loved Alex forever, and I've been afraid of him forever. When I met you, I needed so much and there you were, offering me everything I thought I needed."

"So I was your bandage until your wounds healed."

"If that's how you wish to describe it...but you were more than that. You showed me that I could actually care for someone, that I really do have feelings. I couldn't have made it through these last few weeks without you. I still want us to be friends."

"Friends? That's like poison to a man's ears. I have too many damn friends already. Look I'm not going to pretend that I'm not upset, because I'm pissed. It's partly my own fault. I've known about Alex. I knew he existed. I was just hoping that you would never see him again."

"To be honest, I did everything I could to make sure I wouldn't see him, but I guess my heart overruled my head."

"Right now you have so many different emotions running through you. You're not thinking clearly. You need some time to sort things out; I'm going back to Texas today. When you pick up Robert, I'm going to hop on a flight outta here. Take some time to decide who you really want and I'll be waiting." Maxwell walked over and kissed my forehead.

"Sometimes what we think we want isn't what we really need. Remember, I have the professional training and the bedside manner to help you through this." He caressed my cheek and winked at me as he turned to finish dressing. I couldn't believe it! He was in some sort of denial. I needed to make sure he understood what I meant.

"Maxwell, I don't think you understand what I'm trying to tell you..."

"No, I understand. I just don't think you do. Alex has been your security blanket. You and he were really close. You're going through something. It's only natural to go back to someone who gives you a little stability...you know, like an old faithful."

"No Maxwell, I love Alex. I always have. I want to try and make it work with him."

"Seth, you told me yourself that you have never really let yourself experience love between a man and a woman. It's easy to confuse lust or infatuation with love. The thing is you know Alex loves you, and you are afraid to trust me."

"That sounds so wonderfully philosophical, but you're off the clock and I don't need the psychobabble right now. To be honest, you helped me to realize once and for all, that I am in love with Alex."

"Ok, Seth. Whatever. If you want to continue to be in denial, that's fine. When you come to your senses, and you will, I'll be here." He continued to dress while packing his suitcase.

I was trying to be nice, but I needed to lay it on the line. "Maxwell, do you remember what Alex Young looks like?"

He laughed as if I were asking a stupid question. "Yeah Seth, the whole damn world knows what he looks like. What does that have to do with anything?"

He was still moving around the room, and then he stopped suddenly and placed a single pair of socks in his luggage. He looked up slowly and turned toward the mirror. "Some people have told me that I remind them of Alex." He finally got it. I sat down on the bed.

"Look Maxwell, when I first saw you, you reminded me of someone. I didn't really know who. That day I had the episode in my group session, I noticed something about you, something that was so warm and familiar. Then, that day in your office, when there was the confusion about my changed appointment, your concern made me feel as though I was falling for you. The truth is Alex has never been far from my heart. Not a day goes by that I don't think about him and wonder what if...I'm so sorry Maxwell. I do love you, but every fiber of me is in love with Alex, it's not something that's gonna go away."

I took a deep breath and tried to swallow the lump in my throat as I thought about Alex. I stared across the room and into the mirror as I reminisced about him. "When Alex and I were in college, he had an apartment off of Main and Murworth. You know that Houston is known for its horrible flash floods, well one day the streets were flooded and we couldn't get our cars down his street so, we parked them at a store further down the street and proceeded to walk toward the apartment through the flood water. The further we walked, the more scared I became, because the water was just too high. Alex picked me up and carried me on his back for four blocks. I remember hearing the sound of his legs drudging through the water. His breathing was labored and he was exhausted, but he never complained, he just told me to hold on tighter. For the first time in my life, I let go. I let go of the entire weight that I'd been carrying around for years. I let go of the hurt and pain that filled my soul. I held on to him as tight as I could. It was then that I realized Alex Young was no ordinary man. He made me feel so safe. I felt like he could do just about anything. That day I realized he was the one for me. I was so messed up and broken. I never even realized I couldn't allow myself to tell him how I felt. Yes, Alex has always been safe and familiar, but he's always been the one. Now that I have one more chance to be with him, I have to take it."

Maxwell sat down beside me and took my hand. "Since the first day I saw you at the boutique, I was so overwhelmed by you. There was something about you that I just couldn't shake. I wanted to be with you so badly, but I was scared to say anything to you. Then when you came to the hospital, I guess I used my position to get close to you. I was hoping that somewhere along the way you would fall in love with me."

He let go of my hand and walked toward the window and looked back at me, with a pitiful smirk on his face. "I've known about your history with Alex. I remember hearing Robert and Isabelle talk about how you two were meant for each other. Robert would talk about how much Alex was still in love with you and about the pictures he had all over his house. Isabelle would say that you never really mentioned him, so that gave me some hope. Then the day he came to the store, I saw the way you looked at each other. When you took off and ran out the door, I knew I had my work cut out for me. I didn't say anything because deep down I thought that would be the last we would see of Alex. Right before we left for Georgia, I heard Robert remind Isabelle that Alex was in Atlanta. They talked about how you might be with me physically, but Alex would always have your heart. When you left last night I knew where you were going, but I was just hoping you would come back this morning and tell me you realized you were in love with me.

I stood up and gathered my things; I thought it was best if I dressed in Lauren's room. "I never meant to hurt you and it may seem a little selfish, but I want to be happy with the person who loves me and the one that I truly love. That has been my wish and my prayer for as long as I can remember. I have my sister back, I have a niece, I'm finding out the truth about my past, I'm learning to trust other people and I have found my one true love. I need this to survive, but I also need your friendship. I know it's gonna take some time for you to be comfortable with me again, but I wish you'd try." Maxwell didn't respond, he continued to get dressed. I knew it was going to take time. I knew we couldn't just drop things like we did and simply leave them. There were going to be some awkward meetings, awkward dinners and awkward hellos. I was truly hurting over the way I'd treated Maxwell. It wasn't like a breakup between a boyfriend and a girlfriend. It was more like a friendship that would never be the same. I guess in a way I felt obligated to Maxwell for bringing me to this point.

I left the room while we were still able to be civil to each other. That was the key, to leave while you could still be civil. I walked down the hallway with the squeaky wheels of my suitcase trailing behind me. Lauren's room was two doors down from mine. When I reached her room, I knocked on the door. She answered with a big smile.

"Have you been evicted?"

I smiled back. "No, it was more like a voluntary evacuation." I entered her room and placed my things on the bed. "I need to get dressed here if you don't mind, it's less complicated."

Lauren was already fully dressed. I could she was anxious to get to the city to see what this man had to say. She was smoking a cigarette. I didn't even know they still had rooms for smokers.

"I didn't know you smoked, well I guess not until last night."

"I have been trying to quit, Noel hates it. Right now, I need it."

"I understand that. Hell, after last night I wanted to light up myself." Lauren's mood was really beginning to concern me. She had a sullen look on her face. It wasn't like before. This was different. She mustered up a smile as she asked about my night.

"So tell me, where did you bolt off to last night? Who is Alex?"

"Alex." I said his name and a huge smile took over my face. "Alex is the only man I have ever truly loved, and it has taken me years to realize that."

"Where did you meet him?"

"I met him when Mattie and I moved to Texas. He lived next door to us. We were in the same elementary, junior high and high school, as well. He was my best friend, and didn't even know who I really was. Man, it's hard to describe our friendship. I mean we were best friends, but there was something else between us. At one point, I was doing pretty badly. I had been doing stuff that I couldn't explain. It was like there was some dark force guiding me to do crazy shit. Alex was the one who helped me through the really rough times."

"So through all this unspoken chemistry, you guys never hooked up?"

"That's just it, one night on one of our many vacations together, we slept together. Actually, we did more than that. It was almost spiritual, if I can use that word to describe it."

"That sounds like a good thing."

I continued the conversation as I was dressing. "Well, for someone normal, it would be a good thing, but I've been running from anything that was good all my life. I couldn't handle my feelings for Alex. I knew, as my feelings got deeper, someday I would have to tell him about my past. I never thought I would be where I am now, back here in Dillon. I sure as hell didn't seriously think I would be standing here talking to you." Lauren put her cigarette out in the ashtray.

She ran her fingers through her hair. "Noel saved my life."

I took a seat across from her. "What do you mean?"

After she cleared some ashes that had fallen on the table, she sat down tapping her fingers on the table. "When I became pregnant with Noel, I finally had something that belonged to me. I'd lost everything that I loved the night our parents died. I was so lost. I couldn't even imagine that you were alive. You had hope, but I didn't have anything. I couldn't even love my adoptive parents. I thought I loved Noel's father, but he wouldn't love me back. What did I expect? He was a damn pimp. Noel was my chance to start over. The day I found out I was pregnant with a girl, I knew I was going to name her after you. I have tried to make that child a miniature you. I've tried to make her favorite color orange, her favorite food pizza. I even call her Sugar.

Daddy used to call you "Sugar" and me "Peaches." Together we made a damn peach cobbler. She became my whole life and I started to live again. All these years, I have felt so much overwhelming guilt because I lived and no one else had. Then, I found you and became jealous because you had been raised by someone you knew. Now, I've found out that all these years you and Mattie were like strangers." Tears began to roll down her face and formed into a small puddle on the table. I felt paralyzed. I couldn't move.

She stared across the room, fixated on nothing in particular, and her voice cracked as she continued. She grabbed her cigarette pack and pulled out another one. She let it hang from the corner of her mouth as she lit it, then took a deep drag and placed it in the ashtray. "Last night when Dr. Shaw was telling us what really happened that night. I started to feel so relieved and a weight was lifted off of me, but right here in a little pocket in my heart I'm still empty. You know how you were saved. You know how you began your new life. I still don't know what son-of-a-bitch decided my fate. I couldn't sleep last night in anticipation of seeing that police officer again today. I can just see myself putting my hands around his old neck and chocking him until he stops breathing." Lauren was clutching her chest as if she was actually choking the man.

I reached across the table for her hand. "Lauren, come back, come on back honey."

She shook her head as if she were trying to come back to herself. "I'm sorry. I am just filled with so much resentment and hatred."

"I know honey, I know. I don't know whom to hate anymore. I mean, really, even though Daddy supposedly changed his mind about killing Mama, for money no less, he still had the thought in his head. To have even thought about killing her, or let someone persuade him to murder someone he loved, is some real sick shit."

"I was thinking the same thing. What if he told Dr. Shaw that he changed his mind just to redeem himself. But then I think of how the night he died there was so much pain in his eyes when he told us he didn't mean do to it. Maybe he was remorseful."

"Maybe that pain was just from the bullet and it made it seem that he was sincere."

"Maybe ... It's still all pretty bizarre to me."

"I know you're gonna think I'm crazy, but this morning when I was in the shower, Mommy came to me. She said to beware of a wolf in sheep's clothing. She said something about the devil being an angel once. It was really creepy. I wish I knew what it meant."

"Do you think she meant Dr. Shaw?"

"Oh, no she was clear about being able to trust him." The subject switched tones for a minute.

"You know, when I was in that children's home, and later on when I lived with my adoptive parents, I would cry myself to sleep. It was like I could feel Mommy's arms around me. Sometimes, I could hear her singing me to sleep. I dreamed about her and she would always say she couldn't find her way."

It was like a brick hitting me in the chest, I had that same dream almost every night. I didn't say anything to Lauren because I wanted that to be her memory, her connection to our mother. I could tell things were getting to be too much for Lauren because she was still crying. I looked at my watch and commented about the time flying. Just then, there was a knock at the door.

"Hey ladies, is everyone ready to go? I see Miss MIA made it back safe and sound." Isabelle walked through the door looking fresh and well rested.

"I told you I was on my way back."

"Girl, you're better than me, because I would have stayed there."

"I know that's right," Lauren added her two cents. "What does this Alex look like anyway?"

Isabelle spoke to us from the bathroom. "You mean you don't know Alex Young?"

Lauren looked puzzled. "No, should I?"

Isabelle poked her head out of the door while, as she called it, "adjusting her girls" in the mirror. "He's Alex Young, the professional basketball player. You know—the NBA."

"Well, that explains it. I don't know a thing about sports. What does he look like?"

"You've seen my brother, right?"

"Of course, I know Maxwell, unless there's another one."

"No, he's the only brother I have. Well, Maxwell looks just like Alex and I put them in the correct order, because Alex did come first.

Anyway, the only difference is Alex is like seven-foot-two or something like that."

I began to put on my shoes. "Isabelle stop exaggerating, Alex is only six-six."

Lauren laughed. "That's close enough for me."

Isabelle finished putting the final touches on her makeup. "Well did you break up with my brother gently?"

I went to the bathroom door where Isabelle was, Lauren was in there as well putting on her mascara, and said, "I tried my best."

Isabelle ran a comb through her hair. "Well, it's gonna take some time. We got to get a move on because I have a husband, and he will be arriving soon, so grab your stuff and come on."

I walked toward the window and pulled the curtain back. I watched as Maxwell was getting into a cab. I looked over at Isabelle with questioning eyes. "Maxwell is getting into a cab. What's that about?"

"Yeah, he decided it was best to take a cab to the airport instead of riding with us."

I knew what she meant. " You mean instead of riding with me."

"Well can you blame him? Come on now be real. I wouldn't ride with you either. His pride is hurt."

"I guess you're right." As I closed the curtain, he looked up at the widow and our eyes locked for a moment. I could only imagine what was going through his head. I closed the curtain, grabbed my purse and motioned for us to leave. I put Maxwell out of my mind and prepared for the day. I was sure I'd need an open mind for what I was about to hear.

Chapter Twenty

We pulled up to the nursing home and watched as Dr. Shaw parked in the space marked "PHYSICIANS ONLY." From the outside, the grounds seemed well-kept. We all stepped out of the air-conditioned vehicle into the hot Georgia sun. I was glad I had let my hair air dry, I could feel my roots curling from the sweat. I was dreading my brilliant idea to wear denim Capri's. They were sticking to my skin and the huge cuff at the bottom was hitting my calves and annoying the hell out of me.

I looked over at Lauren; she had a big smile on her face. "I told you to wear your linen pants."

"Oh shut up."

Isabelle reached in her purse and sprayed me with misting spray. I instantly felt cooler. Isabelle was always prepared. She had a purse full of wet wipes, alcohol pads, bandages, aspirin, everything. She really needed to be someone's mother. We walked into the front door and entered through the set of security doors. We were all smiles as we greeted Dr. Shaw. He seemed to be a local celebrity among the staff and the patients. He introduced us as his nieces from out of town. He told the nursing staff he would be there long enough to check on a few patients and we wanted to meet some of the ones he always talks about. He asked how Mr. Brandenburg was doing today and if he was up for visitors. From the nurse's response, it didn't seem that he had many visitors, if any at all. She told us he would be thrilled to have some company. Dr. Shaw introduced us to a few more staff members and patients. When we reached the office that he shared with another physician he closed the door behind us and gave us some instructions.

"Now, I'm going to see a few patients just to make everything look legitimate, but first I'm going to get you settled in with Brandenburg. I'll stay for a few minutes then I'll leave, so you can be alone with him. Remember he's had a stroke and may not remember much, if anything at all. As I told you before, he has never acknowledged that he knows who I am. He may not want to talk to you at all. Tell him exactly who you are before you start asking questions. You don't want to scare him off. "

Lauren said, "I have to admit, I'm afraid of what I might find out. At this rate anything is possible."

Dr. Shaw sat down in the chair across from us. "I know you're both scared, but the only thing we can do is try. I want to get rid of this burden as much as you girls. We're all in this together and no matter what we find out or don't find out today, we can't stop now. The good thing is that we know where Clark is or at least we think we know. If Brandenburg can't help then we go straight to the source, I guarantee Clark knows everything."

Isabelle said, "Yeah, even though we're gonna find Clark, any information that Brandenburg can give will help us prepare for Clark and whoever else we might have to face." We all gathered ourselves in preparation to meet Brandenburg. Isabelle suggested we pray. We held hands and bowed our heads and prayed that God would grant Charlie Brandenburg the wisdom, the knowledge and, most of all, the heart, to tell us what we needed to know.

We entered Brandenburg's room. It was dark and smelled of antiseptic. I assumed the custodian had just left the room. Dr. Shaw commented earlier on how clean they tried to keep things around there. The curtains were closed, so just a hint of light was shining through the room. Brandenburg was lying in his bed with his back turned to the door. The television was on, but the volume was turned down low. We stood by the door as Dr. Shaw turned on the light and went further into the room. Dr. Shaw motioned for us to come in. Isabelle and I stood beside the bed and Lauren stood closer to the foot of the bed waiting for Brandenburg to wake up.

Dr. Shaw announced his presence. "Mr. Brandenburg, how are you today? It's Dr. Shaw. I brought a few visitors for you today." Brandenburg didn't move. He was stiff and I was wondering if he was dead. I thought, please don't let this man be dead, not for my sake, but for my sister's. Please let him be alive. Dr. Shaw called out his name once more. "Mr. Brandenburg...Charlie."

Isabelle grabbed my arm. "Do you think he's dead?" Just then he started wrestling with the covers.

"No, I'm not dead, I just do things on my own time." He was a cantankerous old man. For a man who never really spoke, he made a horrible first impression. I could tell by his tone that his mind was fine. The question was...would he cooperate? He finally freed himself from the blankets and sheets and turned to face us as he sat up. He reached over to the nightstand to retrieve his glasses. I tried not to stare as he sat up. He was familiar to me. I remember the day Lauren was sick and had to stay home from school. I went alone with daddy to get ice cream. Mr. Brandenburg was the man who showed up at the Dairy Freeze. I remembered him because he gave me a five-dollar bill to go and get him a chocolate cone. He told me to keep the change. Even as a child I remembered thinking most grownups gave kids loose change or a dollar, but he gave me a whole five. He commented on how pretty I was and how much I looked like my mother. He patted me on my head and pinched my cheeks. I didn't feel too comfortable with him then, and I didn't feel comfortable with him now. I don't think Daddy liked him either, because he told him we needed to get back home, as he reached into his suit jacket pocket and pulled out a thick envelope and handed it to the man. Brandenburg opened it. Daddy stopped him and told him to count it later. Thinking back there must have been money in that envelope. I looked over at Lauren as she was easing her way down by the rest of us. I stood there survey-ing my surroundings. I noticed his name posted on the wall above his head, Charles Jonathan Brandenburg. Just then I remembered Mattie saying that if anything ever happened to her to contact Officer Charles Jonathan.

Unconsciously, I said aloud, "Officer Charles Jonathan."

As he was adjusting his hands and his sheets, he looked over at me. "Jonathan, Brandenburg, Charles, Chuck or Charlie which ever you prefer we're all the same."

It seemed as though we were dealing with multiple personali-ties here. I wondered who we were going to meet that day. They could be different things to different people, but I bet they all knew the same secrets. Dr. Shaw walked over to close the door, while Brandenburg politely invited us to sit down. We looked at each other as if we were facing sudden death. No one moved too quickly and we kept our eyes on him at all times. He was very calm and soft-spoken. He reached in his drawer and offered us some peppermints. I took a deep breath before declining his offer. He unraveled the paper from a piece of the candy and popped it into his mouth.

He began with idle chitchat, "You know I never thought I would be an old man in a nursing home sucking on hard candy." He said as Dr. Shaw checked his pulse.

"Mr. Brandenburg you are unusually alert today how do you feel?"

To everyone's surprise, Brandenburg pulled his hand away from Dr. Shaw. "I am just fine. I've always been fine Claude. Why don't you call me Charlie like you used to?" The smirk on Dr. Shaw's face meant that old Charlie wasn't as sick as he thought he was.

Brandenburg felt Dr. Shaw's shock.   "You thought I was dead to the world and didn't know who you were. That's good, it was my intention. As long as you didn't say anything, I didn't have to say anything. I knew this day would come though. Hell, I've laid my ass up here in this bed, playing possum long enough. With the life I've led, I needed some rest." Dr. Shaw walked over to the side of the room that we were on and took a seat near Brandenburg and crossed his legs. He was intrigued and decided to stay for a while and listen to another chapter of this mystery.

"I've been waiting for someone to come into this room and smother me with a pillow or give me an overdose of something that would take me on out. I knew it wouldn't be you. Claude you've always been too level headed, for that. No blood on his hands, he just wiped up our messes, and what a mess I've made." He seemed to be venting. I didn't know whether to allow him continue to talk, or start asking questions.

"Look Mr. Brandenburg..." I decided to speak first.

"Call me Charlie."

"Ok, Charlie, you probably don't know who we are. Judging by your interesting dialogue you know that we are here because of something you've done in your past."

"My darlin', I know exactly who you are. You are Nolan and Anna Marie Toussaint's daughters, both of you are. I don't know who the other young lady is." He pointed to Lauren and me, but he used our old names.

I introduced Isabelle, "This is my best friend Isabelle, and she came along for moral support."

Charlie smiled, "Ah, yes support...that's a good thing to have. Some people don't have the love of good friends or family." Just then he struck a nerve, this man seemed a little twisted. It was like he was much too calm; he seemed high on something.

I said, "Listen, Charlie we have a few questions to ask you about our parents' death."

He was acting as if he hadn't heard me or maybe he was simply and blatantly ignoring me. He looked over at Lauren. "Little Lauren... my, how you've grown. You know I gave you that name. It was a beautiful name. You were such a beautiful little girl. When I found you that night, I was so glad that the fire didn't damage your face."

Lauren wrung her hands together as she sat as still as a statue. "You found me? Were you the one who pulled me out of the fire that night?"

"Oh, yes I pulled up just as the other guys were pullin' away. I was hopin' to get there in time to stop the whole thing, but I was too late. I remember hoping that no one was home and they'd just set the house on fire. I sat there on the road and watched the flames, hoping that it was just an empty house. I just happened to look toward the left side of the house, close to the fence and I saw what looked like an animal crawlin' on all fours. Whatever it was, it was movin' and it was on fire. I ran to check it out and I noticed it was a child...it was you. I rolled you around in that grass and I burned my own clothes trying to put you out. That's how I got these burns on my legs. I'm sure the good doctor here thought I got them from setting the fire."

Charlie pulled back the cover and showed us his legs. His skin was shriveled and twisted in certain spots. He pulled the cover farther back to leave his legs exposed. His voice was still calm and creepy.

Dr. Shaw said, "I assumed you were involved, and killing Anna and Nolan wouldn't be too far off."

Charlie smiled. "Claude, I could never hurt Anna's family. I knew when I saw little Nicolette that everyone else was in the house and that they had been killed by the fire." He looked back at Lauren. "I grabbed you up and took you home. My wife was a nurse and she took care of the burns. They weren't too bad and my wife knew just what to do. There was a doctor that Johnny Case used when some of the boys came down with stuff that couldn't be reported in an emergency room, if my wife couldn't handle your injuries I was going to take you to that doctor. I knew we couldn't keep you in Dillon very long. So, one night when a couple was killed in a car accident, I took Lauren to the children's home and said you were found at the scene of the accident. I was the law, who was gonna question me? In those days, it was easy to disappear. It also helped that the couple was from out of state and had no family in the area. Hell, I don't even know if they had any children of their own. Of course I knew everyone, so it was easy to fix the intake records."

I turned to my sister to ask about her burns. She was still sitting very still. "Lauren, do you have any burn scars?" I hadn't noticed any on her body before. Since Brandenburg's burns were so gruesome and defined, I figured she must have had some as well.

Lauren was so enmeshed in her own little world, she didn't hear my question. Instead she looked at Brandenburg. "I don't understand. Why did you save me when you knew I might remember everything?"

"I wasn't worried. I knew you were too traumatized by the whole thing and you were in a mental hospital for children. Who would believe you? I have to admit you're doing much better than I thought you would. I kept up with you for a while, and to my understanding, you were pretty bad off. I didn't think you'd ever function like a normal child again."

I sat there trying to figure out what he meant. He said Lauren had been pretty bad off. I wanted to ask, but the visit was for Lauren and she needed to ask her own questions. I also remembered that she said she hadn't spoken for two years after the fire, so maybe that's what he was referring to. Whatever he meant, it made me uneasy for some reason. I was also becoming preoccupied with the absence of burn scars from her body. As I was sitting there, I thought back to when Mattie gave me his name as a contact.

"Mattie told me once, that if something ever happened to her, I should contact you. It sounds to me like you knew Mattie. So why didn't you just give Lauren to Mattie? You had to have known I was alive."

"That's just it. I stayed away from Mattie until she called me and told me she was afraid of Clark and she needed to leave town. She told me to stop by the house late one night. She took me into the bedroom and showed me that you were still alive, Noel. I couldn't believe i! There you were safe and sound. I couldn't tell her that Nicolette was alive because I knew she would have wanted to take her too. That was too much to explain. I had already hidden her in the home. I couldn't very well just up and move her to an unknown location. She was already listed as a ward of the state. It was too risky. If Clark had known that you girls were alive, he would have panicked, and there's no telling what he might have done. I needed to get you and Mattie out of there quickly. I would figure out a way to get Nicolette to you and Mattie later. I started working on getting you and Mattie out of town. Then, I heard Mattie had a heart attack. I couldn't very well ask about you. I hoped you were smart enough to run away on your own. I never knew what happened to you, but I prayed that you were ok. How did you get away and survive on your own?"

Dr. Shaw raised his hand and said, "I can answer that question. I didn't know that Mattie had spoken to you, so I to arranged for them to leave town. I didn't know anything about Lauren, or Nicolette, at the time."

At that point, I really didn't know how to feel. Mr. Brandenburg was the one person who knew that both my sister and I were alive and he didn't try to keep us together. I didn't understand what the big deal was in removing Lauren from the hospital he'd placed her in and taking her to Mattie before her alleged heart attack. The major question that was on my mind was, if he was such a notorious bad guy, why was helping my family so important to him? Where did he fit into all of the madness? He kept commenting on how pretty my mother was and calling her by her name like they were so familiar. Did he have a thing for my Mama? Was he one of those old southern white men who had a secret desire to be with a black woman? There was something twisted about what he was saying, even apart from the obvious. He, like everyone else in this God-awful saga, had more to tell than I think I wanted to hear.

Isabelle was wondering the same thing. She hunched her shoulders.

"Why would a man like you want to help anyone?"

Lauren looked over at her and said, "You took the words right out of my mouth." Then she turned back to Mr. Brandenburg. "What was so special about my family that created such a warm place in your big ole heart? If you knew who Dr. Shaw was all this time and you've been waiting for him to come in here and kill you, why didn't you say something to him?"

Brandenburg twisted around in the bed. "I guess I felt that as long as he never said anything, maybe my life was just a dream. The truth is I haven't always been a bad person. I got hooked up with Johnny Case, Clark and Nolan and I changed. It was like they had some sort of an ungodly hold on me. They never really trusted Claude. They knew he had a heart and a conscious. I never really knew exactly how much you knew about any of this (he looked over at Dr. Shaw), so I didn't volunteer any unnecessary information. No offense Claude, but you were weak. And just like I was, you were caught up in some shit that you had no business in. I ran away from a family of no good, lying, murdering bigots that wouldn't spit on a black man to save him from burning. My wife, Grace, was black. We never had any children because we didn't want them to grow up afraid and cast out by society. We wrestled with the thought of keeping Nicolette and leaving town, but I was too afraid Clark would find us."

I still wasn't convinced of his humanitarian efforts. So what, he married a black woman. Is that why he wanted to save us good Negro children? Was he one of those Negro loving white folks that loved us as long as we were cooking and cleaning for him? The trouble with that was why did he have a fascination with my mother? She wasn't a maid or a cook. She was rich.

"That's wonderful, you like black folks. That still doesn't explain why you would risk your life to stop my father, and then save both of us," I stated.

"It's simple. You reminded me of your mother and my sister."

"What? You're not making any sense. Are you tryin' to tell me that you had some sick fascination with my mother? And what the hell does your white sister have to do with any of this?"

"I had more than a fascination for you mother, I loved her." Everyone in the room was stunned. Was this bastard trying to tell us that he had an affair with my mother? If he had been connected to tubes, I would have pulled every one of those mutha-fuckas out one by one. After my mother found out what happened to her biological father, she hated white folks. I knew he was getting ready to tell a lie. Even Dr. Shaw's jaw dropped.

Lauren jumped up from her seat and started yelling. "Are you trying to say that you had an affair with my mother?" Charlie swung out of the bed and planted his feet on the ground, he grabbed Lauren's hand to try and calm her. She snatched her hand back.

I sprang to my feet and grabbed him by his throat, "Get your hands off my sister! Do you understand that I will kill you...do you?"

Charlie threw his hands up and said, "I don't doubt that for one second."

Things had gotten out of hand. A nurse and an orderly came in. "Is everything alright Mr. Brandenburg? Dr. Shaw, I didn't know you were in here."

Dr. Shaw said, "Oh yeah, my niece is an aspiring actor and old Charlie here wanted to hear some of her monologue."

Charlie turned and smiled, "Oh, yes I have always wanted to be an actor myself."

The nurse smiled, "Well anything to put a smile on Mr. Brandenburg's face is alright with me. We can't get him to say two words."

Isabelle smiled, "Seth has a way of bringing that out in people." The nurse turned and waved goodbye as she backed out the door. Was she stupid or something? I ran my fingers through my hair, adjusted my clothes, and sat down. I patted the seat next to me for Lauren to take her place beside me.

Isabelle calmed everyone down and said, "Now look, killing this S.O.B. before he tells us what we need to know is not going to help us, plus we don't want to get Dr. Shaw into any trouble."

We all looked at her. I wondered if she realized what she'd just said. I wondered if she would actually let me kill him man after we were done with him. I really didn't want to find out. Just as we were settling down, Isabelle's phone rang.

"Damn, it's Robert. I forgot all about him. I'm gonna see if Alex will pick him up. Do you mind? That way we can all kind of unwind together."

I nodded yes and said, "That's fine with me." Isabelle stepped outside to answer her phone, I wasn't moving. Charlie had made his way into a recliner farther away from us. He was a little slow and feeble. I guessed life had just kicked his ass. He had patches of hair on his head going in all sorts of directions and liver spots all over his body. He walked kind of stooped over and held on to things to keep from falling. I don't think he was as old as he looked. I guess you reap what you sow. He was too old for me to be snatching around. I guess that's why he moved farther away from me. He should have been scared, for a minute. Hell, I was scared of myself. I was also glad that I didn't have a knife or a gun. It would have been a mess in there.

I looked at him, trying to figure him out. I wondered what else he was holding inside. I looked at his eyes. They were sad and they reminded me of my mother. What was this man holding on to? There was something much deeper. Maybe he was thinking of his wife. I assumed she was dead. Maybe he really did love my mother and he was thinking of her or maybe he was thinking of his sister that he'd just mentioned.

Isabelle reentered the room and let me know that everything was set. Alex was going to pick up Robert from the airport. She briefly mentioned how Robert was happy that I'd spent the night with Alex and that I was finally finding the answers I was looking for. I felt truly blessed to have Isabelle. She was like my sister and I finally had my biological sister. My little family was coming together. We all settled into our chairs once again. I guessed Dr. Shaw forgot about the rest of his patients because he was still with us. A part of me felt that I should have apologized to that old man, but another part of me wanted to knock the hell out of him. I did neither. Instead, I waited for him to resume our conversation. He didn't say a word, he just stared out the window.

Finally Lauren spoke, "Mr. Brandenburg, you mentioned you loved my mother. Would you mind explaining that please?" Charlie began babbling about his sister. I thought he was acting that way because of his stroke, or maybe he was trying to avoid the subject at hand.

"You know I had a sister, she was so beautiful. She was the prettiest girl in Georgia. You know I'm from an old Georgia family, the Brandenburg's. We've been around for years. Well, we've all just about died out now. I'm the last of the children. There were only two of us, my sister and me. Oh, my father hated black people. The only thing they could do was work for him and he cheated them every chance he got. My folks owned slaves way back when. I grew up on the same plantation that once housed them." He stared straight out of the window as he spoke.

Lauren was becoming agitated. We all looked at each other, like what was he talking about? Lauren was getting ready to interrupt him and Dr. Shaw put up his hand to stop her. "I'm sure he'll come back around, just give him some time. If he doesn't come back then we'll start asking questions." Lauren nodded her head in agreement.

Brandenburg was still rambling when we turned his attention back on us. "I remember he would use the Lord, Jesus Christ's name and Nigger in the same sentence. He was the meanest son-of-a-bitch in Pickens County. Yes, I had a sister. She was beautiful, just like Anna." He showed all of the teeth he had left as he talked about his sister and my mother.

"I remember growing up there was a handy man who stayed on the property. His name was Nathaniel, but we called him Nate. He lived there with his family. They were what you called sharecroppers. My daddy didn't do much sharing though. There were several black families who lived on our land. I was very shy as a child and kind of mousy. I liked to read and listen to music. My father thought I should hunt and do "manly" things. He always told me I was gonna be a sissy." I guessed Charlie was using the opportunity as a therapy session to release all the pain from the past. He was right about one thing, his father sounded like a real S.O.B.

"Nate was a stout fellow." He continued. "He was strong as an ox and could fix anything. I think Nate was the one black person that my father ever even pretended to care about. He was the only one my father trusted to drive around. Boy, I sure did love old Nate. There were two other boys who lived on our land. They were brothers. They called one Baby Brother and the other Pone. I never knew why they called him Pone, but that was all I knew. Pone and Baby Brother were always nice to me. They weren't just nice to me because they lived on our land, they were really good people. One night, there was a lot of much commotion at the house. My daddy had dogs all in the woods and there were men with guns everywhere. Pone and Baby Brother's mama came to the house. I remember her on her knees begging my daddy to please let her boys be. She said they had done nothing wrong. I saw my daddy spit on that woman and told her to get the hell away from him. Can you imagine that? He spit on that woman, as she was pleading for her sons' lives." Brandenburg seemed to zone out even further. "My daddy disappeared off into the woods. Later on he came and got me out of bed and took me behind the house, into the woods. I remember my sister was crying and my mother was yelling at him, calling him a bastard. What I saw in those woods changed my life forever. I saw Pone and Baby Brother hanging from a tree by ropes. They were just danglin' in the wind by their necks, naked. Their bodies were covered in blood. I looked at Pone and his eyes were gone, ripped right from the socket. Baby Brother's hands had been cut off. Both of their private parts were gone. There was nothing left. I stood there in that spot and threw up all over myself. My daddy grabbed my head and said, "See, boy, you can't trust a Niggra."

As Charlie sat there tears started to roll down his face. I didn't bother to get him any tissue; I didn't even think he remembered we were in the room. I could tell it was more than therapy. It was more of a confession. It was stuff you could read about in antebellum novels or you learned about in history class if you're lucky. Brandenburg actually lived this. My heart was so heavy. I looked at Lauren and Isabelle and saw the tears in their eyes. I'd forgotten what we were there for I, and I wanted to hear more. Charlie was still staring out the window.

After a few minutes, he looked over in our direction and asked us, "Have you ever smelled burning flesh? It's a smell you'd never forget." He wiped the tears from his eyes and continued to tell the story. "While I was standing there, I wanted to ask about Nate, because I knew if Pone and Baby Brother were there, Nate couldn't be far behind. I was too scared to ask so I took off and ran back to the house. My father ran after me and grabbed me. He took me into the house and led me up to my sister's room. He took his foot and kicked the door open. Boy, you see what Niggras do to white women? I looked over at my sister. My mother was on her knees holding my sister and she was holding this tiny baby in her arms. The baby looked like a tanned white baby, but I knew it was black. I knew it had to belong to either Pone or Baby Brother, maybe even Nate. To this day that was the prettiest baby I've ever seen. My sister was begging and pleading for my father to let her keep the baby. My father told her to shut up. He told my mother to get off her knees and leave the room. He yelled downstairs for Nettie our housekeeper or maid, in those days, to 'come and get this niggra baby.' I was still wondering what happened to Nate. Suddenly, Nate came running up the steps. He told my father that he'd found Callie. Callie was a midwife. This old woman came creepin' up the steps. My father took Nate by his shoulders, turning him toward me, and said to me, `Now boy, this is a good

Nigger, he does what he's told and nothin' more. I watch these other niggers around your sister and they all over her: 'How you Miss Virginia?' ' You alright today?' Just a bunch of smilin' Niggras... Nate here don't say nothin' to nobody. He just do what he's told. Nate knows I treat him better than the others 'cause he's a good boy. He knows his place. He knows I'll have his black ass hangin' from a tree if he crosses me.' I knew right then that Nate was the father of my sister's baby. Neither of them said a word. Callie took the baby away and she kept it with her until she died. When Callie died the baby became a ward of the state. My sister Virginia was ten years older than I was. The night your mother was born, I was ten years old. I was just a child, but I grew up that night."

He said that last statement so casual I had him repeat it.

"Excuse me. I must have misunderstood what you just said."

"No, you heard right. My sister, Virginia, was your grandmother. I am your great uncle. You two are my nieces."

I think you could have hit all of us with a brick and we wouldn't have felt a thing. No one said a word. I don't know if anyone ever remembers that moment when you got a whipping and you were so numb all you could do was just sit there with your mouth open until you made that one sound and just let go.

Charlie was staring out the window again.

I looked at Dr. Shaw and asked, "Did you know this?"

He threw his hands up and said, "I had no idea."

Lauren and Isabelle were absolutely stunned. They went from having a bleeding heart for this man who had witnessed an awful act to, "Oh my God, is he serious?" I moved from my seat over to the window in front of Charlie. I knelt down in front of him.

I couldn't help but laugh, I think I was suffering from hysteria or something. "Look, Charlie, forgive me if I don't welcome you into the family. The last two days have been filled with so much vital information which I somewhat expected, but this is just too much. The saddest part is of course, we never knew any of our biological family on either side, so I have no way of verifying this information. My mother never knew any of her family. What makes you think you are my uncle?"

He took a deep breath and finished his explanation. "About a year or so before your parents died, your mother started looking for her family. My mother was dead, my father and even my sister were all dead by then. Nate left town shortly after you were born and to this day I don't know where he is. I was the only one left. Your father tried to help your mother find whoever was left of the family. I really didn't know how your mother would respond to me, so I told your father not to tell her who I was. The truth was, I found your mother a long time ago. She was never really lost. My sister had kept up with her over the years. When my father died, he left everything to your mother. Of course, I was disowned because I married a black woman. When my sister died, she left everything to me and made me promise I would share it with your mother, Anna. Your father helped me fix up a will stating that everything would be left to her. In the midst of getting to know your father, I got into all sort of things, not to mention the fact that I was Dawson's private body guard when I was off duty."

This was another piece of the puzzle. Everyone fitted in somewhere. Every weirdo has his place on my family tree. I remembered my mother talking about a white woman named Ginny coming to visit her. Ginny must have been short for Virginia. My mother was right. Ginny was her mother. She died not knowing that she had a blood relative who cared about her. She never knew how much her mother loved her.

There was really nothing more to say at that point. I didn't feel the warmth in my heart that I should have felt for a long lost relative. I felt sorry for him because he'd carried everything around with him for so long, but he was just another man.

I expressed my feelings, "I'm sorry, Charlie. I really hope you don't think we're going to welcome you with open arms. I'm just not ready for that. We really just came here to find out if you knew who saved my sister and if you could tell us anything about that night that would help us. The family tree was just extra." I.

"I never expected you to welcome me into your family. I don't deserve it. I still think that somehow I could have stopped your father from murdering your mother, but I couldn't. I was too. late that night."

Lauren came over to the window and sat down on the windowsill beside me and said, "No, my father changed his mind. It was Clark who double-crossed him and murdered my family. My father couldn't go through with it. He loved her." Charlie smiled and looked over at Lauren and then at me.

"Boy o' boy, it amazes me at how many people who knew Nolan and Clark, thought Clark was the bad seed. Your father was
something else. He was smart and cunning. He made you think he was
so professional and all about business. Clark was always so hyper and
impulsive. The truth is Nolan used Clark to meet important people.
He couldn't get through, like your father did with his suits and
cufflinks, so Clark was the go between. Nolan was the man next to the
man. Phil was Johnny Case's right hand man. I know the good doctor
told you about Mr. Case. Phil messed up by giving Clark access to the
books and to Case's money. Clark gambled and stole money from
Case. Phil wanted to save him, but he wasn't going to use his own
money. He wanted to use your mother's money to pay Case back. She
wouldn't give him the entire amount he wanted, so he planned to kill
her and wait for the insurance and the inheritance. Your father was
sitting on millions when he died, and it all went to Clark and Dawson.
I had to tell your mother what was going on which meant I had to tell
her who I really was. I even showed her a picture of my sister so she
would remember the woman who visited her. She asked your father
to move out of the house. All of this was in the middle of Clark's
accusations of her being unfaithful to your father. I told her that she
should leave and take you girls, but she loved that house. Your father
told me he'd changed his mind about the hit on your mother, so I
thought we had enough time to get you guys out of town. That was
just for my benefit though. I swear to you, the night of the fire, I got
this overwhelming feeling. I was sitting at home and something told
me to go out to your house. I rushed over and saw it engulfed in flames
and my heart sank. Later on that night, I found out that Nolan was
dead as well. I figured Clark had gotten tired of your father running
him and had simply snapped. The whole thing was strange. I never
really expected Clark to kill Nolan. Clark and Nolan had a weird
relationship. It was almost as if Nolan had some sort of hold on Clark.
Clark was so dependent on him. When Dawson came along, things
started to change between Clark and your father. Dawson Meeks was
Clark's new master. After your parents' murders, a few weeks went by
and Johnny Case, along with a few others, came up dead. Then Clark
contacted me about helping him get away. I read in the paper about
Clark's alleged accident. Every now and then, he would contact me.
Last I heard, he was in California somewhere."

Brandenburg's memory was right on target. I felt like I was getting closer and closer to the truth. There was one last thing I needed to know.

"Charlie, if everyone knows that Clark is still alive, then why haven't the police caught him yet?"

He looked at me and said, "I'm sure the proper authorities know where Clark is and I'm also sure that he has them in his back pocket just like always. There are some people in this world that even the police don't bother."

There was something about Charles Brandenburg's demeanor when he spoke of my father and Clark. There was still a hint of fear in his eyes. I guess he was right; there are some people that strike fear just at the mention of their names. I was becoming more and more anxious about finding Clark. The consensus seems to be that it was my father's plan to have my mother killed. Clark didn't exactly stop it and he may have been the one who pulled the trigger. One thing we do know is that my father ended up dead, so someone had to have pulled the trigger on him as well.

Each time I replayed that night in my head, it seems that I uncovered new details. With each new piece to the puzzle, another casualty seemed to emerge. I couldn't help but wonder why everyone who was twisted up in our story had a history of dysfunction even before meeting each other. It was amazing how those people latched on to each other like leeches. Each one sucked the life out of the other. I was happy for my mother, she'd died knowing that her mother loved her and there were circumstances beyond control that had kept them apart. My great-grand father was a real S.O.B. I couldn't possibly imagine what Virginia and Charles went through living in that house. So, I guess my mother was spared after all. There I was sitting in the room looking at my own flesh and blood. I have embarked on a journey and uncovered much more than I ever expected. To be honest, I only expected to come to Dillon, look at a piece of land and hope the soil would speak to me and tell me what the hell had happened on the night my parents died. Instead I helped two people release years and years of mental oppression. I allowed Mattie to confess her secret without uttering a word. It had been a productive trip for us all. Well I know it had been for me, I couldn't speak for Lauren. I wondered what my mother would do in a situation like that. I mean, there sat my blood uncle, not even three feet away from me, and he was the one who tried to save my mother from her deadly fate. Should I have just walk out the door and never ever acknowledged him or what he said? Should I have learned to accept him as a link to my biological family? The answer, like the answers to my past would definitely take some time to be revealed.

I looked at my watch and realized time was getting away from us. Dr. Shaw was still sitting in the same spot. He hadn't checked on one patient that day. I was anxious to see Alex and I knew Isabelle wanted to see Robert. I checked my cell phone and there were several missed calls, a couple from Mattie and a couple from Alex. I was sure Mattie wouldn't have been surprised to find out about my visit with Brandenburg. She knew he was alive, and that Dr. Shaw would be the one who lead me to him. My feelings were all mixed up. I didn't really know how to feel about my father. Of course part of me wanted desperately to say that Clark had planned the whole thing and my father was blind to everything that was going on. The rational side of me screamed, "Don't be a fool!" Everyone couldn't be wrong about the same thing. I looked over at Brandenburg, he looked tired and worn out.

I said, "Well guys, I think we've worn out our welcome. We've got to get back to Dillon and then come back to the city to meet Robert and Alex."

"Yeah, you're right." Isabelle agreed. "I'm sure the guys are pretty restless by now."

I added, "Alex has called me three times already." Dr. Shaw and Lauren removed themselves from their seats. We rearranged the chairs to the way we'd found them. Lauren thanked Charlie for the information. We said our goodbyes and headed for the door. As we were leaving, Charlie tried to pull himself up from his chair. He reached out his hand and balanced himself on the side of the bed. I was the closest to him. He reached out and grabbed my arm.

"Please, I know I don't deserve this, but you two are the only blood family that I have. I'm all alone in this world. All I have is money that I can't even get out of here to spend. Will you forgive me for keeping you two apart? I really couldn't see another way to keep you together. Please don't let this be the last time I hear from you. I would love some company every now and then, maybe even a phone call."

I placed my hand on top of his and said, "I can't promise you anything, but I will definitely have to think long and hard about what you've told me and draw my own conclusion about your sincerity and place in my life." I pointed to Lauren, "Of course I can't speak for my sister. She might feel differently about the whole thing."

I looked over at Lauren and waited for her response. "With all due respect, Mr. Brandenburg, I think this will be the last time you and I ever see or talk to each other." Lauren was very firm with her statement and she meant every word. I knew exactly where she was coming from. Lauren saw him as the man who kept us apart all of those years. She walked through the door and headed outside. I turned to leave the room as well. I easily walked out and didn't look back. I meant what I said when I told him that I would have to think about continuing contact with him. That was something I would definitely have to pray about.

On the way back to Dillon to get the rental, I couldn't help but feel a great deal of relief. I had mixed emotions, but a good bit of the pressure was off my chest. All those years, I waited to hear the truth. When I was faced with it, it hit me like a baseball dead in my face. Deep down or maybe even on the surface, I knew that my father had a hand in what happened. I never imagined it was quite that deep. I couldn't help but think of Mattie's warning to let the past be the past. I guess if you look for something hard enough, you sure will find it. I can guarantee you won't like what you find. I sure didn't like it, not one bit.

We almost made the forty five minute drive without parting our lips to say a word. Everyone had a million questions rolling around in their heads, but no one said anything. Dr. Shaw kept looking in his rearview mirror to check on my sister and me. He wanted to see if we would break down at any point. When he'd look at me, I'd look over at Lauren, but her attention was focused on whatever was outside her window. I wondered what was going through her head. Most of all, I wondered about the burns that Charlie had from the night of the fire. I must admit I was shocked as well to see that the burns Lauren had surely suffered that night, had healed the way they had. There wasn't a trace of the traumatic ordeal. I guess my ignorance on the subject of plastic surgery, skin grafts, or whatever else she did to get rid of them began to show. I was happy that she was able to erase at least one reminder of that night. I also couldn't help but feel guilty about the fact that I had grown up with money, privileges and someone with whom I had a kinship. Lauren seemed so lost and more troubled than I was. There was something in her eyes that revealed more hurt and pain than she was able to admit. I thought the visit would divide us on the issue of the truth, more so now than ever. She desperately wanted to forget the past while my life thrived on vengeance. I wondered if I would be able to walk away and let things stand as they were. Then again, I thought that if we didn't find Clark, look in his eyes and ask him why, I was going to implode from the mystery of it all. The mind is amazing. You can sit for ten seconds and ninety-nine things will rush through your head. I had to realize that Lauren and I were two different people. Now that I knew that she was alive and seemingly well, I could no longer live for her. I had to live for myself. In order to do that, I had to go one step further.

Most importantly, I was straddling the fence between good and evil. I wanted to pray and ask for direction, but I didn't think God would give me the green light to seek revenge. So who could I have looked to for guidance? Who could've helped lead me to my destiny? After thirty minutes of staring out the window, Isabelle broke the silence.

"I guess I'll call my husband and see if Alex picked him up from the airport."

I'd forgotten that we had left Robert stranded at the airport. I encouraged Isabelle to call.

"Oh yeah, I'm glad you remembered, because I'd forgotten. For some reason I was thinking he had come with us."

Isabelle decided to impose her humor on me.   "I think you got him confused with Maxwell, you know...my brother you sent back to Texas wounded and heartbroken?"

Even though she said it in a joking manner, I knew she was serious. Dr. Shaw looked confused. For some reason, I felt the need to address the subject of Maxwell.

"I already feel bad enough about the whole thing."

Isabelle turned around to face me. "Listen, I've told you before, he's my brother, but I realize you two aren't compatible. Maxwell can't handle you. He's weak when it comes to love. When he should have cussed you out, he didn't. Besides you ended up with just the man you need. Don't blow it this time."

Isabelle spoke sternly and was very candid. There was nothing left for me to say. While I was letting what she said soak in, she was confirming that Alex and Robert were together. "Alex picked up Robert and they're waiting for us to come back to the city. They claim they're starving." I smiled at the fact that I was going to see Alex again.

Dr. Shaw was tired of being out of the loop. He finally broke his silence.   "Is someone going to tell me who Alex is? I already know Robert is your husband. He nodded toward Isabelle.

Before I could open my mouth, Isabelle said, "Alex Young."

Dr. Shaw turned his head, "The basketball player?"

I nodded my head yes, and his interest peeked. "Man, he is one of my favorite players. That boy can play some ball. I've watched his career since college. That's right...you do live in Houston." I was happy that Dr. Shaw approved of Alex.

"Yes, Alex and I were neighbors growing up and we went to college together. We've been friends forever."

"Sounds like more than a friendship to me. Isabelle is willing to sell out her own brother just for you to get with Alex." Dr. Shaw laughed behind his statement. Isabelle gave him a gentle punch to his arm and giggled.

Dr. Shaw looked in his mirror and said, "You know I want to meet him, and I want game tickets too, since I'm in the family again." We all laughed and joked.

I was enjoying the sound of my own laughter when I realized Lauren wasn't laughing with us. She was still staring out the window. Isabelle noticed the same thing as she pulled down her vanity mirror and looked back at me, quite obviously I might add. Lauren's hand was resting on the seat. I reached over and touched her hand. "Hey, are you alright?"

"Yeah, I'm gonna be fine. I guess I'm just taking everything in."

I turned my body so that she could see that I was paying attention to her. "Don't worry, tonight is the night for you to release some of this frustration. Alex is having a party and I know there will be some fine eligible men there." I smiled at her. "I'll make sure he introduces you to some of his more reserved teammates."

"Someone like Alex, huh?" There was a hint of sarcasm behind her comment.

"No, not like Alex. You and I both know how some athletes are. I just want to make sure you find one of the good ones."

"Thanks, I really appreciate it, but I really think I want to catch a flight back to Houston tonight. I wouldn't feel comfortable. It seems more like a couple's thing anyway."

"No, it's not like that at all. Tonight we all just want to have some fun. You know let our hair down."

"Thanks anyway, but I really miss Noel. And I know she's probably driving Mattie crazy by now."

"Well, if that's what you really want to do. I guess we need to call and see if there's a flight going out later."

I was confused. I didn't know if Lauren was bothered by what we found out earlier that day or if she really did feel uncomfortable being the only one without a date for the party. I felt it would be the right thing to do to go back with her.

"You know what? I don't feel much like partying either. I think I'll fly back with you tonight."

Isabelle heard that loud and clear. She turned around. "You do know that you messin' up now. Alex will have a fit." Isabelle didn't understand that my sister needed me.

"Isabelle, Alex is just going to have to understand that I need to be with my sister right now..."

Lauren interrupted, "Isabelle's right, you need to stay here. I promise you I'll be alright. I have a little friend in Houston that I can hang with if I get lonely." Isabelle and I both looked at each other and then looked at Lauren. We didn't even know she knew anyone in Houston, much less had a friend.

Isabelle, (with her crass ass) said, "Go head girl, get you some, I know I can't wait to see my husband." She had forgotten that Dr. Shaw was driving us around, and suddenly put her hand over her mouth. "Dr. Shaw, I'm sorry, what I meant was..."

Dr. Shaw smiled. "Don't worry about it, I wish I had a little friend...Hell I might even go to the party myself." Everyone laughed, including Lauren. Dr. Shaw was good people. He was all right with me.

When we reached Dr. Shaw's house we said our goodbyes. I told him we would definitely be in touch, and to tell Claude Jr. and Victoria what was going on. I desperately wanted to see them. I told him I was going out of town for a while and when I returned I wanted everyone to get together and come out to Houston for a reunion. He assured me that they would.

Before I left, he pulled me to the side and said, "I know where you're going from here. I saw it in your eyes when you found out Clark was alive. For some reason, I know you will be all right, but be careful. You might not want to hear this, but you have a lot of Nolan in you, but Anna Marie helps keep it balanced. Having some of your daddy's ways can help you out in the long run more than you know. Don't fight it. Use it to get what you want and what I know you need. If you need me, call me and I'll be on the next thing smoking. I've waited a long time to see Ellis Clark Winfield pay for what he's done to you and so many others. I think you're the one to make it happen. There's something about you, I can't begin to explain what it is, but all I know is you will be all right. There's something about Lauren too. I know she's your sister, but she just ain't the same. Her spirit is different. You pay close attention to what's going on around you and don't take a damn thing for granted." I embraced Dr. Shaw as if it were our last time seeing each other. I thanked him for his help and tucked every word he'd said to me away for safekeeping. He hugged Lauren and Isabelle and we were on our way back to the city.

Lauren's flight was set to leave at 6:45pm. It was 5:00. The drive was forty-five minutes and the airport was on the way to Alex's house. We drove through the town of Dillon on the way out just as I'd done with Mattie twenty years prior. We passed the old land and I whispered to myself, "I'll be back soon." Once we hit the highway, my eyes became heavy and I fell asleep. Before we even made it out of Dillon, Lauren was fast asleep.

She looked troubled, even in her sleep. Whatever happened to her while we were apart sure did have a hold on her. I felt her problems were deeper than she was willing to admit. Dr. Shaw was right. She was different. I understood the fact that we had not seen each other for twenty years, but she was my twin and I did not feel any closer to her than I did before she came back. I was giving myself too much credit. I felt that I was trying as hard as I could to connect with her, but it just was not happening the way I thought it should. I sensed some resentment and some other emotions from her that I could not explain. Sometimes it bothered me that I remembered more than she did. My memories had become her memories. I guessed some people chose to suppress their past, rather than live it as if I had all those years. Nevertheless, she was my sister and we were going to get that thing right.

As we pulled into the airport, Isabelle yelled for everyone to wake up. She pulled up to the curb where Lauren's designated airline was. We hopped out to help her with her bags. Isabelle and Lauren said their goodbyes. I walked Lauren over to the baggage counter and waited for her to check in. The security guard reminded Isabelle that she could not park for very long...that was my cue to hurry up. I hugged Lauren and told her to call me when she arrived in Houston. I remembered there was not anyone to pick her up and I did not want her to take a cab.

"Hey, we need to figure out who can pick you up from the airport. Maybe Mattie can come out and get you."

Lauren said, "Don't worry, I already have someone to pick me up. Thanks anyway." I remembered the friend she had mentioned earlier, so maybe he was going to pick her up.

She reached out to hug me. "You guys better go...that policeman looks like he's ready to start giving tickets. Have fun tonight, and put in a good word with one of those eligible bachelors." After she hugged me again, she turned and waved goodbye to Isabelle. She was waving so hard, I thought her arm was going to fly off. Her mood was quite different than it had been earlier. Hell, it was different from five minutes prior. Her eyes were lit up and she seemed perfectly happy. She turned and I watched as she disappeared into the crowd.

"We came with four and now we're just two." Isabelle said as I got back into the car. "Wouldn't it be something if Lauren and Maxwell got together?"

I was totally shocked, but it was something to think about. "Isabelle, where the hell did you pull that from? Come on, my sister, Lauren, and Maxwell?"

Isabelle continued to drive and said, "I don't know, stranger things have happened."

I looked over at Isabelle, "You know you would never let that happen. You don't even care for Lauren."

Isabelle acted as if she was offended. "I am appalled! I never said I didn't care for her! What I said was that you should take things slow with her. She just seems a little flaky, you know like she's bi-polar or something. That's all I said."

"Whatever, Isabelle. I think she's just hurt and confused, and she's in a new environment. I, on the other hand, have you, Robert, Mattie and now Alex. She and Noel are all alone."

"She's not too alone. She's going to see some man tonight."

"You and I both know how that goes."

"Yeah, ok. I'm sorry, but you know I have to say what I feel. Just don't expect her to be my lovey-dovey sister-sister self, right away. It may take some time and you don't know everything she's been through. I'm just a little concerned that she can explore ten different emotions in sixty seconds."

"Well, I guess I'll see if Maxwell can talk to her."

"He's not even talking to you right now."

"Oh, yeah I forgot."

Isabelle was right about Lauren, she obviously needed some sort of therapy. I decided to talk to Lauren when I returned to see if she would consider my suggestion.

Isabelle and I decided to meet Robert and Alex back at Alex's house. We pulled up at the gate and the guard remembered me from the night before. "Well hello there. I see you're back and you brought a friend with you."

I leaned over and said, "Can you please just let us in?" He looked at his sheet of paper.

"Let me see...Young. Ok, here it is. I guess you would be Seth St. James. Mr. Young added you to the list this morning."

He leaned into the car and said, "I still don't want any trouble up there." He must have thought he made the joke of the year because he was still laughing as we drove through the gate. Isabelle asked what that was about. I told her that she didn't even want to know. I directed her to the house. As we pulled in the driveway, Robert and Alex were standing around outside admiring one of Alex's old cars. I didn't know a thing about old cars, but that one was clean. They both wore huge grins. Robert walked over and kissed Isabelle. Alex did the same with me. Before I could stand up straight he asked where my bags were. I pointed to the trunk. He knew which ones were mine. He grabbed my bags and closed the trunk. I motioned for him to open it back up.

"Wait, Isabelle has to get her things out."

"No she doesn't," Robert yelled.

Isabelle asked, "Robert what are you talking about?"

"You and I will be staying at the hotel tonight. Alex and Seth have some grown folks business they need to attend to."

I walked toward Robert and said, "Robert please, now get your wife's stuff out of the trunk."

Alex interjected, "Robert please, my ass. He knows what he's talkin' about. You and I have some grown folks business that we need to handle." I guess there was nothing left for me to say. For the first time Isabelle was speechless as well. Robert walked into the house to grab his bags and told Isabelle it was time to go.

I said, "Aren't we at least going to eat?"

Robert said "Yes, we're gonna eat and you two are gonna eat, just not all together." Robert opened the passenger side door for Isabelle and instructed her to get in. Then he ran around to the driver's side and hopped into the driver's seat. As they were rolling down the driveway, he rolled down the window.

"Bye, grown folks!" Alex started to laugh, but I was confused. I was really looking forward to spending time with Robert and Isabelle. Robert had been waiting for Alex and me to get together since I'd known him. Something smelled real funny around there. Alex put his car away in the garage and we went into the house. He told me to follow him as he took my bags up the steps.

"I know the way to the bedroom. I was here less than twenty four hours ago."

He looked back at me and said, "Will you ever just let me be in control for once?"

"Yes, you were in control last night."

"Yeah, I was, wasn't I? He smiled. "I was kind of impressed myself."

"You are so sick."

"And you just love it. Wait a minute, what happened to your sister? I didn't see anyone else in the car."

I'd almost forgotten about Lauren.

"She decided she wanted to get back to her daughter, so we dropped her off at the airport before coming here."

"I was really looking forward to seeing what another you looked like."

"I can't tell...you sent everyone away."

"Well, I was gonna meet your sister and offer her a hotel room."

"You are so tacky."

"No, that's not what I mean. I reserved her a room so that she could stay in the same hotel with Robert and Isabelle. I even told one of my boys about her."

"I guess it worked out for you because my sister was not going to a hotel room."

"Whatever, I guess we'll never know."

I couldn't help but watch his claves flex as he walked up the stairs in front of me. He was carrying my suitcase like it was a piece of paper. I was glad we were alone. I realized we did have some things to take care of. When we reached the bedroom, he opened the door and stepped aside. I walked in and looked around. When my eyes reached the bed, that's when I noticed a dress lying on the bed next to a pair of shoes, a handbag and two black velvet boxes. Everything was absolutely gorgeous. He'd matched everything perfectly. I was really proud of him. Alex would wear jeans or a jogging suit everyday if you let him.

We walked over to the bed and sat down side by side. He handed me the smaller box first. I opened it and inside was the most stunning tennis bracelet. It almost blinded me. I couldn't wait to see what was in the larger box. When I opened it, I lost my breath. Inside was a diamond necklace. It was a larger version of the tennis bracelet. I hopped up and straddled Alex, kissing him. Just when things were heating up I looked into the bathroom and noticed it was glowing. I stopped kissing Alex and got up.

He grabbed my arm, "Wait a minute, baby. Where you going? We're just getting started."

I said, "Hold on, something is going on in the bathroom."

He said, "Oh yeah, I forgot." I walked into the bathroom. There were candles everywhere, and the tub was filled with rose petals. I reached into the tub. The water was still hot. I looked over at Alex standing in the doorway.

"I know how important your bath time is to you, so I thought I would make it as pleasurable as possible for you...and for me."

I let my guard down. He was trying so hard. To be honest, the bath impressed me more than the clothes and the jewelry. I couldn't wait to lie down on his chest and lose myself in the moment. We both undressed and immersed ourselves in the tub water. The water was so calm and soothing. For a while we just lay there quietly. He began to get uncomfortable so he pulled his legs up on both sides of my body. That made it even better. I enjoyed the fact that he was big and strong. I was wrapped up like I was in a cocoon. I felt safe and comfortable. I could have stayed there all night. He wrapped his arms around me and kissed me on the cheek and told me he loved me. I smiled so hard I almost gave myself a headache. The water was beginning to cool down, so I turned on the heated jets, of course rose petals went everywhere.

Alex laughed, "You sure do know how to ruin the moment." I turned the jets off, leaving only the heat on. The water vibrated calmly. Alex took the washcloth and washed my entire body. I turned to him to return the favor, and he stopped me, pointing to the soap dish behind him.

"Use this other soap...here behind my head."

I wondered why he couldn't use my soap, so I asked, "Why can't you use my soap? Don't you like it? It doesn't smell feminine."

"Will you hush...old smart mouth woman. Please, just get the soap from the dish behind me." As I reached for the soap I was about to just straight cuss him out when I took the lid off the soap dish and almost chocked on my words. I grabbed the dish to bring it in closer to my eyes. There, resting on a bar of soap was the biggest diamond ring that I'd ever seen. I looked at Alex and he took the ring from the dish and grabbed my finger. My mouth was no longer flip. In fact, I couldn't say a word. He sat up in the water and I waited for him to speak.

"I've known you all my life and I've loved you forever. I know we've been apart for a while and lived separate lives, but none of that matters. I don't want to waste any more time dating and getting to know you. That's for beginners, you and I are veterans. When I walked into the store earlier this week, this was in my pocket. I was going to give it to you that day. Even Robert didn't know about it. Thirty days before I booked my flight, I fasted and prayed and waited for the Lord's approval. Once I received his yes, I knew it was time to hear yours. At first, I was confused because things went the wrong way that day at the store, but he told me to wait, so I did. When you showed up last night, I knew the wait was over. Seth, will you please honor me with the blessing of being my wife?"

I was crying so hard, I could hardly hear myself saying, "Yes." I must have held on to him for what seemed like an eternity. He slipped the ring on my finger. There was nothing left to say. I leaned back in his arms and rested my body on his.

I was on cloud nine all night long. I could barely get dressed for the party. Alex and I danced around each other laughing and playing. Ever so often, I would glance at my ring and then look over at Alex. I loved watching him dress. There was nothing like a man that looks good in a suit and smells so good, he'll take your mind on a thousand journeys.

When we were just about dressed, Alex called the driver to let him know we were ready to go. He told me he'd hired a driver because he wanted to sit in the back and be fresh with me. I informed him that he would not be messing up my hair or my makeup so he would just have to admire the view. When the car arrived we hopped in, and settled in for a twenty to thirty minute ride. Alex and I marveled at the fact that after all those years and drama, we were finally together. I wanted so badly to tell him I was going to have to go to California, but I just left well enough alone. I figured I should quit while I was ahead. Once we reached the party, Alex and I were pretty much attached at the hip. He introduced me to everyone as his fiancée. I must say I was eating it up.

Isabelle and Robert were late. I could only guess what was keeping them. While I was waiting for Isabelle, I noticed most of the other guys were alone and didn't have their wives or a lady-friend with them. The wives that were there were all huddled up together. I tried not to pay attention to rumors and stereotypes, but there was a colorful array of women in this crowd. I asked Alex where the sisters were. He told me not to start anything. He reminded me to be careful because my hair wasn't exactly can't-cha-don't-cha (Can't comb it and don't even try), and that I did fall into that same stereotype; light skin with long hair. As I was hit with that reality, I was quiet for just a moment, but not for long. I could tell that I clearly did not belong in that group and Alex didn't attempt to introduce me either. I did feel rather awkward as I tried to give Alex his space. I really didn't want to hang onto him all night. I realized we needed a lot of trust in our relationship. I wouldn't attend too many of those events. I stood back and looked at all of the vultures that could smell money buried under a pile of shit. It was amusing to see what some people would do just to say they were with someone famous. Alex was very careful and remained respectful during the entire night.

I waited for Robert and Isabelle for quite some time. Just as I was leaving out to call them, I saw Isabelle sashay through the entrance. As Robert walked in, I watched the women whispering to one another. I was too far away to hear, but I could only imagine what was being said. Isabelle left Robert and ran over to where I was standing. She started talking before she even reached me.

"Girl, I am so sorry we're late. We feel asleep, and then we sat there debating about whether or not we wanted to come. I told Robert you would just die if I didn't show up..."

"Isabelle."

"Girl, there are a lot of people in here and it's hot, like a sauna."

"Isabelle..."

"You look cute, that's not the dress we picked out for you though, why did you change?" Isabelle's mouth was going a mile a minute while I kept trying to get her attention. I was tired of trying to shut her up so I could tell her about my engagement. I simply, and calmly, lifted my hand and put it dead in her face. Isabelle stopped in the midsentence and grabbed my hand.

"Girl that is gorgeous! My God it's huge! Can you even lift your hand? That's why they were acting so anxious earlier today. How did he propose?...Oh my God, I'm so happy." Isabelle was very excited.

I told her, "It was so romantic. You know how I love my baths. Well, he filled the tub with rose petals, and candles surrounded it. After we relaxed for a while and engaged in a little conversation. He told me to grab some soap from the dish that was behind his head, and there was this gorgeous ring inside. I was absolutely speechless. He told me he had brought it with him when came to the boutique."

Isabelle put her hand up to her mouth, "Oh girl, and you just acted a fool. I guess things happen when they're supposed to because you would have been confused with Alex and Maxwell there."

"You know I didn't think about that."

"So how do you feel?"

"To be honest, I am on cloud nine. Isabelle, I am really happy right now. I love Alex with all my heart. I'm just scared I'm gonna mess this up."

"Don't worry. Alex has been patient this long. Plus, he knows what you're going through. Everything will be just fine."

"You're right, as usual, I'm making too much out of this."

After a few more minutes, we decided to leave and go our separate ways. Alex and I had more catching up to do. We were back at his house and we were lying on the couch locked in each other's arms.

"So tell me about your sister. What's her name again?"

"Her name is Lauren. Did I tell you she has a little girl named Noel?"

"Oh, so I have a niece?"

"Yes, you will have a niece. Noel was my name before I moved to Houston."

"That is absolutely amazing. All these years your sister was alive and you didn't even know it. How did she make it out of the fire alive? Where has she been all these years?"

"It's all crazy and confusing and I can never explain everything to you in ten minutes. A police officer who worked with my father found her that night. He kept her for a few days and his wife, who was a nurse, took care of the burns she'd sustained from the fire. Anyway, he took her to a children's home where she stayed until a couple from California adopted her. So, she spent her life in Cali."

"Well, is she married? I forgot to ask before I tried to fix her up tonight."

"No, she's never been married."

"I see. So how do you feel about seeing her again?"

"To be honest, I really don't know how I feel. Don't get me wrong, I love the fact that she's alive and I love the idea of having her back in my life. Half of me wants to do everything I can to make her happy, but the other half worries about her stability."

Alex narrowed his eyes in confusion, "What do you mean her stability?"

"Well for one thing, Lauren and Isabelle aren't quite hitting it off like I wanted them to. They aren't exactly fighting, but there is a lot of tension between them. Not to mention Mattie isn't comfortable with her either for some reason. I'm surprised Lauren let her keep Noel this weekend. Mattie and Lauren keep telling me to take it slow because I don't know anything about her."

Alex didn't hesitate to agree with Mattie and Isabelle. "Baby, they're right. I understand she's your sister, but I'm sure she's been through quite a bit. You know what you've been through and how you handle personal relationships. When the two of you bump heads...I mean really bump heads, because you will sooner or later...it's gonna be very ugly."

"I will admit she does have some peculiar ways. She seems to have these mood swings and there is something strange going on in her eyes. I don't think she'd try to hurt me though."

"Look I don't know her, and I can't begin to understand what you two are going through, but you do need to take it slow. Don't try to push this family thing on her all at once. Follow her lead." Everyone was saying the same thing and they were making sense, but my emotions were getting the best of me and I really wasn't trying to hear anything negative about my sister. If she just wanted money, then she would have disappeared last week when I transferred money into her account. I wondered if I should've told Alex that I'd given her money. I thought for a minute before I spoke.

"Alex, if she was just out for the money, then she would have left after I transferred the money into her account last week."

Alex looked at me with this crazy look in his eye. He jumped up from the bench, "What do you mean you transferred money into her account? Please don't tell me you gave her money."

I immediately became upset. "Yes, I gave my sister the money that is rightfully hers. Half of everything my mother left for us is Lauren's. It's only right. I've held on to it all these years because I knew she was alive. I guess you're gonna tell me there's something wrong with that."

"Hell yeah! You don't know anything about her Seth."

"She's my damn sister—my blood sister. A blood test proved it."

"I don't care who proved what. What if she disappears again?"

"Then that's her right to do so. All I know is the blood test proved she's my sister so, it's only right that she have the money. Frankly, Alex, it's really none of your business. I don't even know why I told you."

"Yeah, you could have kept that shit to yourself."

Alex threw up his hands. "What the hell is in the water in Houston?"

"I put my name on the account Alex!"

"At least you had enough sense to do that."

That's it...I was officially pissed off. I couldn't stand there any longer. "Alex, kiss my ass! What do you mean 'at least I had sense enough'? You know what? I don't even want to know."

Alex reached out to grab my arm. "Seth, I'm sorry, I didn't mean..."

I pulled back from him. "Please, just don't touch me right now. You can't possibly understand the position I'm in and what I'm going through. I could understand if the blood test had come back negative. Lauren is my sister, my flesh and blood. I know she's had it rough. I just want to make sure she feels safe and secure. Even if we never really connect as true sisters, at least I know in my heart that I did the right thing. I am so happy she is alive...that she didn't die that night and I would give her anything. I held on to the money because something inside of me kept saying she was alive, I promised myself, that when she did come back to me, her rightful share of our mother's money would go to her. I'm tired of trying to explain this to all of you. I don't want to ever talk about the money again. Is that understood?" I stormed up the stairs and prepared for bed.

Shortly after, Alex entered the room and stood by the door. "Look I'm not taking this bullshit into the next day and I'm not sleeping on it either. I'm sorry that I upset you, but I'm not sorry for what I said. Now that should be it, because you know I'm right. We are not gonna start this engagement arguing over something that neither of us can control."

He was right, what was done was done. I did what I thought I should've done. The truth was I was tired of not saying what was in my heart to him. We were two grown people, so why couldn't we get past it? I wanted so badly to tell Alex I was sorry as well, but I couldn't part my lips. I was dying inside. My damn pride or stupidity just wouldn't let me give in. I didn't say a word. I simply walked in the bathroom and stepped into the shower. Alex dropped down on the bed and threw his socks at the wall. I felt like a fool. With the water rolling down my back, I started to cry. I was angry with myself because I let my funky attitude and my need to be in control, mess up my relationship with the man I loved. Abruptly, I turned off the shower, grabbed a towel and stepped out. I walked into the bedroom and found Alex staring at the wall. I guess he was thinking about what the hell he'd gotten himself into.

"I'm sorry...that's it...I'm just sorry. I know you don't understand how I feel about this, but I just want you to respect my decision. Can you do that?" I was sitting beside him on the bed.

He turned to me and looked into my eyes. "I can respect how you feel about this whole thing, but I need you to understand that I'm not gonna let anyone, not even your sister take advantage of you."

There was no need to say anything else about the matter. I leaned over and kissed him. As I was heading back to the bathroom to finish my shower, Alex grabbed my towel. "You do know that we're going to have to do something about your stubbornness. I love you, but something has got to give. I know this is you, and you're set in your ways, but something has definitely got to give."

I heard what he was saying loud and clear and I silently agreed with him. I really didn't like the way I treated him at times, but there was something inside me that just refused to compromise. I remember Mattie telling Mrs. Stein one day that if she didn't keep Dr. Stein happy then another woman would. She was trying to encourage her to stop drinking in order to save herself and her family. I needed to step outside of myself to see what I'd become. Sometimes I felt that if I allowed myself to give any part of me in romantic relationships, I would be admitting weakness. I often see love as a weakness and a luxury. Sometimes, when things become so habitual, and we get caught up in the act of it all, it becomes a part of us. It becomes who we are and pretty soon we are unable to control our own emotions. I knew in my heart that I loved Alex. Sometimes I would sit back, look at him and thank God for him. When it came to expressing my feelings verbally everything fell apart. My heart and my head didn't seem to communicate well when it came to love. I must admit, there were some who hadn't even deserved the time that I'd given them and I'd treated them better than I'd treated Alex. I think it was my defense mechanism, and I hadn't been able to disarm it. The revelation was an inconvenience that I could add to a laundry list of others. Alex and I were engaged, and we could only move forward from there.

Chapter Twenty-One

The plane ride back to Houston carried the same sentiment that I expressed coming out to Georgia. I dreaded going back and I was uneasy about expressing the news of my engagement. I knew Mattie would be overcome with joy, but somehow I didn't think that Lauren would be too thrilled. Alex represented one more person that I had to give my attention to and one more "good" thing in my life. I needed her to understand that just because I was more financially stable than she was growing up, didn't mean that I lead a privileged and stress-free life. I could honestly say that I would give up every cent I had if my life would've just gone back to the way it was twenty years ago.

When I pulled up to the house, Mattie's car was parked outside. I parked my truck in the garage and entered the house. I walked in announcing that I was home. Mattie yelled back that she was in the kitchen. I smiled when I smelled food cooking. I was so hungry. I placed my bags in front of the steps and walked into the kitchen. There were pots bubbling and boiling on all of the burners, and the smell of fresh cornbread escaped from the oven.

Mattie checked one of the pots. "I thought you all might be hungry when you got home." She looked at me with a furrowed brow. "Where's Lauren?"

"Actually, she left a day early. She said she was tired and really wanted to get back to Noel."

Mattie looked at me and said, "I don't know about that. Noel is in the room watching television."

I immediately went into the room where Noel was watching television. Sure enough there she was sitting down watching cartoons. "Hi peaches." She sprang up from the floor and wrapped her arms around my waist.

"I missed you. Did you bring me something back?" I found it odd that she didn't ask about her mother and was inquiring about gifts.

I took her hands in mine and said, "Yes, I did bring you something back, I'll give it to you when I unpack, if that's alright with you." Noel laughed hysterically.

"It's alright with me." I kissed her cheek and told her that I was going to help Mattie with dinner. I was confused and didn't know what to do first. Before going back into the kitchen, I stopped by my office and called Lauren.

"Lauren, hey this is Seth. I'm very worried, we're all back from Georgia and Noel is still here. Mattie says she hasn't heard from you, so naturally, I'm worried about you. Please call me and let me know that you're ok."

I hung up and sat for a minute trying to figure out where Lauren could possibly be. I was worried that something may have happened to her. On the other hand, I figured she was still uneasy about our visit to Dillon and may have needed some time alone. I was chewing my thumbnail when the door to my office opened. It was Noel. I motioned for her to come in and told her to make herself comfortable. She came in and sat on my lap with her head on my chest.

"My mother didn't come back with you did she?" I was surprised by her maturity and the lack of distress in her voice.

"She's just going to be a little late. She had to run an errand."

Noel examined the locket around my neck and said, "Don't worry, you don't have to pretend, I know she's gone."

My curiosity and concern was now getting the best of me. "Noel, what makes you think your mother won't come back."

"She does this sometimes. She usually leaves me with one of her friends. She gets really mad and screams really loud before she leaves. Don't worry she always comes back." This news was very disturbing. I needed to know what she meant by 'she gets mad and screams before she leaves.' Was my worst fear becoming a reality? Did my sister really have problems much deeper than I could have imagined? Was insanity another facet of our generational curse that plagued our family? The distressing part was that I had no idea who to call. Noel mentioned Lauren's friends, but didn't know who they were. I'd never heard her speak of anyone, but her adoptive parents. I guess I would start there, I was sure Noel knew her grandparent's names.

"Noel honey, do you know how I can reach your grandparents or any of your mother's friends?"

Noel shook her head. "I really don't know any of my mother's friends, and I've never met my grandparents. I know that I have an aunt, her name is Rachel." This was becoming an even bigger mystery.

I didn't remember Lauren ever mentioning a sister and I seriously doubted there were any family ties on Noel's father's side.

"Is this aunt your mother's sister?"

"She was adopted when my mother was adopted. She lives in a hospital, I think she's sick all the time. It's not a regular hospital though, my mother says we're not supposed to talk about her. She's a special kind of sick."

Lauren had told us that she was an only child and that her adoptive parents had no other children. Now, I was becoming angry. My thoughts immediately turned to the skepticism that everyone harbored about Lauren. I was not questioning her lineage. I was questioning her motives for finding me after all those years. Maybe she did want money from the beginning and someone to care for Noel. Whatever her motives, I was still relieved to have had the burden lifted from my spirit. As usual, my feelings about the situation were extremely conflicted. I straddled the fence from being pissed to feeling sorry for both Noel and Lauren. The fact that Lauren had some unstable qualities was solidified by the information Noel had provided. I was even more intrigued to find out why Lauren failed to mention she had an adoptive sister. The special kind of illness Noel mentioned was weighing heavily on my mind.

"Sweetie, what do you mean by a special kind of sickness?"

"My mommy says that she looks like a grownup, but she's a kid like me."

As I sat there concluding that Rachel must have some sort of emotional handicap, I still struggled to understand why Lauren hadn't mentioned her being a part of her life. Noel fell back on my chest and I held her there in my lap, and caressed her hair. I looked up toward the door and saw a shadow in the doorway.

"Come on in, Mattie." Mattie walked into the office. "How much did you hear?"

She folded her arms and said, "All of it. Don't worry, I'm not going to say a word. There's nothing left for me to say. We just have to take care of the little one and make sure she's all right. I'm sure Lauren will show up with an explanation. I think wherever she is, she's probably better off." I watched thoughtfully as she turned to walk out the door. "Dinner is ready. You all come on and eat before it gets cold."

I think Mattie was relieved that Lauren was gone. Somehow I really didn't feel an "I told you so" coming from her. I decided not to press the issue with Noel. I didn't want to upset her. She jumped off my lap and we headed into the kitchen.

We settled in for dinner. Noel said grace and we enjoyed the good food that Mattie had prepared. We didn't talk about the trip. Mattie and I would talk about that later, in private. I decided that it was a good time to reveal my good news. "Well, I have some good news." I stretched out my hand across the table and let my ring sparkle.

Mattie looked at me and flashed a fake smile. "Well, that's nice. I didn't know the doctor was seeing that many clients."

Mattie was a trip. You know how some people try hard to say the right thing, but once the words leave their brain and pass through their mouth it turns into hot air. Getting her approval was like pulling teeth. Ironically, I knew that cooking the dinner was her way of saying, "Everything is alright between us for now."

I wanted to make sure she had a little crow with her collard greens. "I really don't know what Maxwell's financial portfolio looks like, but I do know that Alex can afford this ring and a whole lot of other things." Her eyes bucked as she grabbed her chest with one hand and my finger with the other. She almost ripped my finger out of its socket.

"You mean you and Alex are engaged?" Somehow her enthusiasm didn't mean as much.

"Yes, Alex and I are engaged." Why couldn't she have been that happy when she thought I was marrying Maxwell? She jumped up, came around the table and hugged me. While we hugged, I got a familiar feeling. It was the same warm feeling I had the night Mattie told me my parents were never coming back and she would take care of me. I felt safe in her arms that night and I felt just as safe right then. That was the first time since that terrible night that I felt that close to her. I embraced her with everything that I had, while we shared that moment. I finally did something that she could be proud of.

Although Noel was confused and really didn't understand what was going on, she jumped up and hugged us as well. I didn't want to tell her what was going on right then, just in case her mother showed up. I wanted to make sure that I was the one who broke the news to Lauren.

We sat down at the table and discussed my engagement over dinner. Mattie was confused about how everything came to be. "Now, help me to understand how you left with Maxwell and came back engaged to Alex."

"Well, after Dr. Shaw took me back down memory lane, I felt so empty and needed a shoulder to cry on. It was so strange. I was sitting there talking to Maxwell about our relationship and it hit me that I wanted to have that conversation with Alex. I grabbed the car keys and drove to Atlanta. I went straight to Alex's door. We talked and I told him everything that had been going on. He told me he loved me and I told him the same. And the rest is history."

"I knew you two were meant for each other, I'm glad you finally realized it."

"I am too. I do know that if I hadn't gone to Dillon, we wouldn't be sitting here talking about my engagement." I didn't really mean to mention Dillon. It just popped up during the course of the conversation. Once I mentioned it, Mattie dropped her head and things were quiet for a moment. Surprisingly, she actually asked me about the trip.

"So, how was your visit to Dillon, did you find what you were looking for?"

"Yes, I found more than I expected and I also found someone that I didn't expect to find." Mattie's facial expression was less than favorable. She looked like she was having some difficulty swallowing her food.

Just when I was getting ready to ask if she was alright, she asked, "Who else did you find besides Dr. Shaw?"

I took a bite from my fork and said, "Charles Brandenburg." Mattie displayed mixed emotions, but there was a bit of relief mixed with the shock on her face.

"Charles Brandenburg? I thought he was dead."

"No, he is alive and well. Well he's alive, at least."

"Just what did old Charlie tell you?"

"He told me enough to know that my father was definitely no angel. Now I have to go to California to find Clark." Just when I was expecting Mattie to jump up from the table throwing flatware, she leaned back in her chair and sighed.

"I'm sure you know how I feel about all of this. I do know that nothing I can say will stop you. If you want to make Alex a widower before his time then you go right ahead." Her sarcasm was much more refreshing than her last verbal outburst over my decision to go to Georgia. I did find it strange that she wasn't at all shocked about the fact that Clark was still alive.

"You're not shocked about Clark being alive?"

"I stopped being shocked about anything he does a long time ago. Besides, I'm his mother. A mother can always feel her child in her soul, just like you are Nicolette's twin and knew she was alive. I have always figured he was out there somewhere."

"Yeah, but you didn't believe me."

"Oh no, it's not that I didn't believe you. I saw that you had hope and you were desperate to believe that Nicolette was alive. Sometimes when things don't turn out the way you hoped they would, you find out that hope is far better than the reality. I always expect the worst, so when good does come my way it's that much better." I looked over at Noel. She had finished her meal and was playing with her milk. I instructed her to go and wash her hands and finish her cartoon. She hopped up from the table and set out for the bathroom. After Noel was out of sight, I asked Mattie to clarify her last statement.

"What do you mean, when it's not what you expect?"

Mattie put down her fork and said, "Do you ever pay attention to the little things, like gestures, eye contact and body language?" I wondered where she was going with this.

"Yeah, but what does that have to do with anything?"

"If you look into Lauren's eyes...I mean really look, you'll see a dark and troubled place."

"Mattie, what are you talking about? Lauren is fine, this is all new to her, and she just needs some time to adjust. Coming here, and thinking that I've had an easy life, was a terrible blow. It's only natural for her to feel jealous or left out. She'll be here to pick up Noel before the night is over." I needed to convince myself because I knew I was sitting up there lying through my teeth. I desperately wanted to believe that Lauren would show up. Mattie swept her plate aside and began to illustrate her point with her hands.

"Covetousness is one of the Ten Commandments and along with this commandment goes all the others. When you have something someone else wants, whatever it may be, you will stop at nothing to get it. You will lie, steal, cheat and even kill. I've been around a long time, and I've come across a lot of trash in my day. It seems like I just I couldn't get away from evil, so I know it when I see it. Now, I don't know Lauren's entire story, but I do know that when I look into her eyes, I don't see whatever it is you see."

"So what, now you think she's out to get me? She tracked me down after all these years just to get what she thinks I have because it rightfully belongs to her? I know Lauren had a hard life and there seem to be things that she's kept from us, but I also know she's my sister and she wouldn't do anything to hurt me intentionally. She's my flesh and blood."

Mattie removed her plate from the table and walked over to the sink. "Cain and Abel were flesh and blood too. Clark is my flesh and blood."

At that point I'd had enough. I didn't know what everyone saw that I couldn't see. I knew Lauren had problems. I just thought she needed some professional help. I suppose if Alex had met Lauren, he would have said the same thing. I wasn't hungry anymore. The conversation had taken my appetite. I took my plate over to the sink and emptied it into the disposal. I rinsed it and left it there with the other dishes Mattie was washing. My luggage was still sitting at the bottom of the stairs. I picked up my bags and walked upstairs to my room, where I unpacked and took a shower. As I stepped into my bedroom, I walked over to my phone to check for any missed calls from Lauren. I also checked the caller I.D. on the home phone. There was nothing from her. I looked out the window and saw that the sun was going down. I stood there and watched as the sun disappeared. The reality that Lauren wasn't coming back anytime soon settled in my bones. I had a major responsibility on my hands. I was at a loss. I didn't know what to do. I didn't know who to call. To top it all off, I didn't know a damn thing. I grabbed my sweats, a t-shirt, my phone and car keys and headed downstairs. I walked into the room where Noel and Mattie were. I called Mattie outside the door to speak to her privately.

"I'm going to ride by Lauren's to see if she's there. Maybe she's asleep or sick or something."

Mattie asked, "Do you want me to ride with you?"

"No, we'd have to take Noel and if Lauren isn't home I don't want her to be disappointed." Mattie agreed to stay home and wait for my return.

I hopped in the car and rode the fifteen minutes to Lauren's house in silence. Her car wasn't out front or in the driveway, so I parked in the empty spot in the driveway. I was hoping it was in the garage. I rang the front doorbell and knocked on the door and then I went to the side of the house and knocked on every window that I could reach. I even positioned myself to jump over her back fence. Just when I'd gotten a good grip on the gate to pull myself up, her neighbor came around the house.

"She's not there. I don't think she'll be back for a while. I saw her earlier today with a big suitcase. I guess she's busy, she just came home with luggage yesterday."

What was he neighborhood watch? "Thank you, sir. She's my sister and I hadn't heard from her. I was concerned. I guess she left a day early for her trip." I didn't want him to think I didn't know where my own sister was, so I pretended to know that she was going out of town and that I just didn't know when.

The man smiled. "Yeah, she looked like she was leaving in a hurry."

I wanted to be sure she was alone. "Did you say she drove herself or did someone pick her up?"

"Actually, one of those airport shuttles picked her up. She didn't have the little girl with her though. I don't know where she is, although she's probably better off."

What did he mean by that? "I'm sorry, I don't understand."

"The little girl, she's probably better off. She seems like such a sweet little girl. You said the lady was your sister? Well your sister has a mouth on her. Let me tell you..."

"Yes, please tell me what you mean."

"She yells at that little girl so loud. I know the child is afraid of her. I'm just a neighbor and she scares me. Sometimes if I'm out tending to my lawn over here, I can hear her yelling at the child. I've even seen her grab her by her arm. Sometimes the mother is all smiles and so pleasant and some days, she'll look you straight in the face and won't part her lips. I wanted to call social services, but my wife said to stay out of it."

"Well, thank you sir..."

"It's Bennett...my name is Walton C. Bennett. I was named after my grandfather. The C stands for Cleveland. Ironically, I'm from Cleveland, but my granddaddy wasn't named after the city though. I really don't know who he was named after..."

Oh my goodness I needed to stop him before I knew his entire family history. "Thank you Mr. Bennett. I can assure you that my niece will be just fine. I appreciate your concern. You're very observant."

"My wife says I'm nosey, but I'm just like you just said, observant. You have to be these days, it's not like it used to be..."

"Ok, Mr. Bennett. I think I'd better head back home. It's getting late." I hurried up and headed toward my car. I walked away waving goodbye to the observant neighbor. I didn't want to give him the chance to start back up. As I backed out, he was standing there in his shorts, t-shirt, sandals, and church socks waving goodbye. His wife was right, he was nosey as hell. This time his nosiness paid off. I began to get really pissed off. Mr. Bennett had absolutely no reason to lie to me about Lauren's behavior with Noel. I wanted to find her just so I could confront her about it. I needed to figure out a way to ask Noel if her mother was abusive. I wasn't sure how much Noel would actually share with me. One thing was for sure, I definitely couldn't tell anyone else. Not yet, anyway.

I rode around for a little while longer, trying to clear my head and make sense of my new situation. Finally, I pulled up to my house. I walked through the door and Mattie met me not even three feet from where my feet landed.

"Was she at home?"

"No, a neighbor, Mr. Bennett, said she'd left earlier with a suitcase." I closed the door and walked past Mattie. I looked back at her and said, "I don't want to hear any more about this." She followed me down the hall and into my office. I sat down behind the desk and turned on my computer.

"I'm not gonna say a word. What are you doing?"

I looked at her and gave her an honest answer. "I have no earthly idea. I don't know what to do. I don't think she's coming back any time soon."

"Do you know how to get in touch with her adoptive parents?"

"No, Lauren never told me their names and Noel says she never met them. The only thing I can think of, is to get a copy of Lauren's adoption records from the state of Georgia, but they may not give them to me. The only name I do have is her alleged sister Rachel, and I think she has problems, too. This is turning out to be one big mess." I hated that I had admitted that to Mattie.

"Ok Seth, calm down. Get on that computer and find out who to contact in Georgia to get Lauren's adoptive parents' names. Maybe they'll know who this Rachel person is as well."

"It's been twenty years, I'm sure there's no record after all these years. It seems like a long shot."

"Right now it's our only shot."

Mattie was right. I looked up the information and found a main number. Hopefully, they would direct me to the right department. I wrote the number down on my scratch pad. I would call first thing in the morning.

I was awake all night pacing the floor, trying to figure out where Lauren could be and why would she leave her own child for weeks at a time. Of all people, she should have known how it felt to be abandoned. I was truly amazed at the way Noel was handling the whole thing. Maybe Mr. Bennett was right, she probably was better off, at least for the moment. I left many messages for Lauren. The last time I called, her voicemail was filled to capacity. I'd been avoiding phone calls from Alex and Isabelle. I wasn't ready to explain just yet. Where would I even begin? I knew I couldn't keep avoiding them. Oddly enough, I found it comforting to know that Lauren disappeared periodically, but she always returned.

While I was on the computer, I pulled up the transaction history of Lauren's bank account. There was nothing unusual. She made a withdrawal of three hundred dollars at an airport ATM. There was no record of a ticket purchase.

I was straddling the fence between anger and disappointment. I wanted so badly for things to work out. Most of all, I was pissed at the way she'd reportedly treated Noel. I picked up my blanket and pillow and tiptoed into the room where Noel was sleeping. I curled up in the chair beside her bed. I wanted to be there, just in case she woke up. I didn't want her to feel abandoned and confused. I laid there staring at the wall, going over Lauren's body language as Mattie had suggested before. I couldn't help but remember the way she'd acted in Dillon. One minute she was hot and the next she was cold. I remember catching her gazing at Isabelle sometimes. It was almost as though she hated her. I thought of us as children, about how she was always so timid and afraid of everything. I couldn't help but wonder yet again, what had happened to her?

I must have drifted off to sleep, but I was awakened by Noel's ear piercing screams. "Mommy, please. I'm sorry, Mommy. Please don't do it. I'll be good."

I ran over to the bed and pulled her close, trying not to startle her. She woke up kicking and screaming. I held her closer and rocked her in my arms, as I told her softly that no one was going to hurt her. Mattie came running in the room. She touched Noel's face. It was dripping with sweat. She ran down stairs to get some water. I sat there wondering what Lauren had done to her. After we calmed Noel down, she asked if we'd both stay with her and we agreed. I picked her up and took her to the chair with me and rocked her to sleep. I didn't want to let her go. I was angry and hurt. I wanted to know what was going through my sister's head. It was happening. This curse of insanity and darkness hadn't ended with me. It had also taken over Lauren.

At that moment, I felt, as though I didn't want Lauren to come back. I didn't even want to think of what I might do to her if she did. And if she would hurt her own child, what would she possibly try to do to me?

Mattie said, "My God, what has Lauren done to this child?"

I looked up at her as I rocked Noel and said, "I don't know, but I hope she stays far away from her until she can get herself together. She better not come back here with this bullshit. You can bet money on that."

My disappointment had now turned to rage. I could feel tears welling in my eyes, and my heart was beating fast. I wanted to find Lauren and smack her around, just as she'd apparently done to this child. I stopped rocking and placed Noel in the bed. I stood there looking down at her and wondered if somewhere deep inside of me I could be capable of hurting her. As I looked at Noel, I remembered my own innocence and how it had been taken from me. I knew that I could never take that from another child.

Daylight had come and we'd made it through the night terrors and emotional roller coasters. I took my shower got dressed and headed to my office to call the state of Georgia. I reached someone who was able to give me general information on how to make a closed case request.

The lady on the other end of the phone told me I would have to make a formal request in writing with the adopted child's full name, date of birth, social security number, date of custody or possible date of custody. An estimated month and year would be acceptable. She also informed me that since this was over twenty years ago and everything was done by hand back then, they would have to locate the case file which could take four to eight weeks. I told the lady that it was an emergency, and I really didn't have four to eight weeks. Of course that wasn't her concern, so she told me to state the urgency in my request letter. I thanked her for her help, hung up the phone and started typing my letter.

Shortly after my phone call, I checked on Noel and then left the house for the boutique. I dialed Alex while I was on my way. It was one conversation I was dreading.

He answered the phone in a very sarcastic tone. "You do know the ring is returnable." He had jokes early in the morning.

"No Alex, it's not, you had it engraved and I know it was made especially for me." He wasn't going to get the last word.

"Whatever. Why didn't you call me last night when you made it in? I called you all night on your cell and at home. What's the problem?"

"I was so tired. All I wanted to do was eat and go to sleep."

"So you didn't see the need to call me?"

"No, that's not it. Look, I don't have an explanation. I just didn't call. Let's not argue."

"Seth you really need to get your priorities straight."

"What does that mean?"

"It means that I am your fiancé and I think about you when I get up in the morning and when I go to bed at night. There are no exceptions."

"I never said I didn't think of you."

"Well actions speak louder than words. I have to go work out...I'll call you later." I sat there for a minute trying to figure out whether or not he'd hung up or not. I didn't think he had.

"Hello?"

I heard, "If you'd like to make a call, please hang up and..." I realized he had hung up on me. A few days ago I would have called him back and cussed him out, but I honestly had too much on my mind. Plus, if I called him back, we would've argued some more.

I knew I was wrong for not calling Alex last night. I should have at least let him know I was ok. Sometimes for me the easiest thing was to just be difficult. I wish I could've been submissive to a certain extent, but the harder I tried the more I failed miserably. If Alex could only see what was truly in my heart and know that I really do love him. I didn't want to lose him, but like he said, actions spoke louder than words.

I arrived at the store and prepared for Isabelle's update on the wedding that had only been in the making for forty-eight hours. When I walked in she had this big grin on her face.

"Good morning, Seth. How are you? Did you sleep well?" Isabelle was always so upbeat. I expressed my sentiment for a restful night's sleep.

"Good morning Isabelle, I had a good night's sleep, and no, I don't want to go over anymore wedding plans, but thanks anyway."

"How did you know I was going to talk about the wedding?"

"You're breathing, aren't you?"

"You know you've got a smart mouth. That's ok though. I know Alex cussed you out this morning."

"And how do you know that?" I asked.

"He called us last night to see if we made it in safely. He said your phone was going straight to voicemail."

"I know...I was so tired last night."

"I understand that, but you can't just not call the man. It's not only about you anymore. And no, I don't want to talk about the wedding. First, you have to learn how to be in the relationship, period. You mess around and you will find yourself, by yourself."

Isabelle was upset. She started cleaning the front window. Her paper towel was coming unraveled, but she continued to wipe the window. I knew I was wrong, but I didn't say a word. Instead I walked into the back and put my things away. The last time I was in my office, Alex was there with me. The relationship thing was not going to be easy for me. I thought it was a mistake to skip dating and go right into being engaged. I didn't have what it took to be in a relationship and I know I couldn't be that man's wife. I looked at my ring. I erased all the excitement for the proposal from my head. I thought about it realistically. I loved that one man all of my life and I didn't even know how to treat him. I'd been in relationships before, but I never really cared for any of those guys. They were here today and gone tomorrow. Something as simple as the wrong shirt or ugly shoes would turn me off. The truth was I was scared to death of Alex and like most people when they're afraid, I wanted to run. Part of me wanted to remove the ring from my finger, put it in a box and mail it back to him. The other part wanted to hold on tight and wait to see what happened. I wondered once again, at what point I would turn into my father. Not only did I have my father's personality to worry about, but my grandfather's as well. And to make matters worse, my sister was acting like Mommy Dearest. They say insanity skips a generation. On my mother's side, she escaped the madness, so it had to be my turn.

I sat there twirling the ring around on my finger. It was a perfect fit and it would take some force to remove it. I thought of how I wanted to say the right things to Alex, but when I opened my mouth bullshit always seemed to come out. I sat with my arms propped up on the desk and my head in my hands. I looked up when I heard a knock at the door.

It was Isabelle. She opened the door and stood there with paper towel debris in one hand and the glass cleaner in the other. "Look, I'm not going to apologize for what I said, but we do need to talk about how you keep shutting Alex out. You can't keep this up and expect to hold on to him."

I leaned back in my chair. "I know I can't, but I don't know what happens to me. When I see him or even hear his name, I want to be that mushy and emotional woman, but I just can't. My heart says one thing, but by the time it reaches my mouth, it's all twisted up and wrong."

Isabelle tossed the paper towel into the trash. "You are scared of trusting Alex with everything in you. Not everyone is your father. And everyone isn't out to hurt you. I know you have twenty years of hurt, anger, frustration and God only knows what else, but you have got to be careful. When you finally let all that emotion out it's gonna be a mess, look at what happened not too long ago, you almost killed yourself because you had all this anger and hurt built up inside. You need to take all that negativity and transfer it into the love that I know you have for Alex. If you love him with as much passion as the hate you have for Clark, that's gonna be some powerful love."

"It's easier said than done, Isabelle"

"I know it's not going to be easy, but you need to start somewhere. And I promise you sex does not equal love. Believe it or not a man needs more. You need to learn how to shut the hell up sometimes."

"I know."

"I know that you've spoken to Alex this morning, and you probably brushed him off, so I suggest you call him back and explain yourself."

"But, Isabelle..."

"But, nothing," she interrupted me. "I know you've known each other forever, and he knows how you are and all that bullshit, but that still doesn't make it right. Sometimes people just like to hear, 'I'm sorry.'"

I sat there for a minute and listened to what she had to say. Of course, she was right. I told her I would call Alex when he was finished working out. I thought about sending flowers, but that seemed kind of feminine. He loved sweets. I contacted the Sweet Factory and sent him his favorite deserts. At least it was a start.

After I'd had my order of sweets sent to Alex, I walked onto the showroom. Isabelle was standing by the window, looking out. I could tell she was still upset.

"There is something I need to tell you, but first you have to promise not to say a word to anyone."

She folded her arms and asked, "What is it, Seth?"

"Lauren didn't pick up Noel when she returned on Saturday and apparently she's left town. Noel is still at my house."

"What?"

"That's not all. According to Noel, she does this every once in a while when she gets angry. She leaves Noel with friends."

"Is she crazy?"

"Apparently...she does have a problem. I spoke with her neighbor when I went over to see if she was home. He told me that Lauren yells at Noel all the time and he's even seen her push and grab her at times. Last night, Noel woke up screaming and hollering, saying she'll be good. She was begging her mother not to do it again."

"What is it? As if I don't know."

"Mattie and I assume she's been beating Noel."

"I know she's your sister, but someone needs to beat her ass."

"Oh no, this time I agree with you."

"I knew she was a little peculiar, but I never would have guessed this. She seems to be so patient with Noel."

"I know."

Isabelle grabbed my arm, "Girl, tell me she didn't run off with the money you gave her."

"That is a possibility, but as of this morning, she had withdrawn only three hundred dollars and Noel did say she always comes back."

"Ok Seth, what would make her return this time? She has someone reliable to care for Noel. She probably knows her daughter is better off without her. The fact that you gave her all that money, she's probably halfway to Mexico by now." Isabelle was being funny, but she was probably right. Lauren was probably long gone.

"You're probably right. To be honest, I don't mind if Noel stays with me, but I don't have anything. I can't register her for school in the fall. I don't have a birth certificate. I don't know her social security number. I don't know anything."

"Don't worry. What you don't have you know you can get. You know Noel was born in L.A. A birth certificate will be easy to get and so is her social security number. You know Robert's brother-in-law is an attorney, so these things are the least of our worries. How's Noel handling this?"

"Surprisingly well, she seems to be ok with it. I guess she's used to it."

"Yeah, and the fact that she's crazy about you helps a lot." Isabelle finally smiled.

"I guess."

I decided to accept the fact that Noel would be with Mattie and me for a while. Each day I found myself looking forward to coming home to Noel. Her big eyes would light up when she saw me. Each day we had a new activity planned. We went to the zoo, the amusement park and the movies. We did everything together. Mattie and Isabelle joined us for most of our activities. We wanted to make sure Noel was happy, so she wouldn't think about her mother's absence so often. I couldn't imagine my life without Noel. She had become a part of me. I began to accept the fact that Lauren was gone and that it was for the best. Noel never once mentioned her mother. She continued to have nightmares though. I contacted Maxwell and asked him to recommend a child psychologist. The truth was I didn't know if I was ready to hear what Noel had been through. I started to think about all of the strangers Lauren left her with. I didn't want to think the worst, but I had to keep an open mind.

After a while, it was like Noel had never even had a mother. Alex absolutely adored her and she thought he was the best thing since sliced bread. Every time he came to visit, which was every week, he brought a suitcase full of toys and clothes. I was a little worried about spoiling her. Noel was wise beyond her years. She was very grounded and levelheaded for a five year old. I guess when the parents are crazy; God gives wisdom to the children, because they just might have to raise themselves.

We were getting ready for Noel's birthday, which was in August. We had planned a backyard birthday blow out with the children in the neighborhood, children from her school and her ballet class. Since Noel told us she'd never had a birthday party before we wanted it to be special.

The birthday party was an absolute success and Noel seemed to be happy in Houston with all of us. Isabelle was the only person who knew I was still planning to going to L.A. Everyone thought I'd forgotten all about finding Clark. No one brought it up, out of fear that I would just up and leave one day. They figured Noel was the only thing keeping my feet planted in one spot. They were partially right. I didn't want Noel to think I was leaving her and not coming back like Lauren had done. She would start school in a few days. First grade carried more responsibility than kindergarten, so she'd be quite busy.

It was time to shop for school clothes. After Kelly and the new girl we'd just hired came in to close the store, Isabelle and I took Noel to the mall. I was thoroughly enjoying motherhood. I still wasn't sure about pushing out any of my own, but I was enjoying Noel. We found so many pretty things for little girls at the mall. We shopped until the stores closed. Noel wanted tacos for dinner. We went to a Mexican restaurant and ordered something to sip on while we waited the fifteen minutes to be served.

"Aunt Seth, I love you...I love you too Aunt Isabelle and Uncle Robert and Uncle Alex and Mattie. I'm glad my mommy finally found someone to take care of me. I know she's sick and she can't always take care of me, but I'm glad I'm here, I don't ever want to leave."

Noel's sentiment took me by surprise. Isabelle didn't know what to say either. I leaned over and kissed my niece on top of her head and told her, "We'll always be here. We're your family."

Noel looked up at me. "It's ok, Aunt Seth. I know I can't stay with you forever."

"What do you mean you can't stay with me forever?"

"My mother says happiness is not real. That's why when you're always too happy, something bad is going to happen."

"Well, Noel I can't promise you that you'll always be happy, but I can tell you I will try my best to keep you safe and happy. I'm gonna make sure I take good care of you."

As I sat there looking across the table at Isabelle, I couldn't believe that I'd just had that conversation with a six year old. Why should a child be worrying about sadness and bad things happening all the time? I could only imagine what else her mother had told her about life. Since Noel has been with me I'd done some research on the effects of children who'd been physically and emotionally abused. Even though she's never blatantly revealed that she's been abused, I knew that Lauren had done something inappropriate to Noel.

However, I had to admit that things had been going so well that I couldn't help but wonder what was going to happen next. My biggest fear was that Lauren would show up while I was in L.A. and take Noel away, and I wouldn't be there to stop her.

After leaving the restaurant, Isabelle went home. Noel and I joined Mattie on the Lanai when we got home. After Noel told Mattie all about our trip to the mall, she and I went upstairs to get her ready for bed. Noel asked me if I would sleep in her room. I tucked her in and told her that I would be in as soon as I took my shower and prepared for bed. After Alex and I finished our nightly conversation, I retired to Noel's room. We'd redecorated her room in ballerina Barbie. She'd been taking ballet lessons after Alex's suggestion and had become obsessed with being a ballerina. I drifted off to sleep effortlessly for the first time in quite a while. Since Noel had been with me I didn't think of the past that much. I tried to make sure I looked toward the future. Everything that I did was for my family. I wanted to make sure that everything remained just as it should.

Chapter Twenty-Two

The next morning, I began my routine. Mattie and Noel had planned to go to lunch and a movie. I was happy to see Mattie doing better with Noel, than she'd done with me. I guess letting go of the secrets of her past had helped her to open her heart to Noel. Sometimes, I looked at them together and couldn't believe she was the same person. Noel knew that her mother was adopted, and she understands that concept. She also knew that I was her aunt, her mother's sister, but I was not sure she understood how that relationship evolved. Noel thought that Mattie was my mother. She called Mattie grandmother and we allowed it. I supposed one day when she was old enough to understand the mess, I would explain things to her. I decided not to keep secrets from Noel. Secrets sometimes become lies and lies turn into something that you can never get over. I didn't want Noel living with the burden of carrying secrets the way her mother and I had.

Noel was still asleep. I showered and dressed for work as usual. I had a cup of tea and a croissant for breakfast. Mattie called it bird food, but the truth was I hated breakfast. It had to be the least appealing meal of the day. I really only ate cold cereal and pancakes, but there was only so much of that one person could take. I finished up my version of breakfast and headed down the highway, enjoying the unusually cool summer day. I could smell the rain in the air and watched as the clouds drew closer together. I could tell it was going to be a stormy day. Although clouds really didn't mean anything in Houston, it would rain and then the sun would shine ten minutes later.

For once, I arrived at the shop before Isabelle. That was very odd. She always made it to work before I did. I placed my things behind the counter, locked the door and turned on the lights. I was there for about twenty minutes, getting ready for the day, when Isabelle pulled up. She hopped out of her car with her usual morning tea and muffin. Her hair was wild and free. She had one of those short cuts and normally curls every strand. She must have been too tired that morning to bother much with her hair.

"Good morning, girl. Don't ask. I know I look a mess this morning. My husband waited until the last minute to get his things ready for camp. He acts like he's going out of state or even out of the city for that matter. He's like a big kid. He had to have this and that, toys and gadgets, just all kinds of shit." I watched her multitask while her mouth was going a mile a minute.

"Do you need to go back home and get some rest? I can call Kelly in for the morning. Mornings are usually slow anyway."

"Oh no, I'll be just fine as soon as I pop a few packets of sugar in my tea. Why are you here so early this morning?"

"I thought I was on time."

"No. I'm only thirty minutes late, you're usually here about an hour after I get here."

"Really? Damn, I guess I'm a real slacker."

"Call it what you want. You're just slow."

"Oooowee, please hurry and drink your tea. Do you need a shot of liquor in that cup?"

"Shut up, you just wait, you'll be going through this with Alex soon. You'll be singing the same sad song."

"No I won't, Alex lives in Atlanta. He will be getting his own things together." Isabelle smacked her lips.

"Alex lives here three days out of the week. The only reason he hasn't moved in permanently is because you swear you need your space."

"Do you really even like me?"

"Why?"

"You're always defending Alex. Alex this, and Alex that...Alex...Alex...Alex!"

"You sound as crazy as I look this morning."

I walked back to the office mocking her, while she yelled out threats of coming back there and slapping me. I sat at my desk, switched on the computer and checked my email. Alex usually sent me crazy emails. I'd left the door to the office open so I could yell out and talk to Isabelle every now and then.

I was sitting there laughing at something Robert's sister sent me, when I heard Isabelle say, "Oh, hell naw." Seconds after saying that, she bellowed my name. "Seth, get in here right now."

I ran to the front to see what was wrong as Isabelle pointed to the window. I looked up and watched as Lauren got out of a new car. She looked like a million bucks. She was neatly dressed and carrying a $2400 handbag with the shoes to match. Don't get it confused, she always kept herself up, but this was different. She had the look of wealth and relaxation. Her diamond earrings were twinkling in the sunlight. I stood there with my hands by my side and fists balled up. I could feel the heat rising from my toes to the top of my head. All I could think was that she was not taking Noel.

"Seth, please calm down. Just breathe." Isabelle knew what I was feeling at that moment. I closed my eyes and took a deep breath. The situation could be volatile and I really needed to be rational. Where had she been for almost two months and why the hell had she come back? From the paper trail she left I knew the area she was in. I figured she was grown and could handle her own affairs.

Isabelle unlocked the door, and I stepped back to let Lauren into the store. She walked in with a huge smile on her face, as if she'd been on a weekend trip instead of a two month hiatus of doing Lord knows what. She sashayed her ass on in, pulled off her sunglasses, and reached up to wrap her arms around me. She hugged me so tight, I thought I was gonna pop open like a can of biscuits. I just stood there with my hands by my side. She twirled around with her hair swaying from side to side.

"Oh Seth, I've missed you so."

I think this broad is bipolar or something. The first thing that should have come out her mouth should have been, "Seth, please forgive me. I'm so sorry." Or better yet, why not go and see her kid, you knew where she was. I continued to stand there and talk to her in my head.

"Isabelle, you look tired. Are you getting enough rest?"

Before I could skip to another thought, Isabelle took the words right out of my mouth. "I guess everyone can't leave their responsibilities to relax like you have."

Lauren stepped back as if she were shocked. "Isabelle do I detect a little hostility?"

Isabelle lunged forward and said, "Bitch, you detect more than hostility! Where in the hell have you been?"

Part of me said let Isabelle whip her ass and the other part of me said stop before the neighbors called the police. I stepped in and said, "Ok, that's enough. What are you doing here Lauren?"

"I know I owe you an explanation, but I just needed some time to myself. I was feeling overwhelmed."

This time I wasn't playing with her, I was hotter than piss on the sidewalk in the summer time. I lowered my eyes and said, "Is overwhelmed another name for psychotic and selfish?"

"Hold on, Seth. You don't know shit about me or how I feel. You had Noel for almost two months. I've had her for five years..."

"Lauren please, whether you've had her for five years or fifty, that doesn't give you the right to just up and leave her. According to her you do this all the time. You leave her with people she doesn't even know!"

"She knows you. You're her aunt."

"How long has she known me? You showed up on my doorstep, did a little song and dance, shed some tears, cashed in and took off. You just said we don't know shit about you. I'll tell you what I do know, you've been doing something to that child that you shouldn't have and if you ever put your hands on her again, I promise you, your next death certificate will be real. Don't even think you're taking her away from here!"

"Are you threatening me? Obviously, you don't know who I am."

"You're right. I don't know who you are. And believe me I don't even want to know anymore."

I wanted her to leave and never come back. I would pay her to stay away from us. I was determined not to let her take Noel away from me. She didn't deserve her. I stood there and tried to find some humanity within myself.

"Look Lauren, I don't want to argue with you. Standing here arguing and getting upset isn't gonna do either of us any good. Why don't we walk over to the café, sit down and talk about this?"

Isabelle looked at me like I was crazy. I glanced at her and focused my attention back on Lauren. Lauren looked over at Isabelle and rolled her eyes. I waited for Isabelle to respond, but she held her tongue. I grabbed my purse and keys and we headed out the door. As

Lauren and I walked out the door I looked back at Isabelle. She rolled her eyes at me.

"Why does Isabelle feel like I need to explain myself to her all the time? I know she's your best friend, but I can't stand her."

There was so much passion in Lauren's voice. She put extra emphasis on the words 'best friends'. I couldn't help but think about what Mattie said about jealousy.

I came to Isabelle's defense, "Lauren, you have to understand. Isabelle is like a protective older sister and even though you are my sister, we don't know anything about you. Then you go and pull a disappearing act all summer long. You have to admit, your behavior is bizarre and that's putting it mildly."

Lauren got really angry. "Bizarre? What the hell do you mean bizarre? So no one trusts me. What do they think I'm gonna do? Do they think I'm gonna hurt poor, pitiful, guilty Seth?"

I stopped in my tracks and turned to Lauren. "What do you mean guilty? Just tell me what you think I should feel guilty about. Should I feel guilty just because I happened to be the one who had material things? Just because I grew up a little more comfortably than you, that doesn't mean I have anything to be ashamed of or feel guilty about. I have suffered just as much as you have. I would have given anything to have my family back. That money didn't mean shit to me, it didn't make me happy. I still cried myself to sleep every night."

Our conversation was taking a turn for the worse out there, and in front of all of those people passing through. The green-eyed monster was definitely making an appearance. Lauren didn't back down. Instead, she became more intense.

"I get so tired of people like you who say money doesn't make them happy. It's always the ones with everything who say that. I bet you never had to work hard, not one day. Everything was given to you. Have you ever had to have some nasty, funky ass man fuck you just so you could have food to eat? Have you ever sucked a dick for spare change? Everyone is so concerned about poor Seth. I know those heifers don't like me, not Isabelle or Mattie. And frankly I don't like them either. And I'll tell you something else, they better watch out, because you are so right...they don't know me and you don't either."

I didn't know what to say. My instincts told me to snatch her in the street and beat her ass for talking to me crazy. I wasn't sure if she just threatened me or not. The loving sister side of me said to calm down and act civilized. I paid attention to her eyes like Mattie instructed me to. They were wild and crazy like she was hyped up on something unnatural. I reached out my hand to touch her arm and she snatched away from me.

"Don't you fuckin' touch me! Don't you ever touch me! Do you understand me? You think you're better than I am? You don't want to cause a scene in public. I guess they didn't teach me any manners in the stinkin' orphanage that I grew up in. I didn't grow up behind a white picket fence." That was it. The sister shit was going to have to wait. I was so tired of the, 'woe is me, poor, pitiful Lauren' attitude.. I guess I just forgot that I was out in public, not to mention, I'm a businesswoman who owns the store we're arguing in front of. I stepped in close enough so she could hear and feel what I was saying.

"Look, I am so tired of your bullshit. If you don't like the way I live and the way I got the money that I shared with you, then you can get the hell on. Yes, I have friends. I have my own business, and a man who loves every inch of me and I'm not going to apologize to you for any of it. Don't you ever tell me how I feel, because whether you believe it or not, I would give anything, I mean anything, to have my family back. I would love to have the chance to be your sister, but I can't force it on you. You're right...I don't know you, and with the way you act I don't want to know you. Now, I don't know what kind of psycho trip you're on, but you need to go somewhere and get some medication. I will tell you this, if you want to play who's crazier, that's fine with me, but you better get plenty of rest and bring your A game. Oh, if you thought my life was so wonderful before, then I guess you should know that Alex and I are engaged, so add that to your list of things too!"

I didn't turn and walk away like in some dramatic scene. I stood there with her eyeball-to-eyeball waiting for anything to happen. She didn't blink or move a muscle. It was like she was contemplating what to do next in her head. For that moment, she wasn't my sister. She was just another woman in the street. I was tired. I'd done all I could to welcome her into my life. I guess you can love someone, but it doesn't mean you have to like him or her. After our moment of silence, Lauren put on her sunglasses, told me she'd talk to me later and walked to her car. That bitch was clearly insane.

Before I could finish my thought, she turned to me and said, "I hope you enjoyed playing mommy, because you'll never see Noel again." My face grew warmer and warmer, and before I knew it, I felt my hand leap from my side. I drew back my hand and slapped Lauren across her face. As blood trickled from the corner of her mouth, she rolled her head around and grabbed the side of her face. Her eyes were wide with shock and amazement. She quickly pushed her hair back from her face. I didn't say a word or flinch one bit. I didn't even feel bad for what I'd just done. As she wiped her mouth, she knelt down to retrieve the sunglasses that I'd knocked off her face. She stood in front of me with her back straight and her head erect.

"Don't worry, you bourgeois bitch, we'll definitely meet again and I guarantee this is the last time you'll ever slap me!" She hopped into her car and peeled off.

I felt something warm drip from my nose. I looked down and I saw drops of my own blood on the concrete. I put my hand up to my nose and felt the blood pouring out. That hadn't happened to me in a long time. For some reason when I got mad, almost to the point of no return, my blood pressure rose and my nose bled. Just a few seconds ago, I had pictured myself ripping my own sister's head from her body. Even though everything was calm now and Lauren had driven off, I stood there with blood dripping, my heart beating fast and my pulse racing. I listened to my heartbeat. I could feel my pulse pounding in my neck and in my wrist. I tried to focus on a car, a bird, a tree or anything to escape what I was feeling inside. I breathed deeper and deeper, while all kinds of crazy thoughts rushed into my head.

I saw Isabelle coming toward me with a roll of paper towels. I looked over and my neighbor, Ms. Katzman, was asking me if I was all right. A crowd of people gathered around me, each of them asking me if I was all right. Isabelle came to me and put the towels over my nose. As she walked me back to the store, she said she could feel how fast and how hard my heart was beating. I snatched the paper towel from her hands.

"We've got to go...she's gonna take Noel, and I'll never see her again!"

Isabelle said, "Ok, just wait here. Let me get my purse and lock up the store." She looked around and found Ms. Katzman. "If anyone comes by tell them we had an emergency and we're closed for the day." She ran into the store, grabbed her things and we hopped into her car. Just as I'd done the first day I saw Lauren, we raced down the highway at top speed trying to get to my house before it was too late. All I could think about was Lauren and Mattie going head to head. Isabelle darted in and out of traffic switching from lane to lane. We were both hysterical. All we could do was pray.

"It's gonna be ok...it's gonna be ok." Isabelle kept assuring me. Finally, we exited the freeway and pulled onto the main road. We darted up the street that led to my house. When we arrived, Lauren was outside throwing Noel's things into the car. Noel was crying and Mattie was screaming.

"I'm calling the police," Mattie yelled at Lauren.

"And tell them what? That a woman who doesn't really exist is coming to get her own child?"

"I'll tell them that you've been abusing this child!"

"Please, do you think they care? They don't give a damn about little girls that get beaten and cussed at all day long. I'm just trying to make her tougher. Everyone can't have everything handed to 'em." She walked over and grabbed Noel by the arm.

Noel screamed, "I don't wanna go, please don't make me go. I hate you. Let me go. I hate you!"

Lauren shouted to me, "You had everything...now you want my child too?"

I ran over to her and tried to pull Noel away from her. Isabelle grabbed Lauren while I was trying to hold on to Noel. Lauren was pulling so hard that she ripped Noel's clothes. I let Noel go, reached up and caught Lauren right under her chin. She and Noel fell to the ground. That's when I saw the gun fall out of Lauren's pocket. I dove to the ground to pick it up, but she got to it first.

"I really don't want to use this. I just want my child. If I have to, I'll do anything to get her back. I need her. I have nothing. She's the only thing that belongs to me. Please don't take her away from me."

Her face was all twisted as she began to cry hysterically. She was pleading for me to give up Noel. I stood there breathing hard and strong. My adrenalin was flowing. Isabelle stepped so close to me I could almost hear her heartbeat. I stretched my arms out toward my sister.

"You don't want to use that gun. If you shoot me then you definitely won't have Noel. Just please put the gun down. We're all a little too wound up right now, let's go in the house and talk this out. I want to help you. You need help."

"I know I need help. I just can't stop these feelings. I don't know what to do. I just need some time to figure things out. My mind won't stop. It just keeps going and going. I feel like I'm gonna snap."

"I know how you feel Lauren. I went through the same thing. I went to a nice quiet place and I got lots of well-deserved rest. You can go there. Maxwell works there. You'll be just fine. And when you come home, Noel will be here waiting for you."

"Bitch, I'm not crazy. I know you want to send me to the nut house so you can take my kid." She'd stopped crying just as fast as she'd started. She kept the gun pointed at us, walked over and snatched Noel up by her arm. Noel hadn't said a word the whole time. I watched as Lauren pushed Noel in front of her and told her to get in the car. Noel crawled over the seat and Lauren jumped in and drove off...just like that. I ran behind the car, screaming for her to come back, she drove faster and faster down our residential street. She cut the curve and did a tail spin. I stopped and watched as her lights disappeared around the corner. What could I do? None of us could afford a police investigation. Isabelle and Mattie ran down the street to meet me. I couldn't hear a word they were saying. My body was numb and everything around me was lifeless and mute. I walked back to the house with Isabelle and Mattie chattering away in my ear. Once I reached my house, I picked up Noel's things that had been thrown across the lawn and went into the house without saying a word. I couldn't speak. All I could do was walk. I left the door wide open. I didn't look back to see if anyone was coming in behind me. I went up the stairs and into my bedroom and closed the door. I dropped down on my bed and just laid there in a daze. I was sure that Mattie and Isabelle knew not to say anything to me right then. No one came to my room. They left me alone. After awhile, I sat up on the side of my bed with my head buried in both hands.

"Lord, have mercy on me." I didn't say a full or formal prayer; I just needed mercy. I didn't want that to be the end of the world for me. Once this was over, I would find Noel again. I knew in my heart she didn't belong with her mother. Not while Lauren was so unstable. I was so pissed at her for what she'd done, but I was still worried that she'd hurt Noel or herself. Not less than ten minutes ago, I found out that my sister was a very disturbed woman, and that we'd crossed that line between love and hate. It was truly amazing how thin that line was. It was like a hair that could be snapped at anytime. The sad thing was that I couldn't honestly deal with that problem. It was much bigger than me. That was the unspoken approval for me to do what I needed to do, and that was to find Clark.

After I settled down and everything seemed normal again, I realized my clothes and hands were stained with blood. I hadn't bothered to clean up. I went to the bathroom and pulled my clothes off. I tried to wash away what residue I could from my clothes and hands. I avoided the mirror. I didn't want to face my own failure. I'd failed to maintain self-control and I'd failed to protect Noel. My conversation with Lauren was still fresh on my mind and weighed heavily on my heart. My emotions were mixed and I wasn't sure how I was supposed to feel. I'd cursed my sister out like she was just another woman in the street. Part of me saw her as just that, another woman in the street, but part of me still wanted to see her as my sister. I thought about what Mattie and Isabelle had been telling me all along. I saw that today with my own eyes. She was jealous, almost to the point of insanity. The look in her eyes was so cold and distant, like she was on a trip somewhere far away. Her exit was even more disturbing. It was like she went from zero to sixty in just three seconds. She deliberately tried to take me to that point of no return. Once I was at the height of my anger her eyes had changed, as though she was satisfied.

As I was standing at the sink, washing my blouse, I heard my bedroom door open. It was Isabelle. "Can I come in?" I welcomed her in with a slight smile. She came and stood at the bathroom door. "I think I need to go home. It's been a long day and it's not even three o'clock yet."

"I know this is one day I don't ever want to relive."

"You do know that you did everything you could. Noel's gonna be ok, she's a strong little girl."

"I know she's gonna be ok. I prayed a prayer of protection for her. I don't think it's her lot in life to suffer."

"We'll see her again."

"I know. The major thing that worries me is that I failed Lauren. I tried so hard to make her a part of my life. Just like that...she walked into my life and then walked right back out. I couldn't even keep my own sister."

Isabelle looked at me with disappointment. "Seth, you aren't Lauren's keeper. She's a grown woman and can do whatever she wants to do. Whether it's a man or anyone else, you can't keep someone who doesn't want to be kept. And as for her being a sister, to some people sister and family is just a word and it doesn't mean shit."

She reached over and took my arm and turned me around to face her. "You forget about this. We'll see Noel again, you can bet on that. You have another mission that's been on your heart for months. Now you get yourself together and go find the man who started this mess." Isabelle could see the disappointment still lingering on my face.

She moved in closer to me. "I saw the look on your face today, it was something that I've never seen on you before and it scared me. It scared the hell out of me. You were standing there with blood dripping from your nose, your heart was beating fast and your pulse was racing. You were on the verge of rage. I watched the two of you go at it, and thought about what my mother always told me, 'If someone makes you that mad, then you need to leave them right were you found them.' I know she's your sister, but when she walked away from you she had a smile on her face. Seth, if you don't have sense enough to move when someone is pissing on you then that's on you. I'll tell you one thing, she ain't my sister and I'm not gonna let her send me into cardiac arrest. I'll drag her ass out in the street and see what happens."

She let my arm go and walked away. She enforced her message with her body language and let me know that she didn't want to discuss it anymore. She had made her point.

Isabelle left me there in my room tending to my stained clothes and my thoughts. I got tired of trying to wash the blood out so I just rung the clothes out in the sink and placed them in my laundry bag. I took the clothes down to the laundry room and placed them on the shelf until morning. Mattie was nowhere to be found. I passed her room and, noticed that the door was closed. I didn't bother to go in. I knew that losing Noel had to be difficult for her, so I just gave her some time to herself. I would check on her later.

I went back into my bedroom and changed into my workout clothes, I needed to run off some steam, but it was too hot outside, so I turned on my MP3 player and started on my treadmill. I began walking at a normal pace. I didn't want to start out too fast or hard. The music became more intense and so did my thoughts. I forgot I was running on a machine and began to run faster and faster. I felt like I was outdoors running on a never-ending road. I could feel the wind on my face as my stride became longer and longer. I ran and ran until my heart started beating faster and faster. My feet moved along with the rhythm of the music. My heartbeat, my footsteps and the music made its own rhythm. I closed my eyes. I thought of the events of the day and each time I saw Lauren's face I ran faster. I thought of Clark and I ran faster. I thought of my father and I ran faster. Isabelle's words kept ringing in my ears, "Watch her. Sometimes sister don't mean shit." I thought of my mother. She never told me that I shouldn't trust Lauren, so how was I supposed to feel? It seemed as though my life was flashing before my eyes. I thought of Mrs. Stein and Benjamin. I thought of my affair with Dr. Stein. Maxwell flashed through my head and finally the memory that I'd been waiting for. I thought of my mother and the moments that I'd spent with her before she died. I remembered the last time I kissed her and the last time I hugged her. I could smell her perfume, and I could see her face. I started running faster and faster like I was running to her. Instead of reaching my mother, I ran straight to the instant the bullets hit her body and she collapsed on the floor. I pressed the button on my treadmill and stopped running. I stood there with my heart beating extremely fast. I didn't know if I could catch my breath. I was so wound up. I stepped off the treadmill with the music still blasting in my ears, my heart beating a mile a minute and my pulse racing. I took off the headphones and unhooked the MP3 player from my treadmill and threw it against the wall. I watched as it shattered into tiny pieces all over the floor, and then I fell down on the floor with my head in my hands and cried.

In the midst of everything I hadn't noticed Alex standing in the doorway. I wasn't expecting him back so soon. I felt his presence as he knelt down in front of me and kissed my knees, then my hands and then my lips. I was excited just to feel his hands on my skin, I didn't bother to ask why he'd come. He kissed my cheeks, my eyelids, my forehead and my lips again. I could actually feel that he was the man for me. Just sitting there, feeling his hands caressing my flesh, made me want to be a better woman. If what I felt for Alex at that point, was any indication that I was capable of loving someone, then I wanted to feel more. I wanted children. I wanted the dog and the house with the white picket fence. He took a seat beside me on the floor, and for a while we sat there without uttering a word.

Finally, he reached over and took my hand and said, "I, ah, ran into Isabelle at the gate and she told me what happened. I'm so sorry. I don't know what we can do. I mean Lauren is her mother."

"I know she's her mother, whether she deserves to be or not right now. There's nothing we can do. Neither one of us needs a police investigation, I'm just too paranoid for that. There's nothing we can do, but wait until she comes back. She has to run out of options eventually and run off again. She knows we'll take care of Noel."

Alex caressed my hand and kissed the back of it. "Seth, I can't begin to imagine what you're going through with your sister and I'm not gonna pretend I do. It just seems like you're letting this whole thing consume you...your body is here, but your mind is somewhere else. I don't mean the fact that Noel's gone, I'm hurting over that too...I mean there's something else, can you please tell me what I can do to make everything alright?" Alex was right. No matter how hard I tried, I just couldn't stop thinking about going to L.A.

I put my hand on top of his and said, "Thanks, baby, but there's nothing that you or anyone else can do. To be honest, I don't know when things will get better inside my head. Every night I pray that I'll wake up and this will all be a faint memory. But, it's the same day after day. You're right, this will probably consume me and I will suffocate."

He became uneasy. "Please don't say that. You're a strong woman and I know you can beat this."

There was silence in the room once again. I was happy to see that he had faith in me, even if I didn't. He got up from the floor and stuck his hand out to pull me up. "You know what? I have an idea."

I pulled away from him and sat down on the bed. "What's your bright idea?"

Alex flashed his pretty white teeth. "Since we're going to become one soon, we'll need to get rid of our property and purchase a house together." I wondered where he was going with that statement.

"I'm sure we'll need to do that at some point. But what's your idea?"

"Well, I have a house in L.A. and before I began playing for Atlanta, I would spend the off season there. Since we're starting fresh, I want to put that house on the market. I just don't have the time right now to do it myself...so why don't you do it for me?" I didn't think Alex knew what he was doing. I couldn't remember if I had told him that Clark supposedly lived somewhere in L.A. I didn't bring it up. I saw it as a sign, and the answer to the question I'd been asking myself. "Should I try to find Clark?" I tried not to show too much excitement. I placed my hand on his knee and leaned over to kiss him.

"You know, I think you're right. A little time in L.A. would really do me some good, and I would love to do some shopping. Yes, I think I will take you up on your offer."

Alex kissed me back.   "Well then, it's settled, now please go take a shower. I know you're a little tart from all that running." I jumped up and wrestled him to the ground. While we were playing around, Mattie stopped at the door, peeked in and shook her head. Alex threw me to the side, got up, grabbed Mattie and gave her a big hug. Mattie laughed. She seemed to be enjoying the moment. She fanned him off and continued to laugh.

"Go on, take a shower." He turned me around and gently pushed me toward the bathroom.

"We are going out to dinner. I've already told Isabelle, and of course she'll tell Robert. They'll pick up my mother since they live in the same neighborhood. Go get Noel ready..." He stopped mid-sentence with an apologetic look on his face. I shook my head and threw up my hand to let him know that it was all right. Avoiding the awkward moment, Alex waved me toward the bathroom again, telling me to get ready.

I was nervous about seeing Alex's mother. I really didn't know why, because she came into the store every occasionally, but it was different now that I was getting ready to marry her only son.

Mrs. Young greeted me with open arms and a bright smile. "There's my girl," she said, laughing as she hugged me.

I immersed myself in the company of my friends and family. Looking around the room, I thought about how each one of them had touched my life and made me feel like I was truly loved. Isabelle was the sister that I'd always wanted. Robert was more like a brother. Mrs. Young was the one who had provided me with the womanly advice I needed growing up. Mattie was the only real connection that I had to the past. Given the circumstances, she did the best she could and finally, I appreciated her for that. What could I say about Alex? There were no words to describe what he meant to me. I realized they might not be flesh of my flesh, but they were family. Sometimes family is more than just a word.

When we returned home, I took a shower and got ready for bed. Mattie and Alex were downstairs shooting the breeze, talking about me no doubt. Just as I'd gotten comfortable and settled under the covers, I heard Alex enter the room.

He went into the bathroom and turned on the shower. I felt cold air on my naked flesh as he pulled back the covers. I lay there wide-awake, anticipating his next move. The hair on the back of my neck began to rise, and my body began to tingle as I felt his soft lips caress my spine. My muscles relaxed as he moved further down. My cheeks quivered slightly as he kissed each one. Pretending to wake from a deep slumber, I turned over and waited for him to explore further territory.

He outlined my lips with his tongue and caressed my neck. He suckled my breasts, manipulating my nipples with his tongue. I made love to Alex as if it were our last time. I wasn't sure what the future held for Alex and me, but I did know that I was going to L.A. to find Clark. Selling Alex's house for him was just the cover I needed. I settled in Alex's arms and enjoyed his embrace. He would be returning to Atlanta in the morning and I would begin my journey to L.A. I lay there, with my eyes closed and prayed that I would return safe and sound.

Alex spent most of the morning relaying instructions to me about the house and how things worked. He gave me security codes, safe combinations and a huge ring full of keys. He telephoned one of his friends in L.A. and arranged for him to leave one of the cars at the airport for me. He told me that he'd arranged to have the Range Rover left at the airport since I was comfortable driving one. Alex knew I liked to sit up high and feel the power of the Rover. I was pleased that he was giving me the responsibility of selling his house. I figured it would give me a chance to see how he had been living out there in L.A. The house in Atlanta was gorgeous, so I could only imagine what the house out west was like. Alex rattled off several other instructions. I took notes and waited for him to ask about the possibility of my seeing Clark, but he never did. I think he was afraid to admit my real reason for going to L.A. I really didn't want Alex to leave, but I knew he had to prepare for camp. As I watched him gather his things and prepare for his flight, I tried to freeze his face in my mind. As he walked past me, I shut my eyes and inhaled his cologne. It seemed like such a sullen time for me. I knew that if I did return alive, I would not be the same person standing before him.

I walked Alex to his rental. That moment seemed to be more significant to me than any other that we'd shared thus far. I felt my chest swell and my throat become dry. After Alex finished putting his things in the car he pulled me close and we kissed. We stood there for a long time, just holding one another. As I rested my head on his chest, I closed my eyes and listened to his heartbeat. I didn't want to let him go.

He looked down at me and said, "I picked a hell of a time to propose, didn't I? I'm leaving the love of my life just a few days after I got her back. How can I keep my mind on the game?"

I smiled and said, "I tell you what, if you get kicked off the team it's over. I only want you because you're Alex Young."

"Woman, please. You have wanted me ever since we were ten years old. I'm not even worried."

I held his hand and told him, "You'll be all right. I'll be home soon, and camp will be over before you know it."

He kissed me on the forehead and said, "I guess." He leaned back against the car. "Seth, I love you."

What he really wanted to say was, "Seth, please don't fuck up." We kissed one last time before he drove away. I stood at the edge of the driveway and watched until he disappeared. I walked back into the house and closed the door behind me. I leaned against it as I reached into my pocket and pulled out a piece of paper with Clark's phone number printed on it. Benson and Hawthorne Realty, Stewart Benson 323-555-5555. The piece of paper had been calling my name since the clerk at city hall in Dillon had given it to me. She told me that Benson and Hawthorne had owned that property for the past twenty years. She also said they got numerous inquiries about it each year, but it hadn't been purchased yet. She didn't go into detail, but spoke of the tragedy that happened years ago. I listened to her as if I was hearing about it for the first time.

I held the piece of paper tightly in my hand and took a seat on the steps. I sat there and listened to Mattie humming the melody to' Amazing Grace'. Her voice was so was passionate and powerful that it trickled down the stairs. She was clearly happy. I looked at the piece of paper and knew that if I picked up the phone and dialed the number there was no turning back. I knew hearing Clark's voice for the first time, would be like a drug to me, drawing me closer to him and forcing me to want to know more about him. I already wanted to know what in the hell he'd been doing all those years. Had he been living off my parent's money and if so how well was he living? Did he have a wife and children? Did he still have that same Louisiana accent that once fascinated me? Just who was Clark and, better yet, who was this Hawthorne person? Whoever Mr. or Mrs. Hawthorne was, I felt sorry for them. I didn't think they really knew who they were dealing with. As I sat there on that step alone, listening to Mattie, I couldn't help but think of how she'd feel if I introduced Clark back into our lives. Like she said, the memories of the past did not just belong to me alone. I contemplated discussing my intended conversation with her. I hadn't yet revealed to her that I had Clark's number. I listened to the happiness and jubilation in her voice and realized that no matter how temporary, I could not rob her of that joy. I placed the piece of paper back in my pocket, pulled myself up from the steps, went into my office, and locked the door behind me.

I looked at the clock. I think L.A. was two hours behind Houston. I pulled the paper out of my pocket, placed it on top of the desk, and leaned back in my chair. I started tapping my fingers as I sat there and watched the numbers on the clock change. Finally, I turned around, sat up straight and picked up the phone. I held the phone to my ear and listened to the dial tone until I heard the recording, "If you'd like to make a call..." I slammed the phone down and started tapping on my desk again. Suddenly, I took a deep breath, snatched the phone up and started dialing. As I listened to the phone ring, my stomach twisted into knots, my mouth watered and I could hear my stomach rumbling. I felt like I needed to go to the bathroom right then and there.

I was about to hang up, when I heard a voice say, "Hello? Benson and Hawthorne, how may I help you?"

When I opened my mouth to speak my voice cracked, "Yes, is Stewart Benson available?"

She was so animated, "I think Mr. Benson is on the other line, may I ask who is calling and what it's regarding?"

"Sure, my name is Seth St. James and I'm calling regarding the property in Dillon, Georgia."

"Ok. Please hold for a moment."

"Thank you." She put me on hold. I listened to the music as I waited for her to return to the phone and tell me that Mr. Benson would call me back.

I was ready to recite my phone number to the perky woman, when I heard a voice say, "Ms. St. James, this is Stewart Benson, how may I help you?" At first, I sat there quietly, trying to process the fact that I was talking to Ellis Clark Winfield after twenty years. I wanted to hang up and forget I'd ever heard his voice, but I couldn't move. His voice went through my body like water. I felt warm, and the receiver became slippery in my sweating hand.

As I tried to figure out what to say next, he said, "Ms. St. James, are you still there?"

I snapped out of my trance and said, "Yes, Mr. Benson, I'm sorry my secretary just walked in and I was a little distracted."

He laughed. "Don't apologize. I understand. It seems like every time I receive a call, someone walks into my office." I tried to listen for familiarities in his voice. His old accent was undetectable. I wasn't sure if it was just his phone voice, or if I had the right person. What if that guy wasn't Clark? What if Dr. Shaw and Charlie had the wrong information and I was about to hit a brick wall. I started to have doubts about the man. I wondered if a person could actually lose an accent entirely. I thought of Mattie. Her accent wasn't as distinct as it used to be, but you know it's different. I took a deep breath and engaged Mr. Benson in conversation.

"Well, Mr. Benson, I understand you're a busy man, so I won't keep you long. I'm calling in regard to the property in Dillon, Georgia on Winston Road. I visited Dillon recently and fell in love with the land. I'm interested in building on it."

He expressed what seemed to be some sort of laugh but I really don't know what it was. Then he said, "Yes, that is a beautiful piece of property, and ideal for a house. There's plenty of space and it's great if you love horses. Unfortunately, it's not on the market. I'm not interested in selling. I'm sorry, but I can help you find a similar property."

The fact that he didn't want to sell the property helped to ease my mind, I started to think that maybe he was Clark.

I tried to keep the conversation going. "Mr. Benson, I assure you that I can offer you a pretty substantial amount for that property, it's just what I've been looking for. If money is the issue, I'm sure we can work something out."

By the change in his tone, I could tell he was getting a little agitated. "I understand your fascination for the land, but it's just not for sale, under any circumstances. Once again, I'm sorry I can't help you."

I didn't want to piss him off so I agreed with him. "I understand. If I were you, I wouldn't part with the property either. I think I will take you up on your offer to find a similar property. I will be in L.A. in a few days taking care of some business and would love to set up a meeting with you."

I could hear him smiling through the phone. "Miss or is it Mrs. St. James?"

I couldn't believe it. Was he flirting over the phone? "It's Miss for now."

"Well, Miss St. James, I would be more than happy to meet with you, I'm sure we can find something that suits your obvious and, shall I say refined taste."

"Thank you so much for your assistance, Mr. Benson. I'm sure we can put our heads together and come up with something that will work for both of us."

"Yes, I'm sure."

"I'll be arriving on Thursday morning. Will you be able to meet around noon?"

"Sure, noon sounds great. I'm usually at one of my other establishments on Thursdays going over paperwork. My secretary will set up the appointment and give you directions."

"Thank you, Mr. Benson. I look forward to meeting you."

"Please call me Stewart."

"Ok, Stewart."

"Miss St. James ..."

"Yes?"

"Just how did you come across my contact information? The property was listed as a private owner."

"Well, Mr. Stewart. I was anxious to acquire the property, so I did some research, called in some favors and found you. I guess I'm just a little persistent when I see something that I want."

Stewart cleared his throat and expressed a little undefined chuckle. "So I see, well you and I should work well together, my job is to give the client what she wants." For some reason our conversation seemed more like foreplay than anything else. Just the way he responded to me told me his weakness was pussy, and if it was attached to a pretty face and a nice body then that made it even better. We said our goodbyes and he transferred me back to his secretary. The perky woman set up my appointment for Thursday at 12:30 pm. She gave me the address. I thanked her, and hung up the phone.

I leaned back in my chair and laughed to myself. I felt good about my trip to L.A. I actually couldn't wait to see old Clark once again. I decided not to tell Mattie why I was going to L.A. and stick to the story about selling Alex's house. Since our episode the previous day, Lauren's apprehension about meeting Clark no longer mattered to me. It was no longer what's best for us; it was what was best for me. Inside I was agonizing over what had actually happened between us because she was my blood sister. Hell, she was my fraternal twin. After yesterday, there was a side of me that just said screw her. I knew I had to tell Isabelle the truth about my trip to L.A. so I called and asked her to come over to the house. I needed to go over some things with her concerning the store. There was also the possibility that I would not return. I needed to go over some important personal papers as well. It all seemed so morbid and final, but I needed to prepare myself for anything. I picked up the phone and called Isabelle.

"Hey girl." She always sounded cheerful.

"Hey girl, what's going on with you today?"

"Nothing much. You know Kelly and Robert's sister are handling the store today, I'm tired. Yesterday wore me out."

"I understand that."

"You should. I'm surprised you're not lying under Alex right now."

"Don't I wish ... He left this morning."

"Oh, I thought he'd be here at least another day."

"No, he had to get back. He has rehab for his knee later today."

"Oh yeah, I forgot."

"Listen, I need you to come by here today. I really need to talk to you."

"Yes, of course. You need me to come right away?"

"No, there's really no rush, just whenever you can."

"Well it sounds like whenever I can means get over here right now. Have you heard from Lauren?"

"No, not since yesterday. To tell you the truth, I really don't want to talk to her anytime soon. Yesterday was too strange for me. I just don't like the way I let her push me to the edge like that."

"Hell, I didn't like it either. You messed up a perfectly good skirt, bleeding all over the place like a faucet." We laughed for a moment. Isabelle announced she would pick up a pizza on her way and would be here in about an hour. After we hung up, I decided my next move was to go upstairs and tell Mattie that I was going out of town. I exited my office and walked upstairs. Mattie was moving around the room, humming hymns. As I walked up the stairs, I smiled and reveled in the thought of us actually being happy for once. The closer I got to the door, the louder she seemed to hum. Something inside of me was beginning to stir. I didn't want to cry, scream or yell. I just wanted to feel good. I leaned on the wall outside of her room. After a moment, I walked over to the door and knocked softly.

"Come on in, Mrs. Young." Mattie smiled.

I laughed and said, "Not just yet."

"Oh yes, we've already claimed this one." She was very happy about my engagement. She was almost happier than I was. I walked over and sat down in the chair next to the window. I watched as Mattie spun around the room putting her laundry away.

"Have you talked to Lauren today?" Her question was fifty percent concern and fifty percent nosiness. She never stopped what she was doing as she spoke to me.

"No, I haven't. I think it's safe to say we won't hear from her for a while."

Matte dropped her head. "I sure do miss Noel. I hate that she's caught up in the middle of her mother's madness."

"I know. It's always the kids who suffer for the parents' insanity."

"Well, I know Noel will be ok. She's a tough little girl."

"That's what I keep telling myself."

"So, how does Alex feel about Noel leaving?"

"He's trying to be positive about it, but I know he's hurt. There was something about Noel that made everyone forget about all this other mess and concentrate on giving her the family she deserves."

"Yeah, she melted my heart, something I thought would never happen."

One thing was sure. Noel was definitely good for Mattie. I was glad that Mattie was able to transfer the love she never got to show Clark or me to Noel. Mattie looked at me and saw the effects of what had happened yesterday on my face.

"Sometimes we want to love someone and want to share our lives with them, but it's not always healthy for them or for you. We don't know anything about where Lauren's been or what she's been through. You need to face the fact that her showing up here might not have been for a fun loving family reunion. Maybe she just wanted to ease her mind and reassure herself that you were actually alive. I don't doubt that she loves you or that she loves Noel, but sometimes love just can't conquer all. You've done all you can do. You invited her into your life. You've treated her just like your sister. Now the rest is up to her. Give her time, when and if she's ready she'll come around. If she doesn't, it might be for the best."

Mattie looked up at me before she continued. "One thing you need to remember, favor ain't always fair. God blesses the child that's got his own. There are always going to be the haves and the have-nots. God ain't gone let nothin happen that's not in His will. What you need to do is pray and ask Him to help you do what is in His will and leave it alone. If it's meant for you two to have the relationship that sisters should have, then you will. The Bible speaks of separating yourself from confusion. Lauren is filled with confusion and chaos."

I thought about what she'd said for a minute. She was right. I reassured her that I was going to let it go and move on.

"Well, I've decided to let it be. I have too many other things to worry about right now. I'm going to L.A. for a few days. Alex wants me to put his house on the market and take care of a few other things for him while I'm there. I won't be long, I'm just gonna do what I need to do and come on back."

Mattie's face was full of disappointment. I waited for her to blast me out once again about some stupid decision I was about to make. I just knew she saw right through my reason for going to L.A. So, I waited to hear what she was going to say. She resumed folding her laundry.

"Ok, just be careful. I hear L.A. is a pretty fast and exciting place. When are you leaving?" I was totally shocked...for once she'd simply said, ok.

I responded before I could give her time to retract her thought. "I'll be leaving Thursday morning."

The words that came out of Mattie's mouth did not match her body language. I knew she wanted to say something negative about my trip, but she didn't say a word. As I was getting ready to comment further, the doorbell rang. I told her it was probably Isabelle. I sprang from my seat and headed for the door. Before I exited the room, I looked back at Mattie. Her back was turned and she had her hand on her head as if she were getting a headache. There was an uncomfortable look of worry on her face. I knew she was afraid of the real reason I was going to L.A., but for once she held her peace. I wanted to reassure her that I was not bringing Clark back into our lives. I was going to make sure that he never surfaced again. At that moment, a new thought entered my mind.

I planned to get rid of Clark for good and that would make me feel complete. But Clark was still her son, her flesh and blood. No matter how evil he was and how much he'd hurt her, he was still her son. How would she respond to me, knowing that I had taken the life of her only child? It was yet another burden that I'd have to bear. As I started down the steps Mattie started singing, picking up where she'd left off, only this time she sang the verses. I never realized what an amazing voice Mattie had, "When Jesus is my portion...a constant friend is he...his eye is on the sparrow...and I know he watches me..."

I opened the door to find Isabelle standing on the other side with a big grin on her face. She was holding my favorite pizza. She walked through the door and went straight into the kitchen. I grabbed a few sodas out of the refrigerator and brought the pizza from the kitchen into my office. I sat on one side of the desk and she sat on the other.

As she served the slices, she asked, "So what's up?" There was no need in sugar coating anything. Our conversation was way overdue.

I took a slice of pizza and said, "I'm going to L.A. the day after tomorrow. I need a couple of days to find a good wig and get some brown contact lenses."

"Wow, this all seems so final. I never really realized how dangerous this is. You have to change your look to protect yourself?"

"He may see my mother's resemblance on my face and I can't take that chance. My eye color and hair are just like my mothers. We even have the same teeth. I thought about cutting my hair, but I don't think I'm ready to make a move quite that drastic.

"I understand. I don't know. A part of me knows that you can take care of yourself, but the other half is really worried about you."

"Don't worry. Everything is gonna be all right. Just like in any other situation, I have to be prepared. I called you over here, because I want to make sure that someone knows where all my papers are." I pulled out a big envelope, "This is my will, and these are the keys to my safe deposit boxes. There are two, in two different locations. This is my bank account information. I went to the bank a few days ago and had your name put on my account. You have ten days to go to the bank and sign your name. This is my financial portfolio. It includes my stocks, mutual funds, and all of my investments. These are the papers for the store. My house, my car and Mattie's car are all paid for. My credit cards are all paid. Nothing will be left for anyone to have to carry as a burden. The house and the car will go to Mattie. The store will go to you. "

Isabelle clutched her chest, "You're giving me the store?"

"Of course, I was going to offer you a partnership anyway. These days you've been running it better than I have. We're family, plus I've always wanted to go into business with my sister." Isabelle smiled. She couldn't believe that I would leave the store to her, or that I would want her as my official business partner. I meant what I said about her being my sister. She was the closest thing that I had to having a sister before Lauren came back into the picture.

Isabelle placed her hand on the desk.   "All this talk about wills and who gets what... I'm beginning to feel uneasy about this. Are you sure you know what you're doing?"

"To be honest, no I don't know what I'm doing. I don't have a clue. I just know that I have to do something. If I don't, I'll never feel complete. I owe this to myself, and to my family."

"Why don't you just let me go with you?"

"No. Absolutely not! This is something I have to do."

"Ok. Then why don't I just go out with you for a few days, get you settled in and then come on back?"

"Isabelle!"

"Ok, but you call me if you need me and I'll be on the first thing to L.A."

"I know that you'll always have my back, but I need you to take care of Alex and Mattie."

Isabelle accepted the fact that I didn't want her to go to L.A. with me. After I went over everything in the envelope, she told me to put it back in the safe. She said that she was sure she wouldn't need the information because I'd definitely be back soon. She walked over to the safe and placed the papers back inside and locked them up. I'd given her the combination, just in case the worst did happen.

I told her that I had actually spoken with Clark over the phone. Or shall I say, Stewart, the man that I thought was Clark. "I called Clark, I mean Stewart, this morning."

"Oh my God, how do you feel?"

"I guess I'm kind of in shock. I won't be convinced that it's really him until I actually lay eyes on him. When I heard his voice on the phone, I froze. I wanted to hang up, but I gathered myself. I told him that I was interested in the property he had in Dillon. Of course, he told me it wasn't for sale, but I managed to set up an interview with him anyway. I'm sure it'll hit me once I see him."

"Clark's seems pretty smart. What if he's changed his appearance as well?"

"I thought about that, but if Dr. Shaw says he's Clark then I believe him. Hell, I'll collect his DNA if I have to."

"Then what?"

"Girl, I don't know. I'm just running out of ideas." We sat there for a moment laughing. "The one thing that worries me is how

275

I'll react to Clark. Sometimes, I can picture myself taking one look at him and blowing his brains out. I don't want to be impulsive. I want to get to know him and catch him when he's weak."

"Well Seth, you're a very interesting and charming woman, not to mention you're beautiful. I don't think you'll have any trouble getting what you want from this man."

"That's what I'd like to think."

"What does that mean?"

"Clark is a very charming man. He's got this certain appeal about him. I can't explain it. If there's one thing I remember about Ellis Clark Winfield, it's his ability to make you want to know more about him. He knows just what to say to get you right where he wants you. He had me spellbound when I was a child."

"Seth, you're not a little girl anymore. You're a grown woman who can damn sure take care of herself. Not too long ago, manipulating and charming men were part of your profession. Besides, he's what, almost sixty by now? How fine could he be after all these years. If he's lived his life like he used to all these years, I'm sure time has taken a toll on him."

"He's fifty."

"What?"

"Clark...he's fifty."

"Ok, he's twenty-two years older than you. I think he's all pimped out by now. Don't you?"

"Yeah, I guess you're right. I'm just acting silly trying to making excuses for my own fear."

"So, you admit you're afraid?"

"I'm scared as hell. I'm scared that I won't come back. I'm scared that I might have to actually take this man's life, and I'm scared of finding out the truth."

"Whew, I'm glad. For a minute I was worried. Fear keeps you from doing dumb shit. Every normal human being has to be afraid of something, as long as you don't let that fear consume you and cause you to make irrational decisions. I now know more than ever that you'll be just fine."

"I can't imagine making it this far in life to let my past destroy me. I mean, I escaped death twenty years ago. I survived a suicide attempt and the nut house. I'm not gonna pass up the chance to look into Clark's eyes, and watch him suffer as he tells me what really happened to my family."

"Just be careful and watch your back. Remember, if he killed once he'll do it again."

I appreciated Isabelle's concern and the fact that she was willing to pick up and take off with me but I needed to do it alone. We sat around for a while laughing and enjoying our time together before I went off into the great unknown. We didn't speak any more about my impending trip to California. We didn't discuss anything that was even remotely related to the subject. Isabelle said that she'd just rather think I was going on a vacation and would return shortly.

She brought a few bridal magazines with her and also sketched out a few bridesmaid dresses. Isabelle could do anything. She always wanted to own her own restaurant and design clothes. I think once she married Robert she was happy and content to put her dreams on hold.

The day before my trip to L.A. was just as agonizing and time consuming as my departure for Dillon. I tried to keep myself busy with odd jobs around the house. I did everything I could to pass the time. The night before my trip, I was like a kid, repacking my suitcase at least five times. I made sure my room was neat and tidy. I hated leaving my house unorganized before a trip. I knew it was strange, but I always thought that if someone broke in at least they wouldn't think I was a slob. I really didn't know what I was worried about since Mattie would be there to keep the house up. I watched television all night, and each time a picture went off, I would say, "That's thirty minutes down." I popped in a DVD. I figured a movie would make the time go by faster. I managed to doze off, but after an hour I woke up and walked outside to sit by the pool where the air was cool and comfortable. I wasn't thinking of anything in particular. My mind was jumping from one subject to the next. I didn't talk to God. I don't think I wanted to hear what He was going to tell me. I knew what I was about to do was wrong in His eyes, and I would need His protection.

Finally, the sun came up and it was time to get ready. I took a shower, got dressed and prepared to change my hair and eye color. I wrapped my hair and placed the thin stocking cap on my head. I put the wig on and took a double take. The short hair made me look a bit older and more mature. In a way I liked it. I did some touch up curling and combing, trying to make it look as natural as possible. I wanted it to look like the hair growing out of my head. I'd paid four hundred bucks for it. I wanted to make sure it didn't look fake and wiggish. I checked to make sure my contacts were in the case. I decided to put them on after I reached L.A. I remembered that I had green eyes on my driver's license. I didn't want any mess at the airport about my ID.

The cab driver met me on the front steps. I handed my bags to him and told him I would be out soon. I stood at the bottom of the stairs and looked around the house. I took baby steps toward the door and inhaled the fresh fragrance of Magnolia lingering in the air. I stood there for a moment. It was time to leave. I couldn't put it off any longer. I walked toward the door and took one last look before closing it behind me. Like Lots wife, I was afraid that I might perish if I looked back, so I kept going and just hoped that when I returned everything would be just as I'd left it.

When I climbed into the cab, the driver asked if I was ok. I assured him that I was fine. I reached inside my bag to make sure I had enough cash to pay him. I came across something unfamiliar. I pulled out a manila envelope. I turned the envelope upside down, and the picture of my mother, father and Clark that I'd found in Mattie's closet fell out. I picked up the picture and held it to the light. I smiled to myself and placed the picture back in the envelope. As we drove off, I placed my chin on the window as I'd done twenty years ago when I realized my life would never be the same. With the same sentiment, I realized once again that things were about to change.

Chapter Twenty-Three

I inhaled the L.A. air and noticed the distinct difference from the air in Houston. Houston had a stifling heat, and it was extremely humid. You could forget trying to maintain your hairstyle. I'd been in L.A. for a total of ten minutes, and loved it already. The moment I stepped off the plane, my mood had changed. I was more confident and comfortable about meeting with Clark. Actually, I was anxious and couldn't wait to finally see him. All I needed to do was lay eyes on him. As I walked through the lot trying to find Alex's truck, I enjoyed the sun.

Finally, I found the car. It was right where it was supposed to be. I hit the unlock button on the remote and listened as I heard the truck sound off confirming that I had the right vehicle. I placed my things in the back and hopped in the driver's seat. The truck was almost identical to mine except the inside had some sort of high technology convention going on. There were all kinds of electronics, I couldn't tell the radio from the DVD player. I was too tired and frustrated to figure out how to use the radio. So, I decided to just hum a tune. When I rolled out of the lot, I reached down and accidentally hit some button and the radio came on full blast. I slammed on brakes and fumbled around until I found the volume button. I felt like an idiot, I was sitting there shaking like a leaf in the wind. When I finally became settled, I shook my head, adjusted my mirrors and pulled out the directions to Clark's meeting place.

I drove through the streets of L.A. enjoying the scenery. I enjoyed seeing palm trees that weren't imported. I'd almost reached my destination when I began to wonder if I was in the right neighborhood. I failed to ask Clark where I would be meeting him exactly. I was looking for Cordova Street. Once I reached it, I looked down at the paper to make sure I had the correct address. The address I'd gotten off the Internet and the address that his secretary had given me matched. I couldn't believe it. This fool had me meeting him at a place called Paradise Island, a strip club. I knew it had to be a mistake, so I called his office to make sure. The phone rang three times before the perky woman answered.

"Hello, Benson and Hawthorne, how may I help you?"

With a frustrated tone I said, "Hello, this is Seth St. James and I'm scheduled to meet Mr. Benson at 12:30. I think I may have written the address down wrong. It appears this address is for some type of adult entertainment club."

The woman on the other end of the phone laughed. "If it's Paradise Island, you're at the right place."

I sat back in my seat and said, "Oh, all right then. I guess I do have the right place, thanks." I didn't even wait for her response. I ended the call and shook my head. I must have sat for about fifteen minutes before going in. I was fifteen minutes early anyway. Finally, I grabbed my purse and got out of the truck.

I opened the door to the club and walked in. The light was dim. I took my sunglasses off and tried to adjust to the sudden change. All eyes were on me as I made my way to the bar and asked if Mr. Benson had arrived yet. The girl behind the bar, and I do mean girl, said he was expecting me, and would arrive shortly. She looked too young to be working in a shake joint. She told me to have a seat and she would bring me a drink. I ordered a rum and coke. As I located an available seat, I looked around the bar and remembered my old college days. The more things changed, the more they stayed the same. I remembered going to those types of clubs with Alex, when we were just friends. I wouldn't dare go with him now.

I sat there and waited for Clark to arrive. I wasn't at all uncomfortable meeting him in one of his establishments as he called it. I did however find it very distasteful on his part to request that we meet in a strip club when he knew absolutely nothing about me. I could have easily been offended. Clark's choice of meeting places helped me understand what I was really dealing with. He was still a piece of funky old trash. It was just like him to own a place like this. I looked around at the men and some women sitting around half drunk watching some young girl or some woman way past her prime swinging on a pole and clapping her ass cheeks to the latest tunes. Didn't these people have jobs? The place wasn't even a high-class joint. It was a smoky cloud of confusion. The nudity didn't bother me, I was used to it. Hell, I used to pimp flesh for a living. Back in the day, that was how I recruited my team. Flesh is flesh. Those women didn't have anything I hadn't seen before. Some had more assets than I did and some had less. I hoped I didn't look like I was having a good time. I wanted to make it clear that I was only there to meet Clark and not for the entertainment. It was the middle of the afternoon and I was sitting in a strip joint drinking hard liquor. As I took my first sip, I laughed to myself.

For the first time, I actually sat there and studied those women. I wondered about their stories, why were they there. Some of those girls were barely legal, not even old enough to drink. They still had milk on their breath and were in there peddling ass. You could tell the ones that were fresh from the Greyhound. They came out to L.A. to fulfill their hopes and dreams of becoming stars. Other women were here trying to make ends meet, working to feed their children or trying to make it through school. Others just didn't give a damn; they loved it and wouldn't have it any other way. I thought about my college days, and wondered how my girls were doing. I wondered which ones were tricked out and at the point of no return. I wondered about the ones who had graduated and were unable to list their work experience on job applications. In a way, I felt ashamed about my past and in another way, I felt as though I did what I had to do. I was no different than anyone of these women. While I was patiently sitting there waiting, a girl came over and proceeded to attempt a lap dance. I politely held up my hand and pointed her to the next two tables over. I definitely didn't want her to think I was interested by any means. I thought about what I was about to do. I wasn't getting ready to swing on that pole or walk the strip, but I was getting ready to pimp myself. I was ready to do whatever I needed to bring that man down and to destroy his world completely. If that meant swingin' on a pole, then I was down for whatever.

I glanced at my watch and noticed that Clark was fifteen minutes late. I hoped he hadn't stood me up, although I wouldn't put it past him. At that moment, I realized I didn't know what he looked like. I thought of what Isabelle had said that he may have changed his features...I mean he was supposed to be dead. I also had to remember that I was meeting Stewart Benson not Ellis Clark Winfield. It was time that I started to refer to him as Stewart. I made a mental note that Clark was dead and I had to think of him as Stewart. It was crazy, but even though I remembered his voice, I could not remember what he looked like. In my mind, his face and my father's face seem so cloudy. I did remember his distinct Cajun-French accent. When I was child I used to love to hear him talk. It was like he was from another country. It was funny how I never noticed Mattie's accent until I found out that she was Clark...I mean Stewart's mother. Mattie's accent had never been as distinct as Stewart's. There was a noticeable difference. I remembered Stewart as being smooth. Back then, smooth was in. I could tell by his many lady friends, that he thought of himself as a Casanova or Don Juan. My mother used to call him "Nickel Slick." I assumed it meant he was sneaky and couldn't be trusted. One thing I did remember about Stewart was his eyes. He had these piercing green eyes. I know it sounds crazy, but they changed color in the sunlight.

My patience was wearing thin, and then I heard a deep voice coming from behind me. "Miss St. James?" I turned to look over my shoulder and there he was, old Clark, in the flesh.

I said, "You must be Mr. Benson." To my surprise, my emotions remained intact, and I managed to maintain my cool. As I stood up to greet him, he extended his hand, and our hands connected. I stared deep into his eyes. Mattie was wrong, I didn't see the devil at all. I saw revenge. I was overwhelmed and consumed with hatred. I couldn't believe the fire that was burning inside me. It was like touching his flesh opened the door to Pandora 's Box. My body was warm from the tips of my toes to the top of my head. I knew there was no turning back. I wanted this man's heart in a jar above my fireplace. I could feel myself changing inside. I'd tried so hard to suppress my dark side, but I could no longer pretend that it didn't exist.

I studied him carefully. I had to admit, he'd held up well. He was clearly not a man riddled with guilt. This was a slimy snake that had more restful nights than I did. Stewart was what we in the south, called a redbone. He was a Louisiana redbone. His hair was jet black with thick silky curls. He was very clean cut with an immaculate hairline that contoured the shape of his face. His mustache and goatee outlined his full lips that led the way to his perfectly straight white teeth. His skin was flawless and smooth, like butter. His thick eyebrows and long lashes accented the shape of his eyes. I didn't realize how tall he was. I guess when I was a child everyone was taller, so I never noticed. Stewart was at least six two and appeared to be in great shape. His suit was tailor made to fit his well-maintained body. The years had certainly been kind to him. If it weren't for the fact that I knew he was a lying murderer, I would say he was fine. Ok, I could admit that the man was gorgeous and he knew it. This was going to be a piece of cake. Stewart obviously thought very highly of himself. I could tell by the way he'd greeted me. He leaned in and kissed my hand. He was the type of man that thought that his shit didn't stink. That was fine with me. I knew just what to do for him.

You see, a man like that wouldn't see it coming. He thought he couldn't be played. One thing that weighed even more in my favor was that I was going to be a challenge for him. He was used to dating women who wanted him just because he looked good and appeared to have some change in his pockets. He went for the women that he could wine and dine. He liked to pay for the coochie. That way he made them feel obligated to take his shit. I bet he drove some sort of high priced two-seater. I glanced at his hands to see if he was wearing a pinky ring, and there it was shining like the North Star.

He licked his lips before he spoke. "I must apologize for being late. My meeting ran much longer than I'd expected." To my amazement the accent was gone. I didn't know it was possible to get rid of an accent completely. "Please, let's go to my office. This really doesn't seem like the sort of environment that you're used to."

"Well, Mr. Benson..."

"Please, call me Stewart."

"Ok, Stewart, you appear to be very perceptive."

"Can I offer you another drink? I see that you were quenching your thirst while awaiting my arrival." Who in the hell did he think he was? Quenching your thirst...awaiting my arrival... what kind of shit was that? If I stood there much longer, I was going to throw up. While he led me to his office, he stopped at the bar.

"I'm sorry, what were you drinking?"

I looked at him without hesitating and said, "Rum and Coke." He raised his eyebrows as if her were shocked by my drink preference. I declined his offer to have another. "Thank you, Stewart. I'm fine for now."

"You sure are." He obviously didn't mean for me to hear him.

"Excuse me, were you speaking to me?"

"Oh, no I was just thinking out loud, I do that sometimes, it's a terrible habit."

"Yes, so I see."

This man clearly did not have an ounce of decency. He had me meet him in a strip joint. He had basically undressed me with his eyes since he introduced himself. My next guess was that he was going to offer to take me out and show me the city. Unfortunately, he would not get the chance to wine and dine me like his many other conquests. I knew just what to do for him. Once we reached his office, I made myself as comfortable as I could in his presence. He offered me a seat on the couch. I declined and chose to sit in the chair in front of his desk. He took the hint and sat behind the desk. He leaned back in his swivel chair and rested his foot on his knee.

"Well, Miss St. James I was shocked when you requested to meet me in person. What's so special about this one little piece of property?"

"Please, call me Seth."

"Ok, Seth, what's up?"

"Well, Stewart it's really not that complicated. I am in L.A. for a few days trying to take care of a few things for my fiancé. We're actually selling the property here in L.A. since he no longer works here. We both have separate homes right now and we want to build something that will be ours. Right now he's working in Atlanta and we want to live outside of the city. I thought that since I was in the area I would see if I could persuade you in person."

"So, you're attached."

I decided to flirt, just enough to leave the door open. "Yes, but I'm not married yet." I crossed my leg so my skirt would rise revealing a prelude to my thigh. I could tell by the look in his eye that he was impressed.

"So, you still haven't told me, why this particular property. How did you even find it? It's not advertised, nor is it even on a main road." I took a chance and prayed that I wouldn't blow it.

"My fiancé's doctor invited us for a barbeque and I just fell in love with the area, it's so quiet and secluded. We need all the privacy we can get. Doc lives right next to the property. He said he's lived there almost forever and he loves it." I watched for his reaction. Even though I didn't mention Dr. Shaw's name he knew exactly who I was talking about. "I just can't believe you have that beautiful piece of land out there and you're not doing a thing with it."

Stewart's expression never changed, I did notice that he was paying more attention my lips than he was to anything else.

"The truth is Seth, I haven't seen that property in a few years, I've actually neglected it. I can't imagine what you find so appealing about it." It seemed like he was fishing for something. Or maybe I was paranoid.

"Actually, it is rather unkempt, but I can see by the other homes around, that it has great potential."

Stewart resumed an upright position in his chair. "Seth, I wish I could help you, but I just can't. That place has a lot of special memories for me. It belonged to someone that I loved very much. Selling it to you would be like dishonoring their memory."

At that point, I think I reached a boiling point. Was he actually referring to my family? He used the word their, he didn't say his or her, he said their. Was his subconscious allowing him to express his guilt or did he have another angle? I took a deep breath before I opened my mouth.

"Oh my goodness Stewart, I never stopped to think that you knew the poor family that was killed in that fire. I must seem so insensitive, I am so sorry."

Stewart looked at me like he just swallowed something that had a bad taste to it.

"Fire, how did you know there was a fire there?" I decided to ease his troubled mind. "Well, Doc didn't know who the property belonged to, so I went to City Hall to find out who owned the deed. It was listed as a private owner and Benson and Hawthorne were the deed holders. While I was there the clerk commented on the tragedy that had occurred, I think she said over twenty years ago."

Stewart eased himself back in the chair. "Did the Clerk give you any other Dillon historical facts?"

I laughed as if to support the fact that he was telling a joke.

"She didn't say anything else." That put him at ease, and he noticeably relaxed. I thought I would bait him once more before we closed the subject.

"Oh, she did mention that it was said to be some sort of crazy love triangle between the husband, the wife and the husband's business partner. They suspected the business partner, but the charges were dropped. I guess it was just one tragedy after another, because the business partner was killed in a car accident."

Attempting to appear apologetic, I placed my hand over my mouth. "Oh, I am so sorry. I'm usually not this insensitive."

Stewart remained calm. "No, I didn't know those people. Actually, I was equally impressed by the property. I purchased it for my fiancée as a wedding gift. Unfortunately just as we were preparing to build she was killed in a car accident."

I sat there totally shocked. I wondered how long it took him to create a fake fiancée or did it just come out naturally? As I was sitting there with my empathetic face on, I was trying not to leap over the desk and choke the shit out of him.

I could see that he wasn't going to budge about the property. That was fine. I really didn't expect him to sell it to me. I wasn't worried. It would be mine soon enough. He reached into the humidor on his desk and pulled out a cigar.

"Do you mind if I smoke?"

"Actually, I do." He stopped in the midst of lighting the cigar, placed it on the desk and rested the lighter beside it. "Thank you for your consideration." I watched as he smiled and leaned back in his chair.

"Miss St. James. I wish that I could help you, but I'm sure you understand why I can't part with the land."

"Yes, I understand. I must admit, I am disappointed. If you ever decide to sell please think of me."

"I'm sure I'll think of you regardless."

"Why, Mr. Benson, are you flirting with me?"

"Is it working?"

"Maybe."

"Then, I'm flirting."

"You do remember that I am engaged."

"Yes, but like you said you're not married yet."

Everything seemed to be falling into place. He was definitely interested and about to burst the seams of his pants. He was practically drooling on himself.

"Listen, Seth why don't you let me show you L.A."

I knew it!

"Ideally that would be great, but I've been to L.A. dozens of times."
I was lying, but he didn't need to know that.

He smiled, "Oh, yeah, I forgot your fiancé has a house here."

"Correct."

"Ok, then why don't you just let me take you out for a drink?"

"I think I've had my quota for the day."

"Well damn, do you eat? Can I take you out to dinner?" I revealed a
smirk and acted as if he'd worn me down.

"I guess that can be arranged."

I agreed to have dinner with him. Of course, I didn't want him to
know where I was staying, so I agreed to meet him at 8:00. He claimed
he knew the owner of Mariano's and promised I'd have the best Italian
meal I'd ever eaten. We exchanged cell phone numbers and confirmed
our "date." After the meeting, and just as I knew he would, Stewart
offered to walk me to my car. He said he was on his way out as well. I
knew he just wanted me to see the masterpiece he was driving. We
walked through the club. The crowd was growing. As we passed
though, the regulars greeted Stewart like he was God, and he was
eating it up. We passed one of the strippers giving a lap dance to some
old guy who looked like he could go into cardiac arrest at any time.
Just as we were about to reach the exit, this tiny little thing with
skintight pants and huge implants rushed over to Stewart. You could
tell she was familiar with him. She was probably one of his backroom
whores that gave him a free taste whenever he wanted it. She tried her
best to look professional with her basement weave and tight polyester
and rayon blend suit. He had probably convinced her that she was his
main piece. Strictly, for my benefit, he pushed her away and told her
he would be with her in a minute.

She looked at him with utter confusion and glanced over at me as if
to say, "Who is this bitch?" Just as I figured, that no class trick decided to make her presence known. She looked me up and down and said,
"Stew, who is this bitch? I know you ain't thinkin' 'bout hiring her.
We don't need any new girls around here."

She didn't even realize how stupid she had made herself look.
Stewart politely apologized and told me she was the office manager.
Office manager? Please...she needed to manage that mess she was
wearing. This atmosphere was taking me to a whole new level that I
didn't wish to reveal. Stewart was trying to maintain his composure.

If I had been anyone else, he would have slapped her. Just as I tried to walk past her, she stepped in front of me and stuck her chest out. She was underestimating my Tahari suit and Stuart Weitzman pumps. I leaned close enough for her and Stewart to hear me.

"You better back up. I'll pop that plastic you're sticking in my face. I promise, you don't want none of this."

I walked past her and made my way to the exit. I noticed a two-door Mercedes coupe next to the truck. Stewart played with his remote to let me know he was driving that fine piece of German engineering. Once I reached the truck, I noticed that little scene seemed to have turned him on.

"Girl you got some fire in you, those eyes, that hair, your skin ... Where are you from?"

I stepped into Alex's Range Rover. Before closing the door, I looked at him through my sunglasses and said, "You'll find out soon enough."

I closed the door and drove off, watching him as he watched me through my rearview mirror. He was obviously impressed.

After I left the club, I checked in with Alex, letting him know I'd made it in ok. I made sure I called at a time that I knew he would be unavailable. I was good for that, probably because I was always up to something. I didn't want to tell him I was meeting Stewart for dinner. I damn sure didn't want to tell him I was planning to use my feminine assets to get close to him either. I hated lying to Alex, but I was willing to risk it.

I finally reached the house. It was absolutely gorgeous. It was about the size of my home, but the architecture was what really set it off. Everything in Cali was pretty much made of Stucco. I punched in the code at the gate and waited for it to open. I drove through and opened the garage. There were three garage doors, and I opened each one. The first one was empty. I guessed that was where the Rover lived. The second one housed a brand new McLaren Mercedes Benz. Behind the next door was a Black Denali. All of Alex's cars were black. I drove into the vacant space and parked the truck.

I bypassed the Benz and walked straight to the Denali. I don't know why I ignored the Mercedes, but something led me to the truck. I pulled out the keys that Alex had given me before I left. I pushed the disarm button on one of the remotes and the Benz started chirping. I tried the next one and the Range went off. The last one unlocked the Denali. I hopped into the driver's seat to back it out for closer observation.

I almost peed on myself when the damn thing started talking. "Hello, Mr. Young, don't forget to buckle your seatbelt." I laughed aloud, as I backed the truck out and walked around it, studying it very carefully. You could tell the car belonged to a man. Every seat had a television in the headrest in front of it. There was a DVD player, a PlayStation and countless other gadgets and do-dads, and it sat on spinning rims. Alex definitely has some hood in him, and I loved it. I stood there for a minute and decided that, that would be my transportation of choice. It was the whole vibe the truck was giving off. It spoke class, but the spinners made it street. Stewart wouldn't know what to expect, when he saw me jump out of this truck, all suited and booted. He would be confused. I parked the truck back in its place and popped the lock on the Benz.

I felt like a kid in a candy store. The car was gorgeous. I opened the door and sat down in the driver's seat. You would've thought that I wasn't used to a damn thing, the way I was acting. I put the keys in the ignition, and things started to move. The steering wheel came toward me and stopped just where I needed it. The seat adjusted to my body perfectly and the pedals came to me. That damn car talked too. "Hello, Mrs. Alexander Young, your husband absolutely adores you."

This time I didn't laugh out loud, I put my hands up to my face and smiled so hard my cheeks hurt. I looked in the mirror because I knew I was blushing. I looked over in the seat and there was an envelope. I pulled the card out and read it. "To my future, this is just the beginning. Sit back and enjoy the ride, Love Alex."

Well, of course, you know I was on cloud nine. I sent him a two-way saying, "Enjoying the ride, love Seth." I sat there for a minute appreciating that moment of freedom from the madness. I prayed for God, to please help me. I didn't want to mess things up.

Chapter Twenty-Four

I put on a pair of black linen pants that fit tight on my hips and flared at the bottom. I teamed that with a black silk blouse, which was cut low in the front. The V stopped just below my breasts. Low enough so that everything would be sure to stay in its place, but let you know they were there. I accessorized with chains around my neck, making sure they were dangling between my breasts and the opening in my blouse. I wore my stiletto heels with the toe and back out, and a simple strap across the top. I hopped in the Denali, arranged my music selection and I was on my way. I listened to my missed messages. Of course there was one from Alex, demanding that I call him before the night was over. "Seth, I don't know what the hell you doin' out there, but you better call me before the night is over. I'm not playin' woman. I do know the way to my own house." I wondered if he meant before the night was over in L.A. or Atlanta. I took my chances with L.A. time.

I pulled up to the restaurant and hoped that Stewart hadn't made it yet. I really wanted some time to relax and prepare myself for the date. I checked myself one more time in the mirror to make sure everything was in place. I grabbed my accessories, hopped out of the truck and handed my keys to the valet. The guy looked at me and smiled.

"This is nice."

I looked at him, smiled and handed him a tip. "Yes, and I want it back just the way I gave it to you, CD on track 8 and everything."

He smiled and said, "No doubt."

I walked into the restaurant and approached the host. I asked him if Stewart Benson had arrived yet. He informed me that Mr. Benson had not yet arrived, but I was welcome to wait in the lounge. I followed his lead, and saw two glass doors trimmed in mahogany wood. I nodded my head and thanked the host. I walked toward the lounge, turned the brass knobs on the door and walked in. Once the doors were open the sultry sounds of R&B filled the air. There was a live band, and a mid-sized woman was sitting on a stool signing her heart out. The place had a nice laid-back atmosphere. I really would have rather be in there than out there with the general population. As I walked in, I made eye contact with the bartender. After he scanned my entire body, from head to toe, he gave a nod of approval. I glanced over the room looking for a place to relax. I spotted a table in a corner close enough to the bar where it wouldn't take too long for my drinks to arrive. The woman's voice relaxed me as she sang' If You Don't Know Me By Now'. It was like a breath of fresh air, and it put me in a tranquil mood. I sat down and made myself comfortable.

The bartender made his way over and asked for my drink order. I asked for his best Cognac. He stood there for a moment and looked at me as if, he were trying to figure out if he heard me right.

Finally, he said, "Yes, I'm sure I can find something special just for you." I requested an ashtray as well.   "Certainly,   I   apologize. There should have been one on the table."

I gave him a smile and said, "Don't worry, it's not a problem. Just don't forget to bring it back when you return." As the bartender walked away, he glanced back at me and smiled.

Just as he was resuming his position behind the bar, I noticed a man sitting at the table directly across the room. I don't know how I missed him. He was very noticeable with his massive size. He was a bald, black man dressed all in black. He was reading the newspaper and drinking some sort of dark liquor. We made eye contact, but he didn't part his lips to smile or even change his expression, he simply went back to reading his paper. I wondered why he was sitting there alone. I studied the others who were sitting in the lounge and wondered about each of them. I wondered why they were there. Some people were alone just like me. Some were with other people. I guess I have some sort of fascination with other peoples' lives. I liked trying to figure out if they could possibly be in situations as bad as mine.

The waiter came back with my drink, and the ashtray. He asked if there was anything else I needed. I told him not right now. I informed him that I was waiting for someone. He gave me an understanding nod and informed me that I have the option of dining in the lounge. I thanked him for the information and sat back in my chair, which was more like a recliner and very comfortable. A person could sit there, get drunk and go straight to sleep. I reached in my purse and pulled out my cigar, clipped the ends, lit it and took a drag. I knew it was a bad habit, and not very lady-like, but some things were just a part of me and I didn't have to apologize for them. I appreciated a good cigar and a fine cognac. Hell, at that point I deserved crack, acid, speed, heroin ... anything to take the edge off. That was the only secret that Robert and I kept from Isabelle. He also appreciated a good cigar. Whenever he bought his cigars, he always made sure he kept me supplied as well. Isabelle would have had a fit if she knew I smoked cigars. I didn't even think she knew that I drank anything other than fruity cocktails.

I sat for a while enjoying myself. For a moment, I was somewhere else. I didn't know where, but I wasn't sitting there waiting for Stewart. I was getting so comfortable that I'd lost track of time. I looked at my watch and realized Stewart was now thirty minutes late. I checked my phone to see if there was a missed a call. There was nothing from him. Even though I was enjoying my solitude, I was becoming pissed off. Being late without calling was certainly a sign of a man who was full of shit. Even though I already knew this, it still didn't make it right. I took a sip of my drink and another drag from my cigar and looked around the room once more. Everyone was still in his or her place. The large gentleman in the corner had not moved, he was still reading the paper. There were now two new people sitting at the bar. They were white women who were obviously having a good time. They were smoking, laughing and drinking. They looked like money. I wondered if I looked like money. It was easy to draw your own conclusion from my aura that day. I mean here I was, driving around L.A. in a Denali, sitting on twenty-two inch rims that spun around like a top. My music of choice at the time was The Game, followed by the ultimate Tupac mix. Not too far behind was a little R&B thrown in. I was sitting at the bar alone drinking Cognac that cost over $300 a bottle and smoking a premium cigar as I waited for a pimp. Sounded crazy to me, but I guess that's where I need to be right then. On the contrary, in Houston, I had a very modest Range Rover with all factory equipment sitting in the garage. Nothing but jazz and blues was in the changer. On an average day I was pretty much suited. I thought to myself, "Why did I pick now to go outside the box?" Whatever was going on, it felt good. I felt comfortable with myself. I was away from home and I could do or say whatever the hell I wanted to. I guess everyone had a little hood in them or at least, they should have.

Just when I was about to take another sip, I saw Stewart walk through the door. He looked straight in my direction, pointed and smiled. My expression didn't change nor did my seat. He stood there for a moment waiting for me to get up and greet him, but I kept my seat. He was very well groomed as usual and he smelled great. That was really the only positive thing that I had to say at that point about old Stew. I pointed to the vacant seat and offered it to him without saying a word. He pulled the seat away from the table, sat down, and made himself comfortable.

"I apologize for being late, I was held up at the club, you know how it is." At that point, I figured I would take the time to point out his unsuccessful attempt at establishing who was in control. I leaned over to make sure that he was the only person who would hear, but I stayed far enough away to keep boundaries.

"No, I really don't know how that is. You were late to prove you can keep me waiting. Well, I'll give you this one, but it won't happen again. The next time you feel that you'll be held up, you pick up the phone and call or you will be sitting somewhere by yourself. I'm a grown woman, I put Barbie up a long time ago, if you wanna play, then you play with those dolls down at the club. I hope I've made myself clear."

I took my eyes off him for just and second, looked back at him without giving it a second thought and calmly said, "I hear the salmon here is quite appetizing." I sat back in my chair and waited for his response. He raised his eyebrow and it was clear he'd been totally caught off guard. He stroked his goatee and motioned for the bartender to come to the table. He had not yet responded to my verbal blast. I really wanted to know what was going through his head. He sat there for a minute looking at me. The waiter came over and asked him for his drink order.

Stewart said, "I think I'll have whatever she's having. It seems to have put some hair on her chest." The waiter confirmed what I was drinking. Stewart looked at the bartender then looked at me. "What?"

The bartender said, "Yes, that's what the lady is drinking, will you two be sharing an ashtray or will you require your own?" I guess Stewart hadn't noticed the smoke coming from my direction.

He looked over, smiled and replied, "I think I'll need my own, thanks." As the waiter walked away, I noticed that the man across the room had left. When I focused my attention back on Stewart, he was staring at me. I asked him if he was hungry, he said yes and searched the table for a menu. He handed one to me and grabbed one for himself. Suddenly he dropped his menu.

"Who the hell are you?" For a minute, I was just slightly thrown.

"What do you mean?"

"I don't know...there's just something about you. I mean I have never met a woman with your confidence before. How many women do you know who sit around, drink top shelf cognac, smoke cigars and act as if it's an everyday thing? Not to mention you had the nerve to check me about keeping you waiting. Earlier today you seemed totally different."

I interrupted him, "It's like night and day, huh?"

"Hell yeah, that's what it is, night and day."

"Well that's me, unpredictable, you never know what to expect."

"I see. How does Alex handle this side of you?"

I think that at that very moment you probably could have peeled me out of that chair. I hoped my facial expression didn't show my uneasiness at his mention of Alex. I thought to myself, I have to remain calm and play along. How the hell did he know about Alex? I just knew my cover was blown.

"Alex accepts me for who I am. He knows exactly what I do, and he can't get enough of me."

"I'm sure he can't." His mind was clearly in the gutter. I took the opportunity to find out how he knew about Alex.

"I see someone has been in my business."

He flashed those beautiful teeth and all I could think of was the devil. It is so easy to be tempted by the flesh. If I haven't said it before, I'll say it now, he was one handsome full grown man. I was feeling the liquor along with the cigar and the emotion that came next was, of course, lust. I sat there and pictured Alex's head on his body. (I would be doing that quite a bit.) Even though Stewart was fine, I needed a little more motivation.

He took a sip of his drink and said, "Well, you know the Garden of Eden was destroyed by a woman. Solomon lost his strength behind a woman and you see Ruth got her man...shall I go on? When you walked into my office I had to do my homework, a whole lotta women would love to see me hemmed up. I just checked the license plate of your truck earlier and to my surprise it was my old friend Alex Young."

This mutha fucka actually knew what happened in the Bible besides "In the beginning..." More importantly, how did he know Alex?

I asked, "And how do you know Alex?"

"Well, I don't actually know Mr. Young. Of course I know of him and we have a few people in common. I can assure you it's nothing to worry about. No one would ever put the two of us together."

"Thanks for your concern, but I have everything under control in the Young household."

He licked his lips and said, "I just bet you do." His lips were like ripe strawberries just waiting to be tasted. I just enjoyed the view.

We finally placed our order. I needed something to cushion the liquor and cigar. While we were waiting for dinner, we engaged in a little chitchat. Stewart opened the conversation with the subject of the land in Dillon.

"Listen, I hope you understand about me not being able to sell the land in Georgia. I just can't part with it."

"Don't worry. It's all right. I think I'll get what I need soon enough."

"Why do I get the feeling that you always get what you want?"

"Well, I've always felt that life is too damn short and you should never say what if. So I set my sights on something and I go for it."

"Really? What's your new...shall I say...`project?'"

"Oh, there's something big that I'm planning to catch."

"Do you think this one will be easy to catch?"

"I've already caught it. It just needs to be reeled in. It won't be much longer now."

Stewart raised his glass as if he were in agreement and took the last few sips of his drink. The food finally arrived, and while we ate, we continued to talk.

"So tell me, do you have a job of your own or does Alex take care of your needs?" He was asking me if I met Alex because I was a groupie.

I politely dispelled the rumor that all women who dated professional athletes are gold diggers and groupies. "No, actually Alex and I have been friends since we were kids. It took a while for us to get together, but we did. I own my own clothing boutique...and no he didn't buy it for me...I bought it myself. And yes, he does take care of my needs, thank you."

"Ok, I was just wondering. You never know, women are a trip now-a-days."

"And so are men."

"Well tell me this, if Alex takes care of your needs, then why are you here with me?"

"Right now, we are just two associates having dinner. It's all very innocent. If I do choose to go outside of my relationship then that's my choice. It has nothing to do with Alex's inability to satisfy me. It's called human nature. People are no different than animals. We're all a little curious. I know the way back home when I'm done."

"What makes you think you'll want to go back home?"

"I'll tell you what...if you can make tears come from my eyes and my flesh ache the way Alex does, then I need to get up from this table right now."

"You never know what you've missed until you try something new. I think it's time that I settled down. I need someone who's got my back and I have a feeling you're down for whatever."

"Well Stewart, let me just tell you. Curiosity is my only motivation for this little meeting. I don't plan on now or ever leaving Alex for anyone. I suggest you keep everything in its proper perspective and remember that."

"You do know it was curiosity that killed the cat?"

"Yeah and it fucked up a lot of dogs too. Don't get your tail clipped."

I was getting tired of our conversation, he understood where I was coming from and I definitely knew what he wanted. My mission had been accomplished. I needed him to see me in a different light. I needed to peak his curiosity even more. The one thing that men love is a challenge. Just the fact that I belonged to someone else was good enough for him. Even more significant, he needed to prove to me that he was in charge, especially since I pulled his player's card earlier. We sat there a little while longer and talked about unimportant things. I asked about children and girlfriends, ex-wives, so on and so forth. He denied having any of the above. He said he wasn't the family man type. He enjoyed having his freedom and being in control of his own life. He said that the older he got, he missed having a steady woman in his life, someone he could trust. He wanted someone who would love him despite his many faults. Basically, he was saying he needed some stupid woman who knew he was a dirty low down snake and didn't give a damn about what he did because she would walk a mile just to smell his shit. He meant that he needed a woman who would accept the fact that he was a murderer and would still be willing to justify his actions. He would need someone who was just as evil as he was, or equally as stupid. My buzz was wearing off. I could tell because he was beginning to make me sick. While I waited for the bartender to bring me a glass of water, I asked Stewart about his past. "So, did you grow up in L.A.?"

Just as proud as he could be, he puffed his chest out and sported his huge grin, "Oh, no baby girl, I'm from the Bayou. Can't cha tell I'm one'a dos ole Louisiana bois?" The sound of his voice cut straight through my heart like a knife and sent me straight back to the night my parents were killed. That damn accent came out as plain as day. I almost choked on my water.

"I see you can turn your accent on and off whenever you like."

"Yeah, it takes years of practice."

"And why would you want to give up that part of your heritage?"

"Some things you just want to forget and leave behind."

I hated that son-of-a-bitch. I swear I did. I wish I had some cyanide or anthrax. I continued with the conversation. "Family is one thing you should never willingly leave behind."

The look on his face told me I'd struck a nerve. "I never said I left family behind. I don't have any family. It's just me. I ain't never had no family. Families don't mean shit to me. Benjamin Franklin, Grant, Washington, they are all the family I need. You'll find out when Alex breaks your heart."

I looked at him just as serious as I could and said, "If Alex ever hurt me, I would slit his throat from ear to ear and drain him like a hog." As I spoke, I pictured Stewart's head exploding in front of me, I think somewhere inside me I meant just what I'd said. I'd had enough of Mr. Slick for one night. I summoned the waiter to bring the check. Stewart reached for the check and I swiftly retrieved it from the bartender. I placed the amount for the bill, including tip, in the case and finished my water. Stewart sat there with his mouth open and his pride on his sleeve. We were only inches apart from each other as we stood up to leave.

"You have to control everything, don't you?"

I stood on my tiptoes and whispered in his ear, "Absolutely everything."

As I turned to walk out the door without saying goodbye, he grabbed my arm. "Hold on, at least let me wait with you while they bring your car around."

I smiled "I guess that'll be alright." We walked outside and waited while the valet brought my truck around.

"So when will I see you again?" Stewart asked.

"I don't know. I'll call you and let you know."

He started to laugh, "You'll let me know?"

I didn't crack a smile. "Yes, I will let you know."

He made one more attempt, "Why don't you follow me to my house? Just to talk, no strings I promise." I wasn't expecting to be invited over this soon. It took everything in me to decline the offer. I was curious to see how he was living, but I wasn't going to play myself that cheap. A day or two makes a good bit of difference, so I declined the offer.

"No, I think I'll take a rain check. I've had a full day and I'm really tired, maybe next time." Before he could respond, my truck rolled around. At that point, the spinning rims were giving me a headache. I wondered what the hell was wrong with Alex. The rims were worth more than the truck.

I extended my hand, and Stewart moved in for a kiss, but I quickly pulled back. He seemed quite agitated. I told him I would call him, and then I walked around to the driver's side of the truck and hopped in. While I was preparing to pull off, a Bentley Continental GT rolled around and parked behind me. Stewart stepped off the curb and hopped in. The smart thing would have been for me to act unconcerned and pull off before he did, but I sat there glaring in my rearview mirror. There he was riding around town in a damn Bentley. I wondered if the head start he received from my parents' blood, sweat and money helped him buy that Bentley. My mother should've been driving that car, hell I should've been driving it. I laughed to myself as my body heated up to the point where I felt like I was on fire. It wouldn't be long before I was driving that car, leading his funeral procession. I was gonna get everything I ever wanted in just a little while.

Chapter Twenty-Five

I made Stewart sweat for a few days. He called me constantly, inviting me out for dinner, lunch, drinks...anything. Days passed and I finally decided to take him up on his offer. I agreed to let him cook for me. I knew I was taking a big chance going to his house and actually eating his food. I kept in mind that I hadn't come that far to be taken down by something as simple as dinner. Stewart's house was gorgeous, and that was putting it mildly. After dinner, we sat in the room adjacent to his large pool, which was equipped with a waterfall and slide.

"I'm sure you do a lot of entertaining," I said once we were settled.

He smiled and said, "No, I hardly ever have any company. I have the pool just for the atmosphere. The entire house is really too big, I'm thinking of downsizing." Oh, what a shame, Stewart was having such a problem with his luxurious lifestyle.

I walked over to the couch and took a seat. He sat down right next to me and rested his arm on the back of the couch, barely giving me enough room to breathe. I realized this might be a little bit more difficult than I anticipated. I had tried hard to down play his apparent physical attributes. I think I was most fascinated by the way he'd held up all those years. Initially the thought of me sleeping with a man over twenty years my senior repulsed me. However, when I saw Stewart for the first time, my natural instinct was to admit that he was fine. I've never denied that fact. I inhaled his intoxicating fragrance. His cologne was fresh and clean. I glanced down at his hands, they were well manicured. As usual, his hair was immaculately groomed and he'd shaved his goatee.

As he began to speak, I focused on his plump cherry lips and hung onto his every word. I envisioned our lips in a luscious embrace. I could feel my temperature rise along with the hair on the back of my neck. I tried to remind myself of who he was. I snapped out of my daydream and gathered my thoughts. I couldn't believe I was letting the physical overtake the mental. It's like it hit me all at once. It's really all in the way you look at a person. I mean physically look at a person. Stewart got up from the couch to refresh his drink. He walked erect and seemed to glide around the room. He was dressed in a pair of linen pants with the drawstring at the waist. He wore a linen shirt with the sleeves rolled up. He was very comfortable. I'm sure he had some sort of fitness regimen. I could see the imprint of his manhood through his pants. He wasn't making it easy for me. I wondered what his secret to looking so young and fit was.

The silence was awkward. Stewart stared at me as if he were trying to read my thoughts. He raised his hand to remove a fallen eyelash from my cheek. "You have the most beautiful eyes."

Before I could respond, he pulled me in closer and kissed me. He held my face in his hands, and I could feel my heart beating at a rapid pace. Feeling that I would soon lose control, I pulled away from him. We sat for a few more awkward moments staring into each other's eyes.

All of a sudden, he removed himself from the couch and walked over to the piano. I figured the piano was just like the pool, a conversation piece. He placed his drink on top of the piano, raised the lid, and proceeded to play. When his hands touched the keys, it was as though the piano came alive. I was truly taken by the fact that he could actually play. His eyes were closed and he seemed to be in some sort of trance, as his fingers floated along the keys. I was mesmerized and equally aroused as I watched him feel the music in his soul. Just when I thought I knew everything about the man that I was supposed to despise, my body was filled with overwhelming passion as my ears were blessed with the melodious sound of his voice. He sang as if he and those eighty-eight keys were the only things in the room. I watched as his body became relaxed and he crooned the lyrics to 'A Change is Gonna Come'. It was almost as if he were telling the story of his life. It was clear that the man was suffering from some sort of unnatural oppression that had taken hold of his soul. I stood there paralyzed and confused as tears flowed freely from his eyes. His voice was soulful and rigid. It ran through me like warm water on an empty stomach, it touched every vital portion of my body. I was so captivated by his pain that I failed to feel my own tears streaming down my cheek. I walked over to Stewart and placed my hand on his shoulder. He was startled by my touch and immediately snapped out of his trance. This didn't stop the flow of the music or the flow of his tears. He continued to play.

I stood there running my fingers through his thick curly locks. It was like I could feel his pain, or was I just reliving in my own. It was funny how that same song, 'A Change is Gonna Come', had a different meaning for two people who shared the same memory. Ironically, I wished that we'd met at a different time, in a different place. The reality was that there was no way that I should've been sharing that moment with him. How could I console this man who I held in such contempt? Just when I'd come back to my senses and withdrew my affection, Stewart removed his hands from the keyboard and ceased his cries of redemption. He turned to me, wrapped his arms around my waist and rested his head on the pit of my stomach. I hesitated to respond, but somehow I was drawn to him like a moth to a fiery flame. I held his head close to me and reassured him that everything would be alright. I took a deep breath and asked him what was wrong.

"Stewart, what's wrong? You can tell me...I want to help you through whatever this is."

Still holding on to me, he stood up and looked down at me. "I'm just an old man with old memories that I can't let go."

As I looked into his eyes I could feel my nipples harden. I said, "What can I do?"

He caressed my face and said, "You've already done it, I think you were sent to save me." The look in eyes was sincere, but haunting. I felt as though he were looking right through me. He pulled me in closer and kissed me. I could feel my right foot as it took leave of the floor. I wrapped my arms around his neck and pulled myself closer to him. I felt his butter soft hands against my flesh as he reached under my blouse. As his hands moved further up my back I could feel my blouse begging to be released from my body.

He whispered, "Your skin is so soft." I didn't say a word. I was enjoying feeling his faint breath on my neck as his lips made the veins in my neck pulsate. I could feel my legs become weak. All of sudden, I no longer felt the comfort or the safety of my feet planted on solid ground. Stewart picked me up and placed me on top of the piano. I sat on top of the cold surface feeling his warm hands as he pushed my panties to one side and fondled me with his fingers.

Everything was happening so fast, my head was swimming with all kinds of emotions and reservations. One side of my brain kept saying, "Stop!" The other side of my brain was saying, "Shut up and go for it." I didn't have much time to say stop or go, because he was inside of me and all I could say was, "Damn."

I was silenced and amazed by his obvious gifts. I mean...come on. This man is old enough to be my father, and I had to open up and prepare myself to take all of him. I wrapped my legs around his waist, closed my eyes and took a deep breath. He grabbed my thighs and rested his head on my chest.

"Got damn," I heard him say. With each stroke I could feel him going deeper and deeper. I tried to catch my breath and retain my balance, but my head was spinning and I'd obviously lost control. Just when I was getting comfortable, he whisked me off of the piano and headed toward the stairs.

As we made our way up the stairs, the little voice in my head was telling me to get down and get a hold of myself, but the little voice between my legs said, "Hold on and enjoy the ride." My legs overruled because the next thing I knew, I was helping him push the bedroom door open. I didn't pay attention to the details of the room. If you asked me to draw a map to his bedroom I couldn't help you at all. It was like there was some sort of force that was overtaking my body and clouding my judgment. I knew there was a possibility that I would have to sleep with him, but I'd planned to be the seducer.

Stewart gently placed me on the bed. That was my opportunity to come back to myself and take control, but then he leaned over and kissed my neck. The heat from his body intensified his fragrance. He smelled like a man, he tasted like a man and he felt just like a man. He opened my blouse and I heard the buttons as they flew to various destinations around the room. He reached around my back and unhooked my bra. My breasts popped out and landed perfectly in place. He definitely knew what he was doing. As my breasts relaxed from the entrapment of my bra, I could feel my nipples become firmer, awaiting his warm touch. He caressed each one with the tips of his fingers and kissed my lips. I outlined his lips with my tongue and sucked his bottom lip like a juicy grape. I pulled his shirt over his head and was utterly amazed at what I saw. Stewart had the most amazing skin tone. It was like smooth butterscotch, and I couldn't wait for it to melt in my mouth. His skin was smooth and flawless. There was nothing old about that man's body. His abs were tight and his arms were strong. My hands longed to touch his bare skin and feel the wonder that my eyes held. I touched his skin. It was soft like cotton and sweet like honey. I ran my fingers through his hair and it felt like I was touching silk. As he removed my underwear with his teeth, he reached my ankles and kissed each one. Somehow, thoughts of my fiancé escaped me.

As I lay watching him undress, I took a deep breath and tugged on my bottom lip with my teeth as the word damn flashed through my head. It's amazing what some people hide behind clothing. He stood in front of me at full attention. Everything about him was physically perfect. He was just the right size, not too big and not too small. His length was proportionate to his width. He lifted his knee placed it on the side of the bed and crawled toward me. On his way up he kissed the inside of my thighs, placed his tongue inside of me and French-kissed my clit. Every stroke of his tongue sent chills up my spine. I grabbed the back of his head and ran my fingers through his hair, closed my eyes and hoped that I would make it out of his bed with my mind intact.

I thought of Alex suddenly, and then the thought disappeared. There was only Stewart. He was there when I opened my eyes and when I closed them once again. I felt him prepare himself to push inside of me. I wrapped my left arm around his body, grabbed the back of his head, pulled my knees closer to me, and flipped him over.

When he landed on his back he looked at me and said, "Damn girl." I leaned in closer, and put my finger on his lips and instructed him to hush. I parted his lips with my tongue, allowing our tongues to embrace. I reached down to make sure he was ready for what was about to happen. I felt his pre-ejaculation excitement and I knew he was more than ready. I raised myself up and sat down on top of him. As I placed my feet on each side of him and eased him inside of me, I watched as his eyes grew wider and wider and all of sudden they shut tight. I watched as he struggled to speak. Once he was completely inside of me, and my feet were relaxed he reached his hands out. I grabbed his hands and locked them inside of mine. I leaned in closer to him, resting my knees on each side and placed his hands behind his head. As I moved up, down and around I looked into his eyes and saw nothing but sheer ecstasy. I sat up and placed my feet on each side of him and rested my hands on his stomach. As I rode him, I watched his eyes and felt his body tremble and listened as my name graced his lips over and over again. Once again I was in control and I didn't think it bothered him one bit.

As Stewart laid there flat on his back, releasing his last moan of satisfaction, I struggled internally to classify what we'd just done. I couldn't believe I'd just been swept away by one of the vilest human beings on the face of the earth. Had I allowed my archenemy to feel pleasure, while I enjoyed every single minute of it? Somehow, I felt a lot differently than I had originally thought I would. As I listened to Stewart inhale and exhale, I heard the sounds of fulfillment. I felt dirty, as if I'd just sold my soul to the devil. I laid on my back with my eyes closed trying to figure out my next move. The only thing I could do was grab my clothes and leave. I definitely couldn't stay the night there. I kept my place for just a few more minutes, and then I stood up, ready to leave. Stewart rolled over and kissed my shoulder. I looked over at him. He was wearing a huge smile on his face. He grabbed my hand and kissed it. I politely retrieved my hand and pulled the covers over my breasts as if I were ashamed. He rested his hand on the top of the sheet.

"You really are something. I have to watch you...you just might give me a heart attack." At that moment I realized that he was pretty old; in great shape, but old. My feelings of repulsion began to surface once again. I moved his hand from its position.

"I damn sure don't want to give you a heart attack. How would I explain that to Alex?"

Stewart was thrown off by the mention of Alex's name. He started to pout like a little boy and turned his back to me. What did he expect? I guess he thought that a little taste of him would have made me forget about Alex. What I could never admit was that just a few moments ago, I couldn't even remember who Alex was. I tried to figure out if I should've let him pout or if I should've said something to ease his ego. I sat up on the side of the bed and began to get dressed. I looked back over my shoulder to see if he was still sulking when my heart almost stopped beating.

Stewart's back was turned to me. That's when I noticed his birthmark. It was a dark, port wine stain that was shaped like a rectangle. I remember Mattie telling us that had been the last thing she noticed before her mother took her baby out of her arms the night she delivered. The birthmark was minor compared to the burn marks that covered his back. I took a deep breath and unconsciously reached out my hand to touch his back. I pulled my hand back and stood there still, not making a sound or moving a muscle. It was clear that everyone had war wounds from that night. Some of us deserved them and some of us were just casualties. As I stared at Stewart's back, I was transported back to that night. I saw nothing but flames. I pictured myself dousing Stewart's body with gasoline and setting him on fire once again. I wanted to ask what had happened to him, as if I expected him to tell me the truth. The longer I stood there preparing to hear his lie, the more I wanted him to die slowly and painfully. I wanted him to feel every ounce of pain that I've felt. I wanted to set his soul on fire/ I wanted to watch him burn until there was nothing left but ashes. I stood there so long, I hadn't realized sweat was dripping from my hands. Just when I felt my nose starting to bleed, Stewart rolled back over and faced me. I guess he realized I was staring at his scars. He rested on his elbow, motioned for me to come closer.

"Don't be scared. The scars are just remnants from my past."

I couldn't believe that son-of-a-bitch called the blood of my parents "remnants" from his past. My mouth welled up as if I were going to spit on him, I tugged on my lip with my teeth.

With a faint almost nonexistent voice I said, "What happened?" I sat down on the bed and waited to hear what was next. Stewart looked down at the bed as if he were trying to gather the strength to speak. As he began to speak, I settled in and prepared myself.

He said, "It's painful. I don't even like talking about it."

I reached over and caressed his hand. "You know it helps to let things out. Whatever it is it seems like you've been carrying it around inside for a long time. Please I'm here, let me help you." I couldn't believe how compassionate I appeared.

He looked at me once again and said, "My life has never been normal. I've done some things that I'm not proud of, things that I am down right ashamed of. To be honest, I should be dead or in jail..."

I wondered where he was going with his confusion. I knew he wasn't going to lie there, butt-naked, and confess his sins to someone he met a few days ago. I was good, but not that damn good. I continued to listen, as he began his story.

"I was a wild and crazy kid. I wasn't scared of anything. One day, when I was about nine or ten, I was trying to burn some ants on the windowsill with a magnifying glass and the curtains caught on fire..."

I couldn't believe that shit. He had actually concocted a backwards ass story about setting the curtains on fire. I mean how Hollywood could you get? This lying piece of shit! The more I listened, the more I wanted to rip his eyeballs out of the socket. I could feel my pulse starting to race and my adrenalin was working overtime. I smiled and nodded my head as if I really cared. He continued the lie.

"The fire got out of control, and I couldn't stop it, and somehow my clothes caught fire. At that time, we didn't know how to stop, drop and roll. Anyway, my foster parents put it out and I have these burns to show for my curiosity." I sat for a minute trying to figure out what to do. Should I slap him in the face or stroke his ego? I decided to go with the flow and play the compassionate role and caress his face. I leaned in close to him, and looked into his eyes as he was trying to appear to be distraught about his past. His obvious mockery of the pain and anguish I've felt all these years snapped me back to reality and reminded of the real reason I was here, which was to take his ass down and destroy him bit by bit until there was nothing there but the stain his blood will leave on the floor. I reached out my hand and gently brushed his cheek, and leaned in to kiss him gently on his lips.

"Baby, everything happens for a reason. Those scars on your back are just like you said, remnants from the past. Don't worry, I'm here to take care of you and make sure that from now on you live the life you deserve. You and I are gonna make our own memories that I promise you'll never forget."

Poor Stewart, he leaned in and kissed me. He thought I was promising him a future of undivided attention and affection. The only thing I was promising him was that I was watching him take his last breath.

With the bitter taste of Stewart's vile kiss lingering in my mouth, he rested his head on my chest, while I ran my fingers through his hair. I lay there staring at the ceiling unable to move. I couldn't erase the memory of those scars from my mind. I lay with him in my arms pretending to console him and at the same time plotting his demise. I listened to him breathing so freely and thought of how he'd taken his life for granted. I thought of my purse that I'd left downstairs and the gun that was resting inside. I continued to lie there and think until there was nothing left to ponder.

I woke up the next morning to find myself in Stewart's bed alone. I was actually glad that he wasn't there. I hated the thought of waking up next to him. I checked the room to make sure he wasn't in the bathroom. I quickly retrieved my clothes from the chair and started to dress. A strange and uncomfortable feeling came over me, something definitely wasn't right. At that point, I didn't know if Stewart was still in the house or if he'd stepped out. I figured he was still around because I couldn't imagine him leaving me there alone. As I reached down to slip on my shoes, I heard the doorknob turn. I looked up and there he was, coming through the door.

"Good morning, beautiful." He plopped down beside me, threw his arm around my shoulder and gave me a kiss on my cheek. He was surprised to see that I was up and moving around so early.

"What's the rush? I was just about to fix us breakfast. I left an extra toothbrush and some towels for you in the bathroom. Why don't you freshen up while I make breakfast?" He hopped up from the bed and spun around the room like a little boy. He came back from the bathroom with one of his bathrobes.

"Make yourself comfortable, I've got to run to the store for some eggs and milk. I won't be long." He really didn't give me enough time to respond. I couldn't stand eggs. They made me gag. If it was going to get him out of the house and away from me for a while, I had to keep that to myself. I could see he wasn't going to take no for an answer, so I agreed to stay.

"That sounds great, but I do have an appointment at noon that I need to get ready for, so I can't be too long."

He flashed those gorgeous teeth of his. "No problem. You're gonna love my omelet. Cooking is one of my specialties, among other things."

He winked his eye at me as if I should've agreed. I hoped he wasn't referring to what he did the previous night. That shit was like having a pap smear random poking with an unpleasant feeling. Who was I kidding? He could eat the hell out of some pussy. I just smiled and winked back at him as he turned and walked toward the door.

He'd shown me his office last night while giving me a tour of the house. I made up some excuse to get inside. "Hey, Stewart I need to have my orders for this week faxed so I can approve them, is it all right if I use your fax machine?"

"Of course, you remember where the office is, just go on in. Feel free to make yourself at home. If you need anything I should be back in fifteen to twenty."

Before he left he grabbed me by the waist and kissed me dead on the lips. I could taste the cigar he'd obviously smoked that morning. He was an avid cigar smoker, they were like cigarettes for him. I managed to pretend to enjoy his kiss. As he walked away all I could think about was how silly it was of me to get carried away.

I was desperate to wash the stench of that night off my body. The thought of his hands all over me made me want to scrub my skin off. I could taste the remnants of cigars and vodka. It's amazing how those things don't bother you when you're caught up in the moment, but once reality sets in, it makes you sick. I ran to the bathroom and brushed my teeth until my gums bled and I brushed my tongue until I gagged. I rinsed out my mouth over and over again. I was trying to wash away any trace of him. Thank God for condoms. If I had to endure him raw with the knowledge that his bare flesh was inside of me, I would've probably slit my wrist with his razor. I looked over at the shower and it was calling my name, but I knew I didn't have long if I was going to try and do some snooping. I didn't even know where to begin. I took my cell phone from my purse and ran down the hall to the office. I picked up his office phone and dialed Isabelle's cell phone. I let it ring three times, and then I hung up. I called her again on my cell. She answered the phone as if she was disgusted.

"Hello."

"Hey girl, did you just get a missed call?"

"Yeah, was that you? Why did you hang up?"

"I called you from Stewart's home office phone, but hung up in case he has some sort of recording device on the phone."

"You think he records his calls?"

"I don't know, but if I was in his situation, I would. I'm sure he's into all kinds of illegal shit."

"Don't you think his office might be bugged?"

"No, I hope he's not stupid enough to have meetings in here with his underworld friends."

"So, you're just a regular Dick Tracy now, huh?"

"No, just trying to be very careful. Look, let me give you his address just in case you don't hear from me when you think you should."

"Ok, let me get some paper...ok go ahead."

"It's 21247 Briarwood Drive and it's in Briarwood Hills."

"Ok, I got it. Seth...How did you get into his office anyway?"

"He ran to the store to get something for breakfast, so I'm just taking a look around."

"Breakfast, that means you spent the night...are you crazy?"

"Yes, very."

"You get your ass out of there! Meeting for dinner is one thing, but spending the night...Seth...did you sleep with him?"

"Isabelle, I don't need this. You knew before I left what my options were. Once I met him, I knew just what to do. Trust me."

"Girl, you are playing with fire. Are you sure he doesn't know who you are?"

"He doesn't have a clue."

"I don't like this one bit."

"Isabelle, what the hell did you think I was going to do? Walk up to him and say remember me...you killed me twenty years ago?"

"Ok, damn. I see your point."

"Look, I gotta go. Oh yeah, fax over the order you placed yesterday. That's the reason I gave him to get into his office."

"Ok what's the fax number?" I recited the number for her. "Ok, I'm doing it now."

I talked to her for a few more minutes until Isabelle was sure the fax went through. While I was standing there waiting, I noticed some pictures and a few plaques on the wall. I walked over and looked at one of the plaques that read, 'In Appreciation for Exceptional Community Service'. It was presented to Stewart Benson and Reginald Hawthorne. I said to myself, "Who is Reginald Hawthorne?" Next to the plague was a picture of Stewart and two other men. There was one man in the middle who appeared sitting down. Stewart and the other man were kneeling down beside him. Just as I moved in closer to get a better look, Isabelle's fax came through. It scared the hell out of me. I jumped and my heart started beating fast.

I must have made some sort of noise because Isabelle started yelling. "Seth, are you ok?" She startled me again.

"Girl, stop yellin'. You scared me."

She yelled back, "Hell, you scared me."

"I'm sorry the fax machine was really loud, I guess I'm a little jumpy. Let me go before Stewart comes back."

"Ok, but call me as soon as you leave. If you don't call me soon I'm gonna call you back."

"Ok, I gotta go!" I hung up, grabbed the fax and headed for the door. I didn't have a chance to look for anything, even though I didn't know what I was looking for. I did wonder why someone who faked his own death, and ran with such an undesirable group of people would be active in the community and take pictures freely. For a minute, I thought he might have been in the witness protection program. Nah, people like that usually lead lives totally different from where they came from. I figured he was either stupid or he was just that ruthless and didn't really give a damn.

As I was walking out of the office, my body began to crave soap and water. Just as I was closing the door I saw the door at the opposite end of the hall open. I thought that maybe Stewart was back and had gone into another bedroom for some reason. I hoped he hadn't heard me in the office speaking to Isabelle. I called down the hall to him.

"Stewart!" There was no response, so I thought he hadn't heard me. I called again only this time I walked slowly down the hall toward the room. I had my cell in one hand and the fax in the other.

I yelled out, "Stewart, it sure did take you a long time. I think I kind of missed you." I stood there waiting as the door opened. It seemed as though Stewart was struggling to open the door, I guess it was caught on the rug. Just then, the door opened and on the other side of it was a man sitting in a wheelchair. I was taken by surprise. I didn't know there was anyone else in the house with us. As I gripped my chest, the man realized he'd scared me.

As he rolled himself out of the door and down the hall he said, "I'm sorry I didn't mean to startle you. I'm Reginald, Stewart's brother."

Finally, I got to meet Reginald Hawthorne. With anticipation, I walked toward him. As he rolled into the hallway under the skylight, the sunlight shined on his face, my legs got weak, and I almost passed out. Everything began to echo in my head. I heard the sound of the paper crumbling in my hand. It was so loud that my head started to pound. I grabbed hold of the wall to brace myself and prayed that I wouldn't faint. I looked up to make sure I was seeing what I thought I saw. My body was warm and beads of sweat outlined my face. I could feel my stomach twisting into knots. I placed my hands by my side and wiped the sweat on my clothes. The sweat was burning my eyes and my contacts were starting to irritate me. I stood there leaning on the wall and stared into the eyes of the devil himself...it was my father.

Chapter Twenty-Six

My father, Nolan Toussaint, was sitting there in a wheelchair not even two feet away from me. He was just as alive as I was. I pushed myself from the wall and stood straight up. I could feel my chest moving up and down as my heart rate rose. I felt like I was going to throw up.

With my voice cracking, I swallowed hard and said with a straight face, "It's ok. I didn't know anyone was here."

He rolled toward me and I took a step back. It took all I had not to pass out on the floor. There were so many things going through my head. I went from joy, to shock, to hurt, to being pissed off all in ten seconds. I kept saying to myself, "Keep it together." I knew I couldn't continue to stand there, but I knew I couldn't turn and bolt out of there either.

My father rolled over to me, stuck out his hand and said, "You must be Seth, Stewart didn't do you justice." My first thought was to spit in his face, knock him out of the chair and beat the hell out of him. Instead, I maintained my cool. I thought to myself, I could kill him right now, and just walk away, but I just stood there and answered him.

"Well, I must be." I couldn't even feel my own mouth moving. I reached my hand out to accept his handshake. The moment our hands touched, I could feel myself breaking down. It was my father all right. He looked just like he did the last time I saw him. His smile was the same, as well as his hair and skin. Even his touch was the same. I looked into his eyes and I was eight years old again. I remembered the day he gave me the locket. Out of habit, I reached up to touch my neck, but the locket wasn't there. It was tucked away in my suitcase waiting for the right time to appear. Time had been good to my father. Like Stewart, he too, had aged very well.

I never imagined that moment in my wildest dreams. My feelings were much different than they should have been. In one instance, I wanted to fall down on my knees, throw my arms around him and hold him close to me. In the next instance, I wanted to blow his head off and ask no questions. I knew I couldn't harm him, but when the time was right I needed to talk to him. Sitting there in front of me was the man with all the answers. The best thing was for me to get the hell out of there and figure something out. I definitely had not counted on that factor.

I let his hand go and said, "Well, Reginald, it was nice meeting you but I really need to take off. Will you tell Stewart that I'll call him later?"

Just as I turned to walk away Reginald said, "There's Stewart, you can tell him yourself." Stewart was standing behind me with a paper bag in his hand.

With a puzzled look on his face he asked, "Tell Stewart what?"

I turned with an awkward smile on my face and walked over to him. I stood on my tiptoes and kissed him on the cheek. "Hi, honey, I was just telling your brother that my appointment was moved up so I have to take a rain check on breakfast. Maybe you can make me dinner."

Stewart looked disappointed. "Well that's fine, but can't you re-schedule?"

"A few more prospective buyers are coming by to look at the house and of course I have to be there."

"Why don't you let me sell your house for you?"

Was he crazy? I wouldn't let him sell my dog's shit. I abruptly said, "And how would I explain to my fiancé that I fired our old, middle aged, female agent for a gorgeous male?"

Stewart's smile spread across his entire face. "Well, I guess you're right."

He looked at Reginald and said, "See man, I told you she was some-thing else." I kissed Stewart and said goodbye to daddy dearest. I walked into the bedroom to retrieve the rest of my things. I asked Stewart to walk me out. I could tell by the way he looked at me that just one more good, toe-curling night would send him over the edge. As I drove away, he stood there with that sly grin on his face. There was something about that smile that was as shady as a weeping willow.

Once I was out of sight, I couldn't hold it any longer. I stopped the truck, barely putting it into park and jumped out. I stood there on the side of the road and vomited, over and over again, until there was nothing left but dry heaves. Nothing else would come up but mucus and air. I sat down in the grass and held my head and my stomach until the uneasiness passed. I heard my phone ringing, but I didn't try to answer it. I wasn't ready to tell anyone what I'd just seen. Then I remembered it might be Isabelle, and if she didn't hear from me, she might have panicked. I pushed myself up from the ground, and tore off what was left of my blouse and wiped my mouth with it. I threw it into the grass and hopped back into the truck. I rinsed my mouth out with some water that I'd left in the truck. I reached in my purse, grabbed a piece of gum and felt the gun. I'd forgotten I had it in my purse. I picked up the phone and saw that it was Alex. This was the call I dreaded, but I knew I had to call him back. I didn't know what to say. "I've been here for a few days. I slept with the man whom I thought killed my parents. Oh but wait my father is alive and well, and I shook his hand a few minutes ago." I couldn't believe it myself. Since lying really did come natural to me, I was sure that I would think of something. My hands were shaking and I could hardly hold on to the phone. I placed my hands on the steering wheel, where they continued to shake. I felt my stomach start to rumble, I opened the door and leaned out, but nothing came up.

Dry heaves are the worst feelings in the world. I sat there for a minute staring up at the roof of the truck. My head was pounding and my stomach was making an awful sound. I put my hands over my face. Then I reached down, poured some of the bottled water into my hands, and splashed it onto my face. As the water dripped from my chin, I sat there telling myself to get it together. I looked at my camisole, it was a mess. I thought about my night with Stewart. I pictured his back covered in burn scars. I could smell the liquor from his breath and taste his cigar. I pictured his body and wondered why he had to be so damn gorgeous. I thought about what a fool I was to let him think I enjoyed having him touch me.

My mind went straight to my father. I didn't know what to think. This was truly unexpected. What was really going on? I screamed at the top of my lungs. I beat the steering wheel and I asked God...why. I needed to know what I had done to deserve this. Things were so much easier when I thought Stewart was the one who had killed my father. That would have made Stewart responsible for this whole mess. I wondered if my father knew who I was. I sat there feeling like a failure. I felt defeated. I wanted to drive straight to the airport, get on the plane and forget any of it ever happened. I sat there staring into space. I didn't realize I was only a few feet from Stewart's house. I was unaware of time, unaware of space and unaware of who I really was. I tried to figure out what I was doing, and how I had gotten there, when all of a sudden the phone rang. I jumped and grabbed it. I pushed talk and put my car in drive.

Alex was bellowing on the other end. "Where the hell have you been?"

I needed some time to gather my thoughts so I said, "What?"

Alex's voice grew louder. "Don't fuck with me, Seth."

"Alex, I promise you, now is not the time."

"What do you mean? I've been calling you all night. I called the house and your cell phone. Isabelle hasn't heard from you, Mattie hasn't heard from you. You called me last night when you knew I was working out."

"Alex, please, calm down. I'm fine. I had dinner with Stewart last night and..." I let my voice trail off. Well, I guess I did know how to tell the truth.

"You did what?"

"No listen. Baby I..."

"Baby my ass...I'm on my way to L.A."

"Now you know good and well that you're not coming here. All I did was have dinner with him. I'm just trying to see how much info I can get out of him."

"A man like that is not gonna to tell you his life story unless you've givin' him some motivation."

"I'm trying to see if I can try to work with him somehow." I could feel my explanation getting weaker with every word.

"Didn't you tell me he owned a strip club?" Damn, I sure did. Why was I telling Alex everything?

"Yes, Alex. But do you remember what I used to do for a living?"

"My point, exactly. Do you know that I will come out there and beat Stewart's ass with one of those poles you might be swingin' on? Not to mention what I'll do to you."

"Alex, calm down. I'm just gonna convince him that I can manage his girls for him since he has so many other irons in the fire. I'm just trying to get closer to him and gain his trust."

"Seth!"

"Yes Alex?"

"Do you think I'm a damn fool?"

"No."

"Well, then act like it."

"What?"

"I knew it! I knew you weren't just goin' out there to sell my house. I know you. I know what you're thinkin' before you do. You know just how to use what you got to get what you want. Or did you think I forgot...Seth? Don't fuck around and get into this so deep that you can't get out of it and lose me in the process!"

"Well, if you know me so well, why did you support my decision to come here?"

"I told you what's mine is yours. You can have anything that I have. If we are gonna prepare for a new life together we need to get rid of things in our old lives. I guess I didn't think this through until last night when I couldn't reach you and I had time to think. I want to help you, but I'm scared. I don't know what to think."

"Please Alex, just trust me. I need this. My life depends on it."

Everything was quiet for a minute. Finally, Alex said, "Just be careful. You need to think long and hard about what's important to you. This man ain't no joke Seth."

"Believe me Alex, I know that now more than ever." I spoke before I realized what I was saying.

With a curious voice, Alex said, "What do you mean?"

It was time to end the conversation at that point.

"Nothing Baby, I gotta go. They're coming to look at the house in a few minutes." Alex hesitated for a few seconds before saying goodbye.

As I pulled into the driveway, I was thinking about how I needed to make Alex understand how serious things were. I have to tell him about my father. That would have made him realize that it was too late for me to turn back. At that point, it was beyond my love for him or our future together. It was deeper than finding out the truth. There was so much more to my past and I couldn't be the Seth he wanted and needed at that time. The moment I saw my father was the moment any good and decent part of me left my body. As long as my father and Stewart were alive, I was just another ruthless bitch with no morals, and no values. I no longer felt as if I were his daughter. He was my prey and I was the hunter. I would take him down by any means necessary.

I took a deep breath and pushed TALK on my cell phone. I needed to reach Alex again. He answered on the first ring. "Hello."

"Listen, I need to tell you something. I need you to make the decision whether you're gonna accept what I tell you and let me do what I need to do. Or do you need to let go now and walk away from me forever...either you support me or you don't."

"Seth, what are you talking about? You're making me nervous. What the hell is going on out there?"

"Alex, my father is alive." Everything was silent, there were no words spoken between us for several seconds. I had to break the silence. "Alex, are you there?"

"Uh, yeah, I'm here. What do you mean your father is alive? How do you know? Did Stewart tell you this?"

"No, Stewart didn't tell me. Please don't ask me to go into detail. I saw him with my own eyes. I even touched him."

"You touched him? Are you sure...or did you want it to be him?"

"Gotdamnit Alex, I know my own father. It's him. He is alive, very much alive. He and Stewart are posing as brothers. They live in the same house. I saw him. I spoke to him. I shook his hand."

"Damn, Baby are you ok, did he recognize you? I mean...what...how...Damn!"

"No, I don't think he knew it was me. I think he was even flirting with me. I just don't know. I was so shocked, I really couldn't think straight. It took everything I had to just maintain some sort of control."

"To be honest I don't know what to say. I'm still trying to get used to you not really being...well, you."

"I know what you mean. To be honest I don't know how I feel either. One second I wanted to throw my arms around him and hold him. In the next second I wanted to kill him. I really don't want to discuss it in detail. I think the best thing for us is that we just don't even discuss it. I just need you to know how serious this is, and that I'm not going to give this up. I couldn't now even if I wanted to. Alex, I will do whatever I have to do to bring my father and Stewart down for what they did. I would rather have you with me, than against me."

"You know I don't like it, but I know I can't stop you. I know you can handle yourself and you know for a lack of a better term, how to have people taken care of if you need to. Seth, I am so scared right now. I feel like a helpless, little bitch. I mean, I honestly feel like I'm marrying the mob."

"Well, isn't that amusing?"

"No, I'm serious. This is some crazy shit, and it just gets crazier every day. Are you sure it was your father?"

"Yes Alex. And don't fuckin' ask me that again. He's in a wheelchair, and I think a gunshot may have put him there."

"I'm just lost...I don't know what to do. I need to get out there quick."

"No Alex. I don't want you involved in this. I don't even want to tell you anymore than I have to. The less you know the better. Isabelle knows how to contact me, if you can't reach me."

"I'll hang back and let you handle this, but you have to keep me updated at all times. Obviously, this is something that I have no experience in and for some reason I believe you'll be all right. You've always had that I'll slit your throat if I have to kind of way about you. The fiancé in me wants to come and get you right now, but the friend in me knows I will do anything I can to help you."

"I need the friend right now."

"Ok Seth, I'll be your friend. You just have to respect the fact that I am your man...your fiancé...and it's my job to protect you...and I'm getting real tired of telling you that!" I let Alex have the last word. I didn't feel like arguing anymore and I wanted him to feel like he was still in control.

When I walked in the house, I let the house air out before the people came to look at it. I opened the windows and French doors in the bedrooms, as well as the doors leading to the pool. I'd been living out of my suitcase since I arrived. As I finally unpacked my clothes, I realized I could be there much longer than I anticipated. I was in the shower when I remembered what Mattie told me about the devil, and knowing him when I saw him. I'd come across several people that were somehow tangled up in everything, but none of them seemed to spook me more than my father...not even Stewart. The fact that he was alive was unsettling enough, but it was his eyes. He had a look in his eyes that I didn't remember ever seeing before. He seemed as though he could look right through you, and control your every move. He had an eerie aura. It made me nervous just being near him.

I remembered what Charlie said about my father, I mean Reginald. I had to remember to refer to him as Reginald, because thinking of him as my father, would force me to feel something for him other than hate. Charlie had said that Reginald was the one who was in charge. It was clear that my father had to be the mastermind behind the whole plan to have my mother and his own children killed. Now that I knew this, I needed to find out why. Was it for money? Was he tired of being married with children...or was he just plain evil?

Now the part about being evil brought me back to Mattie and her mention of the devil. It baffled me that she would say I'd know him when I saw him. Had she led me on that wild goose chase? No, that didn't make sense, why would she have taken care of me for twenty years? She could have easily left me there to die that night. She could have told me about my father at any time. Why would she let me go to Dillon to find out all that information? And when she found out I was going to L.A., she didn't protest. We'd gotten so close over the last few months. I'd begun to see the good qualities in her. I was happy that she was able to show true love to Noel. She was becoming a totally different person. Something wasn't right. I felt the need to call her.

When I finished my shower, I toweled off and went straight for the phone. I called the boutique. Since Mattie was working in my absence, I could kill two birds with one stone. Alex knew the story. It was time to tell Mattie and Isabelle. Also, I needed to decide whether or not to look for Lauren. No matter how twisted she was, Lauren deserved to know the truth. As crazy as she was, I might've actually needed her in my corner. I was very anxious. I didn't have much time. I knew that if I told Isabelle and Mattie together, Isabelle would be able to read Mattie's body language. She was good at that. I decided to use the house phone with the speaker so I could sit comfortably and talk. I felt crazy sitting there in just a towel, so I reached for my robe. I dialed the number and waited for it to ring. Isabelle picked up.

"Good Afternoon, Anna Marie's. How may I help you?"

"Isabelle, I'm glad you answered."

"Girl I have been worried sick about you, are you alright? Did you find out anything?"

"Hold on Isabelle. Where is Mattie?"

"She's helping a customer, why...what's wrong?"

"Let Kelly help them, you and Mattie go to the office and use the speaker phone."

"What? You're scaring me. What's up with you?"

"Please, just do it."

"All right, hold on."

I held the line while Isabelle went to get Mattie. A few seconds passed and Isabelle picked up. "Seth, you still there?"

I replied, "Yes, is Mattie there with you?"

I heard Mattie's voice. It was a little shaky. "Yes, Seth, I'm here. What's going on?"

I hate when people tried to play me for a fuckin' fool. I just shot straight from the hip. "Mattie, I think you know what this call is about." I waited for her response, but she was silent.

Isabelle said, "Mattie what is she talking about?" I could imagine Isabelle cocking her head to one side and looking like she could eat you alive. Over those few months, I found out that Isabelle has a lot of hell in her. I felt closer to her than I did my own sister. I waited for Mattie's response.

I got tired so I just said it, "Mattie, why didn't you tell me that my father was alive?"

Suddenly, I heard the chair hit the wall. Isabelle yelled, "What in the hell...your who...is what?"

I sat there with a smug look on my face as if they could see through the phone. "That's right you heard me." Mattie still hadn't said a word, but I could hear her crying.

Just then Isabelle said, "What the hell are you crying for? You need to explain."

I interjected, "How could you let me come face to face with my father this way? Especially when you were the one who told me he'd been dead for twenty years."

Isabelle said, "There are people poppin' up from the dead everywhere!"

I was so angry, I just blurted out, "Is my mother gonna jump out of the closet anytime soon?"

Mattie finally came to her own defense. "No, your mother, God rest her soul is dead and she's not ever coming back. It's not what you think."

"Then what is it? You so much as admitted that you knew. I should have known I was in for a shock when you told me that I would know the devil when I saw him. I thought you meant Clark. I would never have guessed this in a million years. You let me walk in with blinders on. What are you trying to do to me? I almost lost it today. What the hell is going on Mattie? Have you known this for the last twenty years?"

I heard Mattie get up from her seat. She sounded as if she were pacing the floor. Her voice was fading in and out.

I heard Isabelle say, "Will you sit down and be still?"

Mattie snapped back, "Will you two please quit yellin' at me? I am not a fuckin' kid. I will tell you the truth if you just shut up and listen."

I never thought I would be tempted to hit one of my elders, but I wanted to reach through the phone and knock the dust off her ass. She was acting as if I'd done something to her.

"Mattie, I am about to start taking muthafuckas out, and I need to know if I should add you to the list."

Isabelle started to get worried, "Seth, maybe you do need to calm down. Do you need your anxiety medicine?"

Before I knew it I said, "I don't need any damn anxiety medicine. I was cured today."

Mattie started to speak, "Seth, I promise you, I just found out a few months ago, and no I never planned on telling you. I didn't want to hurt you."

I decided to calm down. Rage wasn't going to get me anywhere. "What do you mean you just found out?"

"Do you remember when you got out of the hospital and I went to the Bahamas?"

"Yes, I remember, but I knew you weren't in the Bahamas. You couldn't even get the islands right. I just didn't know where you were. I figured you didn't want me to know. At that time, I didn't know I needed to be suspicious of you."

"You don't, Seth. I have a gentleman friend that I met at church. I have been seeing him for a while and he wanted me to go to L.A. with him to visit his daughter."

Wasn't that some shit? I had never met him and she was meeting his family. "Why haven't I met this friend?"

"You know you don't do well with strangers. I was going to introduce you when we got back, but that's when Lauren showed up and I figured it wasn't a good time."

"Ok, that's all fine and good. Now get to the part about Nolan Toussaint, my dead daddy."

"Alright, Carl and I, that's my friend, were in one of the airport shops getting magazines for our flight home when I saw your father pass by in a wheelchair. At first, I couldn't believe my eyes. I've never told you, but sometimes I have these flashes where I think I see people from the past. Sometimes I even think I see little kids that look like you or your sister when you were children. After the fire and we moved here to Houston, I would see women who looked like your mother on the street or in the mall. I made a fool out of myself many days running after strangers."

"Mattie, please get to the point."

"Well anyway, like I said, I thought I was crazy until I saw Clark not even two minutes later walking behind him pulling luggage. I almost passed out, they both looked the very same, accept they've matured. I ran out into the aisle and watched them as they disappeared. I knew I wasn't dreaming. I knew it was them because I could feel it. I felt my bones get cold and a chill filled the air. It was an eerie, uncomfortable feeling."

"Mattie, why didn't you just tell me?"

"I didn't want to hurt you. Most of all I didn't want them to hurt you."

"If you knew this why did you let me go to Dillon?"

"I knew that Dr. Shaw would tell you what happened. He knew that Clark was alive, but he didn't know about your father, no one did. I also didn't know that Brandenburg was still alive. I figured he was dead too. When I did find out he was alive and he didn't mention your father, I figured he either didn't know or didn't want to tell you. To be honest, I thought you would think that Clark did it, and just leave it alone."

"That still doesn't explain why you told me that I would know the devil when I saw him."

"I figured, if I saw your father just by coincidence and your sister showed up after all these years that anything was possible. I wanted you to know that if you did see Nolan, he is no longer your father and you should be very afraid."

"That still doesn't explain why you didn't tell me all of this, when you knew I was coming out here to find Clark."

"I was hoping that if I prayed hard enough, you would be ok."

At that point I was tired. I still wasn't convinced, but I still couldn't figure out if she was lying about my father all those years. I was tired of talking to Mattie so I said my goodbyes. I knew Isabelle was going crazy, so I called her back. I told her to watch Mattie very closely. Isabelle agreed to watch her as much as she could. One of two things was happening...either everything was falling apart, or everything was falling into place.

Chapter Twenty-Seven

Most of the day had gone by. I'd washed Stewart from my body and shown the house to a couple of people. I needed to do normal everyday things in an attempt to get past the fact that my father was still alive. After I'd eaten, I called Stewart and made small talk on the phone. I had not yet heard from Alex, and I was about to break my promise I'd made to him about not seeing Stewart again, until I talked to him again. I became restless. Stewart had asked me out again that night, and I told him that I was tired. I really was tired. I needed to relax and accept what I'd just uncovered only a few hours earlier. I couldn't believe how crazy my life had become. Alex was right. I was a part of a mafia, or was it a cult? Hell, I didn't even know. I didn't even know that sort of thing happened to black people. I sat down beside the pool, sipping a glass of wine. The pool was dirty from months of being unattended. For a minute, I sat there waiting for Tupac, Elvis, Jimmy Hoffa and my mama to show up. I really needed to mellow out.

For the first time, I didn't think of my old house and my old life the way I'd remembered it. I realized it wasn't a fairytale or the American dream. There was something definitely wrong with us. The crazy part was that it didn't start with my mother or my father, it started with their parents. What was going on inside my head was genetic. Now, more than ever, I am a firm believer that you definitely need to make sure that your mate's family is stable. Find out their entire history or you could be breeding insanity. If your man or woman tells you they don't know anything about their family history, then you move on. Oh, yes, please stay away from people who hate their parents, unless they're like my father and just ain't no earthly good anyway. I felt so sorry for poor Alex. Did he really know what he was getting into? One thing I could say is that he couldn't be surprised by anything I did.

I thought about my family tree. I was the great-grandchild of a racist white man, who beat his wife and children and hung black men from tree limbs. My grandmother died from a broken heart because she couldn't keep her bastard Negro baby. My great-uncle ran away from my grandfather because he was a bad person only to find my mother and go into business with my daddy. My daddy, who planned the murder of his own wife, his two children and faked his own death. Not to mention, there may have been other family members on my father's side that I knew nothing about. Oh, yes his parents and his only living sibling died in a car accident. None of his family would care for him for free so he was sent to an orphanage. I guess rejection and loneliness turned him into a sociopath.

Let me not forget, I used to peddle pussy. I was sleeping with a man that could roll over at any time and slit my throat. I was now sitting there with a gun in my lap planning to kill my dead father, the man I was sleeping with and possibly the woman who had cared for me all those years. Hot damn, weren't we a can of mixed nuts?

Everything was crashing down on me at once. The reality consumed me. There was a time when I thought I was stronger. I thought I could handle anything. I felt vulnerable and unsure of the future. I must've been in shock, walking around there like that was the norm. The shock factor actually worked in my favor that morning. I could have come completely unglued and ruined everything. I drank one glass of wine after another until the bottle was empty. I turned the bottle upside down and watched as the last drop slowly dripped from the rim and splashed to the ground. I became violently angry and threw the bottle against the wall, shattering it into tiny little pieces. I watched as each of the glass fragments hit the ground, and felt as though my life was crumbling as well. I finished the last of the wine that was in my glass and then threw the glass as well. I sat back down in the chair and bundled myself up in my robe.

I sat with my mind in a whirlwind, moving so fast that I found it difficult to concentrate on a single thought. I was thinking so many things at one time. It made me dizzy. I thought about my childhood in Dillon, our arrival in Houston, my college years, Alex, Lauren, Isabelle, Mattie, Clark, Noel, my father, my mother, Brandenburg, Dr. Shaw, my grandparents. You name it, I thought about it until I could do nothing but scream at the top of my lungs. I held my face in my hands, and curled up in the fetal position, and rocked and cried and screamed. I yelled out to my father as if he could hear me. "You bastard! You son-of-a bitch! How could you do this to me!" I was so angry and frustrated. What kind of man did that to his own children? I sat there and prayed that I wouldn't lose my mind completely, and end up back in the psych ward. I prayed that I would wake up from the dream. I begged and pleaded with God for His help and His guidance.

I jumped up from my seat and paced back and forth beside the pool. I stopped and looked into the dirty water and contemplated jumping in and drowning myself. I needed some relief. I needed to let it all go. It was too much for me to handle. I started pacing frantically and didn't even notice that I had stepped on some of the broken glass that lay at my feet. I looked down and I saw that my footprints were crimson, but I didn't feel the pain. I sat down in the chair and examined my feet. After I saw that the wounds weren't very deep, I placed both feet on the ground and sat there staring at the sky.

With my feet bleeding and my mind still spinning, I continued to sit. I looked at Alex's house and wondered why I didn't quit while I was ahead. In the blink of an eye, I could make one bad decision and all of it could've been gone. Would it have been worth it? My eyes filled up with tears and my vision became blurred. I think I sat there for at least two hours trying to get a handle on things. I got up from my chair and washed my feet in the pool. I was tired of thinking. I was tired of wondering. I was just plain tired. I stared at the doorway leading back into the house, it seemed like it was a million miles away, so I sat back down in the chair, propped my feet up and drifted off to sleep.

I woke up the next morning and the sun was beaming on my face. I felt like a truck had hit me. My head was pounding and the mere thought of moving my eyes was unbearable. My feet were throbbing with pain and my mouth felt like I'd eaten a bag of flour. I got up and tried to avoid stepping into the glass again. I walked into the kitchen, reached into the refrigerator and grabbed another bottle of wine. My plan was to go through the day, either drunk or asleep. I opened the bottle of wine and didn't even bother to get a glass, I drank straight from the bottle. I took the bottle and walked up the stairs to the bedroom, and went straight into the bathroom. I had to pee so badly, I thought I was going to burst. As the toilet flushed, I stared into the mirror. My hair was all over my head and I had crusty stuff in the corners of my eyes. I grabbed the bottle off the counter, took another swig and walked over to the bed, where I sat and watched my phone light up. I had several missed calls and missed messages. I looked at the house phone and saw the message indicator light on. I didn't feel like talking to anyone. I picked up the phone and texted Alex and Isabelle, "Don't worry. I'm fine. I just need some time to myself."

Within minutes they replied, "Ok." I turned my phone off, placed the bottle on the nightstand and wrapped myself in the covers. My hair was a mess, my eyes were all crusted up, my feet were dirty, my breath tasted like kerosene and smelled like garbage. I just curled up in all my filth and went to sleep. I woke up a few hours later, turned over and looked at the clock. The sun was still shining. I got up and closed the curtains and got back in bed. I hadn't eaten since sometime yesterday, and my stomach felt like it was touching my back. I didn't care. All I wanted to do was sleep.

It was now eleven o'clock, the sun had set and I was still alive. I was lying there staring at the ceiling. I caught a whiff of myself and jumped into the shower. I combed my hair, brushed my teeth and crawled back in bed where I slept for a few more hours.

Once I awakened and freshened up, I made my way downstairs, and realized I hadn't locked the door that lead to the pool. My instincts told me to take my gun, just in case. I felt weak and sick from all the wine that I consumed on an empty stomach. I dressed in my sweats and walked downstairs, and out by the pool again. The broken glass was still there waiting to be swept away. With the wine bottle still by my side, I took another sip. It was hot and bitter. My stomach lurched and I put the bottle down. What was I doing sitting there, wallowing in self-pity? And where was my 'rock bottom'? All my plans had been altered. There was more than just Stewart now. There was also my father. I never included him in the equation. I sat there on the edge of my seat, and looked over at the bottle of warm wine and the shattered bottle on the ground, and realized I was no closer to solving the problem than when I started the first bottle. Suddenly, an unexpected burst of wind swept through the area, sending the wine bottle rolling off of the table. I watched it shatter as it hit the floor. I listened to the wind and felt the cool air on my face. Then, I heard the faint voice of a woman ringing in my ears, "I'm so tired, I need to rest."

It scared me. My heart began to beat rapidly. I looked around to see if there was someone standing there. Then I heard the voice again. This time I recognized it. It was my mother's voice. I only heard her. I couldn't see her, but I felt her. I called out to her.

"Mama!"

She answered back, speaking clearly, "Noel, I've brought you too far for you to mess this up. You have to finish what you started. I'm tired and I'm fading. I need to finally rest, but I can't do it without you. You are the only one who can help me and in helping me you will help yourself. Now get up...get past this, please Noel..." Her voice trailed off.

As suddenly as she had come, my mother disappeared. I heard something, a noise from inside the house. I was really feeling the backlash of my liquor. I was starting to hear things. The wind picked up again and I heard the noises inside the house again. I looked around wildly as I thought someone was trying to get into the house. I grabbed my gun and sprang up from my seat.

"Oh, my God, Stewart and Reginald know who I am and they've come to kill me." My thoughts scared the hell out of me. My heart was beating fast. I ran to the front of the house, I didn't see anything. I ran toward the garage, I didn't see anything there either. I ran through the house like a mad woman, looking in every room, checking windows and the doors. I was growing more and more paranoid by the minute, and I kept hearing eerie sounds inside the house. As I headed back down stairs, I stopped dead in my tracks, almost tumbling down the stairs. Resting on the bottom step was a cat. I guess he'd gotten in through the patio doors while I was passed out drunk. I laughed to myself and shook my head. I picked the cat up and opened the front door.

Before setting him outside I said, "Were you the one who scared my mommy away?" I closed the door behind me and went out back to lock the patio doors. Once I made sure everything was secure, I turned in for the night. I locked my bedroom door, just in case the cat wasn't my only visitor.

That seemed to be one of the longest days of my life. I needed to relax, so I made sure I brought the remainder of the wine upstairs with me. I needed something to take the edge off. I felt so wired, I felt like a kid on sugar. I turned the television on and poured a glass of wine and ran my bathwater. I looked around the room for what seemed like the first time. The house definitely belonged to a man. There's nothing frilly or silky about it. All his towels were basic colors, black, blue, red, no flowers or designs. I took the time to be a typical woman left alone in her man's house. I checked for any traces of a woman. I knew most people in his position, financial and so-called celebrity status didn't just bring people home. If anyone had been there, she would have had to be someone special. The only woman I saw was me. There were pictures everywhere, and I wondered just how many he kept around. I could see him taking them down before female company came over. Robert was right. There were pictures of us everywhere. In a way I was flattered, but the warped side of my personality was worried that it bordered on obsession. I found comfort in knowing someone loved me that much, and finally I had to admit that I loved him unconditionally.

I was talking crap earlier about how he could accept me or move on, when the truth was I would be lost without Alex. I mean, even more lost than I was at that time. I'd made the right decision choosing him over Maxwell. Maxwell was a good person, but I didn't think he would've been able to handle me. Alex was more of a take-charge kind of man, which was what I needed. I could get out of hand sometimes. Maxwell needed someone a little more docile with less fire. He needed someone he could talk to as if she were one of his patients. One thing was for sure, he wouldn't be single very long, he had a whole lot to offer.

After I finished rummaging through the house, I tried to call Lauren. She deserved to know what was going on. I sat and thought for a minute before I picked up the phone. What should I tell her... what should I have said? After all I didn't know what kind of mood she'd be in. I stared at the phone, contemplating about how to tell her. While I was holding the phone, it rang. I nearly fell off the bed.

I looked at the screen to see who was calling. I was hoping it was Alex, but it was Maxwell. I was shocked to hear from him, especially at that hour. I hadn't heard from him since he'd left Dillon. I was actually glad he called, although I really didn't know what to say to him. I was so happy with Alex, I didn't want to hide it, but I didn't want to flaunt it either. I hit the TALK button and put on my best voice.

"Hello stranger," he said once I answered.

"Now you know it's not like that."

"I know you've probably been pretty busy."

"Yes, I have."

"I hear congratulations are in order."

"Excuse me!"

"Aren't you engaged?"

I was caught off guard. Was he really congratulating me or was he being facetious? "Yes, I sure am."

"Have you guys set a date yet?"

"Right now it looks to be August 13th. You know we have to wait until the season is over, and of course there's always the possibility of the playoffs. I'm actually out here in California showing the house Alex has for sale." Just in case his motives were twisted, I wanted to make sure he understood where I was coming from.

"Well it seems that everything is pretty set."

"Yes, I'm really excited. I can't wait."

There was a little disappointment in his voice. "So you're really going to marry Alex without really even dating him first?" There we go ... the real reason for this call.

"Maxwell, I've known Alex almost all of my life."

"You don't think that you two might be too close to maintain a romantic relationship?"

"Look Maxwell, the bottom line is I have loved Alex for a long time...real love. Not some watered down, bubble gum, teenage shit. It's not like you and I had a long courtship."

"Sometimes it doesn't take long to realize that two people are meant to be together."

"Maxwell, I think my engagement to Alex proves that you and I aren't meant to be together. I really think you should move on."

"I have. I'm dating someone. That's why I called you." Obviously Maxwell needed some therapy himself. Why would he call me and start some mess, if he'd moved on? I was so glad he'd found someone else. At least I didn't have to worry about him standing up at the wedding confessing his undying love.

"Well, Maxwell if you've moved on, why do you feel the need to discuss it with me?" The conversation was pointless and I was already pretty agitated.

"Look Seth, I guess our conversation took a wrong turn somewhere. I just called to tell you ...," he hesitated, "I've been seeing your sister Lauren."

Whoa, keep it in the family why don't you. I was annoyed by the fact that neither one of them had bothered to tell me about this, plus the fact that it was my sister he'd chosen to heal himself with. I also wondered if he actually cared for her or if he was just trying to get back at me. I really wanted to know if he knew what had happened the last time I saw Lauren. Now the human side of me wondered how long they had been eyeing each other. I remembered them showing up at the airport together. For just a brief moment I was lingering between being pissed and jealous. While I was trying to figure out what to say, I thought about Alex and how he made my spine tingle.

"That's great. I'm glad that the two of you found each other. I've been saying for a while she needs a psychiatrist. You both deserve to be happy." I didn't think that was what he expected. I didn't think he detected my sarcasm either.

"You mean you're ok with this?"

"Of course, I'm fine with it. Lauren has been through a lot and if you make her happy then that's all I need to hear." There was silence for a few seconds. I thought I would let him off the hook. "Hey look, it's good to hear from you, but Alex is on the other line and I need to get that. So, I'll talk to you later."

Reluctantly, he said, "Ok, I'll talk to you later."

Alex wasn't on the other end. I just wanted to end the conversation. I thought more and more about the Maxwell and Lauren thing, and couldn't figure out why she hadn't mentioned it to me. I was also curious to find out how it all happened. Who made the first move? Somewhere in my gut, I thought it started before we broke up. There are some things a woman thinks she knows, and some things a woman feels in her blood. I felt this in my blood. If they had a fling while Maxwell and I were dating well, that was just bullshit. I thought about picking up the phone and calling Lauren, but that would be petty. What did I care? I was happy with Alex. The whole thing just didn't sit well with me, something wasn't right. We couldn't possibly talk about Maxwell together, because she knew what I knew about him. I went back to the day Lauren and I had it out in front of the store, was it going on then? Did she think she was getting over on me? Was she with him when she trotted off and left Noel with me? I guess, maybe she really did want what I had. How the hell should I have felt about it? The more I thought about it, the more the issue changed from Lauren and Maxwell screwing each other behind my back, to that sneaky little heifer.

I put Maxwell and Lauren out of my head. They were small potatoes compared to what I really needed to deal with, and I couldn't let
anything throw me off my path. I shook my head as if to shake all the
unimportant things out of it. I plugged my phone into the charger and
prepared to take my bath. As I was soaking in the tub, the events of
the day began to take its toll. I felt my eyes getting heavier and my
throat got dry. I tried to fight back the tears, but there was no use. I
brought my knees closer to my chest, wrapped myself in my own
arms, and sat there as the tears fell and became one with the water in
the tub. I looked up toward the ceiling and begged my mother to come
to me and help me. She had reassured me before, and right then I
needed her more than ever. I didn't know what to believe. I didn't
know who to trust. I felt like everything was slipping away from me. I
came out there to find the truth and take care of it. Now that I had the
truth, I really didn't know if I had the strength to go through with
taking care of the problems. I felt like walking into Stewart and
Reginald's place and just shooting. I could've actually done that. I
already knew I could get into the house. Reginald was in a wheelchair. How much damage could he do? Suddenly, I didn't care about
the truth. Hell, I already knew it. My father was a low down dirty
piece of shit, and he needed to pay for what he'd done. I sat there
trying to figure the whole thing out. There was something that I was
not seeing. Something that was right there in my face, but I just
couldn't figure out what it was. I thought so hard, I started to get a
headache.

The wine was taking over my body, and I could feel myself drifting
off to sleep. I found myself walking barefoot and naked through
hundreds of trees. I was cold and my body was trembling. I started
running through the trees, looking for a way out, and every time I
grabbed hold of a tree, it disappeared. Everything I touched disappeared. I screamed for help. Suddenly, I saw Lauren standing near a
tree. She was with Maxwell and had a huge smile on her face. I begged
her to help me but she laughed. I ran toward her with my arms outstretched, but I ran right through her. I saw Isabelle and Alex, they
reached out their hands to help me, but the more I ran to them the
farther away they went. Finally, I saw a light and I ran toward it. In
the midst of the light was my mother. I ran right into her. She
wrapped her arms around me, and I felt the warmth from her body

comfort me. She looked at me tenderly, and told me I was almost there, and I would finally find my way soon. She said I needed to take things just as they came to me, and that I shouldn't make waves where there were none. She instructed me to follow my head, and to leave my emotions out of it. She made another reference to a wolf in sheep's clothing. When I raised my head to ask her what she meant, she began to disappear, and as she faded away, she smiled.

"Nicolette loves you. She's waiting for you to save her." She said as she disappeared. I reached my arms out to her, but there was nothing there. How could I save my sister? What was I supposed to do? As I stretched my hands out farther, I felt myself beginning to choke. I found myself drowning in my bath water. My hands were still extended as though I were reaching for my mother. I grabbed the side of the tub and pulled myself up. I jumped out of the tub so fast, I almost slipped on the water that had spilled out onto the floor. I stood in the mirror completely naked trying to get a hold of my senses. When I felt my nakedness, I grabbed a towel, dried off and wrapped myself up. I grabbed another towel and wrapped my head. I pressed my hand to my chest and felt my heart pounding. The floor was still wet, so I carefully walked into the bedroom and sat on the edge of the bed. I was grateful that I hadn't drowned. I didn't have time to think of my dream. I just lay down on the bed and curled up in the fetal position, blinking my eyes fiercely, afraid to fall asleep. My mind was blank, and I didn't want to think of anything in particular.

Chapter Twenty-Eight

When I woke up the next morning, my body and my head felt overwhelmingly heavy. I lay staring at the ceiling for about ten minutes trying to gather my thoughts. For the first time in days, I was thinking clearly. My emotions had taken several turns within the last few days, but the shock of seeing my father was wearing off. I went from joy, to pain, to disgust, to rage and now finally I was just numb. I threw back the covers and placed my feet on the floor, but I didn't stand up. I sat on the edge of the bed staring at the mess I'd made. The room was in disarray, my dirty clothes were everywhere. My eyes were dry, and my head felt like it was going to burst.

I remembered my night with Stewart. Lust is a very confusing emotion. It's one of those things that causes you to step outside of yourself and do dumb shit. I was so disgusted with myself because I had allowed myself to fall for him. I had been totally taken in by that man. His sly grin and his perfect teeth had seduced me. It was just something that couldn't be described, you would have to experience it for yourself. Lust is one of those emotions that make you think you're in love with a mutha fucka. I've learned that a gorgeous smile and beautiful eyes will fuck you up if you stare too long. And let's not even factor in the fact that he was as fine as cat hair. I think it was his mannerisms, the way he carried himself. He knew that at first glance, he had the power to make women fall to their knees. The rest was purely left to chance and conversation. I didn't know what came over me the other night. I was just glad I had the strength to take control of the situation.

I remember Stewart when I was a child, he always smelled so good. He wore this cologne called 'Grey Flannel'. I remembered sometimes when he'd leave the couch he was sitting on I would smell the pillows that he'd held or that had cushioned his back. There was something about that fragrance that was comforting. He was always so smooth or slick as my mother referred to him, and he could dress his ass off. His clothes were always neat and starched. He wore tailor made suits and shoes with good soles and the finest leather. He got pedicures when it was considered taboo for men, and he was always polished to perfection. I remembered that he hated walking on our gravel-covered driveway. Once he made it into the house, he would take out a handkerchief and dust his shoes off.

He was even more meticulous when it came to his cars. He drove this red convertible. He would ride us around in it with the top down, but we couldn't dare eat in it or put our feet on the seats. My father was identically immaculate. I thought of those two distinctly handsome men and wondered what went wrong. Was it something I'd done to make my father not love me anymore? Was it something that Nicolette or my mother had done? Why would he do that to us? Did he even know the hell I've had to live through all those years? I just couldn't understand it. I wanted the chance to sit down and have a conversation with that man, Reginald. I wanted to know if my father was still in there somewhere. Most importantly, I wanted to know if it was hereditary.

Would I wake up one day, look at Alex and say, "I want it all?" Would I look at Alex's wealth and want it all to myself? Was I capable of plotting, planning and executing a plan to murder my own husband and children? The thought of me carrying that genetically heinous gene terrified me. I thought back to the last time I saw Lauren, and how angry I became. I was so angry my nose started to bleed. I remember thinking as I stood there staring into her eyes, just how much I wanted to physically rip her head off. I could feel my fists balling as they rested by my sides. I could feel my body boil from my toes on up to my brain. I really wanted to hurt her. I thought about all the things I'd done throughout my life and the minimal value that I had placed on the lives of others. I had to find a way to control the anger that raged inside of me.

I was tired of thinking, it was making my head hurt. I started removing the sheets from my bed. I balled them up and threw them on the floor with the rest of the dirty clothes that I placed in the corner to be washed. I walked to the bathroom, ran the comb through my hair, pinned it up, brushed my teeth and washed my face. Standing by the door that lead to the balcony, I drew back the curtains, opened the doors, and inhaled the California air. I wondered what the weather was like back home. The air in Houston would take your breath away. If I were at home I wouldn't be standing on the balcony catching a breeze. I did know one thing though. I would give my right arm to be back at home riding around in the heat and humidity. There was no place like home. As I lit my cigar and took a drag, I remembered those words: "There was no place like home." For as long as I could remember, I had been longing to go back home to Dillon, but the truth is my home was not there anymore. My home was where my family was. My family consisted of Isabelle, Robert, Mattie and Alex. I wasn't so sure about Lauren anymore. I couldn't make her love me. I couldn't make her come around. When she finally realized I just wanted to be her friend, my door would be open. I wanted to be her friend first, because realistically speaking, the only thing that bound us as sisters was the blood that ran through our veins. There was nothing familiar between us. We didn't even share the same memories.

I guess I didn't realize that the whole ordeal was probably more traumatic for her than it was for me. Neither Lauren nor I were those same eight year olds anymore. We were grown women who had led our own separate lives. We had different experiences. We believed in different things. I believed in releasing myself from this curse that had plagued my family. I wanted to confront the past and get rid of anything that reminded me of what happened to us. Lauren dealt with the pain we shared very differently. She lashed out in anger, wanting others to feel the pain she felt.

For the first time, I had included Mattie in my family schematic without reservations. During my drunken stupor, I realized life hadn't been easy for her. She had been through a lot. I knew what she meant when she said she had to keep everyone's secrets. I could imagine if anyone should've been in an asylum, it should've rightfully been her. I had to realize that she was really only trying to protect me. She tried to protect me from my father and even from Lauren. I'd always considered myself completely grown up because of the way I'd lived my life. The past year has prepared me to live my life as an adult. I'd opened myself up and found true love. Not only the love that I shared with Alex, but also the love I had for Noel, Isabelle, Kelly, Quincy, Mattie and Robert. I'd learned to trust and depend on others. The people I loved had truly allowed me to show a side of myself that I knew was there, but fought to release. Isabelle had been there for me since the beginning. She had gone along with every crazy thing I'd wanted to do in order to gain my freedom. Mattie had protected me all those years as if I were her own flesh and blood. I knew my mother and Mattie had shared a special relationship. I couldn't help but think that my mother appointed Mattie as my guardian angel.

Then there was Alex. What could I say about him? Either he was totally whipped or he was just a damn good man who loved the hell out of me. I felt spoiled by Alex. He made me feel as though the things I'd lived through were worth going through just to have him. Every time my heart beat, I thought of him. I lived in a realistic world and knew that we wouldn't have the perfect marriage. There are no perfect relationships. I did know that I would give my marriage all that I had and I would give Alex all the love and respect that he deserved.

Before Alex, I thought that, if I showed a man I truly loved and cared for him, it would reveal my weaknesses. I realize now that love is strength. It takes a strong person to love unconditionally. It takes a strong person to throw caution to the wind and put trust in another human being who's not perfect either. As I sat there and admired the L.A. landscape, my heart filled with two very distinct emotions; the love I felt for my family, coupled with the utter contempt and hatred I felt for Stewart and my father. I felt like I was in an emotional tug of war. One minute, I was consumed with warm feelings and the next I was as cold as ice. As I took the last drag from my cigar, I realized I must extinguish one of those emotions brewing inside of me before I was lost once again among my confused and tortured soul. I needed to finish what I started, and that was to destroy the cancer that tore my family apart. I had to destroy the nucleus of that disease. Stewart was a product of his environment and the company he kept. My father was the beginning and the end of this tragedy. I took the cigar out of my mouth and studied it. It had burned down to almost nothing and I had to put it down. There was nothing left, and it had to be extinguished. I looked at the burning end once more, and dropped the cigar on the ground and put the fire out with my foot.

I walked back into the bedroom and picked up my phone from the nightstand. I guess I'd unconsciously turned it on vibrate. My message indicator was blinking and there were so many missed calls, I couldn't count them. I looked over at the house phone and it said the mailbox was full. I dreaded listening to all of those messages. I was hoping they were all for Alex. I didn't even bother to check them. I didn't know who or what Alex had calling the house and I didn't want to mess up and hear a message that would cause me to upset both of us, so I did what any woman would do, I erased them. Neither one of us would know who called. I scrolled through my phone and of course I saw Alex's number several times. I retrieved my voicemail and the first message was from Alex, saying, "Hey baby, it's me. I know you need some time to yourself right now, but I just want you to know, I'm here and I love you. Please call me soon."

There were messages from Isabelle, Mattie, Stewart and even Robert. Everyone wanted to hear from me. Of course, Stewart wanted to see me again and I needed to see him. I wanted to request dinner with him and his 'brother'. I wanted to just sit across the table from Reginald and figure out what the hell was wrong with him. I needed to see if I could actually be in the same room with him and maintain my sanity. I had to admit that seeing him, after a lifetime of thinking he was dead, had me all twisted up. There were so many questions I had rolling around in my head. I listened to Stewart's message. "Hey Seth, it's Stewart. I just wanted to let you know how much I enjoyed being with you. I don't know...there's something about you, I just can't get you out of my head. I really want to see you. Please call me." I had to admit, hearing the desperation in his voice intrigued me. I'd finally reached my last message and it wasn't from Alex. It was from Stewart. "Seth, this is Stewart. I don't know what's going on. I've been calling you and leaving you messages for two days. I hope you're ok. I'm trying to respect the fact that you're in a relationship, but I'm concerned about you. I do know where Alex Young lives and I don't want to just pop up...it's just a thought. I need to know if you are keeping your distance because of something that I've done or didn't do. I know I couldn't have been that bad...please call me and at least let me know you're ok. If I don't hear from you by tomorrow, then I will send someone to check on you."

I immediately hung up the phone and dialed Stewart. All I needed was for some crazy killer to show up at the door. Plus, I needed to see my father and in order to set that up, I needed Stewart. He answered the phone on the second ring.

"Hello."

"Hi, Stewart."

"Well, look who decided to call."

"I know. I got your messages. I've just been really busy. I apologize. I didn't mean for you to worry."

"Well, at first I was offended. I was hoping you hadn't left town without saying a word. I thought maybe you didn't enjoy yourself the other night, but then I became concerned. I hope you're ok."

"I'm fine. And no, it wasn't personal. Like I said, I was just really busy."

"Ok, I understand. I guess I'm not too offended."

I wanted so badly to suggest dinner with him and Reginald, but I didn't know how to bring it into the conversation. So, I just invited him to lunch. "Well, why don't you let me make it up to you? How about meeting me for a late lunch? Let's say around one o'clock?"

"That sounds great, why don't you meet me at Griffin's, you know the restaurant on Patton."

"That's fine. I know exactly where that is. I guess I'll see you then."

"I can't wait. It seems like forever since I've seen you."

"I know. I'll definitely make it up to you."

I didn't wait to hear his response I just hung up the phone. While I was sitting there my phone vibrated in my hand. This time it was Alex. Since I'd been drunk for the past two days and hadn't spoken to him, I was excited. I could finally talk to him with a clear head. I picked up the phone and answered with excitement in my voice.

"Hey baby. How are you?"

By the tone of his voice, Alex was shocked by my excitement. "Well, this is a pleasant surprise. It's good to hear that you're happy for a change."

"Yeah well, I've had a lot of time to think these last two days, and to be honest, I really should have expected to see my father. I mean after I talked to Dr. Shaw and Charlie, I should have known. Not to mention Mattie had tried her best to warn me."

"I understand, but I really think Mattie should have told you about him."

"Yes, maybe she should have told me. You know when I was young-er; I used to think that if I talked about my parents and my sister and referred to them as being dead, I would actually have to admit that they were dead. I honestly think that if Mattie admitted to Clark and my father being alive, she'd have to admit we would never truly be safe. I had to remember that it was not just my life that was altered, it was hers as well."

"I am so proud of you. You do know that a year ago you would not have been able to forgive her."

"A year ago, we wouldn't even be together. I guess a lot has changed for the best."

"Amen, you can say that again. So what do you have up for the day?"

"Are you sure you want to know?"

"No, don't tell me. I don't want to know anything."

"I'm just going to have a little lunch that's all."

"Just make sure the restaurant is full of people. And make sure all you have is lunch."

"Don't worry, Alex. I'll be on my best behavior."

"Yeah, I've seen your best behavior. That's what made me chase you around like a fool all these years."

"You are so crazy."

"Crazy about you. I can't believe you won't let me come out there to my own house."

"I can't stop you from coming out here, but I know that you respect my wishes and you're gonna stay right where you are."

"Yeah baby, you're right. I'm gonna be a little more patient, but I can fly out there at any time."

"I know you can and you will. Look baby, I need to get ready, so I'll call you later."

Alex and I hung up and I began to get ready for my lunch date. I made sure I looked extra good. I decided to show a little more skin, and put on a short little tasteful sundress with spaghetti straps and my stiletto sandals with the straps around the ankle and the toe. The dress was multi-colored with orange, yellow, pink and red. It was bright and brought out my skin tone. It looked great with my short cut and long earrings. I made sure my legs and arms were oiled. I hated to see a well-dressed ashy woman, or man for that matter. I put on a light perfume that was made especially for me. It was really more like oil. I dabbed it on my pulse points. After I finished dressing, I did the sniff test, checked my hair, checked my makeup and grabbed the keys to the Benz. I decided to be a little sporty that day. I wanted to make sure my strut was fierce. As I walked to the car I practiced my walk.

Stewart loved to see me walk. He said it was classy with a little bit of sassy.

When I arrived at the restaurant, Stewart was standing out front waiting for me. I stepped out of the car, handed the keys to the valet, and walked around the car toward Stewart. I flashed a smile to acknowledge my happiness at seeing him. He was immaculately groomed as always, wearing a pink button down linen dress shirt and a pair of camel colored linen slacks. If a man could successfully wear a pink shirt then he could damn near wear anything. I looked down at his feet and checked out his camel colored leather sandals. I didn't normally go for men in sandals, but his feet looked better than mine. His sleeves were rolled up, putting his forearms on display. As I walked toward him, I noticed that Stewart was better looking than Alex. Just to clarify, there are various adjectives used to describe a person. I've heard some refer to me as beautiful. Others refer to me as pretty or even cute. Beauty is definitely in the eye of the beholder. Different people value different things. Alex was just plain sexy. His walk, his smile, his complexion, everything about him was sexy. Stewart had the intoxicating mystic that made you want to know more. Stewart was like this wild buck that you wanted to tie down just for the thrill of the capture. He was the kind of man you could enjoy for the moment, because once you've broken him down, there was nothing left to wonder. He was smooth like silk, but raw like unrefined sugar. Alex was the kind you gave your panties to just because he was big, black and beautiful. Watching him grip a basketball in the palm of one hand with room left for air made you want to nestle in his safe embrace. Stewart took you in and made you feel like you want to be a part of his world, but you knew that he could never truly be the one. He talked a good game and if you didn't watch yourself you could fall for his mack. Stewart told every woman the same thing: "You are so fine. You're beautiful. Girl you know you a bad mutha fucka." Stewart was good for my ego. Alex was good for my soul.

Stewart would tell you he loved you and would almost make you believe it, until his true colors emerged. If you didn't watch him, he would paralyze you with his smooth demeanor, crafty smile and words that glided off his tongue like honey. Stewart was the one your mother warned you about.

I walked up to Stewart, planted my feet, and stood on my tiptoes to kiss him on the cheek. When my feet were once again leveled, I walked toward the door to enter the restaurant. Stewart grabbed me by the arm and I stopped in my tracks.

He said, "Listen, I hope you don't mind, but my brother will be joining us today." While he was speaking, I could feel my stomach moving with nervous tension. I definitely wasn't prepared to see Reginald just yet. "Reginald had a doctor's appointment today, and it ran a little longer than expected. Of course I didn't want to miss seeing you so, I brought him along. I really didn't think you'd mind."

I tried to hide my discomfort as I said, "No, I don't mind, the more the merrier." I turned away from Stewart, arched my back, held my head high, took a deep breath and sashayed into the restaurant. I could feel his eyes on my backside as I walked in front of him, I heard him whisper, "Damn." Before I approached the table, I could see Reginald sitting in his wheelchair. I started to flash back twenty years, to the night I saw him lying in a pool of blood with a hole in his body.

I could hear my mother shriek as she begged for mercy. I could hear the cries of a woman whom I've never heard before, begging for someone to find her and help her, "Noel, help me. Please save me." Her unfamiliar voice and my mental rejection of something new into my already overcrowded memory jolted me back to reality. I put the voices and the vision in the back of my mind. I knew that I would only bring them out later to analyze them. I walked slowly toward Reginald. He rolled away from the table, flashed a smile and extended his hand to greet me. I smiled and extended my hand as well.

As our flesh touched, I heard the voice again, "Noel, please save me." My mind flashed back to the night of the fire. I saw visions of my father and my mother once again. I shook the visions from my mind. I retrieved my hand from his and took my place at the table, as Stewart pulled out my chair. I was sitting between two accidents waiting to happen. I was sitting directly across from one of the sickest mutha fucka's in the world. And sitting on the other side of me, was a man I wished I'd met in another lifetime. At that point I didn't know who was crazier, them or me. I wished I could have crawled into the minds of each one of them and find out just what made them tick. I sat there and pictured little men dressed in black walking around in Reginald's head carefully calculating the work of the devil. Inside Stewart's head

I could see little men as well, half-dressed in gray telling him to listen to whatever the cripple told him. I wondered which one of those sons-of-bitches turned the other one out. Who slaughtered the first sacrificial lamb? Which one of them discovered the power of control first, and then shared his secret with the other?

As I sat there and looked into the eyes of each of those men, what disturbed me the most was all these years I wasted trying to figure out who I took after. I found out that it had been my father all along. We were one in the same. I was disappointed in my biological conception. I'm ashamed to now acknowledge this man as my father.

After the waiter finished pouring our water and taking our additional drink order, Reginald led the conversation. "Seth, I hope you don't mind my joining you two for lunch. You have obviously captivated my little brother. He seems to be quite taken with you. So, I couldn't pass up the opportunity to be intrigued as well."

I glanced over at Stewart and watched the blood drain from his face as he was referred to as 'little brother'. His discontent helped me to understand the true dynamics of their relationship. No matter how long they'd been wreaking havoc together, Reginald still saw Stewart as his "boy." I thought Stewart needed someone to point that out to him.

"Well, I must say, I do enjoy the company of a good man, or in this case good men."

Reginald raised his glass of water and said, "Hey, I'll drink to that." Stewart sat there quietly as Reginald monopolized the conversation. I reached over and touched Stewart's hand and asked if he was alright.

Reginald answered for him, "Stewart's ok. I think you have rendered him speechless."

Stewart smiled only showing half of his teeth. I caressed Stewart's hand, gave him a reassuring wink and continued my conversation. I was curious to know how they would answer my next question. I took a sip of water and put the glass back on the table.

"Forgive me for being forward, but you don't look anything alike. It's almost like night and day."

Of course, Reginald acknowledged my question before Stewart had a chance to part his lips. "We aren't blood brothers. Actually, we grew up in the same foster home when we were kids. Since then it's really only been the two of us. So even though we aren't blood, we're still just like brothers." I looked over at Stewart as he smiled in agreement with Reginald's answer. Just as the waiter approached Reginald inquired about my family. "How about you?"

I knew what he was referring to, but I just played it off. "What about me?"

"Your family...do have any brothers or sisters?"

I really wanted to say, "Of course I have a sister you slimy snake." But I didn't. I just made something up. "Actually, I'm an only child. As for parents, my mother was killed in a car accident when I was eight and my father may as well be dead. He left us long before my mother's accident. I'm sure he's crawling around under a rock somewhere. To be honest, I've blocked him so far from my memory, I don't even remember what he looks like."

Reginald placed his menu on the table and said, "Your mother had to be a beautiful woman. I can't imagine any man leaving a gorgeous woman and a child."

I couldn't believe he had the nerve to utter those words. Hell, he'd left a beautiful woman and two precious children. Oh, I forgot. He murdered his wife and children. The waiter's presence at the table gave me just enough of a distraction to resist the urge to jab my knife through his neck.

Stewart looked over at me and said, "Honey, do you know what you're going to order?"

I wanted to say, Reginald's head on a platter. I said "Yes, I'm going to have the salmon."

Stewart ordered a steak and Reginald ordered chicken. Once the waiter left us alone, I picked up where the conversation had left off.

"Well I know Stewart has never been married, but what about you Reginald? For some reason you seem like the marrying type."

He rested his hand on the arm of his chair and leaned back. "Actually, I was married once, to a beautiful woman."

Stewart leaned in closer to the table as if he were anxious to hear more as well. He had this look on his face like, "I wonder what this Negro is gonna say next."

I baited Reginald along, but I got the feeling he desperately wanted to explain what had happened between he and his wife. I sat back in my chair, so that I could be comfortable while I listened to his explanation. I needed to brace myself for the bullshit that was about to spew from his lips. "So what happened between you two, if I may ask?"

Reginald conjured up a concerned look and said, "It's been so long that I've learned to accept it."

It was obvious he wanted me to drag it out of him. "Accept what?" He was beginning to piss me off.

"My wife and my little girl were killed in a robbery while I was away on a business trip. Like I said, it was so long ago, over twenty years. Like you were when your mother was killed in a car accident, my little girl was eight when my wife died. My daughter was so beautiful. I guess she'd be about twenty-eight or twenty-nine by now. Sitting here looking at you...you've got to be around that age. I'd like to think that she would have turned out at least half as beautiful as you. She had the most beautiful green eyes. I used to call her my green-eyed butterfly."

As he was letting the words 'green eyed butterfly' flow from his lips, I almost choked on my water. I sat as still as a statue and batted my eyes trying to transport myself from that moment in time.

I looked over at Stewart. He had a blank look on his face. That sick and twisted paraplegic asshole was pure evil. I wanted to thank Reginald for his lie that was so close to the truth. His adaptation of the tragedy that was my life helped me to see him for what he really was. There was one of two things going on: Reginald was just an evil bastard or he knew who I was and he was fucking with me to see just how strong I really was. It could've possibly been a combination of both.

Stewart was as quiet as a church mouse waiting to hear what Reginald had to say next. He hadn't said much during the lunch, it was like Reginald had him under some sort of spell. I remembered what Charlie had said about the unnatural hold my father had on him.

I looked back over at Reginald and said, "My goodness, I guess we have more in common than I thought. It's amazing how so many people share the same kinds of tragedy." I took a sip of my water and asked Reginald, "Let me ask you this. Do you ever think about revenge? I mean do you ever want to make the people who did this to you suffer for what they did? Assuming they haven't already been punished."

Reginald twisted his head to the side. "Wow, that's a rather odd question. Revenge is a pretty serious thing. Sometimes you just need to let the past go. Some people have no control over what they do or how they feel. Murder is a crime of emotion and you never know what drives people to stab, shoot or even get behind the wheel of a car drunk. I'm sure whoever hurt you and your family is paying in their own way."

There seemed to be some sort of cat and mouse game going on between the two of us. It had gone from a simple lunch to a carefully crafted game of chess. I fingered my napkin, which was still rolled up on the table and looked over at Reginald.

"I guess you're right. It is a crime of emotion. Even the thought of murder takes a special kind of evil. It seems that there are some things that leave a hole in you so deep you'll stop at nothing to fill it...that is assuming you have human feelings."

At that point, I could feel a lump forming in my throat, and the skin on my face tightening. I must have gone to some other place that I quickly needed to return from. I was letting my emotions take over. Even though I was sitting there with thoughts of cruel and inhumane punishment for Reginald, I couldn't help but feel overwhelmed by his presence. As hard as I tried to accept the fact that he was a cold-blooded killer, I still couldn't get over the fact that he was my father. I couldn't get over the fact that he'd been alive all those years. There I sat at the table across from my father and thought about how I mourned for him. I thought about my nightmares, and the many sleepless nights. On the nights when my mother visited me, I begged time and time again to hear something from my father. I've prayed for his soul to be safe and secure. I thought about the mental anguish that I'd gone through: the suicide attempts, the panic attacks, the insecurities. I watched him die for God's sake, as he lay in that pool of blood. What was I missing? Did I blink and miss something? The longer I sat there, the more heated I became. I felt the words forming at the tip of my tongue. I wanted to yell out to him. I wanted to ask, "Why and how could you do this to me?" I felt the words pass through my stomach and up past my throat.

I opened my mouth and said, "I must apologize for my passion. Sometimes I just get carried away with my emotions."

"It's ok. Grief can be an overwhelming emotion."

"I guess so. There's something in your eyes that tells me you don't have a problem with guilt or grief. You seem so strong and controlled. You appear to enjoy being in control. I mean look at the way you've monopolized the conversation. I'm Stewart's guest, yet I haven't heard his voice since I've been here. These aren't bad things. They are actually strengths. If I were in a fight, I would definitely want you on my team, minus the chair of course."

Reginald found my latter comment amusing. He threw his head back and laughed. He maintained his composure and smiled at me with a devious grin. He leaned back with that smirk still resting on his face and said, "Miss St. James, I must commend you on an adequate analysis. You're absolutely right. The eyes never lie no matter how you try to hide them. They are the windows to the soul. They unlock all hidden secrets. I must say, you have some of the most beautiful eyes that I've ever seen. They remind me of my wife. I'm sure they tell the most captivating story."

The mention of my mother drove a knife straight through my heart. I felt as if he was saying checkmate. There seemed to be some unspoken acknowledgement of our existence. It was as if we had a secret between just the two of us. I felt the conversation could really intensify if we didn't just stop and leave it there.

I placed my hand in my lap and said, "I'm sure one day we'll sit around and swap stories. I'd love to hear what your eyes have to say."

Just as the air between us thickened, the waiter arrived with our food and a wave of relief shot across Stewart's face. "It's about time, I'm starving," he said.

I couldn't believe it. The mute could actually speak. We sat there and had an entirely abnormal conversation and he didn't open his mouth until the food came. I couldn't believe he was the same man who strangled a woman to death.

For some reason, I became calm and peaceful. I was somewhat alarmed by my sudden contentment. We changed the subject and engaged in a more pleasant conversation. We made idle chitchat, discussing the weather and such. I enjoyed my salmon and left the past alone. Stewart was more verbal and interactive, but he still seemed a little uptight. Reginald enjoyed his lunch as if we'd never had a crazy conversation and matched wits. I felt that I'd given my father a chance to exhibit some human characteristics. However, after his initial disregard for my tragedy, I was unable to feel anything but contempt for him. As I was finishing the last few bites of my lunch, one question popped into my head that I didn't recall ever thinking before; why didn't those two dumb asses get plastic surgery? I mean there they are just sitting around in broad daylight, living life as if nothing had ever happened. Think about it, if Mattie saw them at the airport, I could have easily bumped into them at any time and lost my mind. Those two should've really been on America's Most Wanted.

It made me wonder about the people that you saw every day walking the streets. Could they too be notorious murderers? I thought of myself. I was no better than Clark or Stewart. We were the perfect family: a pimp, a rapist, two murderers, me the pussy peddler, and we were all supposed to be dead.

After we finished our entrees, the waiter asked if we wanted dessert. At the same time, Reginald and I said Cheesecake. I guess our natural response was to laugh at our timed responses, but there was nothing fun about being linked to that man.

Stewart said, "Well, I don't want to be left out. I guess I'll have the cheesecake, too." I smiled at Stewart and motioned for another glass of water.

Reginald wiped the corners of his mouth with his napkin. "So Seth, Stewart says you're interested in the old Toussaint property."

I felt a sharp pain rip through my stomach as I heard my old name slip from Reginald's lips like it was natural. I watched Stewart turn red; he seemed extremely uncomfortable. I tried not to show my discomfort as I went with the flow of the conversation. "I don't know about the Toussaint property, but I am interested in the property in Dillon, Georgia."

"Yes, that's it. Toussaint was the name of the previous owners. That is a beautiful piece of land. Too bad it's filled with so much tragedy. I don't know if Stewart told you about the awful accident that happened there." Reginald looked at Stewart as if he were trying to figure out just how much information he'd divulged about the so called accident. I placed the burden of the explanation on someone else.

"Actually, the clerk at the local city hall filled me in on the history of Dillon's tragic event. My fiancé's doctor lives down the road. All I know is that some people tragically died on that land. I don't know any details, nor do I care. I just want to buy the land and a build a house on it."

Reginald seemed to be pleased with my answer. His next comment shocked me, "Miss St. James, you may be in luck. I think we've held on to that property for long enough. If you're still interested in buying it, I'm sure we can come to a fair agreement. It's just been sitting there vacant for twenty years. Neither Stewart nor I have plans to use it. So if you want it, it's yours."

I was so shocked. I didn't know what to say. Stewart filled in the gaps of silence. He looked at Reginald as if I weren't even there and said, "What are you talking about? Man that property is not for sale. We've already discussed it and I'm not selling it. I can't believe you wanna sell."

"Look man, we've had the damn property for twenty years. It's old and forgotten. If you don't want to sell your half that's fine, I'll sell her my half. I'm tired of holding on to it. The responsibility is just too much. Let her build a house, raise some kids and let her dogs shit on the damn lawn." Stewart was very upset with Reginald. I thought I was going to see a real main event, but Stewart tugged at his lip with his teeth and sat there sulking. For a moment there was silence. As Reginald grabbed the check from the table, Stewart snatched it from his hand and threw a hundred dollar bill inside the leather case. Reginald and Stewart sat there like two pit bulls ready to tear at each other's flesh. I could see fire in Stewart's eyes. He was obviously seriously upset, and didn't want any part of the deal. My first thought was to say something to calm him down, but sometimes people have a look that says, don't fuck with me right now. I drank the last few sips of my water and searched for the right words to say.

Just when I was about to speak, Stewart looked over at me. "Congratulations, it looks like you got what you came for. I hope this land brings you and Alex Young as much happiness as it's brought me and my brother."

As he walked off he looked at Reginald as if he wanted to slap him out of his chair. I didn't bother to reply, I simply watched him walk off like a mad little bitch. I'd scored one goal, even though I felt like Reginald was doing me a favor. I really didn't care if Stewart was pissed off. The property rightfully belonged to me and I deserved it. I deserved everything those two rodents had, and I was going to get it. Something good did come out of that lunch.

I knew that Stewart was growing weary of Reginald's dominance. Although, I didn't think Stewart was strong enough to completely break from Reginald's control. I thought that it was going to be fun to play with his head a little and make him think about how Reginald treated him. I didn't understand why Stewart just didn't tie Reginald to the porch somewhere and let him sit in that wheelchair in the hot sun while he starved to death. That was just my thought process. Since Stewart left the table, I felt that Reginald and I had nothing left to talk about. I gathered my purse and told Reginald that it was time for me to leave. I thanked him for the interesting conversation.

"Well Mr. Hawthorne, I must say this was a very interesting and enlightening encounter. I think it's time for me to go so you and Stewart can sort things out. I guess when you two come to some sort of agreement, I'm sure you'll let me know about the property."

"Miss St. James, there is nothing left to discuss. The land is yours. All I have to do is draw up the papers. You'll have to excuse Stewart. Sometimes he acts like a child."

"I guess if you treat him as such, then he'll continue to act that way."

"Don't feel sorry for Stewart, Miss St. James, some people are born to lead and others are born to follow. Stewart knows his place."

"I guess you're right, but even you can't reign forever...you do remember David and Goliath don't you?"

"My, what an interesting analogy, surely you don't think Stewart is capable of what you and I both know to be true. You all but said it yourself, he's weak."

"Oh no, Mr. Hawthorne, we both know that he does only what you allow him to. The mold wasn't broken when you were made, there's someone out there with a sling shot just waiting for you...but I think you know that...my question to you is ... Are you ready to take that final fall? Good day, Reginald. I look forward to seeing again you real soon."

Just as I started to walk away, Reginald caught my attention. "Miss St. James ..."

"Yes, Mr. Hawthorne?"

"I've been wondering since we first met and I just can't shake this feeling. There seems to be a familiarity between us. Do we know each other? Perhaps we were connected in another life."

"I don't think so Reginald, I don't think you're like anyone I've ever known before."

As I walked away from Reginald, I held my head high and put away all the memories of my father. I tucked them away for the times I would need to remember the way he was. As I approached the door leading to the front of the restaurant, I saw Stewart through the window. He was standing off to the side. He stood with his hands in his pockets and was staring at the sky. There was no way for me to avoid him. I handed my ticket to the valet and walked over to where he was standing. He turned to look at me and before he could speak, I started apologizing.

"Look Stewart, I'm sorry about causing tension between you and Reginald. I really am content with not having the land." I lied, but I was trying to win points.

Stewart removed his hands from his pockets and sat down on the white iron bench. "Don't apologize. Actually, this has nothing to do with you. It's between me and Reginald. You can never even imagine what we've been through together. Sometimes I can't believe the shit myself." He looked down at the ground and then looked back up at me as if he were asking me for answers to an ancient riddle.

"Have you ever felt like you just wanted to disappear and leave everyone and everything that you've ever done behind you?" There was something genuine about this moment between Stewart and me.

I took a seat next to him and said, "I think everyone feels that way at one point or another."

"No ... not like this. I wish I could tell you everything about me: my life, what I've seen, what I've done. Sometimes I feel as if I'm caught between two worlds, one good and one bad."

"Stewart, everyone has done things they're not proud of, things they would prefer to never tell a living soul. People make mistakes, but the real test of a person's character comes when they continue to make the same mistakes. When I look at you, I see so much more than Stewart Benson, Reginald Hawthorne's little brother. You can't let someone else control you forever. At some point you have to break away and be your own man. I hated sitting there watching him talk to you like that. You're not his child and you don't owe him a damn thing."

"You don't understand, Seth. Reginald is all I've had in my life. He's been everything to me. Without him, I don't know where I'd be. It's funny how part of me wishes he can live forever and part of me wishes he'd just go ahead and die."

Jackpot! Stewart really resented Reginald, it couldn't get any better. Sometimes people say things out loud that up until that moment they've only secretly wished in the confines of their mind. The fact that Stewart opened his mouth and acknowledged his wish to see Reginald dead, gave me a lot to work with.

"What do mean you wish he'd go ahead and die?"

Stewart sat back and placed one hand on the back of the bench and leaned toward me. "Reginald has cancer. It's spreading throughout his body, and there's nothing that can be done. That's why he's in the wheelchair. His bones are fragile and he's always in pain. He takes pain medication like it's candy. I don't know how much longer he has to live."

It's amazing how karma works. Reginald was suffering slowly and painfully just like I'd hoped he would, but somehow that still didn't seem to be enough. I wanted to be there when he took his last breath. I wanted to be able to tell him who I was. I wanted to be the one to take his life. I wanted to make sure he didn't have time to ask for forgiveness from God so that he could burn in hell forever. I wanted to have that power.

I placed my hand on Stewart's knee, "Stewart, I'm so sorry. I didn't know. I thought he'd been in some sort of accident. I never imagined anything else."

"It's funny how life works. You do so much bad shit all your life and you think you're gonna die because of the lifestyle you chose, and you end up dying from a disease. I wonder what's in store for me."

"What's that supposed to mean? I can't picture you doing anything that horrible. I just can't see it."

Chapter Twenty-Nine

As I left the restaurant, I couldn't help but think I knew better than to let myself become attracted to Stewart. I was letting him suck me in once again. I couldn't help but see the sadness and the regret in his eyes. There was something I couldn't get a handle on. I tried to recap the night of the fire. It was almost like was missing something, but I just didn't know what. I needed to get home and relax. I'd gone the whole day and hadn't given a thought about Alex, and he hadn't called.

Once I reached the house and parked out front, I hopped out of the car and entered through the front door. I threw my purse and keys across the kitchen, and slammed my fist down on the glass table. I could feel my knuckles stinging as I thought about the lunch date. I was seething with anger. My pulse was racing because of the confusion I was feeling. I still couldn't believe how crass Reginald had been. I couldn't shake the voice that had entered my head. I wasn't ready to start having multiple personalities. I needed to calm down.

I didn't know what direction I was moving in. My heart felt like it was going to burst through my chest. I was hot and sweating. I ran my fingers through my hair. It was wringing wet from perspiration. I walked over to the cabinet and grabbed a bottle of my favorite cognac. I reached in the dishwasher, grabbed a glass, poured a hefty portion of cognac and walked down the hall to the den. I needed to calm down. I plopped down on the couch and grabbed the remote, all the while thinking to myself, "Reginald is like a little parasite that sucks the life out of everyone, including Stewart."

As I savored my drink, the phone rang. I sprang from my seat searching for the phone, and finally found it under the kitchen table. It was Isabelle. I quickly answered. I could hear her voice bellowing from the other end.

"Girl, where the hell have you been? Bitch, are you crazy? You are supposed to call me every day."

I stopped her in the middle of her tirade. "Isabelle, I just had lunch with my father and Stewart. Now is not the time."

Isabelle became silent, but only for a moment. Then she said, "Whoa, how did that happen?"

"Stewart brought him along with him. Reginald had a doctor's appointment so Stewart just brought the bastard along."

"Damn, does he know who you are?"

"I really don't know. I mean the whole thing was so weird. I did find out that he is dying from cancer. How ironic is that?"

"Damn, that's crazy. You live by the sword all your life, and something like bad health takes you down. How did you find out that bit of info?"

"Stewart told me."

"So, I guess Stewart is really comfortable with you."

"Yep, now all I have to do is convince Stewart that he's tired of being Reginald's lap dog. The foundation has already been laid."

"Yeah, with 'laid' being the key word."

"Please, girl. All a man like Stewart needs is a woman who seems to want him for himself. Think about it. He has a truckload of money. Women always want something from him. I have my own money and independence, so all I can do is listen to his problems, stroke his ego, and screw him real good. You know yourself, men don't want to hear all that nagging and constant chatter. Hell, I don't wanna hear it. So I simply make him feel comfortable, and give him what he wants."

"I can't argue with that. You're beginning to think Stewart is innocent, aren't you?"

"I wouldn't say innocent, because he still let it happen. He's not clean by any means. Someone pulled the trigger. I don't know if it was Stewart or someone else, but when I look into his eyes, I don't see a killer. I don't know why, but there's something there that I can't put my finger on. Lately my dreams have been changing. That night is becoming more and more complex. All I know is Nolan Toussaint was the mastermind behind the whole thing. He actually had his wife and children murdered. That's the part I can't get past. He is the one I really and truly hate."

"I know. It is pretty twisted. What kind of man does that?"

"Isabelle, he's not a man. He's not even human. That's what I have to keep telling myself."

"You know what? You are one strong woman."

"Thanks. I hope I can hold on until this is all over. I tell you, it takes everything I have to maintain some sort of restraint. My stomach hasn't settled since I saw him. To be honest I'm just barely holdin' on."

I was telling the truth. I was just barely holding on. I didn't even know what I was holding on to. I was dangling in thin air, holding on to my faith I guess.

Our conversation was interrupted by the beep from my other line. It was Alex. I told Isabelle I had to go. I filled Alex in on my lunch date. I left some key points of my conversation out. If I'd told him the details, he would swear Reginald knew who I was, and insist on coming to L.A. I just told him that everything went okay and nothing more. Alex told me he had about three more days of intense workouts. His knee was getting better. He would be coming to L.A. next week. I was truly disappointed, I missed him, but I couldn't risk having him there. I had to act fast. I needed a trump card, something to get me to the next level. There was no way to talk Alex out of coming. He was determined. Each day he'd grown more and more skeptical about the whole Stewart thing. There was nothing for me to do but accept the fact that he would be coming soon. Suddenly, I thought of something to say that might change his mind.

"Why don't we meet somewhere and rest from all of this mess? You've been working out so hard and my brain needs to rest. Why don't we both just forget about L.A. for now and go away."

Alex was quiet for a minute, and then he said, "You'll do anything to keep me from coming to L.A."

I took a deep breath. "Yes, Alex I will. You just don't get it. If you come here, you'll mess everything up. I am so close to finding the answers I need. If this doesn't work out for me, I will forever be lost and I'll never know what really happened. More importantly, if you come out and ruin this for me, I may resent you for the rest of my life. I know you love me, and I know that you're concerned, but I need you to trust me."

He was quiet again. Finally, he said, "Ok, Seth. Ok. I just can't help but wonder if you'll come back to me alive."

"Whatever is meant to be will be. I don't think we've gone through all of this for nothing."

"Ok, I don't wanna talk about it anymore. Just let it go for now. I'll call you later."

After I hung up, I went back into the den, picked up the remote and turned on the news. I listened to all of the gruesome events of the day, when a report came through about the medical condition of a Georgia congressman, Dawson Meeks. For a minute, I sat there trying to figure out where I'd heard that name before. My mind went back to my meeting with Charles Brandenburg. Dawson Meeks was the man that ordered our house to be burned. I turned the television up and listened as the reporter briefed us on his condition. Apparently, Dawson needed a liver transplant to survive and his condition was getting worse. They weren't expecting him to live through the week. I sat there thinking that sometimes when people were about to die they told things they never thought they'd tell. I immediately dialed Dr. Shaw. He picked up on the second ring.

"Hello."

"Dr. Shaw, hi, it's Seth...Noel..."

"Hi there, Seth is fine."

"Listen, I was just watching the news, and I see our old friend Congressman Dawson Meeks seems to be on his last leg."

"Yes, he's pretty bad. A transplant won't even help him now. I was at the hospital earlier today making my rounds, and I stopped in."

"So you do have access to him?"

"Of course, what's on your mind?"

"I want to see him." I stood up and walked across the room and stood by the fireplace. I looked up at the picture on the mantle. It was a picture of Alex and his mother. Of course this made me think of my mother and I became more adamant about seeing Dawson.

"Dr. Shaw, I have to see him before he dies. I can't really explain it to you over the phone, but there's something you need to know, I feel it's best that I tell you in person."

Silence filled the airwaves. Finally, Dr. Shaw said, "Alright, you know you're welcome here anytime. Come on out and we'll sit and talk and then I'll see if I can get you in to see him." Dr. Shaw didn't understand that my seeing Dawson wasn't contingent upon what he and I had to discuss. I was going to see Dawson, if I had to roam through the halls searching for him myself.

With a stern voice, I said "Dr. Shaw, this isn't debatable. I've come too far to be railroaded. I'm in L.A. and I've seen Clark. I've even spoken to him. Now I could tell you more, but I'd rather wait. So please arrange for me to see Dawson or I'll do it on my own."

I could tell Dr. Shaw was shocked that I had actually come to L.A. to find Clark. "Dr. Shaw?"

"I'm here. I'm just a little stunned right now. I can't believe you saw Clark. What did he say to you...how did you...?"

"Don't worry, it's not what you think, he doesn't even know who I am yet."

"Ok. I'll make the arrangements. Just get here as soon as you can."

"As soon as I hang up I'll make the arrangements. It's still early here so hopefully I can get out tonight or first thing in the morning."

"Ok. Call me back with your itinerary."

"Ok. Talk to you later."

I booked the next flight to Atlanta. I thought it best not to call Isabelle or Mattie and tell them about my trip. Hopefully I'd find what I needed and return to L.A. without anyone knowing. I scrambled around the house throwing clothes into an overnight bag. I didn't think about any of my clothes matching or packing my favorite beauty products. I basically packed the essentials, underwear and soap. Once I was all packed I hopped into whatever automobile that the keys I grabbed would fit, and peeled through the gate, headed to find the answers that I'd been searching for.

Chapter Thirty

When I landed in Georgia, the heat was amazing. It reminded me of Houston. I felt guilty about being in the city and not contacting Alex. I exited the plane with my bags in hand and headed out of the airport. Once I reached the outside, I saw Dr. Shaw pulling up to the curb. He jumped out of his truck, hugged me and escorted me to the passenger side. I hopped in, put my seatbelt on, and settled in for the drive back to his house. He was anxious to hear what was going on with Stewart and me. Just as I was about to tell him what was going on, my phone rang. It was Stewart. I answered the phone and motioned for Dr. Shaw to be silent. Dr. Shaw nodded yes and I proceeded to converse with Stewart.

"Hello."

"Hey baby, where are you? I'm at the club waiting on you. Is everything ok, you're not disappearing again are you?"

"No, nothing like that. I have to get back to Houston, there was an emergency at the store, I'll be back by Sunday and we'll hook up then. Ok?"

"Well, I hope everything's all right. Is there anything you need? Anything I can do?"

"No, thanks. Everything's gonna be ok. I promise I'll call you later."

"Ok, call me and let me know that you made it to Houston safely."

"Ok. I will talk to you later."

I hung up the phone and turned to Dr. Shaw. His eyebrows were raised, questioning me. "What's going on, Seth?"

I didn't see any need to prolong it, so I said, "I saw my father

Dr. Shaw was so frazzled, we almost ran off the road. He was so nervous he had to pull over. He jumped out of the truck and ran toward the grass. I jumped out behind him. He started to hyperventilate and couldn't catch his breath. He slid down the side of the truck and rested in the grass. While he was trying to catch his breath, I reached into the truck and handed him a bottle of water.

After he'd calmed down, he said, "Are you sure it was Nolan?"

I was so tired of people asking me if I was sure. The man looked the same as he did the day he died. Of course I was sure.

"Yes, Dr. Shaw I'm sure, he hasn't changed a bit, but he's now going by the name Reginald."

Before I could finish my sentence Dr. Shaw said, "Hawthorne, Reginald Hawthorne...Benson and Hawthorne, how could I not see it before?"

"I don't think anyone saw it. Everyone knew he was dead for sure."

"How did you find this out? Does he know who you are?"

"I don't think he knows who I am. And you don't want to know how I found out."

"I'll take your word for it."

We stood up and got back in the truck. I checked to make sure he was ok to drive. He said he felt fine. He was just shocked. He couldn't believe my father was alive. He said he thought my father was dead for sure. I told him I felt that my father was the mastermind behind the whole thing and that he meant to kill all of us, my mother, Nicolette and myself. I also told him I felt Stewart had been used as a scapegoat. There was something about the way Stewart pleaded for Dawson not to kill us. I informed Dr. Shaw that there was something about Stewart, which led me to believe he regretted the whole thing. It was almost like he wanted to confess to something.

Dr. Shaw said, "Clark has always followed Nolan's lead. The fact that Nolan was dead, or so I thought, made me think that Clark had double-crossed him. I mean, deep down I never thought Clark had actually pulled the trigger or lit the match, but I figured he planned the whole thing."

As I sat staring out the window, a feeling came over me. "Something's not right about that night. You and Charlie told me what you think happened, but neither of you were in the house. I know I can remember more, I just need some time or I need to hear something that sounds familiar. I'm missing something, I can feel it in my blood, but I just can't figure it out."

Dr. Shaw said, "Don't worry. I think Dawson Meeks can help us. I know he'll talk. I'll make him talk." Dr. Shaw seemed sure about Dawson, but it was something he wasn't telling me.

"What do you mean, you'll make him." Dr. Shaw pulled out a glass bottle. It looked like insulin. I didn't know what it was, but I did know that I didn't have to ask any questions. I knew then, that I'd soon find out all I needed. As we approached Dr. Shaw's house, I asked him to go to the old land. I needed to get out and soak up my strength from the spot where my mother took her last breath.

I stood there and looked to the sky. I told my mother that I would find out the truth real soon and she would be able to rest. I stood on the foundation of my old house and made a promise to avenge my mother's death.

After sitting up all night in a chair watching the time change on the clock minute by minute, hour by hour, the sun came up and it was time to face what was ahead. I pulled myself up from the seat, drew back the curtains and looked out the window down the hill where I used to live. I pressed my face against the glass hoping I would wake from this dream. I closed my eyes and prayed to God that this meeting with Dawson Meeks would give me all the answers I'd been waiting for. If Meeks couldn't tell me the entire story, I prayed he could take me one step closer. Dr. Shaw and Charlie had already told me enough so that if Meeks came up dry I wouldn't be totally disappointed. As I was standing there and my prayers came to a close, I heard the same voice of unfamiliarity that I heard at the restaurant when I saw Reginald.

The voice was calling me Noel. She was begging me to help her. For some reason, my thoughts were with Nicolette. I closed my eyes tight and concentrated on this new person in my head. I then realized it wasn't a stranger at all. It was Nicolette when she was a child. Was my sister in trouble? For the first time since she showed up on my doorstep, I could feel her the way I used to. It was funny how, when she was actually with me I didn't feel a thing, but when were apart, I feel her in my spirit. Since I'd been in L.A., I felt her more than ever, but I couldn't bring myself to call her. I feared our conversation would be much like the one we had the last time we were together. I just couldn't shake the feeling I was having. It was a feeling of uncertainty and distrust for my sister. I can't explain the confusion.

On one hand, I knew she needed me. On the other hand, I couldn't bring myself to reach out to her. It sounds crazy but it was almost as if Lauren and Nicolette are two different people, like she had a split personality or something. A part of me loved Nicolette dearly and the other part of me almost loathed Lauren. I know it sounds crazy but that's how I feel.

My feet were unable to part from that section of the room. I could stand there and stare out the window and reminisce for hours. I felt like I should've cried and mourned my past, but my eyes were dry and I had nothing left to cry with. The tears had been replaced with feelings of hate, anger and determination. There was a small lump in my throat and my chest felt like there was a boulder sitting on top, weighing me down. I was so consumed with the idea of revenge. It was like I could taste my father's blood. I was further haunted by the thought that Stewart captivated me. There was something about him that I couldn't shake. I thought more about him than I did Alex. I knew that Stewart and I could never be more to each other than what were, just two people caught up in an unfortunate circumstance. It was funny how before I left Houston, I was gung ho about avenging my parents' deaths, and killing Stewart without answering any questions. However, the day I stared into my father's eyes for the first time, I knew Reginald was the real culprit. Just so everything is clear and understood, I was not blinded by Stewart's charm, and I did recognize his part in everything, but I had to give credit where credit was due. Everyone tried to tell me how evil my father was, but since he was dead, or so I thought, I clung to the fantasy. I truly believed he wasn't capable of anything evil.

In order for me to be true to myself, and to my plan, I had to free my mind of any thoughts of that man being my father. From that day forward I had to declare to my heart, that Nolan Toussaint was dead, and that perhaps he never really lived. I've never had a father, that part of my past has been wiped clean from the contents of my mind. Men who've never been brought to justice killed my mother in a robbery. Those men are unfamiliar to me and therefore I had no emotional ties to them. They were men who came in the middle of the night and robbed, killed and emotionally mutilated my sister, Mattie and me. Stewart was just another man that I had an interest in. It was a fascination, a game that I was caught up in and thoroughly enjoyed playing. Those were the things I told myself in order to survive. I think the thing that really hit me in my gut was that most people who had loved ones pass on had some memories to keep them going. I had nothing of my mother but the pictures that flashed through my mind. The closer I got to the end of that nightmare, the fainter those pictures become. I found myself closing my eyes tighter, trying to recapture her image.

I had fragments of a sister, and sometimes I wished she had never come back. My mother didn't even have a proper grave, tombstone or memorial. She was up there on that land restless, in the midst of the grass, weeds and soil. I wondered if there was anything left of her, or did her entire body perish in the fire. Did they find her wedding ring, earrings, or the hairclip she wore? I wondered if she was actually dead when I saw her lying on the kitchen floor, or was she burned alive in the fire? I would've liked to read the autopsy report, something to let me know how my mother really died. I replayed the night over and over in my head, wondering if I remembered everything exactly as it happened. Did I witness my mother taking her last breath? Did I see my father lying there bleeding and begging for forgiveness or was that what I wanted to remember? Maybe my mind fabricated a memory, which was easier for me to handle. I tried to compare notes with Lauren, but she couldn't remember a damn thing. Whatever did or didn't happen, I hoped Dawson Meeks could tell me what I needed to know. He was possibly the only man who was there that night, that maybe...just maybe, I could get a straight answer from him.

I started to drift off to a place I possibly wouldn't return from with a sound mind, when my phone rang. Its sudden chime shook me and I felt the ringing throughout my body. I looked down at the nightstand and saw that it was a call from my own home. I figured it was Mattie, so I reached down on the table and retrieved my phone.

"Hello."

"Hi there, I hadn't heard from you in a couple of days. I was getting a little worried."

"I know. I'm sorry. Things have been really crazy for me...you understand."

"Yes, I understand. You still think I betrayed you?" There was a bit of uncomfortable silence. Just as I was getting ready to break the silence, Mattie spoke. "Seth, I hate to start the conversation this way, but I need to apologize for keeping the fact that I knew your father was alive. You have to know that I didn't mean any harm, I thought I was protecting you."

"Mattie I..." She stopped me before I could tell her that I understood and I wasn't mad anymore.

"Please, Seth, just listen for once. I mean really listen to me. This whole thing is crazy on so many levels, but you're right, we need to end it, we need answers. I don't exactly know what happened that night. I've replayed it over and over in my mind every day, trying to understand. Sometimes things are clearer than others, so I don't know if I can help you. I know your mother really is dead. Lauren is your sister, and you love her, but I don't, and I'm not going to apologize for the feelings I have about her. What happened to our family is a mystery that only you can solve. It's your duty to find out what happened. There is one person I believe can answer your questions. He's the only man besides your father and Stewart who was there that night. His name is Dawson Meeks, he's a congressman now and he can tell you everything you need to know. I saw on the news that he's gravely ill and might not make it to see tomorrow, but if you leave for Atlanta today, I think the Lord will spare him just for you. I figure he owes you that much."

Listening to Mattie express her willingness to help me, made me feel warm all over, it was a feeling of love. I didn't tell her I was already in Georgia and would be seeing Congressman Meeks in a couple of hours. I wanted her to feel like she was helping, like she played a key role in finding the truth. I wanted her to feel good about trying to let go of the past, and I didn't want to take that feeling away from her.

"Thanks Mattie, this means more to me than you know. I really appreciate your willingness to sacrifice your memories to help me..."

She stopped me. "This is to help us, Seth."

"Yes to help us. I'm going to make my flight arrangements right now. I'll call you when I get to Georgia. I'll let you know if he was of any help."

"Please be careful Seth."

"I will...Mattie, and thank you. I, uh ... I love you."

There was another silent moment. This time it wasn't awkward, it was just right.

"I love you, too, Noel."

For the first time, I was proud to be called Noel. I finally got Mattie's approval. It was going to be a good day.

As Dr. Shaw and I pulled up to the hospital, he informed me that he was going to introduce me as his niece, who was visiting from L.A. I was supposed to be accompanying him on his rounds, since I was studying medicine. We parked in the physician's parking lot and entered through the private entrance. He found a lab coat and a visitor's pass for me to wear. He even gave me a probe light, a stethoscope and a few other items for ambiance.

He looked down at my feet, smiled and said, "Real doctors don't wear three inch heels when doing rounds."

We both laughed and I said, "Well we all know I'm not ordinary."

We laughed for a few moments, then his brow furrowed. "Are you sure you want to do this?"

I put my hand on his shoulder and reassured him that I was ready and couldn't wait any longer. As we walked down the corridor of the hospital leading to Congressman Meeks room, I felt surprisingly calm. I wasn't nervous or uncomfortable at all. I was totally aware of everything around me. I could clearly hear conversations going on nearby. Sounds became more vivid. I moved to the rhythm of my heels hitting the tile floor. Dr. Shaw and I didn't speak a word. He smiled and greeted his colleagues as they passed us, and to my surprise, no one stopped us and no one inquired about who I was. I was anxious to reach our destination. We finally reached the elevator.

Dr. Shaw pushed the button for the fifth floor. Congressman Meeks was in a private room in ICU. Once we stepped off the elevator, he stopped me. "Remember...you're my niece, Seth, from L.A. You're a medical student accompanying me on my rounds today."

He handed me the visiting physicians pass, and instructed me to follow him. Once we reached the doorway, Dr. Shaw swiped his card. I heard a loud click and the doors flew open. As I passed each room I glanced in and saw different people hooked up to tubes with all kinds of fluids pumping in and out of their bodies. The unit was filled with sickness and sadness. Dr. Shaw greeted everyone at the desk and reached for Congressman Meeks' chart. Before reviewing the chart, he introduced me. "Everyone, I would like you to meet my niece, Seth. She's in her last year at Strickland in L.A. She's going to follow her dear old uncle around today."

Dr. Shaw beamed with exaggerated pride. I silently wished I were his niece. A part of me even wished I was his daughter. Everyone extended a hand and welcomed me to the hospital. They told me my 'uncle' was the best and I was lucky to have him. The funny thing was no one knew just how lucky I was. Once the ordeal was over, it wouldn't be the end of my relationship with Dr. Shaw. I needed him to remind me of what it was like to be around a real father. He asked if Meeks had any visitors. The nurse told him that no one had been in to see him so far and that he seemed to be getting weaker. The nurse informed us that Meeks wouldn't eat and he hadn't spoken since sometime yesterday. Under any other circumstance, the news would've been devastating and I'd feel compassion for him, but at that point I didn't care anything about Meeks' health. I was just hoping he'd hang on until I found out what I needed to know.

Dr. Shaw informed the staff that I would be accompanying him to Congressman Meeks' room. I smiled and told everyone it was nice to meet them all. Meeks' room was located on the other side of the hallway. There were only four rooms in the unit. There was a room on each side of the nurses' station and two rooms directly across from it. We walked over to Meeks' room and showed the security guard our passes. The guard recognized Dr. Shaw, and greeted him. He introduced me once again, and the guard greeted me as well. I took a deep breath and followed Dr. Shaw into the room. I closed the door behind me and stood to the side, while Dr. Shaw drew the curtains. I looked at Meeks lying there asleep struggling to breathe, he looked like death.

His skin was as white as snow. His lips were chapped, and his face and hair were wet from sweating. His eyes were deeply sunken and he was emaciated. I immediately thought about Mrs. Stein just before she died. I never thought I would ever see another human being look so morbid. The only difference was I cared deeply for Mrs. Stein, and Meeks was just another unfortunate victim of his lifestyle. I knew it was probably wrong of me to think it, but I felt like he was getting what he deserved. I was sure I wasn't the only person who Meeks had ever wronged. I wondered how many other people were sitting on pins and needles waiting for that piece of crap to die. I stood by the door, hesitating to move.

"What exactly is wrong with him? What's his prognosis?"

"Well, to make a long story short, his liver is failing. He has a long history of alcoholism and Hepatitis. Of course with media attention, we're just saying he needs a transplant."

"So what are his chances of getting a donor?"

"At this point, it really doesn't matter. He has so much infection flowing through his body, he'll be lucky if he makes it through the week. It's really touch and go. Eventually, the infection will kill him."

I looked up at the IV bottles, which were hanging from a pole, and asked which one was his pain medication. Dr. Shaw pointed to the drip on the right. He pulled the vial that he'd shown me yesterday, out of his coat. I held up my hand and said no. I guess he read my mind because he instructed me on how to stop the pain medication. I walked over to the machine and did as Dr. Shaw had instructed. I stood there by the bed waiting for him to wake up. Dr. Shaw assured me that he'd feel the pain and wake in a few moments. I stood there looking around the room. Standing over him triggered a memory. That was the man behind the voice, the man who had instructed them to burn down a house with two innocent children supposedly sleeping upstairs. I replayed everything in my mind. I heard the wheels of the car against the gravel. I heard Reginald tell Mattie, Nicolette and me to go outside. I heard him tell my mother to stay there. That was the first time I'd ever remembered that. I heard my mother tell him she would stay right there, she wouldn't leave. As we ran out through the back door, Nicolette and I broke away from Mattie. We hid in our respective places. From my hiding place, I saw the faces of everyone. I saw Stewart (Clark), Meeks, and two other men I didn't know. The other men were insignificant because they were just the muscle. Just as I could hear my mother speak, I was jolted back to reality by Meeks groaning in pain.

He moved around and began to breathe hard. His eyes popped open like a jack-in-the box. With his head resting on his pillow, he moved his eyes and located Dr. Shaw, and then without expression he moved his eyes in my direction. It was as if it was too painful to move his entire head. He fixed his eyes on me. "Who are you?"

I didn't feel any need to prolong the meeting. I rested my hands on the bed railing. "My name is Noel Toussaint. I'm the daughter of Nolan and Anna Marie Toussaint. I'm sure you remember me."

Suddenly, the odor of strong urine filled the room. That dude was so shocked that he'd pissed on himself. "You can't be. You're supposed to be dead. You just can't be."

"Sorry to disappoint you, but I'm alive and well. Unfortunately for you, my sister and I weren't upstairs sleeping that night, we were hiding. You were pretty sloppy. You should have double checked. Now, because of your incompetence, I can identify you as my mother's murderer."

He was clearly in pain, and could hardly speak. He raised his hand and put it on top of mine. I immediately pulled away.

"Don't you ever touch me again, or this disease won't kill you. I will."

"I am so sorry about what happened. Believe me, I have paid for the mistakes from my past. Please let me die in peace...please."

"Don't worry, Dawson. I'm not going to turn you in to the police. It's not even worth it anymore. I'm sure nothing would happen to you anyway. I have my own form of justice in mind."

"Listen, Noel..."

"Actually, it's Seth. Noel is dead, remember?"

"Seth, please, you have to understand, that was ages ago. Things were different then..."

"That's where you're wrong, Dawson. It seems like yesterday to me, and I can never forget it, but I'm here to make sure you remember."

"I'm sorry I can't help you, I've put everything from that night behind me."

I became even more agitated with Dawson Meeks. I looked over at Dr. Shaw. He stood to the side, silent, and showing no emotion. I turned the drip all the way off. Dawson started to move erratically. He looked over at Dr. Shaw, his eyes pleading.

"Please don't let her do this. Claude. You've always been level-headed. I promise I'll scream."

Before Dr. Shaw could answer I said, "And if you utter one word other than to answer my questions, I'll crack your skull and shatter it into a thousand pieces. I pulled my gun from the back of my pants and held it to his face. Dr. Shaw was surprised, but not upset. Meeks struggled to swallow as he lay there frozen.

I leaned over him and said, "It is very important that you understand this is not a game we're playing. The information you are going to share with me is not optional. I will kill you and not even think about it. So, let's just be clear on what's going on here."

I heard the door creak, and jumped back. I removed the gun from his face. The guard cracked the door open and asked if everything was all right. Meeks and Dr. Shaw nodded, yes at the same time. The guard backed out and shut the door.

Meeks looked over at me and said, "Well, you sure do have your daddy's personality, how is the sick bastard?"

Meeks' acknowledgement of my father's existence secured my belief that I'd come to the right place. "So you know my father's alive?"

"Yeah, don't you?"

"Actually, I just found out. I didn't exactly grow up with him."

"Don't feel bad. I thought he was dead too, until he needed a favor. When I heard his voice I almost pissed on myself. That man has killed me slowly for years. He won't let me forget the past. He's like a tumor that grows and grows. I hate that mutha fucka more than I hate this shit that's killing me. I can't even imagine what you did when you saw his twisted ass for the first time. You're standing here, so I'm sure he has no idea who you are."

Meeks let out a wicked laugh, which was labored by his inability to breathe properly. He started choking. Dr. Shaw leaned in to help him. I got him some water. I didn't want him to choke to death yet.

"What makes you so sure he'd kill me if he knew who I was?"

"Nolan Toussaint or Reginald as he's known now-a-days, is not human. He's like no other man I've ever met."

"The more I think about it, he had to know I was alive all these years. When you came to my house that night, he sent us out the back way."

"Listen, if he sent you away, he did it for a reason, and I don't think it was love. He wants something from you, and believe me, he will collect. This is a man who killed his own parents and brother."

Dr. Shaw interrupted Meeks, "What do you mean? His parents were killed in a car accident."

Meeks started to laugh again, "Please, Claude, you of all people should know Nolan Toussaint. You should know that accidents don't just happen around him."

Dr. Shaw was becoming agitated as well, "Why don't you just say what it is you're trying to say Meeks."

"When he was ten years old, Nolan's parents had another baby. He was jealous of the child because his parents were spending more time with his brother. Nolan had this fascination with bees and snakes, anything that could hurt you. He kept these bees in a jar with a piece of honeycomb. His sick little ass carried the jar everywhere. When the family was riding in the car one day, Nolan opened the jar and let the bees go. His father was stung; he had an allergic reaction and ran into a tree. Nolan's mother, brother and father were in the front seat and went through the windshield. Nolan was in the back seat and didn't get a scratch on him."

Dr. Shaw knew my father was crazy, but he still doubted Meeks' story. "Meeks how do you know all this? I grew up with him and I never heard this story."

"Well, Claude, you have always been the weak one. I don't think you could have taken that story."

"Bullshit! You asshole! How did you find this out?"

"Nolan needed to convince me that he would definitely kill me if I ever double crossed him, so he told me the story, lucky for me I was worth more to him alive than dead."

"I'll be damned!"

"Oh yeah, that girl that Clark killed, she was Nolan's cousin. She was the daughter of his mother's only sister, who refused to take him in when his parents were killed so he killed her daughter or shall I say convinced Clark to do it!."

I couldn't believe my ears. I didn't understand why I was still shocked. After hearing Meeks' story, my whole body became cold. I didn't know how much more I could take.

"Ok, this is a bit much. Let's get back to the subject at hand. So you're saying you thought you killed Nolan and my mother that night, until you heard from him years later."

"That's right."

"So, you killed my mother, and doubled crossed Nolan...Reginald...whoever he is."

"No, no I'm not the one who pulled the trigger on your mother. That one I won't take credit for. Hell, I didn't even shoot your father that night."

"Ok, wait a minute, you did more than that. You sent two guys upstairs to set my sister and me on fire. I remember that much. I know I heard that.

"I don't know what you think you remember about that night, but you've got your order of events all mixed up."

374

I was allowing that man to confuse me, and send me back to that night. I began to remember things that I never had before. As Meeks began to talk, I started to reminisce. Just as my mind started to drift, Meeks grabbed my hand again.

I pulled my gun from my pocket, and said, "I told you about touching me." Dr. Shaw ran over and grabbed my hands. Meeks started to apologize and cough at the same time.

"I'm sorry, I just want to make sure you listen to what I'm about to tell you. I'm only telling you this because I believe in heaven and hell. I've asked God to forgive all of my wrong doings. Whether you think so or not, I have been haunted by the thought of two little girls who were the same age as my own daughters, being burned alive. I've always hoped that when I died and went to heaven, I would get a chance to ask you and your sister to forgive me."

I couldn't believe he was asking me to forgive him for what he'd done. "Please, can you say what it is you have to say? We've been here too long already and I have a plane to catch."

"Seth, believe me, I didn't shoot your mother or your father, and I didn't order to have you and sister burned alive either."

"Got dammit. If you didn't, then please tell me who did. I'm tired of this cat and mouse game we're playing. Tell me the truth."

"Nolan shot your mother. He told Clark to have the guys go upstairs and throw torches in your rooms. I guess he knew that you guys weren't really up there, but we were paralyzed at the thought of this man killing his own children. Clark was tired of your father's shit and he drew the line at killing the two of you. He refused to do it, so your father pulled a gun on Clark and ordered the men to set the house on fire..."

"Hold on a minute." I held my hand up. "I can't believe this. I've never remembered the entire night before, just bits and pieces."

I stood there and replayed every word he spoke. But there was still something wrong, Meeks couldn't escape his role in all of this.

"At this point I can go along with everything you're telling me, but I know I remember you saying, you wanted everything in the house burned to ashes. You and Clark even talked about who was the executor of the estate. I know I'm not confused about that."

"You're right and I'm not proud of that moment, but greed got the best of me. I figured since you two were going to die anyway, so why shouldn't I get the money?"

"It's interesting how quickly you can turn your conscious off...please continue with your story, Mr. Meeks. I'm anxious to hear the rest."

He took a deep breath, adjusted himself in his bed and picked up where he'd left off.

"Your father shot himself to make it look like a robbery. He begged us to help him get out of the house. The fire spread quicker than anything I've ever seen. Your father collapsed on the ground, and we saw that as an opportunity to finally get rid of him. As we were leaving the house, a piece from the ceiling fell and landed on Clark's back and he caught fire. I put the fire out, but I left him lying there, helpless. I left him and Clark in the house. Before I left, I ran to the safe to get what I could and to make sure there was nothing that would trace him back to me other than the fact that I was his attorney. I figured everyone was dead, until a few days later, when I got a call from Clark. He told me he'd managed to pull himself up and out of the house. He said one of Johnny Case's doctors tended to his burns. He demanded that I give him his share of what I took from the house or he would kill me. After that, I never saw Clark face to face again, and then I heard that he had died in an accident, but somehow I know he's still out there..."

I took in a big gulp of air and answered Meeks' suspicions with a faint voice. "They found each other."

"What?"

"Clark and Nolan ... Well, Clark is now Stewart Benson. They're living in L.A. as brothers. I don't think Stewart knows who I am."

"I guess some things never change. They're meant to be together, master and slave. It's important that you know what really happened that night. You have to know I'm on my last leg. I'll be lucky to make it through the night and I don't want to take this bullshit with me to the grave. The truth is, everyone thought we double-crossed Nolan. Believe me the thought crossed my mind, but Clark was unbelievably loyal to Nolan. He was even going to kill your mother for him, but he got nervous and couldn't do it. When your father called us to the house that night none of us wanted to go, we didn't know what the hell to expect. If it's worth anything, I swear to you I am so very sorry."

I believed every twisted word that Congressman Dawson Meeks uttered. I believed that my father was a sick twisted bastard capable of anything. I also believed that I was capable of anything as well. I leaned over the bed and whispered, "I'm glad that you believe that you will be forgiven in the hereafter, but her on earth you get nothing from me. You left me and my sister for dead. You thought we were burning alive upstairs in our beds while you were downstairs stealing my money from the safe. I hope that the hell you rot in is worse than the one that I've lived here on this earth for over twenty years..."

I looked over at Dr. Shaw and reached my hand out. He handed me the vile and looked away. I took a syringe out, filled it and injected the contents into his IV. I stood over Meeks as I watched his eyes bulge and his face twitch. Dr. Shaw advised that he was going to die very slowly as his body functions would slowly shut down.

I stood there as I watched tears stream down his face. Meeks reached out his hand and mouthed words help me! I just stared into his sick and evil eyes and thought of my mother reaching out to me begging for me to help her as she faded away, only this time I didn't shed a tear.

I felt my heart grow hard and cold. I felt a rush of adrenalin and my body felt almost orgasmic as I watched the man that helped to ruin my life slowly fade away. Meeks was paralyzed and he couldn't speak. He could no longer yell for help, all he could do was just lie there and die slowly.

Suddenly, I could feel a struggle going on inside of me. One side was saying stop this now. The other side told me to savor the moment and enjoy the power. There was a battle going on inside my head and I felt like I was going to burst. I couldn't take it anymore. I looked over at Dr. Shaw and said "I need to leave right now!"

Just as we exited the room I could hear Meeks strained voice saying "I'm sorry, I'm so sorry!" I ignored his plea. I'd once again left a human life to die. I walked out of the room just as easily I'd come closing yet another doorway to my past.

Chapter Thirty-One

I didn't remember boarding the plane. I didn't remember it taking off. I didn't remember turbulence. I didn't even remember the landing. I reached the house on a wing and a prayer. My mind and my body were tired. Reginald was like a virus that attached to peoples' souls and rendered them helpless. He had reduced some of the most notorious men to nothing. The devil was real and he was alive. I couldn't believe he was of my very own flesh and blood. There was nothing left for me to think about or contemplate. I'd been away from home too long. I had a wedding to plan and a life to lead. I needed a good night's rest, the next day it would all be over.

With a peaceful mind, I entered through the front door of Alex's home. I put my bags down on the steps, walked into the kitchen, grabbed a bottle of water and walked toward the den. Once I reached the den, I sat down on the couch and dialed Isabelle's number. When she answered, I didn't say hello.

"Well, I found out who killed my mother." There was a brief silence. I could hear her taking in a breath of air.

In a soft faint voice, she said, "So tell me what happened. What did you find out?"

"Everything that I've thought all these years has been so wrong."

"What do you mean? What's happened?" I told Isabelle that I'd gone to Atlanta to talk to Congressman Meeks. Of course she was a little angry that I didn't tell her beforehand. There was another moment of silence. Finally, I broke the awkward moment.

"Well, it turns out neither Stewart nor Congressman Meeks killed my mother. My father pulled the trigger and then the crazy bastard shot himself to make it look like a robbery."

She let out a gasp that almost turned into a laugh. "Come on now, did you let that man make you believe that?"

I took a sip of water. "No Isabelle, unfortunately it really happened. After I heard it come out of Meeks' mouth, I remembered it like it was happening right then. It was so weird. I've seen one thing in my mind all these years and today, just like that, everything changed."

"Oh my God! Are you ok?"

"Yeah, I'm fine. You know the funny thing is I think somehow this all happened for a reason. I mean, can you imagine being raised with this man as your father? I don't know, I just don't know."

When I realized I was sobbing, I tried to gather myself. I said, "After seeing Congressman Meeks today, I really don't think there's anything else for me to find out. I'm ready to go home to my family and my future husband. I've decided to finish my business with Stewart and Reginald tomorrow night."

"Are you sure you can do this alone? This just doesn't sound right. I'm on my way out there."

"Isabelle, if you come here, I swear I will never speak to you again. I have to do this on my own. Please don't come here. I have everything planned and I don't need any surprises. Just sit tight, please."

Isabelle was very upset. She was determined to come to L.A. "Seth, I'm not gonna make you any promises. This shit is serious!"

"Look, I am ok with this. Reginald is not my father. He never was. He's just another menace to society as far as I'm concerned."

"What about Stewart? I know you two have gotten pretty close."

"Don't worry. It's just physical. I have to admit that I do have a little soft spot for him, and I feel sorry for him. He's like a little, lost, wounded puppy, and like most dogs that are maimed you have to put them down so they won't suffer anymore. He needs to be put to sleep."

"I understand all that, but these bastards are dangerous. All I'm saying is I am willing to risk losing your friendship, if it means saving your life."

I could see that there was no reasoning with Isabelle. I said, "You do what you gotta do," and hung up the phone, and then I threw it on the floor beside me and put my feet up on the ottoman. I flipped through the channels and found the news. The first thing I heard was "Georgia Congressman Dawson Meeks dies of complications from liver disease." I leaned back in my chair, took a deep breath and closed my eyes. I must have been extremely tired because when I woke up the clock read 10:03pm. The television was still on the news station. I switched off the television and realized I was still in my good clothes. I climbed the stairs and undressed and prepared to get some well-deserved sleep.

Before going to bed, I thought about Alex. I knew it was late, but I needed to speak to him. I wasn't going to tell him about my visit with

Meeks, though. After I brushed my teeth and washed my face, I settled under the covers and speed dialed his number.

"Hey baby, I've been waiting to hear from you." Alex's voice made me melt. Hearing him on the other end put everything back into perspective.

"Hi honey, I miss you."

"I miss you too. How are things out there?"

"Everything is going well. I'm ready to go home. I think I'm just gonna prepare to leave, I'm tired."

"What's wrong? You're usually so gung ho about this whole thing."

"I know...it's so crazy. I think I've learned all I need to know. I don't know if I can live with someone else's blood on my hands. I just want to walk away and pretend like none of this ever happened."

"Are you sure this is what you want?"

"I'm sure. I'll probably be back in Texas by the end of the week."

"What brought this on?"

"To tell you the truth, I don't know. Before I picked up the phone to call you, I was ready to make everybody pay. When I heard your voice it just put everything back into perspective for me. I just want to marry you and live a normal life."

"Now that's what I'm talking about." We both laughed and made more small talk, and finally ended the conversation on a good note.

I lay there for a while after our conversation with a smile and comforting thoughts. I realized I'd just lied to Alex and to myself about wanting to walk away from this. I also realized I was suffering from a popular disease called anger.

Anger is one of those things that become part of you. It can consume you and ultimately destroy you if you let it. It was almost eleven o'clock, and I was lying in the darkness, seething with anger. I was so wound up that my body became warm, and I could feel heat rising from my chest. I sat up on the side of the bed for a moment and grabbed my cigarettes out of my purse. It was clearly a habit I desperately needed to break. It was ironic how I enjoyed a good cigar every once in a while, but since I've been out here in L.A., I'd acquired a taste for those cancer sticks. With the pack of cigarettes clutched in my hand, I walked toward the veranda doors and flung them open. I took my seat outside and enjoyed the night air. I sat down in the chair with one foot on the ground and the other propped up meeting the inner thigh of my right leg. I lit my cigarette and took a drag. It was like a refreshing pick me up. I inhaled the smoke with pleasure, closing my eyes and basking in the nicotine buzz. I drew the cigarette from my mouth and studied it as I'd done so many times before. It was so amazing how that little skinny stick made of paper and poison was so powerful. It had the power to control one's mind, leaving them totally dependent, causing them to risk health and sanity. You see people walking around wearing little patches filled with act-right juice and gorging themselves on snacks trying to fill the void of that little stick. As I stared at the cigarette, I realized that must be the power that Reginald yields over people.

Reginald has made grown men in positions of power live in panic, and cringe at the mere mention of his name. It was like something you saw on one of those mob movies; only the dynamics of the characters have changed. It seemed completely unnatural that one man could possess that much power. I took another drag of my cigarette and studied the smoke as it escaped my lips. In the midst of the smoke, I was transported back to the night my mother was killed. This time I remembered everything in vivid detail the way it had really happened.

It was the first day of spring. The night air was peaceful and smooth. There was a cool breeze blowing through an open window in the den where my family spent their last night together. My mother had just called Nicolette and me and told us to get ready for bed. We loved watching the lightening bugs flutter outside the window at night. We longed to break away from our parents and catch them in our jars. We weren't away from the window more than ten minutes when we heard a car pull up into the driveway. I could still hear the tires rolling against the gravel making a loud snapping sound that echoed through the window. My mother looked at my father, and I could tell she knew something was wrong. My father went to the window and pulled back the curtain.

He said, "It's Stewart and Dawson." He closed the curtain calmly and turned to us with his hands by his side. He nodded his head in Mattie's direction and said, "Take Nicolette and Noel outside so they can catch a few lightening bugs before they go to bed. Mattie hopped up from her seat. As she grabbed our hands and headed toward the kitchen, we walked past my father and he mussed our hair with his hand. My mother sprang to her feet and stood still. My father didn't say a word. He just gave her a look that I'd never seen before.

I heard my mother say, "Don't worry, I'm not moving a muscle, whatever happens, you just make sure you take care of my babies, do you understand me?" My father walked to the door and it popped open. I lingered behind Mattie and Nicolette. When I turned my head, I saw Dawson, Stewart and two other men entering the house. I saw them as plain as the nose on my face. I was standing behind the door staring. To this day I don't know why I couldn't move.

I heard Dawson say, "What's wrong, Nolan? What couldn't wait 'til morning?"

I heard Stewart say, "Yeah man. I was out with one of my girls. What's up?"

My father seemed agitated. As if my mother was invisible my father said, "I told you earlier that I needed you tonight. Don't pretend you don't know what's going on. I need this to look like an accident."

My mother began to yell, "Why don't you just let me take the girls and leave Nolan? Just let me go. You can have everything. Just give me my children."

My father snapped back at her, "It's too late for all that. I told you the only way you will leave me is in a body bag. Did you think you were gonna leave me and take my kids? I'll kill all of you before I let anyone leave me. Do you know who I am? I run this house and you! You leave when I'm ready for you to leave. You don't respect me anymore. You don't need me anymore. If you don't need me, then you've become a danger to me. I let you know too much about every-thing. You'll take the kids and then start runnin' your mouth."

My mother started to plead with him. "No, Nolan. I'll move away and you can still see them whenever you want."

"Bitch, I'm not stupid." Just then Mattie must have realized that I wasn't with them, she came back in and put her hand over my mouth and tried to drag me out of the door. I must have kicked her because she dropped me on the floor. Nicolette came back in and we heard the footsteps come closer. Nicolette and I hid in the kitchen in different locations. Mattie couldn't find any place to hide so she ran out the back door.

I heard Clark say, "Look man, this ain't right. She's your family. The mother of your children. She loves you. Just let her go. She's not stupid. Think about this."

As I peeked my head from under the buffet, I heard my father raise his voice. "Let this be a lesson to every mutha fucka in this room, don't fuck with me! No one is above suspicion with me and no one, including my wife and kids, will be spared. You need to understand and recognize that I am the one in control, and what I say goes."

I saw my mother backing up in my direction. Then, all of a sudden, I heard a gunshot. I saw my mother fall to her knees. I heard my father say, "This wasn't in the plan, this wasn't how it was supposed to go. You two were supposed to take care of this, now I've got to get my hands dirty." Another gunshot rang out. My mother's body fell backwards with her knees still bent. Just like I'd always remembered, I stared into her eyes as she opened her hand to reach out to me, and took her last breath.

I knew the rest of the story and I knew how it ended. So, there was no need to remember my father shooting himself. The truth is I don't think I ever witnessed that. I was too focused on watching my mother as she lay there with blood pouring from her body. Maybe this was the same thing that Lauren remembered, and she too had locked it out of her memory, refusing to unlock that part of her mind. At that point, it was neither here nor there. My eyes were dry and I couldn't find a source for my tears, so I sat there puffing on poison and getting lost in the haze of the night air.

I sat there for a few more minutes before I put my cigarette out and grabbed my phone. I dialed Stewart's number.

"Hey baby," he said.

"Hey...what are you doing?"

"I was just sitting here thinking about you." What a normal player response.

"Good, then we must be on the same page. Listen I know it's late, but I want to see you."

"I thought you were out of town."

"I was. I came back earlier. I missed you."

I could hear Stewart smiling through the phone. He said, "Now that's what I'm talking about. A woman who's not afraid to call her man and tell him what she wants." He actually thought I was his woman. That was too cute.

"Yeah, so are you available or what?"

"I'm always available for you."

"I'll be there in a few minutes."

"Actually, I'm at my new club. I'm checking things out for the grand opening. Why don't you meet me here? I'm on 35th and Hopkins." Reginald gave me the directions. When he told me he was at his new club, it gave me an idea. I put on my slip dress and headed out. When I arrived at the club, he grabbed me, and kissed me like we hadn't seen each other in years. After he let me go, I slowly strutted into the club so he could get an eye full.

He said, "Are you trying to give me a heart attack? You know I'm old enough to be your daddy."

"Well, that's not the kind of daddy I want you to be." All he could do was laugh. He walked over and grabbed me again. He couldn't control himself. He started rubbing and touching and lifting my dress. I pushed him away and told him to be patient.

I asked, "Is your sound system hooked up yet?"

He looked confused and said, "Yeah, what's up?"

"Just point me in the direction of the DJ's booth."

He pointed to the left. I walked over behind the booth and searched for the right music. I finally found what I was looking for. 'Darling Nikki' by Prince, the extended version. I pulled a chair out and motioned for him to sit down. Once he was seated, I gently kissed his lips. I stepped up on stage and let the music move through my body. I grabbed the pole and wrapped my warm legs around the cold steel. I felt relaxed as my hair fell freely into my face. I gently tossed my hair around and continued to move my body to the music. I slowly wound my body around the pole, took my final spin and placed both feet on the ground with my stilettos keeping me balanced. With one hand still resting on the pole, I slowly moved up and down grinding my pelvis, slowly moving to the music. I began to lose myself in the moment. I was so comfortable and confident. I slowly moved away from the pole, walked to the edge of the stage and stepped out of my dress. I stood in front of Stewart wearing nothing but my heels. My breasts were erect, and I could feel heat radiating from my thighs. I slowly stepped off the stage and walked over to Stewart. With both feet firmly planted in front of him, I kissed his erect manhood and explored every inch of him with my mouth. I could feel his firmness between my lips. As I caressed him with my tongue, he explored my depth with his fingers. My mouth was gentle, yet strong. It was wet and warm. Once I felt him getting firm and unable to contain himself, I retreated from my position and stood in front of him. He was panting like a dog. He shook his head as if he were trying to focus. I straddled him, placed both feet on the floor and gave him the lap dance of a lifetime. I could feel Stewart's excitement as he grasped both sides of the chair. I could hear him breathing in my ear. I felt the moisture from his hands, as they moved up my spine.

I stared into his eyes as he looked at me and said, "Lord have mercy on me." I smiled and kissed him on the lips. Then, I kissed his neck. He was about to explode. I thought I might need to hurry up and get this over with because he wasn't gonna make it. I moved vigorously and listened to the sounds of his moans and groans of pleasure in my ear. I could feel my body tremble as my mind started to get weak. I struggled to focus on a concrete thought. My body exploded as he grabbed me and pulled me closer and let out an overwhelming sound of satisfaction. We both sat still for a moment paralyzed, trying to catch our breath. I kissed his forehead and got up from my seat, picked my dress up from the floor, and sashayed off to the bathroom. After freshening up, I stood there and stared at him as he sat with a blank stare on his face. He was still sitting in the same chair, dazed and confused. I kissed him once again and walked out the door leaving him in the same spot.

When I reached the house, I parked the car in the garage, and walked in through the side door. Once inside, I made sure everything was secure and started up the stairs. Just as I reached the third step, I glanced over at the side window and noticed a shadow moving past. I quickly grabbed my gun from my purse and dashed off the steps, the shadow was too small and curvy to be a man. I turned out the lights. There were so many windows in that house. The shadow moved from window to window toward the front door. My heart started to beat faster and faster. My hands started to sweat as I gripped the gun tighter. I didn't know what to expect. I knew whoever it was, was trying to come through the front door. I stood there contemplating my next move. I realized I was wearing nothing but a thin dress and heels.

I kicked of my shoes in case I needed to run. I walked closer to the door, drew my gun and turned on the outside lights, so they'd know I could see them. I took a deep breath, counted to three and opened the door. I stuck my gun right in the person's face. My eyes grew wider and my heart sank to my feet, it was Lauren. I just stared at her. With my gun still drawn, and in her face, she held her hands in the air.

"It's me. Don't shoot," she said.

I asked, "What are you doing here?"

I don't know why, but I still had the gun pointed at her. Finally, I put the gun down by my side. I guess she realized I wasn't going to let her in. She looked down at the ground, and then up at me.

"Look, I flew all the way here from Houston to apologize to you, and to see if we can squash whatever this tension is between us. I know my behavior was totally out of control and I'm sorry. Sometimes I lose it and I don't know what to do."

"I just don't know, Lauren. I invited you into my home once and gave you half of what I owned and you still acted like some ill-mannered street trash. Oh, not to mention you were fuckin' my boyfriend behind my back. Have I left anything out?"

She stared at me like a homeless dog, so I stepped aside and motioned for her to come in. As she walked past me and set her bags down on the floor, I wondered how the hell she knew where the house was.

"How did you find this place?"

"Well, I am a real estate agent. I knew you were coming to L.A. to sell it, so I checked it out."

"Uh, hum." I placed the gun on the table, reached down, grabbed her bags and told her she could sleep in one of the guest rooms. I asked her if she was hungry. I told her there wasn't much in the refrigerator and I really didn't know if there was anything open that late. She told me she wasn't hungry, but she could use something to drink, wine or something stronger. Once we placed her things in the guestroom we went back downstairs, where I poured her a glass of wine. I didn't want to see anymore wine, I didn't even want to eat a grape. I'd had my share of alcohol. From the time she arrived, there wasn't much dialogue between us. I had to admit I was at a loss for words, and didn't really know how to respond to her. I was still upset over what had transpired before I left Houston, but somehow I just couldn't turn her away. I knew she was sick and needed help.

I guess I developed the same eerie feeling in my gut that Isabelle and Mattie felt. At that moment, I couldn't dwell on it. I had other things on my mind. Once everything was said and done, I would deal with her and her problems. I decided I wasn't going to mention Stewart or Reginald to her. I didn't see any sense in getting her involved since she seemed to resist anything concerning the past. I figured it would be extremely rude of me if I didn't talk to her at all, so I made small talk.

"So...how are things in Houston?"

"Things are great. Hot, but great. I've been so busy trying to establish my clientele I don't have time for much else, except for Noel of course."

"How is Noel?"

"She's fine. Actually, she sent you a little gift, something she made in school."

"That's sweet of her. I do miss her."

"Yeah, she talks about you all the time. She can't wait to see you again." The small talk was very small, and difficult, but I kept it going.

"How's everything with you and Maxwell?" Her expression changed, but she was reluctant to display any real signs of discomfort.

She responded, "Maxwell is fine, but we're no longer seeing each other. He broke it off."

"Oh, I'm sorry to hear that, really I am." I really was sorry to hear that.

"Are you really? I guess if I were you, I would be...ah I'm looking for a word here."

"Well Lauren, when he first told me about it, I was a little pissed off..."

"He told you about it? I figured you heard it from his sister."

"No, he called and told me about it himself."

"Uh, hum"

"Anyway, I was upset because you didn't tell me, and I felt like you betrayed me in the beginning. But I got over it after I realized it didn't matter anyway because you really don't owe me any type of loyalty. Besides I have Alex, and that's all I should be concerned about. Maxwell is a good guy and I figured he would be good to you and treat Noel right."

The look on Lauren's face indicated her discomfort about something I said.

After I finished my statement she said, "What do you mean I don't owe you any loyalty."

"Well it's true. You are my sister through our bloodline, but we don't know a thing about each other. It's like we're total strangers. Hell, technically we are strangers. I think I was so overwhelmed and happy when you showed up that I simply tried too hard to make something happen that just wasn't there at the time. But I realize my mistake now, and I'm dealing with it."

"So what does all that mean?"

"This is what it means, you are my sister in blood and name. I did right by you when I gave you half of what was left for us, which you were entitled to. Just because we're sisters, doesn't make us best friends. When you acted the way you did outside my house, it made me realize you obviously have some issues and resentment where I'm concerned, and that makes me uncomfortable. I did everything I could to welcome you into my home and my family and you still showed me nothing but contempt. I have lived my life watching my back, watching the people around me, wondering when they were going to turn on me. Trust doesn't come easy for me. When I feel threatened, I shut down. And when I feel like my life may be in danger, there's no telling what I'll do to defend myself. I can see the same thing in you. So with all that being said, I think it's safer that we just take things extremely slow and get to know each other first before we start having family dinners and start singing 'We Are Family'. I finally got my life straight with the people I love and who love me, and I'll be damned if I'm gonna be in another mental institution tied up in a strait jacket."

Lauren took a sip of her wine, and put her glass back down. "I guess that's fair considering my behavior. I understand how you feel, but I was jealous of you. It just seemed like you had everything and everyone loved you. That's something I've run away from all my life."

"It didn't come easy for me either."

"Yeah, I know."

"Look that was then, this is now. Who knows what the future will hold. Just because I don't completely trust you I'm not gonna mistreat you. While you're here you're welcome to anything that I have."

I started toward the doorway leading to the garage. I asked Lauren to follow. I picked up the keys to the Rover along the way. I handed them to Lauren and opened the door.

"I'm sure you don't want to be stuck in the house all day. I do remember you telling me that you spent some time out here, so I'm sure you know your way around. These are the keys to the Rover. The Denali is Alex's pride and joy, and the McLaren is mine, so you're welcome to this truck here."

We walked over to the truck and I told her to pop the lock. She looked over at the Mercedes. "Did you buy that since you've been here? It's nice."

At first, I was reluctant to tell her that Alex had bought it for me, but then I thought why not. "No. Actually, it's an engagement present from Alex. It was here when I arrived." I didn't put much enthusiasm into my explanation. I pretended it didn't faze me. She walked over to the car and looked through the window. I reached inside the house and retrieved the keys. I handed them to her and she popped the lock on the Benz. She sat inside the car and admired the interior. I was hoping she wouldn't have any jealous rage episodes. She put the key in the ignition and the car said, "Hello."

She jumped back and started to laugh. "This is crazy. The car talks!"

I smiled but I didn't want to get to comfortable. "Yeah, I need to have that message changed."

After she finished admiring the car, we stayed up a little longer. We laughed and shared pleasant conversation. I guess it could have been considered a tender moment. I was still watching my back just in case one of her alter egos showed up for a performance. I told Lauren I was tired and needed to go to bed. I offered her full access to the house and said goodnight. She said she was tired as well, so we both went upstairs for the night. As usual, I locked my bedroom door. Over those last few months, I learned that crazy is as crazy does and I was sure Lauren was still unbalanced. Even though it seemed as though she was ok for that moment, I still didn't trust her ass!

Chapter Thirty-Two

When I woke in the morning, I found myself lying outside on the balcony. The sun was beaming down on my face, making it moist from the heat. I was ready to get back to my life. I'd made a careless mistake by allowing myself to be captivated by Stewart. What the hell was I thinking and what was I thinking with? I wondered how things would be between Alex and me. Even though we never really discussed how I'd gotten close to Stewart, he knew what was up. Could he really deal with it? Lauren's visit has thrown everything out of whack, but it was just as well, it was time for things to end.

As I prepared myself for the day, I stopped for a moment, and fell to my knees asking God for forgiveness for what I was about to do. Ironically, I asked for strength as well, strength to carry out justice that was long overdue. After I was exhausted and couldn't utter another word from my lips to God's ears, I stood up and looked in the mirror. For the first time in a while, I didn't want to dress up. I didn't want to put on any makeup. I just wanted to throw on something and ride all day. I didn't feel too much like making a production out of getting dressed. I ran a comb through my hair and wore it straight. I put on a pair of distressed jeans with the tears and holes in them. I accented it with a fitted t-shirt. I wore sandals that I could slip my feet in and out of. I checked myself in the mirror and grabbed my purse. I was hoping Lauren was still asleep. I needed to prepare my mind for that night.

Before leaving I went down the hall to check on Lauren. I knocked on the door and when she didn't respond, I turned the doorknob. Lauren walked up behind me and said, "I'm not there."

She was like a cat. She scared the hell out of me. I released the door handle and turned to face her. She was fully dressed as if she were going somewhere.

I looked at her and said, "Good morning. How'd you sleep?"

"Oh, I slept great. That bed is so comfortable." I started walking toward the stairs.

Lauren said, "Are you going somewhere this morning?" Her whole vibe was pretty weird.

I answered her question. "I'm just going to run some errands today. I need to clear my head and figure some things out. I think I'll just take a ride around L.A. and see some sites. You know, just hang out with myself." I made the 'myself' part clear, so she wouldn't want to tag along. I walked down the hall to my room. I'd forgotten to dab on a few drops of Serenity.

Lauren followed me down the hall. "I understand. I need some time to clear my head as well. I think I'll do some shopping."

I could definitely agree with that. She also said she wanted to pick up a few things for Noel.

When we entered my room, Lauren followed me into the bathroom. That day she seemed more childlike. She hopped up on the counter and looked at me. She had a weird look in her eyes. There was nothing familiar at all. I was afraid that the whole thing with Reginald was making me less compassionate. I looked at her, thinking she should go play or something. I took the bottle of perfume from the cabinet and put some on my pulse points.

Lauren looked up at me and said, "What's that? It smells wonderful."

I guess because I remember everything about my childhood, I expected her to remember as well. I looked at her and said, "It's Serenity. Don't you remember?"

She hit herself on the side of her head and said, "Oh, yeah I remember. It just smells differently than when you wore it before."

I don't know what she was thinking, but it smelled just the same to me. Then she said, "Where did Alex pick that up from?" I could see she'd forgotten that our mother wore that scent all the time.

I didn't want to make her feel bad, so I just said, "You know, I don't remember." I placed the bottle back into the cabinet and walked out of the bathroom. I looked back and Lauren was holding the bottle in her hand.

She put the bottle down and said, "Is it still ok that I take the truck today?"

"Yes of course, for as long as you're here."

"Are you sure Alex won't mind, I know how he is about his cars."

And how did she know that? I guess she read my mind because she corrected herself. "You know, all men love their cars."

I smiled and said, "I know." Then she ran her fingers through my hair and said, "He sure does love you. That's a nice car he bought you. How much was it...about $400,000?"

It was the weirdest thing. I let her play in my hair. "I really don't know, I think it's somewhere in that ballpark. You should know. You have a nice Benz yourself."

She looked at me and didn't even crack a smile, "Yeah, but I didn't have someone like Alex to buy mine. I had to get it on my own." She was staring at me like she was in some sort of trance. Now the conversation could've gone in several directions; I could've just knocked her on her ass for being funny or I could've just ended it right there. So, I just ended it. I told her I needed to get going. As I walked out the door, I could feel her standing there, watching me.

When I reached the garage and hopped in the car, I started to think of how jealous Lauren was. I tried not to think that she went after Maxwell because she was jealous, because I knew he could have easily seduced her. Her entire vibe was troubling me. As I pulled off and glanced up at my bedroom, she was just standing in the window. I blew the horn and drove away.

I needed to talk to Alex about it. I hadn't talked to him that morning. He had called earlier, but I was in the shower. I pushed my speed dial, but it came up empty. I thought that I must have mistakenly erased it or reset it, so I just went to the A section in my phonebook and pressed talk. He was the only A in there. It rang and then went to voicemail and I remembered the time difference. He was still working out. I didn't leave a message. I just hung up and figured he'd see my missed call.

I washed the car and rode through the neighborhoods. Since I did listen to some rap music, I was curious about Compton and Inglewood. I was enjoying my drive and loving the fact that I could say I'd been to Compton, and rode down Crenshaw. I forgot I was riding around in a very expensive car in a place that I knew nothing about. I decided to just do what I did best, shop. I found a mall somewhere, I really didn't even know where I was, but I couldn't get lost with the navigation system in my car. I walked through the mall eating everything in sight. I ate cookies, ice cream, pretzels, and drank slushes. I was like a kid. I just went from store to store trying on shoes, clothes, hats, and jewelry. I was actually enjoying myself. I had lunch alone. I also had a pedicure and a manicure. After I'd exhausted all possibilities in the mall, I left and went to Rodeo Drive. I really didn't know why, it wasn't anything spectacular. I just wanted to go because I could. To my surprise it was pretty crowded. I realized my paranoia about being outside of Houston was really holding me back. I felt free. I was roaming the city, doing whatever I wanted. I could've been doing that all those years. Deciding to walk, I parked the car.

I happened to glance across the street, and did a double take. Stewart was standing across the street staring at me. I didn't want to seem alarmed, so I smiled. His expression didn't change. I looked away to gather my thoughts and figure out how to address the obviously awkward situation. I felt uneasy, thinking to myself, "I know he's not following me." I looked back across the street and he was gone. Just as I turned around to locate him, he was standing almost on my heels.

The first thing out of my mouth was, "Are you following me?"

He smiled and said, "Well, yes and no."

"Which one is it, yes or no?"

"I was in the neighborhood earlier and I saw you driving around, I knew it was you, because I saw YOUNG 1 on the license plane. I was wondering what you were doing out that way, so yes, I started to follow you. I just wanted to make sure you were ok. That's all." I hadn't even noticed my license plate.

For a minute that seemed logical, but I did say, "Ok, after I left the neighborhood and I came over here, did you think someone was going to get me on Rodeo Drive?"

He started to laugh. "No, woman. I was hoping I could treat you to lunch or help you with your shopping."

I bet he did want to treat me to something. I apologized for my accusation and expressed my wish to be alone. "Look Stewart, I appreciate the offer and the concern, but I'm just kind of enjoying being alone right now. You understand, don't you?"

"Yeah, I understand. I understand that I can't stop thinking about you. I don't want you to leave L.A. I want you to stay here with me.

"Come on, Stewart, you know that I'm engaged to Alex. We discussed this from the very beginning."

"So what, you think you can just come here and get me all twisted up. Make me feel like you really want me and then just forget about me? It's not that simple."

"Stewart, what the hell is wrong with you? 'It's not that simple' ... What does that mean?"

Stewart leaned over and whispered in my ear. "It means how do you think Alex is gonna take it, when he finds out that his sweet little California Sunshine has been giving private lap dances."

"Are you threatening me?"

"I wouldn't call it a threat. I'm just protecting my interest in a future investment. Seth, I want you and I'm gonna do whatever I can to keep you." The look in Stewart's eyes was truly unsettling. It took long enough, but Clark finally showed up. He stood there with an unyielding look on his face. I knew he was telling the truth. He would definitely tell Alex about us. I was no longer blinded by what I wanted him to be. He was just who he'd always been. In almost an instant, his looks began to change. He was no longer that suave handsome man I was falling for.

I gathered my thoughts and said, "I'll tell you what, why don't we discuss your pending investment over dinner tonight?" He flashed a smile that was even more disturbing than the way his eyes had changed.

"That sounds good. I'll even cook my famous fettuccini for you."

"Well, it sounds like a date. I'll be there around eight then."

He agreed and kissed me on the cheek before he walked back across the street. As I watched him walk away, I thought of him as the walking dead.

Chapter Thirty-Three

Visiting a few shops, I felt myself winding down. On my way to the car, I checked my phone and Alex still hadn't called. I was really beginning to worry. I'd called him several times, and he failed to answer or return my calls. I was getting even more worried. I just knew he and Isabelle were on their way to L.A. I was in such a state of confusion I didn't notice the Corvette roaring in my direction. I'd stepped off the sidewalk into traffic. I stood there holding onto my purse and my packages for dear life. I stood there paralyzed as the passenger side door flew open. I leaned in to tell the driver how sorry I was for almost causing an accident. The driver leaned over the passenger seat. It was Stewart. "Get in!" he yelled.

After the encounter that we'd had earlier, I was reluctant to get in the car. He patted the seat. "Come on. Get in the car. You're holding up traffic." I looked around as if I was looking for someone familiar, but I didn't see anyone. I just hopped in the car and hoped for the best.

Stewart peeled off, looked at me and said, "What's wrong with you? You look uncomfortable." Uncomfortable was an understatement.

I looked at him and said, "I'm just a little jumpy. I think I just need to lie down for a while. My car is just around the corner, you can drop me there." We turned the corner and passed my car. I sat up in the seat and said, "Hold on, you just passed my car."

He put his hand on my knee and said, "I know, just calm down. I'm gonna take you someplace where you can relax." He continued to caress my knee and look at me with those piercing green eyes and sly smile. I tried my best to relax, but I wanted to open the door and jump out.

We drove for what seemed like forever, through the mountains, up hills, twists and turns. Stewart let the top down. Under normal circumstances, this would have been the ideal adventure. I looked around and this was the perfect place to hide my body. I tried to text Isabelle several times, but I couldn't get a signal. I finally saw a sign that said the beach was three miles ahead. Just over the hill was the most breathtaking sight I'd seen thus far. The ocean was sitting directly to the right of us. As Stewart drove further, I could see more and more of this wonderful sight.

He put his hand on my knee and said, "Isn't it beautiful?" I nodded yes. We drove about a mile down the road before we turned toward an iron gate. Stewart punched a code into the keypad. As the gates opened, we drove through the gate.

There were palm trees and beautiful flowers everywhere. At the end of the driveway was a house that looked as if it were made entirely of glass. I was so taken by the landscape and the architecture that I forgot I was a little uneasy.

Stewart rolled around to the front and said, "Well, here we are!"

I looked back and said, "Where are we supposed to be exactly?"

He turned the car off and said, "This is my oceanfront hideaway." I was so confused I didn't know what to ask first.

He said, "No one knows about this place, not even Reginald. Sometimes, when I want to get away, I come up here to relax. You are the first woman I've ever wanted to show this to."

I thought to myself, "Negro, please. I know how you like to impress." I was more than certain he had brought some hoochie up here before. I looked at him and said, "Stewart, please."

He grabbed my hand. "No, Seth, I'm serious. A man like me can't afford to get too comfortable. I'm not exactly what you call your typical man. I don't need attachments and some woman manipulating me trying to get her hands on what I got."

"So what makes me different? Why bring me up here after only knowing me for such a short time?"

"To be honest, I have no idea. There's something about you, I feel like I've known you forever. I didn't wake up this morning and say, I'm gonna bring you up here. After I saw you on Rodeo, it felt like the right thing to do. So while you were looking at jewelry, I picked this up for you." He handed me a small bag. I opened it and pulled a string bikini out.

He smiled, "It's for swimming, unless you want to skinnydip. I figured we could enjoy the water." Man, oh man. I'm out here in the middle of nowhere. Stewart is gonna drown my ass out there in the ocean.

Stewart put the top up on the car, and we entered the house. The house was exquisite. I stood in the middle of the floor and turned around and around like a kid.

Stewart said, "I've finally impressed you."

All I could say was, "Yeah." My mouth was wide open.

He said, "Come on, let's get changed." He took my hand and led me toward the elevator. As we were elevated to the third floor, I looked out over the ocean, it seemed to never end.

While I was changing, Stewart went downstairs to the kitchen. When I finished, I joined him. He was preparing wine, fruit and cheese. I must say, he had classy moves. He placed everything into a picnic basket and we headed for the beach. He spread a blanket out on the soft sand, and we enjoyed the sun. We drank wine, ate fruit and played in the water. I was enjoying myself too much, again allowing myself to be thrown off track. I began to wonder who was playing whom. Stewart walked over and pulled me close to him. His kiss was different. It was filled with passion, not just lust. He picked me up and carried me to the blanket, but the blanket couldn't shield us from the sand for long. We rolled around in the gritty sand making love like two animals. Our tongues touched with force and excitement. Stewart was so excited. He seemed much larger than before. I gripped his back leaving my fingerprints in his flesh. My mind spun around and around and everything seemed to disappear around me. All I could hear were our moans of ecstasy. I couldn't help but call his name.

"Stewart, Oh Stewart." I wanted to scream, "Here, Stewart just take me. It's yours and only yours."

I tried to compose myself, and get some sort of grip on reality, but I couldn't. I tried to gain control of the situation, but it was too late. I'd lost that one. All I could do was charge it to the game. I started to get dizzy and my vision was hazy. I felt my legs tremble and my whole body shivered. I tried to hold the words in my throat, but somehow they escaped.

"Oh Stewart, Stewart...please...oh, my God...Stewart" After a few moments all I could do was lie there and look at the sky as he kissed my lips, then my neck, my breasts and finally my lips again.

We laid there for a while, completely spent and silent. Finally, he turned to me and broke the silence. "My God you are so beautiful. You remind me..." He stopped in the middle of his sentence.

I caressed his face and said, "I remind you of whom?"

He dropped his head and said, "No one. I guess I'm just getting caught up."

"It's ok to get caught up as long as you know how to release your-self."

He gave me a sincere look and said, "So, why are you here with me?"

I didn't know how to respond. "What do you mean?"

"Well, I am clearly much older than you. You don't need my money and you seem to be very levelheaded. You're engaged to Alex Young. So what are you doing here with me?"

"I don't know. To be honest, I've asked myself that very question. I haven't come up with a concrete answer yet. I'm just here."

"Can you honestly walk away from me? I mean, I know there is something between us that's beyond physical. Hell, I can't even explain it."

I removed myself from the blanket and looked toward the ocean.

"Stewart, I have to walk away from you. Who are we kidding? I don't belong in your world. I'm an everyday ordinary woman who owns an overpriced boutique. You own strip clubs and God knows what else. I can't live my life the way you do. Look at us we're out here in the middle of nowhere, hiding from the rest of the world. There's something about you that's dark, mysterious and unhappy."

He looked down at the sand as if he were searching for a response. Then he looked at me and said, "You're right. I am unhappy and you wouldn't believe some of the things I live with. Yes, I do more than just real estate and own clubs, but I am tired. I do everything from dealin' dope to sellin' ass. Do you know how it feels to be fifty years old, still worrying and looking over your shoulder every minute of every day? This life never ends. For every lie I tell, I have to tell another one to cover that one up. For everybody I bury, I have to bury another one. I don't think you know who I am. I have the power to do anything I want in this world, except to be free."

I didn't know what to say at first. Then I walked over to him and touched his hand. "Then why don't you just walk away?"

He pulled away, "It's not that simple, I can't leave my brother behind. I feel so guilty because every morning I wake up, hoping that he died in his sleep. I swear sometimes I think I hate him."

"Don't say that Stewart, he's your brother." I couldn't very well say, "Yeah let's kill the son-of a-bitch."

Stewart looked at me and dropped his head, and just when I was getting ready to probe further into his contempt for Reginald, I looked down the way at a boat that was docked behind the house. Somehow, I'd failed to notice it before. The boat seemed so very insignificant, I couldn't figure out what drew me to it, until now.

Stewart placed his hand on my shoulder and said, "Seth, are you alright? What are you looking at?"

I blocked the sun from my eyes with my right hand.

"I don't know, I just noticed you have a boat."

"Yeah, I bought the boat shortly after I bought this house. We can go down there if you want."

"Yeah, come on. I'll race you." We both took off down the beach toward the boat. As I approached the boat, I could see the name displayed on the side. The sand became heavy on my feet. Finally, I stopped dead in my tracks. The name on the side of the boat read, "Anna Marie."

In my haste to explain my shock, I looked at Stewart and asked, "Who is Anna Marie?"

He walked past me and climbed aboard the boat, reaching out for me to join him. After finding a comfortable spot, he looked at me with despair in his eyes, which had changed yet again. They were soft and beautiful, as he looked off into the clouds.

"I keep telling you how beautiful you are. I think it is your eyes that drive me crazy the most. I can't explain it. They're so beautiful and rare."

"There's nothing rare about brown eyes."

"It's not just the color. It's the shape and the way they dance when you smile. You have a way of looking at me that makes me...I can't even explain it. There was only one other person in this world who could make me bow like a trained puppy and she had eyes just like yours."

I struggled to wrap my mind around the idea that Stewart was trying to tell me he was in love with my mother. At that point, anything was possible. Was Stewart the man my father had thought my mother was cheating with? Was there really an affair wrapped up in there somewhere?

I took a deep breath and asked, "Was this Anna Marie?"

A calm look came over Stewart, almost as if he was coming down off some sort of high. "Yes, her name was Anna Marie."

My heart sank to my feet. I was paralyzed, but I wanted to know more. "Can you tell me about her? What made her so special?"

Stewart looked over at me, "No, that was so long ago. Anna is gone now and she's never coming back." I prayed that he wouldn't bring me that far and then just drop it. I moved closer to him and caressed his back. I could feel the scars from his burns through the soaked t-shirt. Something inside me started to boil. I wanted to say, talk to me, tell me something. I sat there on the edge teetering between sanity and insanity. I could feel myself growing anxious.

"Please tell me about her. I want to know who made the mighty Stewart Benson fall in love. Where is she now?"

Stewart removed himself from his seat. "She's dead!"

"Oh, I'm sorry. I didn't know!"

"It's ok. I killed her."

I stood there trapped inside this dark tunnel in my head. I was the only one there and there was a big boulder sitting on my chest. Somehow, I thought Stewart's confession would be different. I thought I would feel different, but I was numb. I was confused. Dawson Meeks had just told me that my father killed my mother. Someone wasn't playing by the rules. I'd gotten my wires crossed somehow and had been fed some wrong information. I tried to snap out of my trance. I wiggled my toes and then my fingers. I batted my eyes and breathed deeply, just to make sure I hadn't passed out. Once I was free and clear from confusion, I found myself standing face to face with Stewart. I suppose he could feel my discomfort.

I placed my hand on my chest and said, "What do you mean you killed her?"

"Well, I might as well have done it. Anna was Reginald's wife."

"What?"

"Yes, she was his wife. She was the most beautiful woman that I have ever seen until you walked into my life. Reginald didn't appreciate her. He thought she would always be there when he was tired of playing around, like a good wife should. From the moment I laid eyes on her I knew she was someone special."

"But she was your brother's wife."

"I know, but my brother has to be one the most selfish sons-of-bitches on the face of this earth. I really don't think he's human."

"Come on Stewart, he can't be that bad. He seems charming, arrogant, but charming."

"You don't know my brother, and believe me you don't want to." The look in Stewart's eyes was fear. It was the same look I'd seen in Mattie's eyes when she talked about the devil, the same look in Dr. Shaw's eyes and Charlie's eyes and then in Dawson Meeks eyes. I wanted to know more about his feelings for my mother, but more importantly why did he say he'd killed her.

"Stewart, I still don't understand why you say you killed her."

As he rubbed his temples, he began to speak. "A few weeks before she died, Anna found out how evil Reginald could be."

"What do you mean?"

"Reginald had another woman on the side in the city. The girl threatened to tell Anna. Reginald invited the girl out to the house and made her tell Anna what had been going on between them. It had been going on for years. Just to show the girl that he couldn't be controlled. To put fear in Anna, he shot her in front of Anna. He dared Anna to leave him. Anna came to me scared out of her mind. I'd never seen her so scared in my life. One thing led to another and we ended up making love. After that, I couldn't get her out of my head. I just wanted to take her and run away."

What do you say after someone tells you something like that? I don't know if I should believe him or not. Every time I turned around there was something new to factor into the equation. I was intrigued by his story, so I kept it going.

"So what did you do with the girl's body?"

Stewart looked at me and said, "We buried her in the woods behind Reginald's old house."

I sat there staring at him trying to figure out just what to say. What could I say? The fact is I didn't really care about the dead girl. I'd figured out why Stewart was so taken with me. He was in love with my mother and I was the closest thing to her.

"I thought his wife died in a car accident."

"It was no accident."

"Were you driving?

"No, there was no car accident. I was shocked when he told you that."

"So, how did you kill her? Damn, just be honest. I'm so very tired of this bait and switch game."

"I told Reginald she had been cheating on him with someone else. That planted the seed in his head. That's when he devised a plan to kill her. I had convinced him to believe she was going to leave him, and take all her money with her. I thought he would just leave her, and let her go, but I was sadly mistaken. I tried to convince him that killing her was too risky. I thought I'd gotten through to him, but before I knew anything she was dead...he even had his own children killed."

"Oh my God Stewart, why are you still running behind him?"

He jumped up in a rage. " He's my brother damnit. And I'm not running behind him, he needs me."

"Not even ten minutes ago, you sat there and said you were waiting for him to die. You said it at the restaurant. What the hell is wrong with you? Either you're tired of this man murdering and manipulating, or you enjoy it. It's one or the other."

"Look Seth, you don't understand what it's like to be me. You don't know what it's like to walk around at night because you can't sleep. I hear Anna's screams in my sleep. I can smell her blood."

Before I knew it, I'd yelled out, "What happened to her children? What about them?" Stewart looked surprised. "Did you do anything to try and stop Reginald from killing his own children?"

He closed his eyes and in a faint voice, he said, "No."

I was struggling for my next thought, and my voice began to crack. "So you were in love with your brother's wife? That's not exactly taboo. Just because you planted the seed, that doesn't mean you killed her."

I was trying to give him a way out. I was trying to spare him. He sank down in his chair, and held his hands together and looked at me with tears streaming down his face.

"When Reginald asked for my gun. I froze. For a minute, I was paralyzed. I said to myself this is the time that you take a stand against Reginald and say, 'No.' This is where you draw the line. He asked a second time and then a third and finally, I handed it to him. I just handed him my life. I did nothing as I watched him murder the woman I loved. I could have done something. I could have held him off until she got away. I could have shot him and been rid of him forever, but I just handed him the gun."

There it was, right there in my face. There was no way in hell I could let him go. He was right, he could have done something, but instead he did nothing. He was the man who put the gun in my father's hand. Ironically, I was disappointed in Stewart. I was hoping I could blame everything on his weakness and inability to be a man, but he failed me. Somehow I believed he loved my mother more than my father ever could.

With a heavy heart and confused mind, I sat there in silence, waiting for Stewart to say something. He stared into space as if I was no longer there. I gathered myself and walked over to him. I leaned over and kissed him and threaded his fingers through mine. I told him it was getting late and I needed to get back to the city.

We went back into the house, where I took a shower and prepared to go home. I walked over to the bed and picked up my cell phone. I noticed it was flashing. I must have it on silent. I looked at the caller ID. It was Maxwell. What did he want now?

"Hello."

"Yes, Hello"

"Who is this?"

"Who did you call?"

"I called Lauren Davis."

"Maxwell, this is Seth you called my phone by mistake."

"Seth, I'm sorry but I pushed number three on my phone and that should be Lauren."

What the hell was going on? Did I pick up her phone accidentally? But I called Alex from that same phone earlier. "Look Maxwell, can you please hang up and try again. I need to check something out."

Maxwell agreed and called right back. "Yeah, Seth, you have Lauren's phone. This time I dialed the number directly."

I'll be damned. I could hear Maxwell calling my name as I dropped the phone on the bed. My head was swimming. Why would Lauren have Alex's number in her phone? And how did I end up with her phone? I was trying to make sense of everything when the phone rang again. It was Isabelle.

"Seth, are you ok? I received several texts from you saying you were riding with Stewart. And why are you calling from Lauren's phone? There is something that you need to know..."

I was so dazed I couldn't listen to Isabelle ramble about anything. "Look Isabelle, I'm fine. Now is not the time. Something weird is going on, and I need to figure it out."

"I know, Seth...I have to tell you something..."

"I don't have time to talk right now."

"Seth, the information you requested from the State of Georgia came back. There's something you should know."

"Look Isabelle, just hold on to it. I mean it can't be that important."

"Seth, what's wrong with your phone..."

"What... I don't know. Listen, I'll call you later." I hung up. My body began to get cold. I held my purse close to me and rushed toward the bathroom. I locked the door behind me and sat on the commode with the lid down. I searched through the phone and located the phone information section, I pressed ok and selected the My Phone Number option. 972-555-9607 popped up on the display screen. It was Lauren's phone. I scrolled through the phone and found Alex's number. What in the hell was going on? Why would Lauren have Alex's number programmed in her phone? At that moment, I had a few more hunches I needed to check out. I scrolled through to find Stewart's number. I exhausted every possibility of how he could be listed and I came up empty. My next move was to see if Reginald's number was stored in Lauren's phone, and there it was R. Hawthorne. It was clear to me that I was being screwed. Alex, Stewart, Reginald and my own sister were playing me like a fiddle, but why? What did Alex have to gain by any of this and how did he know Lauren? I felt like I was dangling from the end of a rope and one of them was waiting to tighten the noose around my neck. Clearly, it was too late for me to turn back. I didn't have time to think or to prepare. I never saw that one coming. My back was against the wall. My mind began to race, and I started to panic. Tears welled up in my eyes. Stewart and Reginald knew who I was and they were going to kill me for sure. I leaned my head over in the sink and drank some water from the faucet. I paced back and forth trying to figure a way out. It was just my luck that this bathroom doesn't have a window.

While I tried to gather myself I thought of my mother. The wolf in sheep's clothing had been revealed to me in the form of my sister. Or was it Alex? I guess I was too caught up with the reality of Lauren being there, that I never stopped to think that she could be my nemesis. I was really baffled by Alex's role in all of it. I just couldn't imagine that he would be this pissed off with me for rejecting him in the beginning. I heard Stewart outside of the door asking if everything was ok.

I yelled out, "Yes." I realized I couldn't stay in there forever. I didn't have time to try and figure out everyone's connection. I looked in the mirror and took a deep breath and stared at myself.

I started to call on the spirit of my mother. I said, "Mama, I found my wolf in sheep's clothing. Please lead me to the truth and get me out of here alive." In that same breath, I said, "Lord, I know you didn't bring me this far to drop me off." I closed my eyes for a few seconds. I didn't shed a tear. I leaned over, popped my contacts out and removed my wig to reveal my natural hair. I stood there staring into my green eyes. I was ready to face whatever was next. I took my gun out of my purse and held it close. I took one last deep breath, opened the bathroom door and found Stewart waiting on the other side. There we were standing face-to-face, Noel and Clark. Clark was thrown by my sudden change in eye color.

"What the hell is going on, Seth? What happened to your eyes? They're green." I placed my gun in his face.

"Yes Clark, this is the natural color...green. My mother Anna Marie's eyes were brown. My sister Nicolette's eyes are brown. My father Nolan's eyes are brown. I'm the only one with green eyes. Remember?"

He backed up and crashed on the bed like a sack of potatoes. "Clark? Where'd you get that name? I haven't heard that in years."

"Yeah, twenty to be exact ..."

"Who the fuck are you?"

"I just told you who I was, weren't you paying attention Clark? I'm Anna's daughter, Noel."

The blood drained from his face as if he'd seen a ghost. "Look, I don't know who you think you are or who you think you're playing with, but Noel is dead. I don't think you know who you're messin' with. You better tell me where you got your information from."

I gripped my gun firmly in my hand, and raised my voice.

"And I don't think *you* know just who you're fuckin' with." I reached over and grabbed my purse with my gun following him steadily. I grabbed my locket and threw it at him.

"Not too long ago you were pouring your heart out to me telling me how much I remind you of my mother. You were ready to bare your soul to me. Hell, you did bare your soul. Why did you do that? I was really starting to love you, Clark. I was hoping you had nothing to do with my mother's death, but you gave that evil bastard the gun...how could you...you weak muthafucka!" Stewart held the locket in his hand as he got up and walked toward me.

I didn't pull the trigger. I was so enraged, my thoughts weren't clear. I started to yell, "You might as well have pulled the damn trigger." I ran up to him and shot him in the arm with the gun.

He screamed, "You crazy bitch ... What do you want from me? You're supposed to be dead!"

I leaned down in front of him and said, "So are you."

He started to breathe hard. "Please, I told you I didn't do it. Your father killed your mother."

I jumped up and said, "Yes, because of the lie you fed him when you were the one going behind his back."

I started to say things that I didn't even know I felt.

"If it weren't for your lies my family might still be here."

Clark laughed. "Do you actually think Nolan wouldn't have killed your mother sooner or later? He didn't need me to give him a reason. After your mother inherited that money, he was thinking of ways to get his hands on it. He tried to convince her that I had him in debt, but she soon found out he was just a greedy S.O.B."

"What I don't understand is if he is so evil...why haven't you killed him and gotten rid of him?"

Clark lowered his head, "I can't kill Nolan Toussaint. I don't know if anyone can actually kill him. He's got some kind of power or control over people. He can sell contact lenses to a blind man." He managed to straighten himself up on the bed. "I can't believe you let me fall for you. Were you planning to kill me all along?"

"Yes."

"Damn. Nolan always said pussy was gone kill me one day."

"Stewart please, I didn't ask you to pour your heart out to me. Dawson Meeks had already cleared you for the murder. You just had to free your conscience. Why couldn't you just shut up?"

"You talked to Meeks?"

"Yes. I also talked to Dr. Shaw and Charles Brandenburg."

"Damn, you've done your homework."

"Damn, that shit is a trip ain't it?"

"Little Noel. Damn girl you sure did grow up to be a fine woman. Who would have thought you would kill me? I thought one of those bitches in the street would have taken me out by now." He took a deep breath and grabbed his shoulder. "How did you survive that night anyway?"

"Mattie, Nicolette and I ran out the back and hid in the woods until it was safe."

"So where were you when I came to Mattie's house that night?"

"I was hiding in the closet."

"So you and Nicolette are both alive...what have you been doing all these years?"

"I have been living a life of hell. Nicolette is another story that you don't have time to listen to."

"How is Mattie?"

"Oh, you actually care?"

"When you get your ass whopped by time like I have, you start wishing you could have done a lot of things differently. Would you tell her that I'm sorry?"

I couldn't believe that man had a conscience. He had to be the biggest pansy on that side of the ocean. I agreed to deliver the message to Mattie. He handed me the locket. "So what's next? Are you gonna kill me now or do I have to wait?"

"You have to wait. We are going to see Reginald now. I figure since you two are so tight, you should die together. Now get up so we can go. I'm ready to get this over with and go back to Houston. Oh yeah, if you even think about trying anything, I will blow a hole straight through your head."

Stewart struggled with his wound. I grabbed my things and we headed out the door. I decided I didn't need to take any chances so I made him get in the trunk. We stopped in front of the trunk. I opened it. "Get in."

"What?"

"Get in the trunk."

"Oh, Hell naw, I'm not getting' in my own trunk."

"If you don't get in on your own, I will make you."

"Fuck you, do what you gotta do. I'm not lettin' some crazy bitch stuff me in my own trunk."

"Oh, Clark. I thought you loved me, and wanted to make me happy."

"Fuck that! You tryin' to kill me. I told you I didn't kill Anna. I loved her and I thought I loved you."

"Bullshit, mutha fucka."

I clocked him in the head with the gun. He fell over into the trunk. I didn't know if he would fit in there, but I managed to stuff him in there real good.

I had no idea how to get back to the city and back to Reginald. I was going on a wing and a prayer. I kept saying to myself there's no turning back. Someone other than me was driving the car. Perhaps it was anger. I was seething at the thought of Alex and Lauren making me feel stupid. Just then I remembered how bizarre Lauren started acting when we were in Atlanta. It all started when Isabelle and I were talking about seeing Alex later. That's why she left early. She didn't want to see Alex. I didn't understand what Alex would get out of this. I started to cry at the thought of being betrayed by him of all people. My vision became clouded with tears. I wiped them away as I tried to convince myself to hold on. "Get a hold of yourself, you silly bitch. He's just a man." One thing was for damn sure, if I made it out of this alive, Alex would definitely pay.

Chapter Thirty-Four

As I drove toward the iron gate, which led to Clark's house, I checked my rear and a side mirror to see if anyone was following me. I didn't see anyone. My heart became heavy and my hands started to sweat. There I was a 5'8, 130 pound black woman against what seemed to be the devil and his advocate. I figured I must have had the patience of Job and no matter how wrong I was someone somewhere was looking out for me. I drove through the gate and parked directly in front of the house. I hopped out and opened the trunk. Clark was still knocked out cold. I felt his pulse to make sure he wasn't dead. I had no idea what I was going to do with him. I closed the trunk and fumbled to find the house keys on Clark's key ring. It was funny how at certain times a person's identity seemed to change for me. When I wanted to see something good and decent in the man, I referred to him as Stewart. Once I knew actually had a hand in killing my mother, he's back to being old Ellis Clark Winfield.

I finally found the right key. The lock popped and I turned the handle and entered the house. I closed the door behind me. As I moved through the house I noticed a light on leading to the kitchen. I walked in the direction of the light. I could hear movement. I walked slowly into the kitchen with my gun in my pocket and stood by the door. I watched as Reginald sat at the table cutting vegetables.

He looked up at me and said, "Come on in and have a seat. Where's Stewart?"

I pointed in the direction of the door, "He's outside in the car. He's having a little trouble."

Reginald laughed. "I can imagine."

My stomach was tied in knots, I wanted to stop in my tracks, but I kept going. As I walked toward the table and pulled out an available chair, Reginald spoke and expressed his concern for my absence over the last couple of days.

"I missed you these last few days. I thought maybe you didn't enjoy my company at lunch the other day." He never stopped what he was doing, nor did he look in my direction. His demeanor was calm and eerie.

I smiled and said, "I'm glad to know that I've been missed. Actually my sister, Lauren popped into town and we've been hanging out."

Reginald raised his eyebrows alluding to his confusion. He commented, "Really? I didn't know you had a sister named Lauren."

I just went with the flow, "There are a lot of things you don't know about me."

Reginald cocked his head to the side. "You have the most beautiful green eyes. I was wondering why you were hiding them behind those awful brown contacts."

"Well, I guess we all have masks that we hide behind in order to cover up our many sins."

"Ah, yes, sin. What a misunderstood word."

"How so?"

"Sin is one of those tricky commandments. People think that if you just think of committing a sin then you're off the hook. Why be a hypocrite? Just go ahead and do the damn thing."

He looked up at me with a devious grin, "Do you have any sins to confess, Miss. St. James?"

I took in a deep breath and then exhaled "No, Mr. Hawthorne. My sins are no different than anyone else's."

He laughed again. "You believers in God are all alike. One sin is no greater than the other. You're no better than me. You committed sins equal to mine when you fornicated with Dr. Stein on that hot summer night. Your sins were equal when you decided to be a pimp and launder money and drugs with your old partner and guardian angel Monica Delany...How is Monica? Oh man, that was the best piece of ass I've ever had. Did you really think she just showed up in your life one day? Did you forget about that little backstabbing whore Angel, who found out the hard way not to fuck with you? Who do you think disposed of her body and saved you from a murder rap? Oh, and let us not forget that night with Robert that Isabelle and Alex don't know about. Let me see your child would have been about three. You can blame it on the cognac and cigars, but it is what it is...sin."

His voice started to elevate as he yelled and laughed at the same time and threw his hands in the air, "I am all knowing. I know everything about you. I covered you when you thought you had no one and you had no clue."

I sat there paralyzed, only able to move my eye muscles. My lashes blinked a thousand times. How did he know all of that? How in the hell did he know about Robert and me? That was a secret that I planned to take to my grave. A few years before Robert was traded to Houston, he and Isabelle lived in separate cities for the most part. I went to a black businesswomen's conference in D.C. Robert and I met for drinks after one of his games. One thing led to another and we slept together. A few weeks later, I discovered I was pregnant. Robert and I went through a very unpleasant and uncomfortable period in our lives. He wanted kids bad and I wanted no part of motherhood. Not to mention I was his wife's boss. I know people always say they never meant to hurt the other person, but I truly never meant to hurt Isabelle. The crazy part was when I looked at her, I didn't give it a second thought. Up until then, the entire event had been erased from my memory.

I was at a loss for words. I wondered what other skeletons he would drag out of my closet. I settled back in my chair and studied Reginald. I wondered at what point in his life he had turned into what I saw before me. I sat there with my purse in front of me and asked myself, "Should I just take my gun out and blow him away right now?" I was truly restless and had no formal plan as to how I should handle the situation. I was obviously dealing with someone who wasn't of this world. He belonged in his own little bubble with people just like him. I didn't know what to expect, everyone I trusted turned out to be a joke. I felt like an amateur sitting there, neither one of us cracked a smile or changed our expressions.

I sat there in the midst of that awkward moment wondering what to do next. Reginald continued to prepare his dinner. We were sitting there, as if nothing had ever happened, as if we were about to have a family dinner. Reginald chopped his last carrot.

He looked over at me and said, "Would you mind washing these for me?" I nodded my head yes and retrieved the cutting board. I made sure I collected the knife as well.

As I was washing the vegetables, Reginald said, "So Seth, tell me what can I do for you..."

I heard the door slam. I knew Clark had somehow managed to get out of the trunk. I could hear him breathing hard as he approached. He fell into the kitchen holding his arm, and his head was dripping with blood. He was panting like a sick dog. He looked at me placing the food into the boiling water.

He looked dazed and confused, he struggled to speak, "Reggie, man she's not Seth...she's..."

I stopped, placed the top on the steamer and walked over to the table. Everything was so calm it was like something was going to breakdown at any moment. Clark was still standing there bleeding. I reached on the counter and retrieved a dishtowel and wrapped some ice cubes in it. Then I went over to Clark and reached out for his arm.

"Bitch, you must be crazy if you think I'm gonna let you touch me after you shot me in my damn arm and then clocked me in the head with a gun!"

I snatched Clark's arm as he yelled out in pain, "Shut up and stop crying like a little bitch. I'm not gonna do anything to you ... yet."

"'Yet?' Reggie, man, do you hear her? Why aren't you doing something?"

Reginald smiled at Clark. "Man what do you want me to do? I'm in a wheel chair. What can I do but sit here and wait?" I fumbled through the drawers looking for another towel. I wet a smaller towel and wiped the blood from his forehead. They both had no choice but to sit there.

I looked down at Clark and said, "As long as you sit there like a good little boy and cooperate you'll be ok."

He looked over at Reginald, "Reggie do you know who she says she is..." I pushed the homemade ice pack hard, squeezing his arm, and he let out a loud scream.

With a grimacing tone, I said, "Ok that's enough of the name calling around here, let's use our real names. You are Clark, you are Nolan and I am...let's say it all together now...Noel." I was getting really agitated at this point. "You see I'm getting real damn tired of being called Seth, nowadays. Daddy Dearest you gave me the name Noel, you gave my sister the name Nicolette. You named us after your brother who you killed, along with your parents when you were ten years old."

Nolan clapped his hands together. "Bravo, you did your homework."

"Yes, of course, like father like daughter. I've done a lot of research on you. No matter what I seem to uncover, you just never cease to amaze me. Tell me Nolan, what happened to you?"

Clark parted his lips to speak. Nolan raised his hand for Clark to be quiet. I sat there feeling ten pounds lighter and waiting for what would happen next.

Clark asked again, "What the hell is going on here?"

Nolan said, "Shut up and sit there. If my parental instincts are correct, this is my daughter, Noel."

You could have bought Clark for a penny. He was clueless. "So it really is you?"

I began to get angry, "Shut up, you dumb ass. I told you that earlier. Clark, cut the bullshit, it's over. You and this piece of shit know exactly who I am."

Nolan interjected, "He didn't know. I'm the only one who knew you were alive."

Clark sprang from the table. "How could you keep something like this from me? Were you just gonna let her walk in here and play me?"

Nolan said, "You played yourself. You let her flash her ass in your face and you just opened the door. You are weak, you always have been. I don't know why I've kept you around this long. The shit is over. I'm tired. It's over."

Stewart looked at Nolan and then at me. "Over? It's not over until we all leave this earth. So tell me Noel, why show up now? What could you possibly want after all these years?"

Before I could answer, Nolan said, "If my hunch is correct, she is here to kill both of us. She's already started on you."

Stewart was still ranting and raving. "So, what? You were gonna just let her come up in here and take us out?"

Nolan quickly responded, "No. You were. You're the one who got caught slippin'."

Clark snapped back, "So what the hell makes you so smart? How did you know who she was anyway?" I wanted to know the answer to that question myself.

"Yes, Nolan, how did you know who I was?"

"I know you because you are my child...my flesh and blood. Did you think a haircut and some contacts would throw me off? You are my daughter."

"Please, don't remind me."

"The first time I looked into those contact lenses I could still see straight through you. You look just like your mother when she was your age. You are and will always be my little green eyed butterfly...I gave you that name."

"Don't you dare mention that! You have no right to call me that, and you have not right to talk about my mother, you sick son-of-a-bitch. You have no right to call me anything."

"I have every right. She was my wife and whether you like it or not you are still my daughter. When I first saw you and how scared you looked when you discovered me, I wanted to reach out to you. Yes, you are who you are because of me."

"Mutha fucka, please, you tried to kill me, or did you forget?"

"I can never forget. I didn't try to kill you. I sent you out into the woods where you'd be safe. I never meant to hurt you and your sister."

"Oh yeah, just Mama."

"I admit, I did intend to kill your mother, she betrayed me. She was having an affair and she was going to leave me, and I couldn't let that happen. Everything was so complicated and twisted back then, and I can never make you understand, but not a day goes by that I don't think of you. I saved you."

"Oh, I understand. Thanks to Charles Brandenburg my long lost uncle, Dr. Shaw and Dawson Meeks I understand perfectly. I know all about you and Clark and the sick twisted games you play. I bet you didn't know that Clark set you up. Mama didn't have an affair, not with who you think. She was sleeping with good ole Clark over here. He wanted her for himself. While you round here recitin' my sins, did you know that one?" We were now back at level one, they were now Clark and Nolan. There were no more aliases.

My father turned to Clark. "What is she talking about, man?"

Clark didn't dare part his lips, so I answered for him. "You mean, all these years, Clark, you've never told your old buddy that you were the one who had betrayed him. You've been so jealous of Nolan all these years. You knew that, through it all, my mother loved that piece of shit over there until the day she died, and probably still does. What is this hold my father has on you, Clark? I mean it seems really obsessive and unnatural. It kind of makes me wonder if you two are screwing each other or something. I mean...what is it? Help me out, dear old Dad. Are you a homosexual? I mean is Clark here your boytoy? Is that what this is all about?"

Clark turned red; he got up from his seat, as the chair hit the floor he began to pace while he talked to me. "Do you know what it's like to be completely alone? From conception, I was a fuckin' mistake. I'm a legacy of outcast. When my father raped my mother, everyone rejected her. I was born from a reject. I was bounced from place to place. I was beaten and molested and thrown away. I grew up on the streets, sleepin' in alleys and eatin' rotten shit, I'm from the gutter. Nolan was the first person to tell me from his mouth that he loved me and he would always be there for me. This is my brother, my only family in this world."

At that point I had to interrupt him. "Please, Clark, give me a break. Mattie. Do you know her? Your biological mother? She tried to love you, but you rejected her."

Clark placed his hands on the counter and lowered his head and looked back at me. "Did you hear what Nolan said? The minute he saw you, he knew who you were and he wanted to hold you after all these years. That evil mutha fucka over there let his love for his child break him down. I watched for years while my mother, your beloved Mattie, gave all her love to him," he said as he pointed to my father. "When she first saw me, she thought I was trouble. Oh yeah, when she found out who I was she wanted to act like my mother, but I didn't need her."

Clark looked at Nolan. "Man, I just couldn't let them take you away. Noel, you and Nicolette were a mistake. I didn't mean for you two to get caught up. I honestly don't know what happened. When Nolan ordered you two to be killed, I didn't know he'd sent you away. No, I didn't do anything to stop him. I didn't even want your mother to die. I just wanted to pick up and move and leave everyone behind. Things just got outta hand, but eventually you two would have gotten in the way and he would have killed you anyway. So, I guessed everything worked out for the best."

While I was listening to Clark, I realized that he was truly a sick individual. He wasn't evil at all. He was just sick and he should have gotten some help a long time ago. He had actually rationalized his actions. I really felt sorry for Clark, but not sorry enough to spare his life. He reminded me of a wounded wild animal that continued to suffer until someone came along and put it out of its misery. If my father was all Clark had, he really didn't have much. My father sat there like a deer caught in headlights, they'd obviously never had that conversation before. Nolan rolled away from the table.

"I don't believe you let this bullshit destroy my family. You let me believe my wife betrayed me, and she was really gonna leave me. I killed my wife and lost my kids for this shit?"

For once, Clark jumped to his own defense. "Mutha fucka, please. You killed your wife because you are a selfish bastard, who has to control everything. I didn't have to convince you to do what you did. You did it because you wanted to. I even told you I didn't want to go through with it. That's why you had to pull the trigger. You see all this. Everything we have here is because you are a greedy bastard. You run everything and I just say `yes sir, yes sir boss.'"

I was getting tired of this self-help, and revelation therapy that was going on. "Listen, this is all touching, but who gives a shit who runs what? I just need to know why. Why we're sitting here today at this point in time? Why aren't we back in Georgia living as one big happy family?"

Nolan rolled over to me, "I can't tell you why. Clark is right. I did it because I wanted it all. I wanted the American dream, to have more money than I can spend in this lifetime. Do you know that I'm a multi-millionaire? I've got the whole world right in the palm of my hands, and you might find it hard to believe, but I regret how things happened and I have missed you. I love you more than my own life, that's why I didn't acknowledge who you were. I know you came to kill me and I'm ready. I can't take back what I did. I know you've been through hell and I want to give you your life back. I'm ready to turn everything over to you. I wish I could give you and your sister everything that you've lost."

That brought me right to my next question. "So let's talk about my sister, Lauren."

"Lauren?"

"Lauren is the name that Nicolette is going by now. She showed up at my house in Houston. Somehow our phones got mixed up and I want to know why she has your number."

I pulled out the phone and dialed his number.

Reginald looked at me. "This number you called me from belongs to Melanie Davis."

It seemed like at that point everything started to turn gray. My body was overwhelmed by heat and I began to sweat. "Who the hell is Melanie Davis?"

Clark yelled out, "Melanie Davis used to work for me at one of our clubs. She's a damn slut, that's who she is."

My mind was swimming with questions, I asked, "Are you sure her name is not Lauren? I mean she knows things only Nicolette would know. She had the old locket...Oh my God, Nicolette really is dead."

I was starting to fall apart. Nolan smiled. "No Noel, Nicolette is very much alive, she's in a sanitarium about thirty miles north of here. I checked her in after I found out where she was."

Just when I thought it couldn't get any more confusing, I got back on the roller coaster.

"Sanitarium, you mean mental hospital. I don't understand. Why is she in there?"

"Well, Nicolette was never the same after the night everything went down. She suffered some emotional and physical damage. She lost her sight in the explosion, and she is emotionally unstable..."

"You mean she's crazy. Don't sugar coat it, you made her crazy."

"If that's how you want to put it, then fine. Yes, she's crazy. She doesn't even know who she is half the time. She just sits there, day after day, rocking back and forth and talking out of her head. Actually, Melanie brought her to me."

I threw my hands up in the air and started yelling, "Who the hell is Melanie and how does she know my sister? Can someone please tell me what the hell is going on here?"

Nolan began to explain. "Nicolette was adopted shortly after she arrived at the orphanage in Georgia. Melanie and Nicolette were adopted together. The family moved out here. The couple that adopted them got a divorce and the woman couldn't handle Melanie's behavior and Nicolette's emotional problems so they were put in an institution. They continued to stay together until they were both admitted to a state Sanitarium. Melanie said Nicolette used to sit and rock and talk to herself. She would talk to herself about her mother and father and sister. She would tell the whole story, but everyone thought she was crazy, so no one paid any attention. Nicolette was very protective of that locket that I gave the two of you. It was one of a kind, so it stood out..."

I had to stop him, because I couldn't believe it. At that point, I wanted to know where my real sister was and how Melanie knew Alex.

"What hospital is Nicolette in, and how do I get there?"

Nolan settled in his chair and Clark was hanging on his every word, he picked up the chair from the floor and settled. "I don't believe this shit. Even I wanna hear the rest." He had no clue that my father had been keeping this secret. Damn, the devil was deceiving the devil.

Nolan replied, "She's in a place called Westwood Meadows, it's in Westwood Hills. They are expecting you to check her out soon."

"And why are they expecting me?"

"I knew once I told you the truth, you would want to take your sister back to Texas with you."

"How do you know so much about my life, and what is Alex's connection to all this?"

Just then from nowhere, Lauren or Melanie or whoever the hell she was right now, waltzed into the kitchen holding a gun. She said, "I can answer that question for you." Then she turned to look at Clark. "You should really lock the doors behind you."

No one seemed to be fazed. She walked in and paced around the kitchen holding the gun with her hand on the trigger. No one moved. All eyes were on her. She walked over to Nolan and planted a big sloppy kiss on him. Then she stood over by the sink as she began to speak. She spoke to everyone individually like she was late for a dinner party.

"Stewart or Clark, Reginald and yes my dear sister Seth, or is it back to Noel? I apologize for my unannounced visit, but I have a few things to take care of before I leave town for good."

I really didn't need the formalities. I stood up to confront her. "Why, Melanie? Why me? You don't even know me. I've never done a thing to you."

She shook her head and the gun at the same time. There I was in a room full of emotionally unstable people with weapons. I suddenly remembered that even I had spent some time at the psych hospital.

Melanie walked toward me waving her gun. "Bitch, sit down. It's my turn and I do know you. I know you too well."

I sat back down and waited for her to explain. "You see, it's simple. When Nicolette came to the group home back in Georgia, she was so fragile and scared. Inside, I was the same way, so I attached myself to her because she was helpless and she needed me. When we got adopted together even though she wasn't all there, I still had someone to take care of. Boy was I wrong. All she ever talked about was her sister and I knew she was telling the truth because she was so passionate about it. I even started letting her call me Noel. Sometimes on her good days she would talk to me and tell me little details about your family. She even talked about the neighbor kids, Claude Jr. and Victoria. I wanted to be a part of this family, I wanted to be Nicolette's sister. When our adoptive parents broke up, she was all I had, but she was always somewhere else. It was that damn locket that she couldn't live without."

I interrupted her. "So that's how you knew all those details about my childhood, but how did you pass the blood test?"

Lauren said, "It really wasn't that hard. I just found out what lab the blood was going to and paid the technician. That's why I was late that day we took the test. When I met you all getting on the elevator, I'd just made my transaction. I know it's straight from the movies, but it worked."

I still needed to know how she knew Alex. "So how do you know Alex?"

She smiled and started to blush, it was like she was reliving something in her head. "Oh, Alex ... Now that was purely coincidental, it was like a bonus. I met Alex one night at a club and of course we hooked up. I thought he was the greatest thing God ever made. Alex made it clear that he wasn't looking for a relationship, but he treated me better than any man ever did. I fell for Alex Young and I fell hard. I knew I needed to find a way to get close to him, so I made friends with him. He already felt sorry for me because your father had Clark beat me near death one night. I ran straight to Alex that night and he took care of me real good. I got myself together and came back to town and decided that Alex was the man for me."

I interrupted her again. "I don't understand, why did Clark try to kill you?"

She seemed to become agitated. "Please don't interrupt me again. I will tell you everything you need to know before you die, ok? Just shut up."

Surprisingly, I wasn't afraid of her. I was getting impatient. "Now let me finish. Reginald tried to kill me because we used to fuck like rabbits and I got pregnant. He said he didn't want a whore having his baby, so Father Knows Best over here," she said as pointed to my father, "wanted to teach me a lesson for trying to trap him. I tried to get Clark on my side, so I started fuckin' him too, but it didn't work. I stole some money from him and the rest is history."

Just then Clark jumped to his feet and reached for Lauren's gun. Lauren pulled the trigger and shot him right in the chest. Blood went everywhere. He didn't even have time to grab his chest, he just fell to the floor like a sack of potatoes. He was standing so close to Lauren when she shot him that his blood spattered all over her face, and hit my clothes. A shiver went through my body and I was paralyzed. Lauren didn't bother to wipe the blood from her face.

Nolan reached for his gun, which was on the side of his chair. Lauren pointed the gun at him and advised him not to move.

Then she said, "I said don't interrupt me...Clark interrupted me, and I don't like it when people interrupt me. Now let me finish...I need to finish." At that point I realized this bitch was absolutely crazy. I settled in my chair and let her finish.

Those names were getting confusing, so I said, "Look, I just need to know what to call you. I mean is it Melanie or Lauren?"

She said, "Actually, it's both. My name is Lauren Melanie Davis. These names are fuckin' me up to...you're Seth, this is Nolan and that was Clark. Is everyone clear?"

She scratched her head with the barrel of the gun and said, "Now where was I? Oh yeah...Alex...anyway, I convinced one of Alex's friends to let me in Alex's house one night to cook dinner. When I arrived at the house, there you were, everywhere. Your pictures were everywhere, but each picture had the same thing in common, that damn locket. I started to think about Nicolette and the more I stared at your face the more you started to look like Nicolette. I thought about those damn green eyed butterflies she draws and hangs all over the room. I rummaged through Alex's drawers and found a picture that I figured he wouldn't miss. I took it with me when I visited

Nicolette the next day and tried to compare facial features. I showed Nicolette the picture and she called you her mother. I now knew who I needed to try and pattern myself after.

"The closer I got to Alex and pretended to be his friend, the more I saw how in love he was with you. I would let him talk about you so I could find out just who you were and what you were made of. Just by talking to him, I found out your favorite food, favorite movie, your strengths and your weaknesses. It was hard because you appeared to be a coldhearted bitch. And so, that's just what I became. I became you. The two people that I loved most in this world didn't want me, they wanted you."

I wanted to ask her how she knew Reginald was my father, but I wasn't ready to die. I guess she read my mind.

"Let me guess, you want to know how I knew he was your biological sperm. Well, daddy here and his partner love to support the community, for tax purposes no doubt. They were being honored for donating money to a community center and there they were in the Metro section of the paper at a ribbon cutting ceremony. When I was visiting Nicolette one day I was reading the paper and she went crazy when she saw his picture, she started yelling, 'Daddy, daddy...Uncle Clark.' She was so excited, she had to be sedated. I grabbed that paper and came straight to Reginald. My plan was to merely mention it to him, but he told me the whole story. It was then that I decided to blackmail him. Let's just say it didn't work, so I needed to leave town for sure. I made a little stop, over in Dallas and then on to Houston. I brought your little sister. Noel is Reginald's daughter. Because you wanted me to be Nicolette so badly, you made it easy for me. I never intended for you to try to find your father, I figured you needed a sister and I needed a free ride, but you just couldn't let it go."

She was pacing back and forth waving the gun in the air. "I mean you just had to go to Dillon. After that it was over for me, I began to believe I was Nicolette, and I truly wanted to know what happened to her. When I found out you were out here, I knew it would be just a matter of time. So I'm here to end it...did you get all that?" I figured it was safe for me to ask questions now.

"So Alex isn't in on this at all?" I asked.

She laughed. "Girl please, he hasn't got a clue, but he will real soon. After I kill you, I'll be there to comfort him. I should be Mrs. Alexander Young by this time next year."

There was one more thing I needed to be sure of. "So Noel is Reginald's daughter?"

She waved her hands in the air. "Yes, bitch. That's what I said. She's the child that Reginald wanted me to kill. She is your biological sister. That's why she looks so much like you. I figured if you didn't think I looked like you, you couldn't possibly deny her. And naming her Noel was a nice touch."

Well, that explained a lot of coincidences. This chick became the person I feared most in life. I was no longer afraid of my father, I knew what he was capable of, but she was on the edge. She was mentally unstable and irrational. I didn't want to end up being one of her victims.

My father just sat there. He knew there was nothing he could do. Finally he opened his mouth to speak. "Melanie, I will give you anything if you simply leave, and let us go. I'll give you a million dollars in cash right now."

She turned to him with a crazy look on her face. "I don't want your damn money, this ain't about money. This is between Noel and me. I want her life. I want to be Nicolette's sister and Alex's wife. Just look at you, you are willing to pay me a million dollars to save her life. I am sick of this bitch. Do you hear me? I am sick of her! I am Noel! I am Nicolette's sister and Alex's fiancée! I am your daughter now...Please, Daddy...can't you see that I love you? You, Nicolette, Alex, and little Noel can be one big happy family. We can move back to Dillon out in the country in our house down the road from Dr. Shaw. We can be a family. I'll be good...Daddy, I promise...please."

For one moment in time, I felt so sorry for her. I had no idea who she was anymore. I looked down at Clark and I felt sorry for him as well. There we were. A room full of emotionally disturbed and abandoned orphans, some of us learned to cope, and others became victims all over again. I knew better than anyone what it felt like to be alone. Just then I knew that I was blessed. Mattie had nothing to do with any of this and I needed to redeem our relationship. I had Isabelle and Robert. And I was marrying Alex. I refused to die in that house.

While Lauren was having her melt down, I grabbed my gun out of my purse and pointed it at her.

"Lauren, I don't want to kill you, but I will. You need help. Just give me the gun. We can walk out of here and I promise to get you the help you need."

Lauren ran toward me at top speed. "Go ahead, Bitch. Shoot me."

I had no choice. I pulled the trigger, but nothing happened, she was still coming toward me. I pulled the trigger again, and again nothing happened. She laughed, "Now don't you think that when I switched cell phones I saw the gun in your purse and emptied the clip, I can't believe you missed that."

She reached into her pocket and pulled out the bullets. She cocked her gun and said, "You are one stupid heifer." As she was coming toward me I reached my arm out and took a chance at landing a punch. My fist connected with her jaw. And she fought back with another punch. I hit her again and she lifted her foot to kick me in my stomach. I grabbed her foot and spun her around. She landed by the sink, and caught herself on the counter, where she grabbed a knife and lunged toward me, cutting my arm. I didn't have time to think about pain. I picked up an empty pot from the drain rack and tried to hit her with it, but I missed. I ran around to the other side of the island where we stood face to face. I reached over and tried to grab the other knife from the counter. Like a cat, Lauren reached over and grabbed her gun, which had landed in the sink. She pulled the trigger. Suddenly my body was consumed by an intense burning heat. I caught a bullet. I didn't exactly know where I was wounded, but I knew I was in trouble. I felt my flesh burn like someone had poured acid on me. I looked over at the pot boiling on the stove. I picked it up with all the strength I could muster, and threw the boiling water at her. She screamed out in agony. Just then, I reached behind my back and pulled out my spare pistol and pulled the trigger. The bullet from my gun landed right between Lauren's eyes. As she fell to her knees, she looked up and whispered, "Damn, this bitch shot me," and fell to the floor.

I looked down at her as blood poured from her head and yelled, "I'm not as dumb as you think, bitch."

I remembered what Mattie told me about being prepared for anything, so I had packed an extra gun in my waist just in case something went wrong. I stood there trying to catch my breath. I looked down and saw Clark struggling to breathe. I leaned down and looked him in the eyes. I held his head in my hands. As the light in his eyes began to fade he called out my name "Seth, please help me. Seth, I still love you."

I leaned in and kissed him on his lips and said, "Maybe in some other place and time." I looked into his eyes and watched the tears fall from the corners. Then, I twisted his neck and heard it crack. I let his head fall to the floor. I was sure he was dead that time.

I walked over and sat down across from my father with blood pouring from my arm. I could feel the blood running down as it dripped on to the floor. The pain was so intense that I could not imagine anything worse at that moment. I wondered how fast it would take for me to bleed to death. I thought about blood clots, but most importantly I thought about Nicolette, the real Nicolette. I would've literally given my right arm to see her face. In my mind, I begged God to let me make it to see her. I deserved that one thing out of life. As I looked at my father, I thought of how his eyes lit up when he mentioned caring for her. I remembered his tone when he spoke of still loving me and I longed to have my father back. I pictured all of us at my wedding enjoying being a family. I felt the warm tears roll down my face, it felt like the blood that was running down my arm.

I wiped my face and realized my father was sitting in front of me. He was holding my hand and caressing my hair. He said "Are you ok? Everything is going to be alright." I found his touch oddly comforting. I grabbed his hand and held it close to my face. Oh, how I wished my mother were there. He let go of my face and sat back in his wheelchair. As he winced in pain, I could see that his bones and joints were bothering him and he needed some relief.

I tenderly said, "Are your legs hurting? Do you need your pain medication?"

"Yes, but it's upstairs."

"It's ok. I have some Ibuprofen that I take for my migraine headaches. Actually, I could use one myself. Would it be all right if you took some Ibuprofen?"

He nodded as he looked up at me. "I know this doesn't mean much, but I am so sorry. This is all my fault...Clark, Melanie, everything. I'm just a man, a sick man, a man who destroys everything he touches."

I put my finger to my lips and motioned for him to be quiet and I assured him, "Don't worry, everything will be all right."

I handed him the pills. As I walked to the sink to get some water for him, I stepped into my own blood. I stepped into Lauren and Clark's blood as well. I made a pathway through the blood as it blended together. It was all mixed together connecting us once again. I struggled to work the faucet with one hand. I looked over at my father as he sat there in what it seemed like excruciating pain. I thought about the last time I saw him in pain like that. It was the night he was shot as he laid there telling us he hadn't meant for any of that to happen. Somehow, I wanted to believe him. For years I'd held on to that one statement hoping my mother's death was truly a mistake. I now had the answers. There were no mistakes. One man had planned everything. Only one man could take responsibility for all of it. Like it or not, that man is my father.

I made it back to the table and sat down in front of him. I watched as he took the medicine and waited. He swallowed the last drop of water and asked, "What can I do to make things right? How can we leave this all behind us and move on?"

I looked at him and said, "You just made everything all right." I leaned over and kissed him on his forehead, and then I looked into his eyes. I watched as his eyes became larger and larger and he began to turn a dark shade of blue. His lips started to swell and his entire face resembled an inflated balloon. His hands twitched as he reached up to unbutton his shirt and clutched the arms on his wheelchair. He was gasping for air. I sat back and watched as he tried to help himself. He began to cough violently until blood spewed from his mouth. He begged me to help him, but I could care less. I watched as his body twitched in pain. Blood and foam flew out of his mouth as he began to lose his body fluids. He began to smell like a landfill and looked like he was in pure hell. I looked at my watch and noticed it was about 10:30. It was taking a little longer than I'd thought. His body stopped moving, and his tongue rested on the side of his mouth. I stared into his eyes as they slowly blinked. All he could do was blink as horrible sounds of unbearable pain released from his body. Finally, he blinked, his chest rose and his eyes turned cold. I reached over to check his pulse. I stared into his eyes and saw emptiness. My father was officially dead and I hadn't missed one moment of it. The only person I really felt sorry for was the woman lying there with no real identity. Lauren or Melanie had been her own worst enemy, looking for love in all the wrong places. She just chose the wrong family to be a part of.

I could have easily shot my father and gotten it over with, but I ran the risk of him dying instantly and not actually feeling it. When Clark told me about my father's illness, he informed me about how excruciating his pain was at times. He would have to take pain medication for relief. Well, one thing my father passed along to me was the allergy to any type of drugs that contained sulfur. We couldn't ingest any medication with sulfur in it. An excessive amount can be fatal. Before I left my house, I filled the gel caps with sulfur, in addition to that, I had injected whatever it was that Dr. Shaw had in the vial he had when we visited Meeks. I didn't know what it was, but I figured if he was going to use it on Dawson Meeks, then it must be lethal, so I took a chance.

Before I left, I looked around the house and tried to gather my strength. I was ready to leave that place and never return. My work there was done and I could start to live my life just as it should've been. I walked throughout the house and looked at each person lying on the floor. I picked up a cell phone and called 911. I informed them that there were three people dead, and I was wounded. Before I could make it out of the house, I could see a trail of police cars coming over the hill. I walked as far as my tired weak body would take me and collapsed in the driveway. I laid there in the dark, on that cold asphalt. I felt peaceful, and I had no regrets. I laid there waiting for someone to find me and rescue me. Pretty soon, my thoughts began to run together and I drifted off into my own little world. I could no longer feel the pain from my wound, nor could I feel the burden of that night twenty years ago. I was finally truly free.

Chapter Thirty-Five

For some people revenge is like food, or their drug of choice. It's what sustains them, and keeps them going. When you're set on getting even with someone, you eat, sleep, drink and shit revenge. Ironically, once it's over, you're still empty inside, waiting for that next defining moment.

I have waited for this moment most of my life. When I found out Lauren had been a fraud, I thought I was past the point of hope, but fate has given me another chance.

As I walked down the hall of Westwood Meadows, the thought of seeing Nicolette for the first time was not one of joy. It was of reluctance and fear. I feared that the meeting might be yet another cruel joke or trick at the hands of my father. I prepared myself for another scam or con. Everyone was waiting in the lounge for me to return from my visit. I wanted to do it alone. I expected the person at the end of the hall would be some half-baked clone of me. As I walked down the corridor, I could hear the sound of my heels meeting the tile echoing through the hall. I peeked into each room at the residents. I wondered what each one was thinking and their reason for being in that place. I thought of my days at Serenity Springs and wondered if anyone's story was as colorful as mine. I wondered how many of them were dying inside from loneliness. I wondered how many of them were living with dark secrets that haunt them even when they were awake.

The administrator walked in front of me. We remained silent during our journey. As I got closer to the last door on the right at the end of the hallway, the echoes of my steps grew deeper and my stride seemed longer. My arms were swinging and moving with the rhythm of my feet and my hands became heavy. I could hear my heart beat like drums in my ears as the pressure made my head feel tighter. Just as I felt that my head was about to explode, the administrator, Ms. Tolbert stopped and turned to me. We reached our destination. The door to the room was closed.

Ms. Tolbert said, "Rachel doesn't like to have her door open, she's very particular about who enters her room. She's quiet and she doesn't like noise." She touched my shoulder and lowered her head. Then, her tone changed. "Listen, I know you probably want this to be a fairytale reunion, but don't be alarmed if she doesn't warm up to you right away. It takes her a while and you have to earn her trust. She is severely, emotionally disturbed and the older she gets the worse off she'll be. I don't think she will ever function properly without institutional care."

"Rachel," that name cut through me like a knife. She kept referring to her as Rachel. I wanted to say her name is Nicolette, dammit.

I touched Ms. Tolbert's arm as her hand rested on my shoulder. I looked into her eyes and said, "I have never had the luxury of believing in fairytales, so don't worry about me, I'll be just fine."

Ms. Tolbert removed her hand from my shoulder and turned to knock on Nicolette's door. She hesitated for a moment and turned back in my direction. "Miss St. James, I was so sorry to hear about your father, he was such a nice person. We always looked forward to his visits. I know that before Rachel arrived here, she and Miss Davis were in another hospital together, but Melanie always seemed to have everything together when she came to visit. I guess you never know. We just want you to know that you have our deepest sympathy."

I thanked her for her condolences and motioned for her to open the door. When I heard the lock click open, I jumped and my heart started to beat faster. I stood there for a moment before I moved to enter the room. I grabbed hold of the doorway for support. I was ready for anything. When I entered the room she was sitting in a seat in the windowsill staring through the window, rocking back and forth. I looked over the room. It was decorated with pictures that I assumed she'd drawn and painted herself. There were pictures of butterflies with green eyes everywhere. There were fresh flowers randomly placed around the room. The room smelled like my mother's flower garden in the spring. I didn't say a word and neither did Ms. Tolbert. Nicolette had not turned in our direction. I wondered if she even knew we were there.

As I moved closer to the window, I glanced over at her nightstand and noticed something that seemed rather odd to me. I adjusted my eyes to make sure I wasn't hallucinating. I picked up the frame that was resting next to the lamp. It was my graduation picture. I'd taken it on the day of my college graduation. I stared down at the picture in my hand.

"Your father brought in all these pictures for her. I'm surprised she hasn't said anything yet. She doesn't like anyone to touch them. Maybe she's having a good day."

I could not begin to imagine how or why my father acquired those pictures. Just when I think I knew who Nolan Toussaint really was, I am surprised all over again. Sometimes it was so easy for me to hate him and remember all the bad things about him. Other times all I wanted was to remember the first eight years of my life when I knew him as my loving father.

I placed the picture back on the nightstand and walked over to the window. Nicolette was still staring out the window. She had not yet made a sound or an attempt to turn in my direction. I had not prepared myself for a tearful heart wrenching reunion. All that had been wasted and stolen by Lauren's act of deception. That time was different. Could I look at that woman who I believed to be my real life biological sister and feel some sort of emotion for her? And if so, what would that emotion be? I wanted Lauren to be Nicolette so badly, that I was careless and naive. She literally walked in off the street and I welcomed her into my home without reservation. Did I have the strength to go through that again? Whatever energy I once had to deal with the reunion had been spent already.

I walked over and sat down next to her. I didn't touch her. I didn't say a word. I simply sat there and waited for maybe fifteen seconds, without moving a muscle or even looking her way.

"Serenity," She said. She was wearing a huge smile on her face. Her comment was unexpected and it caught me off guard. I looked over at Ms. Tolbert and she shrugged her shoulders. I was afraid to set her off, so I waited yet again to hear more. She continued to stare out the window rocking back and forth with her knees resting on her chest and her arms wrapped around her body. With an effortless and calm tone Nicolette said, "When I was a little girl my mother used to wear Serenity, it smelled like flowers in the springtime."

I exhaled, and let out a long breath, it seemed like I'd been holding it in forever. My chest was full and my eyeballs felt like they were weighed down. I wanted her to look at me. I wanted to look into her eyes. I could see her reflection in the window, but I needed to see her face. I touched her hand and she put her hand on top of mine. I looked over at Ms. Tolbert and she smiled. We sat together for a few seconds with our hands touching, both of us looking out of the window at nothing but time and space.

Finally, she turned away from the window. She unfolded her knees and rested her arms in her lap as she looked at me with her head tilted. "I'm ready to go home now, please take me home."

I sat there trying to find a spot on the wall to focus on so I wouldn't lose control. I searched the room to find that one solid object to focus on. Everywhere I looked was covered with pictures, paintings and drawings.

There we were, sitting in that little room that was like a high priced jail cell. All these years, I wondered how my sister lived and what was going through her mind. I wondered if she was ok, if she was eating and sleeping properly. I looked around and realized that all my faculties were intact. My senses were in order and sometimes my mind worked the way that it should, but Nicolette was the lucky one. She still lived in 1983, and for the most part, she was still eight years old. I was certain she had no idea who our father really was. She would always remember him for who he was back in the day, and who he showed her he was during his last days. For one moment I envied her. I leaned over and took my sister in my arms and held her close to me, so close I could feel her heartbeat. After a moment, I couldn't tell my heartbeat from hers. She rested her head on my shoulder as we embraced. It was the sweetest most endearing moment I'd ever experienced. It was nothing like the moment I thought Lauren was Nicolette. This was just how it should've been. There were no formalities and no excitement. This was warm and gentle.

I moved from our embrace and looked at her face. She was so beautiful. Her skin was smooth and rich like caramel. Her hair was long and straight. She looked just like my mother the last time I saw her alive. She not only resembled my mother, but she was almost a carbon copy of me. We looked more like identical twins than fraternal twins. The feeling was definitely different. I couldn't explain it, but I knew that was Nicolette. I didn't need a blood test, and I didn't need confirmation from any place else. I could not help but sit there and stare into her eyes. I felt like I could sit there all day. There was no need to ask questions. I knew all I needed to know about her. I just wanted to take my sister home. We sat there for a little while longer, enjoying breathing the same air. Nicolette gripped my hand tighter. "I'm glad you're not lost anymore, and the wolves didn't get you," she said.

I was taken aback by the comment and asked her what she'd meant. Nicolette replied, "Mommy told me you would come. She told me not to be scared and to wait. So, that's what I did. I just waited. She told me you were lost and you were trying to find your way." I understood exactly what she meant. I was relieved that my mother had been her guardian angel all those years and had kept her safe. What I didn't understand was the part about the wolves.

I caressed her face. "What about the wolves?"

She became excited as she sprang up, and sat on her knees. "I had a dream that you were in the woods, and you were being chased by wolves, only they had human faces, I was so scared they were going to eat you."

Just then, I remembered my mother's reference to a wolf in sheep's clothing and I thought of Lauren. I couldn't help but smile at Nicolette's innocence. She had become so animated all at once. Ms. Tolbert couldn't believe how alive she was. I helped her gather her things. I took only the pictures and left everything else. I just wanted to get out of there.

Nicolette and I walked down the hall hand-in-hand. I was hoping that meeting everyone wouldn't be too much for her. Alex, Isabelle, Robert, and Mattie were all waiting for us to walk through the door. I hadn't given a second thought to Nicolette's reaction to Mattie. It was too late now. We were just about to open the doors to the waiting area. Mattie was standing by the window with her hands folded. She looked nervous and uncomfortable. When Nicolette saw her, she ran over to her and let out a high-pitched scream. She hugged Mattie so tightly, she almost knocked her down. For the first time in twenty years, Mattie shed tears. She embraced Nicolette, and held her so tightly you couldn't tell where Mattie ended and Nicolette began. Nicolette started to cry as she called Mattie's name. "Mattie, Mattie. My Mattie." I looked over and there wasn't a dry eye in the room.

Mattie looked at Nicolette as she ran her fingers through her hair and studied her face. She looked at me and said, "This is the real Nicolette. This is your sister."

I walked over and embraced both of them. We stood together holding each other. I was so overwhelmed, I cried and cried. I cried tears of joy. I released every ounce of pain, hurt, and heartache. I was healed. I was complete. I felt whole again. I finally knew who I was. I was Seth St. James soon to be Seth St. James-Young. I would hold on to Seth, because it meant second chance. Twenty years ago, I was given a second chance. My life was spared. Even though it had been one struggle after another, three people have never forsaken me: The Father, The Son and The Holy Spirit. What I did to Stewart, Lauren and Reginald was wrong, but I knew that I had been forgiven.

There is a very thin line between good and evil. The only difference is those who are truly evil have no desire to be good. I struggled with the choices that I'd made, and I desperately wanted to do the right thing. If there was one thing that I was afraid of, it was hell. If hell was anything like what I'd been through on earth, then I knew I didn't belong there.

Chapter Thirty-Six

For years I wondered why I couldn't feel my father's spirit. I now know that I could not feel him because he was not of this world. His soul was dead. I couldn't connect with him because God had his hand on me. As much as I'd like to, I can't change what happened. After that night I prayed for God's forgiveness. God has forgiven me and I have forgiven myself. If someone were to ask me how I felt about my father I would say Nolan Toussaint and Reginald Hawthorne were two different people, but yet one in the same. One could not have existed without the other.

I loved Nolan Toussaint, the man with whom I spent the first eight years of my life with all my heart. He was my father and nothing could ever change that. Reginald Hawthorne, his alter ego, was a man that I had a brief encounter with and did not care to know. When I first looked into Reginald's eyes, I thought I found remnants of my father. On the night I sat in front of Reginald, watched him take his last breath, I found a small piece of what used to be my father. For one brief moment, I felt the comfort of Nolan's hands on my face. I had my father back and that is the man that would always be a part of me.

So much has happened since I walked out of my father's home and closed the doorway to my past. I am happier than I have ever been. I made peace with my past, and am embracing the possibilities of the future. Alex and I are married and our wedding was absolutely beautiful. We flew to Tuscany and exchanged vows in the country. I am expecting my first child and so is Isabelle. Actually, I am beyond my due date. Alex and I live in Atlanta now. We are building a house on the old land in Dillon. We purchased the two properties on both sides of the land. I want a stable full of horses and open space to ride them. Isabelle is holding things down in Houston. I have a store in Atlanta as well. Mattie married her mystery man, and they are doing great.

Dr. Shaw and Charles Brandenburg continue to be part of my family. My little sister, Noel lives with us. I can't help but wonder if she will be what is considered normal. She has an old soul and seems to be nothing like her mother or father. All I can do is hope for the best.

After I was treated for my gunshot wound, and was no longer a suspect in the murder of Reginald, Lauren and Clark, I went to the hospital and discharged my sister. She now lives with us. She will never understand how or why things happened, but she does know that she is safe. Some days she seems fine, and other days she is still eight years old.

I love my family with all my heart. I don't regret a minute of the way that I found my peace. I don't know what I will tell my child or Noel of their heritage. I just know that I never want to relive another minute of it. Sometimes I still can't believe the first twenty-eight years of my life. I do know that it has made me much stronger.

The night I avenged my mother's death, the entire crew, including Maxwell, was there to help pull me through. It turned out Alex became alarmed when I called him from Lauren's phone earlier that day. He put two and two together and realized the woman I thought was my sister, was actually Melanie, who had been stalking him for years. He couldn't reach me so he called Isabelle. Isabelle tried to warn me, but I didn't have time to talk to her. She received the file from the state of Georgia. It listed Rachel and Melanie as being adopted by the same couple. They sent a picture of Melanie and my sister from their files. She'd Melanie also flipped out on Maxwell one night and he decided to check her out. He found out that she'd been in an institution in Dallas. He made a call to a colleague, and got the low down on Melanie, aka Lauren. She was a very troubled woman, who just needed to be loved. Alex, Robert, Mattie and Isabelle hopped a flight and met in L.A. Isabelle still had the address to Stewart's house, from when I had first given it to her.

While I was recovering from my gunshot wound, I learned the extent of my father's power. The day he saw me for the first time in twenty years, he knew I was coming to take his life, but he just didn't know how. He arranged to have me cleared of the charges posthumously. Even in actual death my father remained on top of the world. Lauren's instability actually played in my favor. Since she was found at the scene and had a long history of mental illness, plus the fact she'd had a child by Reginald, the entire crime was blamed on her. The paper read, "Mental Patient Goes on Shooting Spree in Jealous Rage."

Consequently, I was considered next of kin for everyone. Lauren, Stewart and Reginald's bodies were released to me. I felt it was my duty to give them proper burials. Actually, it was selfishness on my part. I wanted to make sure they were dead and gone. I had each of them cremated. I stood and watched every single move the mortician made. I stood in front of the crematorium and watched as each body burned to ashes. It was funny how all that evil amounted to a pile of dirty ashes in a jar. After it was over, I took Stewart's boat out and spread their ashes over the ocean. I didn't feel much emotion. I just felt it was the right thing to do.

There is a truth that I dare not speak aloud. In a moment of weakness, I fell for Stewart. It is something that I will never be able to explain to anyone or even to myself. One night I looked into his eyes, and saw pain and regret. I also saw a man who needed to be free. I saw something more than the man I tried to condition myself to hate. If he had been innocent, would I have left Alex for him? Well that is something we will never know.

A few days after my return to Houston, I received a hand-delivered envelope without a return address. Inside the envelope were two platinum heart lockets covered in diamonds. On the inside the inscription read, "New Beginnings." There was also a hand written letter and a copy of my father's will with instructions on finding money that was hidden in the house and other places. My father left Nicolette and me, everything he had. The things that were illegal, and could not be mentioned in the will, were accompanied by instructions on how to properly handle them. I sold the house and relinquished all illegal activity to some of Uncle Charlie's associates. They effectively severed all unlawful ties that my father and Clark had. Everything that belonged to Clark went to my father and was subsequently passed on to Nicolette and me. Let's just say we are two very wealthy women. After I reviewed the will and the instructions, I found a quiet place to read the letter my father had written. After reading it I carefully folded it, placed it back in the envelope and locked it away in my safe. I kept it, just to remind myself that what I'd been through wasn't a dream.

As I sit here and watch my family enjoy the spring breeze, and watch the butterflies flutter in the wind, I have one wonderful memory of my father. That is the day that he made me feel special, the day that I became his green-eyed butterfly!

To My Green Eyed Butterfly

To My Green Eyed Butterfly,

As I sit here writing this letter, I feel the end for me will soon come. I have waited for an eternity for you to find me. My biggest fear was that this cancer would consume me before I had a chance to see you one last time. The words, "I'm sorry," can never make up for the years you've lost, so I won't waste your time with an apology. The truth is I am who I am. I can't ever change that. I have done things that I will pay for beyond my time on earth. I could blame my lifestyle on my lack of having a stable family as a child, but the truth is I find pleasure in other people's pain. That is how I came into this world and that is how I shall leave. Sounds pretty sick, doesn't it? I guess it would be crass of me to expect credit for admitting that I'm a bit of an eccentric.

I am sure that you have wondered all these years what really happened to our fairytale life. Well here's your answer. I realized at an early age that I had the power to make people do whatever I wanted. I have always had a fascination with God, and how people worship him and how He has the power to control life and death. The more I learned about God, the more I learned about the devil. I found that the devil was once an angel, but he fell from grace. The devil realized the power he had to control others, and decided to stick with what he knew best. The first time I took someone's life, I realized I had the power to control life and death. There is something about that divine power that will make a man do things a human being with an ounce of moral fiber can never imagine possible.

I did truly love your mother. I loved her as much as I could love anyone. For years, she was the perfect wife. However, once she asserted herself and found her independence and realized she didn't need me to survive, I lost control. I couldn't live knowing she'd find happiness with another, so the only way to rectify the situation was to get rid of her, forever. Life is too short and there is no room for second chances. Second chances give you hope for the future, and as long as you have hope, you will remain content. For me, contentment is not acceptable. It has to be all or nothing. You have to live everyday like it's your last. I know you were expecting me to say I killed your mother because I was in debt or some other reason justifiable in your eyes, but I am what I am and I killed her because I wanted to.

When you were born, I knew in my heart that you possessed something special. I looked into your beautiful green eyes and saw the color of ambition. I knew you could hold your own and take care of yourself. The night your mother died, I sent you girls off into the woods where I thought you'd be safe. I have always known where you were, and every move you've made. It would have been easy for me to show up one day and explain what happened, but all things come in time and timing is everything. When I left Dillon that night, I never looked back. Somehow I knew you would find your way back to me and set yourself free. In the wild, when animals reach the age of accountability they are sent off to fend for themselves, and learn to survive. Some fall prey and some adapt to their environment and act accordingly. Your sister, Nicolette, fell prey to her circumstance. She could not fend for herself, and could not control her own actions. She became weak and vulnerable. You adapted to your environment and did just what your instincts led you to do.

Finally, you truly needed me. You needed to be set you free and I was the only person who held the key that could open the door to that freedom. You are flesh of my flesh, and bone of my bone. I wanted you to feel the power I felt. I know that taking my life will give you that power and that is my gift to you. I don't know how, when or where, but I know that you will adapt to your environment, follow your natural instinct and end my life. Love is a luxury that a man living in my world cannot afford. Nolan Toussaint was a weak man who was forgotten shortly after his demise, but Reginald Hawthorne will forever live in your mind. He's the man who took your life away when you were eight years old, and motivated you to take it back. He is the man who gave you the power to control life and death. He will always be part of you, and you can never escape that.

Love,

Your father